DEAD OF THE WINTER SUN
THE SPIRITS ARE WEEPING
THEIR TERROR
A LORNE TURNER MYSTERY

First Published in Great Britain 2022 by Mirador Publishing

Copyright © 2022 by Joe Talon

First edition: 2022

Mirador Publishing
10 Greenbrook Terrace
Taunton
Somerset
UK
TA1 1UT

DEAD OF THE WINTER SUN
THE SPIRITS ARE WEEPING
THEIR TERROR
A LORNE TURNER MYSTERY

JOE TALON

PROLOGUE

Horner 1952

HE STOOD OVER THE GRAVE, the heat of the summer's day making his blue serge RAF pilot's uniform stick to his clammy skin. The words of the local vicar, paid well to keep his mouth shut about the unconventional burial, slipped over him. A meaningless drone from an old man. The end of the war with Germany meant the entire country felt numb to burials, and this quiet corner of a Somerset field, rather than the church graveyard in Luccombe didn't cause much comment. None of the villagers stood by the grave, just family, and the woman in charge of the Institute.

The coffin looked so small in the hole. The harsh summer sun didn't make it down to the coffin. Only shadows kissed the plain wooden surface.

He'd seen men burn in downed planes all over Europe, but this small body in her tiny box ripped at his heart more deeply than all the shrieks of those dying heroes.

He remembered the screams of his child most, what parent wouldn't?

Night after night. They shivered his bones, shredding his self-control until he wanted to strangle her, just for a moment's peace. A moment to be free of the pain he couldn't stop.

He never had, he'd never hurt her, but her broken mind wailed her grief and confusion into the world and the world stared back, uncaring, deaf and mute to her agony.

With so much woe, how could the world hear one small voice? Millions lay in graves. Millions more suffered and would for many years to come. He'd witnessed the terrible devastation in Berlin for himself, had saved his future wife and her child, eventually *their* child, from war-torn buildings, hungry soldiers, and the rampant hate swirling around the city.

His eldest daughter didn't deserve this death, to be left and forgotten in a graveyard no one knew existed. Secrets, they all had too many secrets.

The small frame of his younger daughter pressed against his leg, and he managed to release the tension in his fists long enough to hold her shoulder. She wouldn't remember any of this; his wife would give her medication and alter the memories. The institute specialised in that, making memories vanish.

He wouldn't let them steal his memories. Despite the horrors dogging his waking and sleeping worlds, if they took his memories who would remember the brave lost souls?

He did understand why she wanted to help her broken daughter, *their* daughter. It hadn't worked, nothing worked. The poor child's trauma went so deep.

The slim fingers of his wife's hand slipped into his free hand, and he managed to raise his eyes. Her deep sadness, the sorrow at her failure, made his jaw tighten. He had to maintain a stoic presence at the graveside. He held the rank and authority of a captain in the Royal Air Force. Others looked to him to set an example. An Englishman didn't weep at a graveside, not even for their child. His father certainly didn't when they'd buried his brothers during the war. Or what was left of his brothers.

After all they'd gone through to find the frail child, all she had endured to try to leave her memories in the past, she'd died from something as common as tuberculosis. The injustice of this, of watching her madness finally succumb to the drugs, only to die from...

The vicar stopped talking, and he knew he had to be the first to throw dirt on that small dark box placed so deep inside the cold earth.

He didn't bend. He knelt, picking up a handful of the summer hard, thick, clay soil.

"Daddy?" whispered his living, breathing, beautiful daughter.

He plucked a smile out of thin air and managed to hold it on his face just long enough for her to be reassured. "Yes, tadpole?"

"I don't want to say goodbye to Bee." She whispered this, his beautiful girl, with a nervous glance at the stern woman on the other side of the grave.

How he wished that woman lay in this cold grave. Maybe his eldest daughter would still be alive. Maybe his beloved wife would still have her smile. Maybe his youngest daughter, his true daughter, wouldn't have to know such sorrow.

Tapping his little girl on the chest, he managed to say, "We are only saying goodbye to Bee's body, tadpole. Her heart will always live here and your memories will keep her alive. Her soul is…" He couldn't say it. That lie died on his lips because he no longer believed.

They said every soldier becomes a believer when in a foxhole. They all cry out for God to save them. It was true. He'd heard it many times on his comms units as his brothers in arms dropped out of the sky, burnt up, exploded, or merely died from flak devastating their flimsy fuselages. No one ever saved them. Ever. They all died screaming; some in fear, some in pain, some in defiance.

No, he didn't believe in anything.

He squared his shoulders and looked his daughter in the eye. "Her soul is held by you, in here," he stroked her head. "Help me say goodbye to her body then she can find peace."

Her eyes, a shade of grey which switched to the palest blue in a softening light, swam with tears, but she dropped to her knees in the grass beside him.

Reaching across her father's bent knee, her tiny hand grasped a handful of grave dirt. Their eyes locked and time paused. He heard the wind in the tall grasses. The distant twitter of blackbirds and sparrows, the scream of a buzzard overhead and the mocking call of a black coated crow. How he hated those companions of death. They littered every battlefield he'd flown over. His little tadpole broke eye contact, and he hoped his gaze didn't betray the rage drowning his soul.

"Goodbye, sweet girl," he murmured, dropping his handful of soil on the wooden box. It clattered, hard from the dry summer.

"Bye, bye, Bee. See you soon," whispered his daughter.

The words hit him like machine gun fire. He wrapped his little tadpole in his arms and stood, then took his wife in his other arm and pulled her away from the graveside as her sobs began again.

1

Horner ~ Present Day

I REMOVED MY SUNGLASSES AND squinted. The sun weighed down on the fields, and they soaked up the hot embrace. After the terrible snow of the winter and the dramatic flooding during the spring, nature had decided Exmoor deserved a bucolic summer. The oak trees surrounding the field I stood in were dark green and grand. Their companions, the beech and a few surviving ash, were just as dominant. The arboreal version of titans.

I glanced up. The sun-bleached blue of the sky, streaked with high white clouds, played host to an ancient battle. A juvenile buzzard didn't stand much of a chance against the crows, discouraging his interest in their treetop homes. Jet pilots would envy their aeronautical display.

A noise disturbed my relaxed pondering, and I put my sunglasses back on, then adjusted my khaki cap, an essential item for the summer if you didn't have hair.

"So, what do you think?" asked Eddie Rice as he wandered up the overgrown track towards me.

"I think you have a lot of work to do, but it's beautiful, Eddie. A really lovely spot." I gazed over the green fields, cattle grazing in the distance, bee hives nearby filling the still air with a soft and lazy drone. England didn't get much more perfect than this, and I had the privilege of living just the other side of the hill.

He stood beside me and turned to look out over the view. After retiring from the police, just a few weeks before, Eddie already looked like a different man to the one I'd met during the winter. He'd lost weight, gained a tan and smiled a lot.

"Yeah, it is. I can't believe we could afford it in the end." He wiped sweat off his brow and replaced the straw hat his wife made him wear. I liked Lilian Rice, a good woman, with a sensible and practical mind. She'd been a bookkeeper and made some very canny investments over the years, so despite being a public servant all his working life, Eddie had enough to retire to a small patch of dreams in rural Somerset.

"Lot of work, though. It's a really rundown property," I said, focusing on the small cottage about fifty metres south of our current location.

"I know," he said with a glee I didn't understand. "I can't wait to get stuck in. Finally, a real project. Our Bristol house was never much of a challenge."

I had to wonder if Eddie's DIY skills were really up to the rebuild necessary, but Lilian seemed confident. For now, they were living in a couple of mobile home caravans, and seemed blissfully happy.

From our vantage point, an elevation of about twenty degrees to the top of his land, I could see Ella pottering about. We'd been on sticky ground for a bit after the fire and escape from Scob. I'd hurt a lot of people and the collapse of the women's refuge had damaged her confidence. She and Thomas still wrestled with the insurance company, but they wouldn't be rebuilding The Rectory. They'd sell the land and find somewhere else.

The police investigations continued, Prescott's madness playing out in the press almost daily, but I remained safely hidden. No one in Scob wanted to give them my name. Sadly, I didn't have that luxury when it came to Eddie's old boss, Tony Shaw. I'd be giving evidence via video link at his trial, come the late autumn. Eddie and I didn't discuss it much, because he knew they didn't have the whole truth out of me, and he didn't want it. He was a practical copper, and I hadn't hurt any innocent people. It made our friendship easier if I kept my secrets close.

"So, you own all this and a stretch of the woodland behind us?" I asked, turning to look at the dark march of deciduous trees to our rear.

"Yep. We don't have planning permission for anything on that site but keeping the woodland we do own in good heart, is a priority."

"And Lilian's okay with living next door to a graveyard?" I asked, nodding at the field we stood in.

A few headstones reared from the field, scattered about from where a Methodist Chapel used to bury their congregation. The chapel was next door to Eddie's cottage and long since sold. It looked well-maintained and empty. He said they were incomers from London.

He shrugged. "You live next door to a graveyard."

I did, and it often made it hard to sleep, but then I had an interesting relationship with the dead. Willow was trying to help me understand what kind of relationship. I pushed the thoughts away. Today would remain bucolic, and I would *not* fill my head with unhappy thoughts.

"I think the dead here will be lucky to have you and Lilian to look after them." From nowhere, a chill wind caressed my back, cooling the sweat. Prickles raced up my spine. I twisted to look over my shoulder, feeling as if a sniper's scope had zeroed on our position. I forced the feeling down. We stood in a graveyard, it was bound to be weird.

"They say the local plague pit is down there as well. They took the dead from Luccombe and the other hamlets around here."

"Cheerful thought, Eddie, thanks." I raised a smile, the sense of being watched still making my muscles too tense.

He grinned at me. Now free of his police duties, the bag of spanners' face was considerably less hangdog.

A shout from the cottage meant lunch waited for my attention, so we ambled back down the track, avoiding the brambles and stinging nettles with some difficulty.

On the way, Eddie asked, "How's things with your young Heather Wicklow?"

I smiled. Thinking about Heather always made me smile. "Yeah, good.

She's off with the Taunton Army Reservists this weekend. Four days of training. So far, she's loving it, but we'll see how it goes, I guess. Heather's not the best at obeying the rules and if she makes it to the passing out parade I'll be surprised."

"You did good there," he said. "She was on a path to nowhere and you gave her somewhere to go."

"Wasn't just me. Ella had a great deal to do with it as well."

"It's Ella's job to rescue people. You did it because you care. Says a lot about you, Turner."

I didn't know what to say to that. Heather did the work. She put in long hours on my business when she was home, long hours on her training for the AR, and she'd started studying for her college courses that began in October. Heather was on a mission to leave her past so far behind it would belong to a different person by the time she'd finished.

"I just want to see her happy," I mumbled, embarrassed.

Eddie's approval shouldn't mean so much to me, but it did. He represented my idea of a 'good family man'.

Considering how easily I'd hurt people in Scob and murdered Heather's ex-boyfriend, along with my lack of a traditional family, I found myself admiring Eddie Rice.

"Come on," Lilian called out. "It might only be salad for lunch, but it would be good to eat before the sun melts the lettuce."

ELLA SAT NEXT TO ME in the old Nissan Warrior I owned. "Can we make a stop on the way back to the bungalow?" she asked.

I glanced at her. "Sure. Is there a problem?"

"I just need to check on someone. You don't have to be there, though. I can walk over later."

"Ella, it's fine. I'd like to help. I said I was happy to be taxi for the weekend." The Rav, Little Gem, hadn't coped too well with the flooding in Scob and needed an overhaul before the next MOT. Ella didn't have a car for visiting in her vast parishes, so I volunteered for today's run arounds.

She nodded, then turned away and stared out of the window. I was worried about Ella. She'd become withdrawn over the summer and was not her usual dynamic force for good. More of a weak breeze of good intentions. I didn't know how to broach the problem. What if it was womanly health problems? If she wanted me to know, wouldn't she just tell me? Heather was so busy with her life that she hadn't noticed.

"Where am I going?" I asked.

Only a mile and a half separated the tiny hamlet of Horner from Luccombe, so she needed to tell me where in the village we were headed.

"Go past the church and down Holt Ball Steep. I'll tell you when to stop."

"Roger that."

We slumped into silence again. This wasn't normal. I didn't like it. Time to do something.

"What's wrong?" I asked, fearful of the answer.

She turned to look at me. "Nothing."

"Ella. For God's sake, don't lie to me. You and Heather, you're family, what's wrong?"

Her attention returned to the fields and twee cottages we passed. She sighed. "I'm waiting on test results from a breast biopsy."

What the hell did that mean?

"You have cancer?" I asked, my heart going faster than it would during combat.

Ella's eyes widened. "Lorne!"

I stood on the brakes. A tractor loomed, the back end in sharp focus and intimate detail.

"Bugger." I took a breath and coaxed my old truck into a gateway, the hawthorn hedge deep green and thick.

"Okay, tell me," I said.

Ella wiped her hands on her thighs. She wore lightweight cotton trousers and a t-shirt. Now I was paying attention, I realised she'd lost weight.

"They've done the biopsy. It'll be a few weeks before I get the test results. It might just be a benign lump. Or something."

"When did you find it?" I asked.

"June. Thought I'd give it a few weeks to go away. When it didn't, I went to the doctor."

"Christ, Ella, it's the end of August, that's months."

"It doesn't grow that fast." She finally looked at me.

"Tell that to my mum." She'd been diagnosed too late to make any difference to the outcome. I'd made it home long enough to say goodbye, but not to be of any practical use. I regretted it every damned day. "Why didn't you tell me?"

She shrugged. "Girly stuff."

"Ella." I couldn't believe she'd said it or how much it hurt. I took her hand in mine and made sure to hold her eye contact. "You are my closest friend. I will be there every moment you need me and probably several you don't."

She managed a small smile and nodded, trying to fight the tears. "I didn't want to tell anyone until I knew if I'd need treatment or not, but... I'm scared, Lorne."

"Of course you are. I would be. An enemy we can't fight with weapons and it's hard to win. Next time you go to the hospital or doctor, just tell me and I'll be there. Okay? Promise?"

A small nod.

"Are we telling Heather?" I asked.

"I'd rather not. At least not yet. She's so focused on work."

I pondered this for a bit. "She'd want to help. I think we should. I can do it if you can't deal with the emotions. She's very fond of you, Ella."

"Okay, but we'll pick our moment and do it together. She'll need you as well."

The growing ache in my chest, its source fear, thickened my voice. "Hey, I owe the pair of you. The last few years you've held me together, Ella. I don't think I'd have survived without your gentle handling. You've been a rock in a world turned to soggy marshland around me. Your kindness towards Heather has been unlimited. I know she's living at my place, but you're just as important to her. The pair of you keep me sane and straight."

Ella managed a soft chuckle. "At least one of us is straight."

I laughed and the thick atmosphere shifted gear. "If you were straight, Ella, you'd still be too wise to get tangled up with an idiot like me."

"True. Talking of which, how is Heather?"

I pulled the truck back on to the lane and we pottered off, now going through the small village of Luccombe with its huge church.

"Fine, why?" I needed some context here or this conversation would go south really fast.

"I just wondered if anything had changed."

I glanced at Ella. "What does that mean?"

She shook her head. "I'm not getting involved in that pickle, Lorne. You're on your own. I'm sure you'll figure it out one day." She nodded. "We're there, pull over. You can come inside if you want. Peggy will like you."

I had to admire Ella's ability to box her problems in favour of helping her parishioners, but I wondered how much it cost her. I used to find it hard work in the army. As one of the squadron's long-term survivors, I'd become the agony aunt, but there weren't many who could listen to me if I needed them.

You can put that in a box as well, mucker.

I climbed out of the cab of the Nissan and followed Ella up a path that looked like unintentional crazy paving. A garden, given over to meadow flowers and grasses, pressed against my bare legs and rambling honeysuckle climbed the white cottage. More twee Exmoor village properties.

My mind offered up the bombed-out shell of an Afghani hospital as a counterpoint. It had been on my mind a great deal the last few months. Heather had watched with concern as I pored over newspaper reports until she took them all away and banned the radio and TV. During the weeks following the collapse of the Afghan Government, we'd done a lot of running and firearms training to keep me busy and focused on my new life, not my old. Bless her, the girl was fast becoming another of my rocks. Her slim shoulders proved strong.

"Pull it together," I muttered as Ella knocked on the green front door.

I had to be strong for Ella. I had family in trouble. I couldn't do anything about the Taliban, and it wasn't my job any more. I had to stop thinking about the wasted lives or I'd lose what was left of my marbles.

The front door opened, and a woman made of cardigans and white fluffy hair stood in the doorway with a wide-open smile and sparkling eyes. I'd never met my maternal grandmother, but I hoped she looked something like this; my paternal grandmother had resembled that De Ville woman from the dog book in personality if not looks.

"Ella, how lovely to see you. I have home-made lemonade, and is this your boyfriend?" She looked up at me.

"Hello, Peggy. I'm Lorne Turner. Just a friend of Ella's." I held out my hand.

She slipped a small, dry, and delicate hand into mine. I offered a gentle squeeze rather than a shake. "Oh, I had hoped she'd met someone. She's such a dear, she deserves to be all settled down."

I had the feeling Ella would disagree with that sentiment, but she just smiled and ushered Peggy into the cottage. A very strong odour of lavender filled the cottage. The décor of the interior fuddled my mind until I managed to untangle the contents. Peggy clearly loved her crochet and knitting. Every surface had something knitted on it in a blaze of colour, many of which defied nature.

Ella and Peggy chatted about the upcoming *Bring & Buy Cat's Protection Society* sale and fun run.

I listened with half an ear, knowing I'd be running, but not really concerned. I mean, three miles through nice tidy lanes was hardly a challenge.

Peggy poured us cool drinks, and I saw lemon drizzle cake on the small kitchen table. Peggy noticed and smiled. "It's been so long since I fed a man. Let's get you a slice."

I liked Peggy.

"Then perhaps you could help me with some plumbing?"

There's always a cost for a woman's lemon drizzle cake.

2

WHEN I FINISHED CLEANING THE drain in the kitchen, I found Ella and Peggy in the living room. Ella tried to smother her grin. She'd brought me over just for my manliness with drainage issues. I wasn't overly impressed, considering she knew how to dismantle a u-bend.

They were watching something on an old projector Peggy had set up.

"What's this then?" I asked, drying my hands on a dishcloth.

"A mystery, dear, and one I just don't understand," Peggy said.

She had a large, ancient, black Kodak projector set up near an LCD TV, but the projector pointed to the wall behind me. With great care, I edged into the small room, stuffed with cushions, armchairs and more china than I felt qualified to be around. They were watching something.

"You see, that's me," said Peggy, pointing.

I looked at the pale image on the wall. A small girl with blonde pigtails and the brightest smile, raced into view. She headed towards another girl, older, with shorter hair and a somewhat dour face, though her eyes softened as she gave her hand to the young Peggy, and they headed off to a pond. The person recording followed their happy skipping. The images bounced a little, and I watched as both girls pulled off their neat summer dresses and shoes before racing into the water. We couldn't hear them, but we watched their squeals of laughter at the cold.

"I don't know who that is in the background. She's not my mother."

I glanced at the other figure. A woman in a tweed suit and sensible brown shoes. Neat dark hair and an austere face. She watched the children with the dispassionate gaze of an observer, rather than a participant, in the unfolding scene. A tingle started in my spine and the feeling of a hard black feather being dragged over my scalp brought on a shiver. From nowhere, the image on the film expanded like looking through a gun scope, the woman's face now vivid in the pale film. Behind her, a shifting blackness of squirming shadows rose like a portal from a horror film. My mouth dried and sweat broke out on my palms. A physical reaction to genuine fear. How could I be scared in a cottage full of knitting and old lady?

I glanced at Ella; she didn't seem at all fazed. She didn't see what I did, which meant this came from some broken part of my mind. Maybe a residue of my nightmares? They'd started to push and strain the usual narrative, changing and keeping me off balance. I had less of them now Heather lived with me, but when they breached my unguarded sleep, they arrived even harder than before.

"I have no memory of this," Peggy whispered in the present.

"Of the event, or the film?" I asked, trying to shake the dread pooling in my guts.

"The event, the film, all of it," Peggy whispered. "If I didn't know better, I'd have to say this isn't me in the film. But I know it is." She pointed. "That is me. But I don't remember the other little girl, or the woman, and I don't know who is filming. I suppose it must be my father."

"Where did you find this film, if you've never seen it before?" I asked.

Ella raised a hand. "My fault. Someone found it in the village hall and recognised Peggy's maiden name on the box."

The scene broke before the next recording.

Now the girls stood together, the older one looking... odd somehow. It was in her eyes. They stared out of the scene, clear but blank, and even the younger Peggy appeared sombre.

The woman, once again, occupied a detached space in the background. This time in a dark suit. At a guess I'd say the fashion looked to be early fifties, but I wasn't an expert on these things.

I took more interest when a building appeared, it made me force away the strange *otherness* I saw on the film. "That's Eddie's place." I pointed to the cottage in the background.

"Is it?" Ella asked. "I haven't seen it from that angle."

"Yeah, if you stand at the top of the old graveyard he's bought, that's the exact view. Only the house is in one piece in the film." At the moment, Eddie had a roof and four walls but sweet-f-a inside the house. "See, the graves are clearer where someone is tending the field."

The camera panned around, and I watched in surprise. "Where's that?" I asked.

"I don't know, dear," said Peggy, and she sounded almost scared. "I don't understand any of this."

I frowned and continued to watch. Dominating the near distance, a large building of recent construction for the time, spread out in a single storey of glass and concrete. It certainly wasn't a converted farm barn. The trees stood behind it, dominating the skyline as they did now. The structure resembled some of the old army buildings I'd seen on bases in countries that once belonged to the British Empire. One in Kenya came to mind, it was still being used as a clinic and hospital. I saw another woman at the large entrance to the building. Despite the grainy picture, she gave the impression of being worried. No black shadows behind this woman.

"That's my mum," Peggy said. "But I really can't remember the building."

"There's nothing there like that now," I said. "The trees come down to the graveyard." Filmed more than sixty years ago, the trees I'd seen at Eddie's matched the time spans involved. Mature but not old. The film panned back to the children, who now walked away, hand in hand, backs to the camera.

The image vanished just as the projector clicked and ran out.

I glanced back at Peggy. She looked a little lost.

Ella moved and drew my attention to her. "I do have some news, Peggy. Why don't you sit down?"

Peggy sat in what was obviously her chair, judging by the pile of wool next to it. "What did you find out?"

Ella removed a notepad from her bag. "I went through the church records and yes, I found your baptism, Peggy. Under the name, Westbrook, your maiden name. So I went forwards a few months and found another under the same surname. Bettina Westbrook was baptised," Ella checked her notes, "on the thirty-first of October nineteen-forty-eight. She was already three years old."

"I had a sister then? That's my sister?" Peggy asked, hand on her heart, voice paper thin in her surprise.

"It certainly seems likely," Ella said.

"That woman in the suit is not my mother, so who is she?" Peggy asked.

"You really don't remember the girl or being here as a child?" Ella asked.

"I remember being here in snatches, but I don't remember my sister at all." She covered her mouth and tears fell down her round, soft cheeks. "Oh, that's so sad. How could I have forgotten someone I loved?"

I kept my counsel.

Ella, though, reached over and took her hand. "You were a small girl, Peggy. We don't know what happened yet, but I've requested details from the diocese's archives. There might be more hidden away we can discover. Also, I've been in touch with Somerset House and maybe we can do a DNA test on you so we can find other relatives who might know something. These databases are huge now."

"We can really do that? Find more family? It's just been me and my son for so long. It would be nice to think there was more out there somewhere. Maybe my sister is still alive?"

Considering her baptism was over seventy years ago, I doubted it, but being honest benefited no one. Ella just smiled and nodded.

I couldn't escape the weird sense of warning and dread creeping over my skin as I'd looked at the woman in the old film footage. Something about this didn't feel good. Then I realised—the graves in the film—some of them looked freshly turned. Eddie had told me the Methodist chapel had stopped burying people in the grounds during the eighteen seventies because of worries about the plague pit in the area. Ella needed to know this, but Peggy didn't.

Being a well-trained man, I collected up the plates and tea things, taking them to the kitchen. I ran some hot water and started washing up. While I did so, I gazed out into the back garden. Neat and tidy compared to the front, and full of veg, with a herb patch. Peggy loved her garden. I wondered what her story was. She obviously came from the area, but she had echoes of the Black Country in her accent.

I tried very hard not to think about Ella's news. I needed time to process the implications and what I could do to help. The farm had three bedrooms. Heather had my old room, I had my parents', and we used one as an office, but we could move that downstairs. Or even into one of the barns. I didn't like the thought of Ella being alone if she needed treatment.

Heather and I would draw up contingency plans. Diet plans needed considering. Treatment plans. Willow would know of alternative practitioners who worked with the traditional treatments for cancer. We needed to mitigate the side-effects from the possible radiography and chemotherapy, this must be a priority. I could organise it for her. The previous vicar for the parishes, Thomas Hearn, he'd step up and help organise her people so she didn't have to chase curates to take the services she couldn't manage. We'd do that between us. I had good oversight now, it made me calmer.

"Lorne, you'll wash the print off the plate if you keep cleaning it like that," Ella said from beside me.

"What?" Startled, I nearly dropped the plate in the sink. Not a good idea—it was a Belfast sink.

"Time to go, big man."

"Okay."

"Take me back to the bungalow?" she asked.

"Of course."

We said our farewells to Peggy, and I took the rest of the lemon drizzle cake. Heather would be pleased when she came home tomorrow.

I drove Ella through the narrow village roads to the tiny new-build estate and her bungalow. The vicarage had been sold off years before for a ridiculous amount of money. It had five bedrooms and a vast garden. A bit over the top for a modern C of E vicar.

When I pulled into the drive, Ella turned to look at me. "Listen to me, Lorne. I know you're already planning how to deal with my problem, but I need you to remember one thing." She waited until she had my full attention.

"What?"

"This is *my* problem."

"Ella—"

"No, Lorne. My problem. I'll need your help, but you aren't 'white knighting' this—understood?"

I felt my jaw bounce. She maintained laser focus on me.

I caved. "Understood."

She nodded in her business-like way and left the vehicle. "I'll call you in a couple of days."

"Yeah. If you need anything—"

"I know—you are always going to be there." She smiled. "It helps, telling you. Thank you."

She patted the open window frame to the truck door and left. I watched her walk into the bungalow before driving away.

THE SCREAMS ECHOED THROUGH ME. The call to prayer bellowed over the top. The screech of a jet engine tore underneath.

My breath clawed to escape in my blocked throat.

Dust and sand.

I scrambled at my flak jacket and webbing, trying to suck in a breath of clean air. Wishing for the cooling scent of a summer's morning, full of the taste of lawn cuttings and fresh hay.

A weight sat on my chest, preventing my ribs and diaphragm from doing their jobs. I forced my eyes open to look. Was it going to be concrete? Stone? The side of a bomb blasted vehicle?

I couldn't breathe.

I was going to die.

I looked up and saw the shadow of a creature in long robes and a shemagh sat on my chest, arms crossed, long legs folded. Black, almond-shaped eyes stared down at me, glaring and hard. The weight on my chest grew.

Why? Why are you killing me?

I can't breathe! Help me!

My hands weakened on my equipment as I tried to release the straps to free myself.

I was dying and my desert companion sat there, making it happen...

"Lorne! Lorne! Wake up."

I floundered in the bed and knocked against something soft that grunted. Hurling myself away while sucking in lungfuls of sweaty air, I landed with a thud on the floor and scooted to the nearest corner to protect my heaving flanks.

"Lorne, it's Heather," came a muffled voice from the other side of the bed.

It meant nothing to me.

"Lorne?" A small figure. Low to the ground. Short dark hair around a delicate face.

This was no monster.

"Lorne? I need you to listen to me. I need you to stop making that noise."

Noise? What noise? That whine was the jet engine screaming overhead. Right?

No.

Me?

Yes.

I looked into the big blue eyes peering at me from around the bed and snapped the noise off.

The elfin face nodded and smiled. "You need to breathe in and back out. Nice and slow. Count with me. Pinch that spot between your thumb and finger. It'll be dawn soon. We'll have light. Right now, I need you to count. One... two... three... in... hold... out..."

This continued for some time.

"Help."

The small body scooted over the floor, remaining low, and came within arm's reach.

"Heather," I whispered.

"Right here, Lorne. Right here." She gripped my arm hard, pressing into the scars.

I shifted body position and Heather took it as an invitation. She pushed into my flank, holding me tight, and allowed me to bury my head in her neck. Her delicate scent filled my nose. Nothing smelt this good in the army.

I shivered despite the hot air leaching through my open window. She stroked my head and back, her fingers coming and going depending on the scars.

Quiet and still, we huddled in the slowly lightening dawn. When I finally relaxed, she pulled back, and we sat shoulder to shoulder looking at the tangle of sheets I'd dragged off my bed.

"It's been a while since you lost it that badly," she said, not looking at me.

"Yeah, sorry I woke you."

I felt her shrug. "Too hot anyway. I wasn't really asleep."

"Did I hurt you?" If I had, I'd never forgive myself.

"No. You didn't hurt me. I just landed on my arse."

I glanced at her and for the first time realised neither of us wore very much because of the summer heat. I turned my eyes to the front.

"Want to talk about it?" she asked.

"Different dream."

"What's happened to cause it?"

I sighed. "I had a strange time of it with Ella the other day."

"You went to Peggy's, right? I found the cake in the fridge." She blushed. "We might not have cake in the fridge."

I chuckled and it felt wrong, forced somehow. "Peggy showed us an old cine film of her as a child with a sister she doesn't remember. There's something really wrong about it but I can't work out what. It's... Christ, this is going to sound mad, it's like the djinn is demanding something but I don't know what. I just don't understand."

She nodded. "Well, maybe he'll find a way to tell you."

"Until then I get to wake us both up in a sweaty mess?"

"There are better ways to get sweaty," she muttered with a tinge of exasperation.

Heather had lost a lot of her long hair during the explosion at The Rectory in Scob and since joining the Army Reservists, she'd taken it short and spiky. It made her face harder, older, stronger. "If you spent the day with Ella maybe you can tell me what the problem is? She's lost weight. What's she not telling me?"

Oh bugger it, I knew she'd figure it out. "She's had a breast tissue biopsy."

Heather heaved in a breath, shock widening her eyes. "Cancer?" A word full of horror and fear.

"We don't know yet."

Tears welled, and she did battle to control them. She won. "Why is she not telling me?" But keeping the wobble from her voice proved impossible.

I laced my fingers through Heather's. "Because she doesn't want you to worry until we know the result. She only told me two days ago. You were away."

"We have a plan?" she asked. Her hope and confidence in me simultaneously rewarding and worrying.

"We will when she needs us most. Right now she's closing the portcullis and pretending it's not happening."

The phone rang downstairs, the landline. We looked at each other and rose as one organism.

I grabbed a t-shirt and Heather raced off for the phone. I made it downstairs the moment she picked it up.

"Ella, calm down. Yes. Okay, just tell me... Oh no, Ella. Yeah, sure, okay. Here he is."

She handed me the phone. My gut filled with rocks. Had the nightmare been a warning?

"Lorne?"

"What's up?" I almost asked for a sitrep. Idiot.

A big sniff. "Someone's killed Peggy," she sobbed.

It took me a moment to locate the name and the sentence Ella just dropped over me like a bucket of ice. When the fluffy cardigan came into my head, and the taste of lemon drizzle cake filled my mouth, I felt my heart break a little.

"Give us ten mikes and we'll be there," I said.

3

ELLA STOOD OUTSIDE A POLICE cordon with Lilian Rice when we pulled up on my bike. We'd managed to make it down from the moor in eight minutes. I strode over to Ella, and wordlessly, she buried her head in my shoulder.

I looked at Lilian. Her round, kind face bled with sympathy and sadness. "Ella found her. It's bad. Eddie's talking to the locals, locking down the scene before the DI from CID gets here."

"Bristol?" I asked over Ella's shuddering breaths.

She nodded. "DI Mackenzie, Kate to her friends. She's young, but Eddie liked her. She asked for his attendance until she arrives. They're short of experienced CID officers in Minehead at the moment. More bloody cuts." I heard the anger of a woman used to dealing with the impossible hours her husband gave to a job that all too often let him down.

Good on DI Mackenzie for using all her resources in the area.

The sky had woken in shades of pink and blue, the day set to be beautiful. Not a cloud marred the soft pastel shades, and song birds rather than crows filled the air with a musical joy. Nature, with her ability to just roll ever onwards regardless of what happened to the creatures living within her bounty. It always reminded me of my place in this world. Somewhere below irrelevant.

I peeled a soggy Ella off my chest. "What happened?"

Heather handed her a flask of water from her ever present daysack.

Ella sniffed and drank some water. "I couldn't sleep, so thought I'd go for a walk. Came past the cottage. Saw the door open. I was worried. Thought Peggy might have fallen in the garden or something. Went in and…" Her eyes filled with tears. "She was in the kitchen. Someone beat her to death, Lorne."

The tears fell.

"Who would do that to her?" a wail of loss and grief.

I knew she'd be dealing with this better if she weren't so damned stressed over the test results. She was scared and feeling alone. Finding Peggy made it all so much worse.

"Can you get Ella out of here? Back to your place?" I asked Lilian.

She nodded, slipped an arm around Ella's shoulders, and guided her away.

"You want to go with them? I can pick you up later?" I asked Heather.

She shook her head. "I knew Peggy. I liked her. Did some work in the garden for her during the winter and spring. I'll wait with you."

I hadn't known. "You okay?"

"Not really." She looked at me. "Who would do this?"

I saw Eddie in the doorway to the cottage. "Turner, get your arse in here."

He didn't look like the Eddie Rice I'd spoken to just a few days before— this version knew about the darkness in the world, and it exhausted him. He wore a hairnet, coverings on his shoes and gloves, as well as a full white body suit. The forensic team and photographers were busy in the background.

A special constable stood at the gate, white and blue police tape everywhere. Cars now filled the lane, the forensic team parked on the narrow verge and in the field next door. Taking careful note of our names on her action sheet, the special constable lifted the tape for me to walk underneath. Heather came on my heels.

I walked through the small meadow of weeds and late summer wild flowers, everything now tainted with a shade of grey I found depressing. The evil of the world shouldn't touch old ladies like Peggy in places like Luccombe. Or anywhere else come to that.

"Where's the vicar?" Eddie asked.

He stopped us long before we entered the cottage and made sure to keep me on the stone path, rather than the dirt. He wanted to preserve the scene, so I let him manhandle me to where he deemed it safe.

"Gone to your place with Lilian."

He grunted. "Okay, I'll let the DI know when she arrives. Ella said you were here the same day you came to my place?"

"That's right."

"Take me through it. I'll need to take a statement."

I balked at that. "Why? It was days ago, Eddie." I didn't want to get involved in another death on the moor. Too much official paperwork tracking me. "We were just here for tea, cake and I fixed the u-bend in the kitchen sink."

"So you might be one of the last people to see her alive? To be in her house?"

Shit.

"Maybe."

"Then we'll need a statement."

Damnit.

"Okay," I said and managed a smile of compliance.

Eddie's eyes narrowed. He knew we were hiding too many things about Scob, he just couldn't figure out what. As with all police, non-compliance made him twitchy. "We'll also need Ella's, but I don't think she's in any condition right now. Can you walk us through where you were and what you did in the house?"

"Can I ask a question?" Heather piped up.

"Miss Wicklow, can I stop you?"

Heather's eyes narrowed. She didn't trust the police, and it annoyed her that Eddie was becoming part of our lives.

"Ella needs to know—did Peggy suffer long?" Her voice cracked.

She wanted to be just as used to death as me and Eddie, just as tough. In moments like this, I mourned a little for her desire to leave this innocence behind. I didn't want that life for her; I wanted to protect her from the darkness in the world.

Eddie's eyes softened. "No. I don't think she knew much of what was happening, Heather. I think she surprised some burglars, and they attacked. There's a large wound on her head. It would have killed her instantly."

His kindness, and lies, proved to be enough for Heather. She looked up at me. "I'm going to Ella. Let her know."

"Okay, kid. I'll pick you up. Remember, what we talked about stays between us. Ella needs to tell you in her own time."

She nodded, and I watched her walk away, the bike helmet now attached to her daysack keeping her hands free.

I turned back to Eddie. "What's the truth?"

He shrugged. "Can't tell for sure, obviously, not until the autopsy, but it doesn't look good, Lorne. I've rarely seen something this savage."

"Why, for God's sake?"

Eddie shrugged. "Like I said, burglary gone wrong? Can I get you in some booties? Maybe you can see something obvious. I take it you're still hyper-vigilant?"

I nodded. "Hard habit to break even now."

"Come on then."

"Eddie, one favour?"

"Sure."

"I don't want to see the body."

He looked momentarily baffled by my request. "Okay—can I ask why? After everything…" He twigged. "Oh, okay, yes."

I nodded my thanks. There were too many dead bodies in my head. Too many dead I'd cared about. I didn't need another vision to fill my idle moments when I forgot to monitor my thoughts.

After covering my boots and pulling on some gloves, I stepped into the cottage. The calm chaos of Peggy's existence wailed in confusion the moment I stepped over the threshold. The walls looked like they shivered in shock. I paused and drew in a slow breath. The air still held the soft scent of lavender, but the stink of death oozed through it with sticky fingers, tainting everything good.

Over the last few months, I'd been working with Willow on visualisation exercises to help me understand the peculiar talents I'd spent a lifetime ignoring. Apparently, I needed to open myself up while protecting myself. This struck me as such a contradiction I struggled and fought it all the way— much to Willow's annoyance. Though, everything I did tended to annoy her sooner or later these days.

One of these weird abilities had been the 'atmospheres' I picked up on in troubled locations. That's why I'd always had a talent for knowing violence lay behind the doors we were kicking in. This cottage screamed violence.

Glancing down the hallway towards the kitchen, I saw the white suits of the forensic team and various small yellow plastic triangles with numbers on them. The flash of the camera made it easy to see the blood pool and Peggy's arm thrown out, her legs askew, her dress pushed up too high to be decent. Christ, this hurt my heart in a way I'd not known for a very long time.

A shadow shifted, something contrary to the light in the room, a blackness I didn't understand. It mirrored the shadow I'd seen on the cine film. My breath shortened and my heartrate soared, sweat sprang out all over my body.

The image of a child wearing a dress flickered into focus. She knelt in the pooling blood near Peggy's twisted legs, head bowed, dark hair in braided pigtails down her back. I wanted to reach out, pull her from the blood. Cover her small body in mine to protect her from the violence. I twitched, ready to move, when a soft hand on my arm stilled my progress.

"Lorne?" Eddie snagged my attention.

I realised he didn't see the child. A forensics officer stepped into view and the child flickered, blurred, vanished.

I looked at Eddie, unable to find the words for the panicked flood of dread sloshing about in my guts. A man like Eddie wouldn't understand and I didn't want to become some floundering mental fool around him. I had some pride left.

"Yeah," he said, "I know. I know…" His sadness echoed mine, but he didn't understand the shadow or the child.

Soon, I knew, I'd feel rage, but right now, the confusion of this senseless death made me terribly sad. The shadow must just be that sadness. This was all because of the nightmare, a trick of my PTSD. The child, nothing more than a flicker of the light forming a shape, reminding me of the old film we'd watched.

How many times do I have to explain this to you, idiot?

I shook it off like a wet dog. Walking into the living room gave some relief from the pain vibrating in the hallway from the kitchen.

"Wow." I looked around at the chaos.

"I guess it wasn't like this when you came to visit?" Eddie asked. He sounded about a thousand years old.

"No," I said. "No it wasn't."

The armchairs were still in one piece, but that was it. To my experienced eye it looked like someone had taken great delight in gathering up every moveable item, piling them into a blanket, then playing bumps with the pile until everything scattered about in pieces. Much of the crochet had been ripped in the process and tangles of wool were scattered like demented cat toys.

"Can you see if anything is missing?" Eddie asked.

I sighed. "Yeah." One obvious thing. "There was an old Kodak projector with some film in it. She had it set up in that corner." I pointed to where the remains of a TV leaned. "I guess they thought it might be valuable."

"Right. I'll make a note, and have it put on the system so the local second-hand shops can be warned."

"You think it was a burglary?"

"What else can it be? Not like she was the type of person who could be attacked as a hate crime."

A shiver of feathers raced up my spine and over my scalp. The taste of dust and sand filled my mouth. I expected the jolt of fear, the memories of Syria to rush to the forefront, but it didn't happen. The dust and sand usually presaged the djinn's anguish and rage, reflecting the horrors of war living in my head. Not this time. What was my desert companion trying to tell me?

I said, "Peggy showed us a film of her sister."

"So?" Eddie asked.

"She doesn't remember having a sister, but they were both in the film and it was taken outside your place. In the graveyard. She's never been to your house, not since she moved back into the village."

Eddie frowned. "Seriously?"

"Hmm." I looked around with a more clinical eye. "This isn't random, Eddie. We used to toss rooms all the time looking for weapons. This is a systematic search, the way the drawers have been rifled. I think the destruction happened afterwards to hide the initial intent." My heart started to beat harder in a good way, as I let my mind race through possibilities, ready for a hunt. "How did they break in?"

"They didn't. She let them in. Or that's the working theory I have at the moment. There's no damage to the doors or the windows."

"Ella found her early in the morning?"

"That's right."

I turned and looked out of the window. A sleek BMW Z-series was pulling up. I wouldn't have much time left in the cottage. This had to be the new detective inspector.

"Do you have an approximate TOD?" I asked.

"Probably before midnight, but after dusk."

"You think she'd let strangers in after dark?"

"Not likely, but it's possible."

"Was she beaten before or after she was killed?"

"Jesus, Turner."

"What?"

"You're a dark bastard. As it happens, the ME thinks it might be she was slapped about a bit, then killed with blunt force trauma. The blood flow suggests she was rendered unconscious and died of her wounds. Her heart was beating long enough to lose several pints of blood over the kitchen floor."

"So there's some possibility they were after information?"

"That's a hell of a leap."

"There was something about that film, Eddie."

"How would anyone know she had it?"

"Because Ella's poking about in archives. You know as well as I do how easy it is to set a worm on a system to flag a warning when certain search terms are used."

A woman, younger than me and taller, flashed her ID at the special constable and strode up the garden path. She wore a full white body suit, hood, gloves, mask and booties. Professional to a fault.

"Just think about it, Eddie. Please?"

"Yeah, okay. I'll flag it with the DI."

"DS Rice, you taking my name in vain?" The woman walked in with the energy of a highly trained guard dog. Alert, powerful, intelligent and dedicated. "Who are you?" she asked.

I couldn't see much of her face under the surgical mask, but her eyes were the kind of amber you found in a wolf's glare, focused and cunning, her skin a warm brown. Her hairnet didn't bulge, so I guessed she had short hair.

"My name is Lorne Turner. Eddie knows me and I was one of the last people to see Peggy alive in the cottage. I'm just helping him understand if anything is missing."

"I've made extensive notes, ma'am. I'll be sure to give you a full report." Eddie stepped in front of me.

"Okay, well, let's minimise the civilian invasion, shall we?" She held out her arm, a clear indication I needed to leave the scene. Her accent was non-regional English.

To be honest, I wasn't going to put up much of an argument. I wanted out of the cottage. The death of its gentle, happy owner reverberated with a sense of unquiet misery, and something more. It niggled on the edge of my awareness.

"Yeah, sure." I moved towards the front door, keeping my back to the kitchen.

Eddie showed me out. "Can you tell Lilian I'll be home as soon as I'm done here?"

"Roger that." I turned away.

"And, Turner?"

Glancing over my shoulder, I said, "What?"

"I want to hear more about this film you mentioned." The dark frown on his face made me nod with just as much seriousness. His cop instincts squeaked in harmony with mine.

4

I MOUNTED THE BIKE AND rode slowly through the village, now full of rubber-neckers. The press vultures would soon be circling. The ethereal beauty of the dawn became a long distant dream. I realised all the memories of Peggy and her sweet home now suffered under the burden of a coloured filter of red anger and black sadness. It felt terribly unfair.

Pulling up at Eddie and Lilian's place, I climbed off the bike and saw Heather at the top of the field containing the graveyard. Rather than go to the caravan with Ella and Lilian in it, I walked up to Heather's position.

"You alright?" I asked.

She shrugged. "Who would do that?"

I answered honestly. "I have no idea."

"Can we trust the police to find out?" Those big blue eyes, like captured sky, were trained on me.

"I think we can trust Eddie to make sure the police stay honest." Last time, a friend of Heather's was the victim, and the police turned out to be more corrupt than the bikers she'd lived with. Without my interference, his death would have ended with the wrong people prosecuted.

"Forgive me if I find that hard to believe." She kicked at a crooked headstone in the summer burnt grass.

The birds' post-dawn quiet left an empty hollow in the soundscape of the morning. The tail end of summer rendered their mating displays redundant. I watched a blue tractor heave a plough over the stubble of a wheat field, churning the soil to leave red welts for the seagulls and crows to pick over. Their screams and cries failed to reach us.

"How's Ella?" I asked.

Another shrug. "How serious is the threat of cancer?" Heather's voice held a small weakness I didn't hear often any more.

"Don't know. We just have to wait and see. Keep her safe in the meantime."

Heather shifted, leaning against me, and I obliged by putting an arm around her shoulders. "Should I move back to the bungalow?"

I gave it all of five seconds of thought, realised it was the last thing in the world I wanted to happen, so I managed, "We'll see. Let's not make any rash decisions. She could come to the farm."

We were quiet for a moment. Then Heather said, "Why are we stood in a graveyard?"

I chuckled. "Yeah. Eddie bought a graveyard. Weird, huh? What's even weirder is that a cine film showing this graveyard was in Peggy's house, but now it isn't. And as far as I know, only Ella and I saw it."

Explaining the details of the film to Heather as we walked down to the caravans, brought each frame into sharp focus. Who held the camera, though? The father? Peggy said the woman with the shadow wasn't her mother. But why would Peggy have no recollection of her sister?

Why indeed? The thought flashed into my head with the memory of my desert companion suffocating me in dreams of bullets and terror. I shook it off, cryptic messages didn't help with real world grief.

Ella came out of the mobile home the Rices used for living in rather than sleeping. She looked pale, and much smaller than usual. "The police need to speak to me?"

I nodded. "But I don't think it's too much to worry about. Eddie knows where to find you. I can take you home if you want?"

"I managed to get hold of Peggy's son."

"Really?" Odd, I didn't see any pictures of him in the house.

"He's on his way down from Cheltenham. Should be here soon. I ought to wait for him."

"Ah, that explains why there are no photos of a son in the cottage."

"What?"

I'd twigged to the significance. He must work at GCHQ. The secret-squirrel-data-collection-hive-mind of the British Government. "He works for the Security Services."

Ella managed a weak smile. "You're sharp this morning, Lorne."

I grunted. "We've been awake a long time." I glanced at Heather.

She wandered over to Lilian, who now sat outside with a spinning wheel and fleece. She showed Heather how to tease the wool. Christ, I taught her how to field strip an assault rifle when she should be learning things like this, gentle crafts and hobbies.

Yeah, because women shouldn't know how to do both?

Fair point.

"Why?" Ella dragged me back to our conversation.

"Nightmare."

"Sorry."

I shrugged. "They happen less often. This morning was bad. Heather woke me." I tried to keep the emotion out of my voice. The sense of panic I'd endured as my breathing closed down. The fear that had left me a weakened, trembling mess on the bedroom floor. Did this dreamscape now act as an augur for events in the real world? My mind replaying my final calamitous mission in various forms to act as a warning?

My gaze slid up the field to the old graveyard, and I tried to convince myself the shadows came from the passing clouds overhead, rather than rising from the sunbaked soil below. The curling dread in my stomach reared up, serpentine and dangerous. The shadows started to coalesce, formed flickering images I struggled to interpret.

When I realised I saw men, many of them in uniforms I recognised from previous conflicts, bile surged up my throat, sweat broke out all over my body, and the coppery tang of blood filled my mouth. I'd bitten my tongue to hold back a whimper. One of them became more visible than the others in the hard sunlight. He wore a tin helmet, chin strap under his jaw. The dull brown woollen uniform would make a modern soldier weep in despair, especially in this weather. He carried a Lee-Enfield bolt action .303 rifle in his hands.

Even at this distance, I saw the sergeant stripes on his arm and the insignia of Devonshire Regiment from the Second World War.

Unlike the child, this man, he stared at me. Face impassive and emotionless, but the energy rolling down the field towards us—

"You know it's her birthday soon?"

The images vanished.

Once more dragged into the present, I glanced at Ella in alarm. "Really? Shit, when?" All I needed to do was concentrate on the present, on the moment. Whatever, *whoever*, lived in Eddie's field did not exist. My fist closed and my nails dug into my palm, the pain helping to keep me calm.

Ella smiled. "Middle of September."

I sagged in relief. "Not like tomorrow or anything scary?" This was important and real.

"No."

"What do I get her?" *Focus on the people who make you happy.*

Ella laughed at me. "Oh, the panic in your voice. Anything you like, Lorne. I'd say a nice item of jewellery, but I don't think that would work for your friendship, so maybe something for the bike she's saving up for?"

"Oh, yes, okay. Or her own shotgun on my licence?"

Ella shook her head and moved away. "If you think that's what she'd like the most from you? Then you go for it."

It left me a bit confused. I walked after her and changed the subject. "Eddie wanted to know if anything was missing from the house."

"Was it?" she asked as she sat in the chair next to Lilian.

I explained again about the projector.

Ella's hazel eyes sharpened. "Only that was missing?"

"Far as I could tell."

"That doesn't make sense."

I didn't want to fill her head with my suspicions, so I kept my thoughts private for the moment. Instead, I said, "They probably thought it would be an easy thing to sell."

"Maybe. It's a bit of a bloody coincidence that Peggy is murdered just days after she finds that film and I start asking about her sister."

Guess I wasn't the only one with a naturally suspicious mind. "How did it come into her possession?"

Ella stretched out her legs and I noticed Heather paying more attention to our conversation than Lilian's explanation about how to tease wool with the best technique.

"That was all a bit odd as well. She bought the cottage ten years ago, knowing she lived in the village as a child, but she never knew where exactly. Both parents are long dead, obviously, and she had no other family apart from her husband and son. Her husband died shortly after they moved down here."

"That's sad," Heather said.

Ella nodded. "It certainly broke her heart. Anyway, the long and short of it is, the village hall is having a clear-out and someone found a box among the amateur dramatics group's belongings with her father's name on it. Sherry, who helps me out with the cleaning of the church, knew the family name."

"Sherry has a scary brain," Heather added.

"How so?" I asked.

"She seems to keep all the parish records in her head. She's like ninety odd and she's never forgotten anything she's read or heard."

I looked at Ella, who nodded. "It's true. She'd be one of those detective geniuses if she'd been born in a different era. She's lived in Luccombe her entire life and remembers everyone. She knew Peggy had lived here as a child, knew the family name, so figured the box belonged to Peggy."

"How could a box that old have survived?" I asked.

"Have you ever seen into the bowels of a village hall? Seriously, you could find the Arc of the Covenant in some of these places."

I didn't really understand. The army specialised in keeping things squared away or top secret. Then I thought about all the paperwork I'd generated, and it had to be stored somewhere, along with all the files every soldier had ever completed. Yeah, okay, maybe a box stored away somewhere could be preserved for decades.

Ella's phone rang. She took it out of her jeans' pocket and grunted. "Peggy's son."

"Do you want me to take it?" I asked.

She rose and moved away, already accepting the call.

Heather caught my eye as I watched her. "She'll need someone with her to deal with the son."

I nodded. "Don't worry. I'm not going anywhere."

"You have clients tomorrow."

"Then we cancel if necessary." Though the money would be handy with Heather's birthday now on the horizon. I wanted to get her something special. She'd been a huge help with the business and her family had pretty much abandoned her—or she'd abandoned them. I could never quite get to the bottom of their relationship.

She frowned. "No, you can't cancel. It's a corporate team-building exercise. You know how important they are. We're supposed to be teaching them how to navigate without a map and compass."

I laughed. "Most of them don't know what a compass is and can't read a map. If it doesn't come from a bleeping machine saying left and right, they can't go anywhere."

"And that's why you need me. You're not exactly tactful." She shook her head in mock dismay. "I'm sure that's how people felt about paper maps when they were first created."

Ella returned, preventing our squabble from heating up. "He's here already. I need to go back to the cottage."

"I'll drive you."

Heather rose as well and Lilian.

WE WERE FORCED TO LEAVE Ella's fully restored Little Gem SUV in a layby a long way from the cottage. The press had arrived and more police vehicles, making the lane impassable. Lilian saw Eddie and rushed to meet him. They shared the kind of embrace I wished for in my life.

Just as we reached the police cordon, I caught sight of a man with the detective inspector. It took me a while to place him inside my memory banks. We hadn't been face to face for years. "Damn me, that's Paul Cole."

Ella said, "That's Peggy's son."

My mouth dropped open. Paul Cole, my GCHQ contact, stood front and centre. I still used his ridiculous ability to corral ones and zeros if I needed intelligence on someone or something. The last time I'd used him had been during the debacle in January. He helped me realise I'd been targeted by a covert group called the Gnostic Dawn, bent on a disturbing occult domination plan. I had no idea his mother lived in Luccombe.

Paul glanced over to our small group, grief written in every line of his face, but no awareness of me. He started to argue with DI Mackenzie. I shot a look at Eddie, and he nodded in concern. No other male officers stood nearby. Paul stood at over six feet and spent more time in the gym than the average computer wizard.

DI Mackenzie asked him to back off, but Eddie and I knew it wasn't going to happen. Bollocks, I didn't want Paul arrested for being an emotional idiot the day his mother was murdered. He'd never forgive himself.

"Cole," I snapped out in my best sergeant major voice. "Stand down." I marched towards him, angled to place myself in front of the detective inspector.

Startling him worked. Paul broke off and turned towards me with confusion. It took a moment. The last time we'd met in real life my face had been in one piece and I still had at least some hair.

"Turner?"

I reached him. "I am so very sorry about your mother."

He struggled to maintain his composure. "They won't let me see her."

Reaching for his shoulder, I looked him square in the eye and said, "It's for the best, fella. DI Mackenzie is just trying to protect you. Let them do their jobs and you can see her later."

His jaw trembled. "It might not be her..."

"It is, Paul. I am so sorry, but it is Peggy."

A hand went to his belly, and he let go of a sob, doubling over in agony. I heard reporters and knew neither of us wanted our pictures in the press. We needed to move out.

"Come on. We have somewhere you can rest." I glanced at DI Mackenzie. "I'll get him back to Eddie Rice's place, that okay?"

She nodded and mouthed a silent 'thanks'.

"Come on, Paul. We don't need to draw press attention to us right now. Let me help you."

I put an arm around his shoulder and guided him towards the others. Eddie broke up the press at the barrier and, keeping our faces turned away, we made for the SUV. With too few seats in the vehicle, Lilian and Heather offered to walk back to the cottage. Eddie and Ella came with me and Paul. We sat him in the front and retreated from the circus around the cottage.

"How are you here?" he asked me.

I glanced at him. The chestnut curls and warm brown eyes hadn't changed, but he'd lost his puppy fat face and now sported designer stubble and defined bone structure. He was at least five years my junior, and I had the sudden desire to hide Heather away somewhere until he left the area.

"I live just up the road. Ella called me when she learned of Peggy's death. I met your mum the other day. She was a lovely woman, Paul."

"Ella? The lady that phoned me."

"Hello, Paul," Ella said from the backseat.

He turned to look at her. "You're the vicar?"

She went on to explain how she'd found the front door open and called him as soon as she finished phoning the emergency services. Peggy had given her the number some months before in case of 'old people accidents'—her words, apparently.

We pulled up at the caravans, debussed, and Eddie started making tea.

Paul seemed to be struggling to take in the facts, so while we bustled about, Ella explained once more what she'd found at the cottage. By the time she'd finished, the others had arrived.

Heather came straight over to me. "You know him well?"

"I did. He was MI6 when I was posted in Helmand. This was before 2014. We worked together for several tours. He was young, and it was my job to keep him alive. Turned out to be quite the challenge most of the time. He opted to move to GCHQ after the last tour and took a promotion. We've been in touch over the years, but I haven't laid eyes on him for at least seven. He doesn't know why I left The Regiment."

"He doesn't know about the PTSD?"

"No. And I'd like to keep it that way."

Heather understood. She had more than a few secrets she didn't share with anyone, including me. "You didn't know his mother was here?" she asked.

I shook my head. "No. He didn't realise I lived just over the hill, either. Guess we never thought about it."

"Men, the great communicators," she muttered.

Paul came out of the caravan. "Lorne, tell me everything you know."

His eyes focused on Heather for the first time, and I watched him take in her elfin charms. It's hard to be a ladies' man in Afghanistan for obvious reasons, but even there, he'd managed to find willing participants. I felt my fists tighten and forced myself to relax. Heather would handle him, and I had no right to prevent her having a bit of fun.

"You going to introduce us?" he asked me, still looking at Heather.

"Heather Wicklow, Paul Cole." I didn't elaborate on my relationship with Heather.

"I wish we'd met under better circumstances," he said to her.

I watched the slick ladies' man switch on, but it felt flat and broken. No soaring eagle of suave sophistication, more of a broken winged chicken.

"So do I. Your mother was very kind to me. I helped out in the garden and house sometimes."

"You live in Luccombe?"

"I live with Lorne." Her arm came around my waist, almost making me flinch, it was so unexpected. I twigged as to her intent and wondered why she wanted to place such a barrier between her and a good looking, wealthy bachelor. My arm encircled her shoulders.

Paul's eyes widened a little. "Lucky man."

Well, now the pecking order had been established, he turned back into a person, rather than a man on the hunt for game. "Tell me everything, Lorne."

So I did. I went through it all again. Minus the dark shadows, flickering child image, the soldier in Eddie's field, and my sickening dread. The thought of demonstrating my mental illness in front of Paul made me feel irrationally angry.

"And you think that's why she was killed? Whatever was on that tape?" he asked when I'd finished.

"I don't know, Paul. It's just a theory. It could be the police have it right and it's a burglary gone wrong. I just..." I shrugged.

"Your instincts are some of the best I've ever worked with, Turner. If you think there's more to this than just a B&E gone wrong, then I'm putting money on it."

I sighed. I had a horrible feeling that might happen.

5

HEATHER REMAINED CLOSE AT HAND, earwigging, but she knew when to keep quiet. During her time in the motorcycle gang, she'd learned some interesting habits that would make her a good spy, listening being one of them.

"I understand why you want this to be a bit more than just a simple and tragic attack, but I think you should wait for the police to do their job," I said, glancing at Eddie. "Right?"

We sat outside. Sandwiches and bowls of crisps laid out on a table. None of us were hungry, but I knew better than to turn down an opportunity to eat.

Eddie finished his beef sandwich, clearly of the same opinion as me. "A few weeks back, I'd have agreed with your statement, Lorne. But... DI Mackenzie has to operate on the evidence, and at the moment she doesn't have any evidence this cine film even existed. There's no case for it in the house and no camera. She'll look for it, have the pawnbrokers and second-hand shops visited, but mostly, she'd need a damned good reason to consider a bigger conspiracy. She'll not have the budget or manpower to go poking into an old woman's life." He glanced at Paul in apology.

I let my head drop between my shoulders. "Look. I think I'm better off out of this, Paul. I've the court case with Shaw coming up—"

"How many times have I helped you out?" Paul snapped at me.

Heather flinched. It wasn't hard to miss as she'd pressed herself tight against me. I stiffened in response to Paul's words, but I couldn't blame him.

"I know, I owe you, but this really isn't the kind of thing I should be tangled up in. The police—"

"Are going to be sweet bugger-all use, Turner." He glanced at Eddie. "No offence."

"Some taken," he muttered.

"It's been a long day, Paul. Let's get some rest and figure out what to do tomorrow. Things will be clearer. The police will be in touch, and you'll know more about the direction of the investigation." I glanced at Eddie.

He nodded. "They'll be wanting statements from you all."

At that moment, two cars pulled up into Eddie's drive, one of them the BMW Z-series DI Mackenzie had been driving.

Eddie rose. "Or, they'll be wanting statements now. I suggest you get it over with, then you can go home and get some rest."

THEY DIVIDED ELLA AND ME up and took statements in the overgrown garden at the back of Eddie's house. Wisely, Eddie kept Heather out of it, and she remained unobtrusive. She watched Paul with a wary alertness I found disconcerting.

I had the pleasure of talking to DI Mackenzie while Ella sat under an apple tree with a detective sergeant. An older man cut from the same cloth as Eddie Rice but called Trevor Mann.

"Eddie told me what you used to do for a living," DI Mackenzie said.

I grunted. "Eddie talks too much."

"It explained why he let you into the crime scene."

"I have an eye for details. Ingrained habit after twenty years touring the world's shit holes." Not really fair, they were only shit holes because of idiots like me with guns, bombs and agendas.

"You never met Mrs Peggy Cole until your vicar took you down there?"

"Never. She was a nice woman. Gave me lemon drizzle cake." Why the hell did I say that?

DI Mackenzie managed to give me a small smile. "You didn't notice anything else missing, just this..." she made a pretence of looking at her notes. I knew she didn't need to; I could see she knew how to do her job. "Projector?"

"Yep, one of those old ones that played film over two large reels." And some dirty great shadows which only a soldier turned madman saw hovering around and about.

"And you believe the film has something to do with the attack and subsequent murder of Mrs Cole?" Her eyes were sharp, watching for the lie.

"Yes." Not much she could do with that.

"You saw the film on…" again with the checking of the notes, "Saturday afternoon?"

"That's right."

"And the murder occurred last night, Monday night?"

"Apparently."

"Where were you?"

"Asleep at my farm in Stoke Pero."

"Your girlfriend can confirm that?" she asked.

"My friend, with whom I share the house, can confirm I was there at five thirty this morning because I was busy having a very violent panic attack and nightmare. I have PTSD and it's not pretty."

I realised my mistake the moment I finished speaking.

"A violent panic attack?"

My jaw bounced in annoyance. "You ever have dreams so horrific they send you crashing into walls? That kind of violent."

I held her gaze, and she had the good grace to look away first, the colour rising in her cheeks. I didn't want to play nice in this sandpit.

She changed tactic. "What time did you go to bed last night?"

"I went at about ten. Heather would have gone up later. She had some work she wanted to do. She'd just returned from a weekend with the AR." Mackenzie looked blank. "Territorial Army, as was. They changed the name. Army Reservists now."

"Oh, interesting. Okay. So they can confirm her whereabouts all weekend if we need to ask?"

"They can but why would you need to?" I asked.

"Because we're looking into all the unusual visits Mrs Cole had over the last few weeks. Someone she knew, or someone she thought she could trust, did this to her. There is no sign of forced entry. Miss Wicklow has something of a chequered past I understand?"

I felt the beast inside stir for the first time in months at the implied threat to my life. Heather and I had enjoyed a peaceful summer, and he'd been content to lie down and sleep inside me for long stretches. The nightmares didn't disturb him, they only troubled me, because I didn't understand why they'd changed after all these years.

"Miss Wicklow is getting her life together, and I'd be very careful of accusing her of anything to do with Peggy's death. She cared for Peggy a great deal."

"She also had access to the house."

My fists closed. For a moment, DI Mackenzie's eyes flickered with something like trepidation. "Do we need a lawyer, officer?"

"No, just trying to get the facts straight of who is in Mrs Cole's life currently. Violence comes more easily to some than others. I would suggest you and Miss Wicklow remain in the area for the foreseeable."

"Don't make the mistake of looking at Heather for this. She is a good woman, with a kind heart, but she's been abused for a long time. Give her a chance, DI Mackenzie. She won't let you down. I can promise you, she had nothing whatsoever to do with Peggy's death."

"I'm just doing my job, Mr Turner."

I grunted. Looking for a scapegoat more like.

"Anything else I can help you with?" I asked her.

"This film you and the Reverend Morgan claim to have watched? Can you give me details?"

So I did. I went through everything I remembered again. Everything about Ella's investigations into the parish records, all of it. Except for the shadows and the flickering illusion of a child. They remained mine. I gave the DI all the details possible to make the damned police look away from me and

Heather. She certainly listened with more attention than DI Shaw had back in January. It made me respect her, even if I didn't like her very much right now.

"What's next?" I asked when I'd finished.

"Nothing is next for you, Mr Turner," DI Mackenzie said.

"Good."

She looked surprised. "Okay then. I think I have all I need for now, but as I said, don't leave the area."

All this talking wore holes in my patience. I needed some quiet. The nightmare from this morning left me ragged, and I hadn't found a chance to recover yet. I wanted to go and stare at the sea for a bit, preferably with Heather.

We often rode out on my KTM Adventure to North Hill and walked to the furthest point to watch the sun melt into the sea and draw the night sky over the land. We'd stay, sometimes with sandwiches, and wait for the stars. Their bright silence soothing us, and we'd potter home feeling rested. The last few months had brought me a level of happiness and peace I'd never experienced in my brutal life. I also knew that if I had to be brutal to keep it, I wouldn't hesitate.

I stared out over the sun-kissed valley, a buzzard circling in lazy loops overhead, rode a thermal from the hill behind me. Horses dozed, flicking their tails. Cows slept in the distance, lying down in the green grass as nature intended. The hills on the opposite side of the valley rose in a dim haze, crowned in woodland. I didn't want to get involved in this madness— whatever it might be—I wanted to continue to enjoy the peace of the land. The season would shift soon, the deep green of the oak turning golden, the autumn storms dragging the sea into the shore and battering the cliffs. I needed to watch those things happen, knowing I had someone at home I trusted, someone I cared for, a reason to go on with life.

I did not want to endanger this fragile, mundane, and perfect existence.

IT TOOK ANOTHER COUPLE OF hours, but eventually I exfiltrated myself and Heather from Eddie Rice's new home. I tried to convince Ella to come with us, but she was determined to remain in her small bungalow. Paul had her spare bed, needing to stay close to his mother's cottage.

Returning to Stoke Pero felt like the gift that kept on giving. As evening descended, I sat in the garden, tamed thanks to Heather, and drank beer. The warmth of the day hugged the land, and the bats came out to dance their wild jig through the twilight. The local tawny owl even put in an appearance. Blissful, iconic, a British summer evening.

I worked hard not to think about the brutal dawn awakening, Peggy's legs showing through the kitchen door, the small child kneeling in her blood— could it have been Peggy's soul trapped in the cottage? I pushed the thought away, the ramifications too complex for now.

And, of course, Ella's news.

I tried to remain in the moment. Willow said it would help improve my awareness of, and relationship to, my past. The beer helped.

Heather wandered out with more, and sat next to me on the other sun lounger.

"You organised for the next set of clients?" she asked.

I grunted. I'd forgotten.

"Everything is printed out, the handouts and notes you'll need, as well as their names." She sounded resigned to my lack of organisation.

"I was getting to it."

She picked up the empty bottle of beer number three. "Clearly."

I tried not to smirk. "Thanks."

"That's okay. It stopped me thinking about today for all of five minutes." She picked at the label on the bottle.

"Ella will be okay. The police will find out what happened to Peggy."

She looked at me, those blue eyes in shadow, unreadable. "And you? This morning was rough."

I watched the bats. "It's been so much better the last few months I thought it might be easing for good. Then this morning... I don't know—maybe it's trying to tell me something." *It* being my hitchhiking djinn who lived in my head. Or, if you didn't believe in spirits, I should be on heavy anti-psychotics.

"You think?" Heather's sarcasm made me grunt.

"Willow says it might be the case. She wants me to talk to a professional medium she knows. She thinks it might be a spirit guide." Sceptical didn't quite cover my feelings on this one.

Heather knew this, but her assessment of the weird hinterland my mind resorted to under pressure, sat firmly in the *'try it, you never know it might help'* category. "She could have a point. When she's coming up again?"

I heard the strained question. She knew things were drifting with Willow. "Nothing firm, as far as I know."

"Lorne—"

"Leave it, Heather. Willow needs to make up her mind. She has to give testimony at Shaw's trial, and she isn't protected by the same mechanisms I am—it's shaken her, and my issues don't help."

We slumped into silence and night fell over the moor, the stars leaking out of the blackness. I drifted into sleep, content to ride the peace of the night for the moment.

I stood in a green swathe with small headstones dotting the sloping land. A cottage rose from the field, a white, harmless carbuncle among the trees and hedgerows. I recognised the view, and it made me feel safe. In the distance, I saw two children, both girls, and they held hands as they skipped up the immaculate path towards my location. The older of the two had plaits down her back.

The youngest smiled and laughed. The elder appeared sober, indistinct, full of a gravitas beyond her years. They stopped on the path and watched me for a moment. I couldn't quite read their expressions. The summer-kissed freckles blurred and shifted if I focused for too long.

The older of the two lifted her free hand, the left, and pointed behind me.

I turned, expecting to see woodland. Instead, in the distance but also coming closer all the time, stood a building made of glass and concrete.

A woman stood in the doorway. Dark hair pulled back off a face made of angles sharp enough to cut steak. Not a face to smile, unless it had no choice. Behind her stood a figure made of shadows.

Dust and sand filled my mouth, and I coughed. It began to tumble out of me even as I breathed in. Sand poured over my feet. Red sand.

The shadow figure moved. It—he—wore the thob and shemagh.

I wanted to warn the woman, but I couldn't talk while sand poured from my mouth to my feet.

It didn't scare me, but it was very odd.

I tried again to warn the woman. He, my desert companion, moved and suddenly stood before the little girls. The older one lifted her free hand once more and grasped his robe. She whispered to the younger, who looked a little scared.

Moving for me was not possible, but I watched the djinn walk with the children back down the path to the cottage and into its embrace.

I glanced back at the woman in the doorway. This time the shadow behind her loomed, a vast blanket of thick black energy, thrumming with pain and hate. Now the woman smiled, and it turned into a rictus of—

My phone rang, wailing through the armistice between the events of the day and my soul deep need for quiet, tearing me from the dream or vision. I jolted out of the sun lounger. Scrambling for reality.

Heather picked up the phone. "It's Ella."

I took the bleating instrument of doom from her hand. I noticed the phone trembled, and I tried to tighten my grip. "Turner."

"Can you come down here?" Ella asked.

"Now?"

"Please, Lorne. We... we found something in the cottage."

"It's covered in police tape. You shouldn't be in there," I said.

"I know, but Paul needed to see it and I... I'm sorry... I couldn't say no. I have a key—so..."

I sighed. "Sure. Give me twenty. I need a shower."

"Thank you."

I hung up. "Shit." I rubbed my face and pushed thoughts of the dream back. It was already fading, the images becoming less vivid, but not the feeling of hate surrounding that cold woman. I didn't tell Heather.

6

WE COULD HAVE TAKEN THE Nissan, but we opted to ride the bike down instead. Heather's small frame hugged my back. Gone were the days she'd sit at a distance holding the sissy bars. Now she sat tight to me as I rode too fast through narrow lanes, relying on headlights to warn us of oncoming traffic. Not terribly responsible, but we all needed a sin, and speed was mine.

It also kept me distracted from the residue of the dreamscape. Two images seemed burned onto my retinas. That of the woman, with her shadow of hate, and my djinn with the children. What the hell did it all mean?

Pulling up outside the bungalow, Heather dismounted first. "You're a lunatic."

"You didn't seem to mind."

She smiled at me, and her eyes filled with something I didn't understand for a moment, before she glanced away and sniffed. "Ella's cooked something."

"Ella's reheated something someone else cooked."

We walked up to the slightly shabby bungalow and let ourselves in with a yell of welcome. The wall of photos in the hallway now had plenty of Heather and me. We were family, and it felt good.

When we arrived in the kitchen, Ella sat, looking pale and small, while Paul faced the glow from a laptop's screen.

A pot bubbled on the stove.

Ella smiled up at me, but dark circles shadowed her usually bright hazel eyes and I had an irrational urge to throw Paul out of her home.

"Thanks for coming down," she said.

I put a hand on her shoulder and squeezed. "Always, you know that."

Heather moved to the stove. "Is this Mrs Jackson's hotpot?"

"Yes, it is. I was worried you and Lorne wouldn't have enough food in the house after today's events."

Heather grinned, her face wolfish. "Mrs Jackson's hotpot. Score." She made herself at home.

The kitchen table was barely visible beneath a pile of papers, scattered photographs, and a large cardboard box.

"Lorne, good. I need you to look at something," Paul said, turning the laptop to face me.

"Nice to see you as well, Paul," I muttered by way of welcome.

He grunted.

I sighed and sat at the table, trying to focus tired eyes on the screen. "This is a GCHQ database." I glanced at him. "Are you supposed to access it off a laptop?"

He shrugged. "I'm looking at old files. Nothing that'll red flag on the system and I used a small backdoor those of us who are trusted know about. It can't be easily traced back to this location."

"I bloody hope not, Paul. I don't want Ella's place raided in the middle of the night because they think she's a terrorist trying to hack the British Secret Service."

He waved my concerns away. "Just focus on what I found."

I read the screen. Old reports, copies of paper files that must have found themselves placed onto microfiche at some point, then digitised by some administrative mole in the bowels of the country's secret warehouse.

The report referenced the arrival in the country of a young woman brought over the North Sea via RAF airlift from East Germany in 1947. The young woman was a scientist. A blurry photo was there, but it could have been of Eva Braun for all I knew.

"Here." Paul shoved more paperwork under my nose. Actual paper this time.

"Paul, what's going on?" I asked, unable to hide my pleading despair.

I remembered this behaviour from Camp Bastion. He'd find intel on a local Taliban encampment and become almost manic until he'd unearthed every facet of the location. We'd take his intel, present it to the higher-ups, turn it into something actionable and go hunting. Paul, even then, was a highly effective operative. Many times I put my unit's reputation on the line to back him up, and he always came good. The downside of this genius evolved into an obsessive desire to understand the root and branch of every secret he uncovered. This looked like turning into one of those times.

He blinked frequently, making it clear long hours at the computer blurred and red-rimmed his poor suffering eyes. The tidy hair now sat on his head in a mussed, and almost sticky-looking, mess. Rolled-up sleeves and rumpled, unbuttoned, linen waistcoat, with shirt tails escaping, all gave the impression of a man about to fall off the edge.

"How much coffee have you drunk?" I asked.

"Just look at this," he said, shaking the paper in front of my face again.

I took them and placed them on the table. "Paul, sit. Eat. Have some water. You're no use to me like this, you know that."

Heather watched him from the corner of her eye and Ella remained calm, but I knew his behaviour worried her.

"Lorne—"

"Just do it, Paul. Then I'll read the papers."

He huffed and pouted, but I managed to get him to sit. Heather wordlessly brought a bowl of stew, a chunk of dark brown bread and a glass of water to the table. She set them down next to Paul and looked at me. A shared brief smile between us made Heather organise something similar for me.

I focused on the paperwork.

"Where did you find this?" I asked Paul.

"The cottage. Mum had a box in the shed full of paperwork. It had her father's name on the box—Captain Dick Westbrook. I've never seen it before, and I helped her move into the cottage. I think it's where the film she showed you came from."

"Then you should hand this over to the police."

He snorted. "Please, don't make me laugh. That DI seems okay, but she's not going to understand the importance of this intelligence."

Well, I tried.

Also, despite my best intentions, I was curious. I had work the next day, a demanding group who I intended to 'lose' on the moor for a couple of hours. Heather and I would leave trackers in the rucksacks we'd supply, and I'd go find them when I needed to rescue them. Sometimes the groups split up, which gave management a great overview of who functioned well with which team, and who needed to be moved. I'd also be taking another of Smoke's groups at the weekend. His lads, and some of the girls came over once a month and I taught them real survival skills. Heather didn't like being around them, and I didn't blame her. Smoke and the motor cycle club represented her past, but they also paid the mortgage.

I enjoyed working with them despite their murky backgrounds. We'd forage, learn to make simple field dressings, collect plants used for dyeing fabric, and on the days that were too wet, I'd teach things like felt making. People often forget that survival isn't just about hunting and building fire, you need to know how to clothe yourself, to make bedding and simple medicines. I'd been working on my knowledge with medieval and Iron Age experts. Heather and I were booked on a course in October to live in a medieval village for a week, learning how to make tools from flint axes to bronze spearheads and knives. I couldn't wait.

Right now, all that seemed a long distance away. What I held in my hands took a turn for the surreal.

A photo of a young woman, who could be the same as the one on the laptop report, stood outside a building in the snow. She wore a uniform.

"That's Russian military." I glanced up at Paul. The insignia was unmistakable. The red star with the golden hammer and sickle.

He tapped the photo while spooning stew into his mouth. "That's my grandmother."

"What?"

"Yeah, you'd think working for the Security Service this would be flagged on day one of the interview process. I had no idea, obviously. Read the letter."

I scanned the accompanying letter. "It's a love letter."

"Yep. From my grandfather to my Soviet grandmother. She defected through Berlin before the wall went up."

I laughed. "That's stupid." I glanced at him and sobered at the serious expression. "Sorry."

"It's a fact, Turner. From what I can gather, she was a very young Soviet scientist in the late nineteen forties. My grandfather was posted in the British section of Berlin before, and during, the Soviet Blockade. She was smuggled over the border from East Berlin. They wouldn't want to let her go, so it was all very hush-hush, and quite the coup for the British Government, because the Americans wanted her for some reason. She and my grandfather fell in love."

"Surely your mother would have said something?"

He shook his head. "She barely remembers her childhood here. There was some kind of accident, and she suffered such bad concussion she lost her memory, forever. She doesn't," he swallowed hard, "*didn't* remember anything before the age of ten."

"She would have remembered a mother with a Russian accent."

"Not if she didn't have one by then."

All the Russians I'd met in theatre had strong accents; it wasn't one that could be wiped away easily. I also knew little detail about the Cold War because I was busy fighting the War on Terror. I preferred my history considerably older.

"Okay, your grandmother was a... what? Spy?"

"Scientist."

"Who settled in Somerset?"

"Yep."

"And?"

"I don't know, but what if this is the reason my mum was murdered?"

Christ, I felt for him, I really did, but this was bonkers. He needed a reason for the senseless death of his genteel and elderly mother. Losing my mum to cancer had been awful. I couldn't imagine how something like this would devastate me. I'd want someone's head on a pike, and ensure it happened with as much pain and anguish as possible.

Paul needed help, and as the one with *boots on the ground*, it was going to be my job until a closer friend could be found to take over and make him see sense.

"Is this all the information you have?" I asked.

"So far, but I plan on digging in further."

By which he meant digging through deeper archives if necessary.

"Paul, is this a good idea? We need to think about what's best for your mum. You'll need to contact any family, friends, arrange the funeral. I know it's hard—"

"It's not hard. It's life—or rather death—and we need to find out why. That's the important mission. That's what I can do for my mum. I can find out why." His eyes, a hard brown in the florescent light of Ella's kitchen, were utterly focused on his task.

I sighed. "Okay, we'll start digging, but we put together a dossier that we can hand over to the police. I can't get involved beyond that."

"Why?"

"Because I have a business to run and..." I thought about the disturbing dreams I didn't need.

"He has PTSD, which we're still trying to manage," Heather said. "Sorry, boss, but he needs to know." She leaned against the kitchen sink, eating. "You can't push him into something this disruptive. It doesn't do him any good."

My little protector.

I held my hand up to prevent any more private information from leaking out. "It's not quite that bad." Both Ella and Heather huffed at this. "But Heather's right. I've had a rough few years with the inside of my head and

I'm trying to..." What? Put the ghosts to bed? That clearly wasn't happening after this evening's little dreamscape interlude and that soldier... "I'm trying to find some balance in my life, which will calm things down."

Paul scoffed. "The Lorne Turner I served with would have said 'Get your head in the game and get on with it'."

I felt my fist close under the table. "I know. I am not that man. Not any more. Syria broke me, Paul. Look up my damned file. I'm sure you can recover the bits that are redacted for most eyes."

Paul muttered something like, "Syria broke me, my arse."

"I think that's enough," Ella said, standing. "We've shared the information with Lorne, as you asked, but that's it now. We all need some rest. It's getting late." She looked at Heather. "Time to get him home."

Heather nodded.

I ate the rest of the hotpot and bread as if it were the last meal I'd ever consume and rose from the table. "Listen, Paul, let me have a think. Okay? You'll still be around over the next few days, and we can catch up and re-examine the intel with calmer heads. It's been a terrible day for you, mate. Just get some rest."

Ella showed us out.

We stood on her dusty lawn in the darkness. The local residents tried to keep the outside lighting to a minimum for dark skies all over Exmoor. I loved it. Heather wandered over to the bike and leaned against the tank.

"You going to be okay?" I asked Ella.

She nodded. "Yeah, he was just so manic. He was desperate for me to contact you."

"Sorry, mate. He can be a bit intense. That's why he worked with me most often. I listened, actioned his intel but kept him under control. The man's a genius but doesn't advance in his career because the higher-ups just can't manage him. Besides, he's doing what he loves, sifting through endless reports, looking for patterns and interpreting data most of us can't fathom. The man sees meaning in a murmur of starlings."

"Some would call that madness."

"It can be, but he's the real deal. Saved my life more than once, also put it in considerable danger more than once. He knew more about the tribes and family groups in Helmand than almost anyone else I met. Helped us figure out the local police were as corrupt as the Taliban."

"Do I want to know?" she asked.

I shook my head. "No, you don't need those thoughts in your head. Too many lives lost. I worked with him until we were re-deployed to Iraq."

"He's not dealing with his mother's death at all."

"He is, just not the way we would expect. He'll throw himself at this mystery until it's solved, then he'll fall apart for a bit." I stared at the bungalow. "He's safe though. Couldn't hurt a damned fly, that man. I had to put a weapon in his hand once. He almost fainted in terror. It's why he works at HQ rather than in the field."

"Okay, well, I'll see you soon."

"Sure."

I watched her walk into the bungalow and close the door before returning to Heather. "You okay?"

"Yeah. I don't like the way he looks at me."

"He's a ladies' man."

"I don't like it. I'm not a prey creature to be hunted."

I put a hand on her shoulder. "Hey, he won't hurt you. He really is harmless. You'd scare him witless if you threatened that pretty face."

"I know I can scare him, I just wish it wasn't necessary. I wish I'd just be treated like a person."

"Well, you're too beautiful for that, so I'm afraid it's never going to happen."

She looked at me oddly for a moment, then shook her head. "Thanks, I guess."

We climbed on the bike but this time she didn't hug my back. She sat up. I wondered what I'd said to disturb her, but decided she'd tell me if my behaviour troubled her. At least, I hoped she would.

7

HEATHER OPTED TO GO TO bed, the stresses of the day taking their toll. I had the feeling she needed the space to process Peggy's death. She wasn't the only one. I sat on the sofa, beer bottle on the side table, while I stared at the empty fire grate. The night aged while I brooded. With just my thoughts for company, I kept playing the events of the last few days over in my head. Meeting Peggy, seeing the terrible aftermath of her death, the tiny, mysterious figure of the child kneeling on that kitchen floor, and that soldier. The man who stared into me. What did he want? I'd never seen a spirit so clearly.

Who would kill an old woman with such violence? What possible use was the old cine film? If this had happened in my old life, I'd be looking at the cine film with deep suspicion. I'd be thinking about who was in it, why they were there, why the tape had lain hidden for so long. It seemed very convenient that a box belonging to Peggy's father turned up, and days later she's killed. She must have gone out and bought the Kodak projector. No one owned an ancient projector unless they collected old film stock. Watching it couldn't have triggered this attack because they didn't leave a digital trace, so Ella's investigation must have done some damage somewhere, but why? These were seventy-year-old secrets.

It made no sense. I needed more intel, and I needed to keep Paul out of it for now. His distress made him manic, and I wanted space to think.

"Bugger it," I muttered, rising from my armchair. I grabbed my bike keys and boots.

Once outside the farmhouse, I pushed the bike out of the yard and started the engine some way down the hill so I didn't wake Heather. The night air tickled over my bare arms and scalp. I breathed in the heady scent of the dark moor, taking the longer route down to Luccombe just to enjoy the sensation of freedom that came from riding without all the safety equipment. Stupid and irresponsible, but at 02:30 hours the only thing I'd meet on this road would be a fox or a badger.

I pulled up outside Peggy's cottage, the police tape over the front gate and door still intact. Kicking down the stand on the bike, my senses lurched in warning. Someone else was in the lane. I turned my back to the hedge and shifted my weight to my toes. It wouldn't help against a bullet, but if a fist came in my direction, I'd be prepared for the fight. With muscles primed, breathing calm but heavy to give me fuel for sudden action, I waited.

Soft footsteps, coming from the east. The moon, long gone from the night, offered no help, but the tenuous strands of starlight gave just enough ambient light to show me a figure emerging from under the wide branches of a hedgerow ash tree. A familiar gait and shape.

"Ella?" I called out.

A small startled yip followed by a very unvicarly curse. "Lorne," she finally managed. "Bloody hell, you scared me witless."

I stepped out of the shadows. "Sorry. What are doing here?"

"Same reason as you, I expect. Insomnia. Only I live in Luccombe so I'm justified in wandering about the lanes at silly o'clock in the morning. What's your excuse for being here?"

"Needed to check some things in the house without Paul snapping at my heels. His energy is destructive to some of my less conventional senses."

"Isn't it just," she muttered. "What's the plan?"

We turned as one and looked at the cottage. I said, "Break in, spend some time in the house just trying to replay events a little. I don't pretend to know what's going on, but I need a better connection to Peggy, or the past, or…"

"Or something?" Ella asked.

I nodded. "I haven't told Heather, but I saw more than just Peggy this morning." The words slipped out of me with all the grace of a toddler learning to walk. Finding the words to describe the eerie image I'd seen this morning would give it significance, a reality I wasn't ready to face.

Ella picked up on my reluctance. "The kind of something Eddie couldn't see?"

I grunted.

"Well, let's go take a look."

I glanced down at her. "Really? I didn't think you'd want to go back in there after Paul's antics."

She shrugged. "It's different with you. Easier. Considerably calmer. Besides, I have a key, so you don't have to break in." A jangling noise came from her hand.

"Handy," I muttered. "Come on then. We can jump over the wall to get into the garden."

In the end, I jumped, Ella climbed. Once we'd both made it to the wildflower lawn, we went around the back. Pausing for a moment, Ella looked up at me. The pale shadows of her face asked in silence if I really wanted to do this. I offered a nod in response. She slipped the key in the lock and pushed the back door open. We ducked under the police tape and entered the kitchen.

Standing together in the silence, we adjusted to the gloomy interior of the cottage. The damage to the lounge didn't track in this room. The cupboards still contained their cargo. The sink had Peggy's bone china mug, and the plate she'd used for her supper. Local fruit filled the bowl on the table, Cox's Apples, Victoria Plums, and rhubarb, probably meant for a crumble or pie. The bread-knife on the breadboard lay askew, but whether from Peggy's habits or her attempt at grabbing a weapon, I couldn't tell.

We needed more light, and yet neither of us moved to find a switch. I slipped a hand into my combat shorts and found my small Maglite. I wanted to wait for the right moment to break the seal of darkness covering the crime scene.

Remaining still, I closed my eyes and for the first time, I unravelled that extra sense. When kicking in doors of possible enemy combatants, you don't have much time to be subtle. This talent of mine, for knowing of a potential attack behind a closed door, worked in an adrenaline fuelled environment of controlled panic and fear. When we had time to scout a location, to lay a trap, or follow an enemy, I'd relied on training and practiced skills. I most certainly did not rely on some weird sixth sense coming from a connection to another layer of reality most people couldn't see, hear, or understand.

In this new life, I wanted to carve out for myself, the reality of my talents now made it clear I had to at least try to harness this weird ability. Maybe I'd glean more information if I just let myself *feel* the cottage and its memories. All this couldn't just be my PTSD playing tricks in my head. At least, at nearly 03:00, it became a great deal easier to believe in myself than it did during daylight hours.

Starting with my breath, as Willow taught, I took in the smells of the kitchen. All kitchens have odours, and this one smelt of blood, and other bodily fluids. Trying to ignore this obvious stink of misery, I searched for more. The room held the chemicals used by the forensic teams and someone's cheap aftershave. Pushing deeper, I smelt baking, a bin in need of emptying, the cooker's greasy oven and the washing up liquid. Then the smell of Peggy. A subtle scent of a warm and gentle woman, lavender, roses, and lemons. I held on to that remembrance of a living, breathing person. A good soul enjoying her cottage, her garden, the church, and village life. Perhaps a little lonely, especially after the death of her husband. Her son working so hard he had few opportunities to visit, but she had a good life nonetheless.

I opened my eyes.

"They woke her in the living room," I said.

Ella shifted beside me. "How do you know?"

"If she'd been in bed, she'd be in a nightgown. She still wore her dress. That meant she fell asleep in the living room. She didn't let them in. A skilled person broke into the house without damaging anything. Someone used to doing houses, softly and quietly."

"So she didn't know her killer?" Ella asked.

I shook my head.

"What made her come out into the kitchen?"

I mulled this over, understanding human nature from a different perspective to most people. "Maybe she had a weapon? Maybe she shouted at the intruder and chased him? I think the latter is most likely."

"So what made him attack her in the kitchen rather than the living room?" Ella asked.

"Maybe the burglar isn't the one who killed her," I suggested.

"Does it matter?" Ella's bleak voice made me sigh.

"No, it doesn't." I broke the spell, keeping us rooted to the spot, and stepped fully into the kitchen. Switching on the Maglite, the beam very narrow, I did a sweep of the bloodstains on the floor.

I'd seen more than my share of gore. Everyone in a war zone knew what made up a fleshy body under the skin. Be it animal or human. Seeing violence like that in a place like this? It hit me harder than I expected. How did the police do it? How did they see this violence, however rare it remained in Britain, on a regular basis? I'd never had to see civilians die in my country, never fought in Northern Ireland, not really. I'd done stints there in covert reconnaissance, but they were almost training exercises these days. The death of a woman like Peggy, it hit hard and made no sense.

Ella joined me. "I still don't understand why this happened. We only did some research into her family tree, and a few internet searches about her parents in the local records library. Nothing big. She just wanted to know more about her childhood. When we uncovered her sister, it was such a shock."

"When did she find the film?" I asked.

"Straight away, but it took time for me to find the player."

"How long have you been looking into this for her?"

Ella picked up a fallen tea towel and folded it neatly. "About a month, I suppose."

In the stillness of the summer night, we both froze at the sound of a board creaking overhead. I glanced at Ella, her eyes very wide. Putting my finger to my lips to indicate silence, I stepped over the bloodstain. The creaking increased.

The atmosphere in the cottage shifted with the speed of a charging rhino, and all the subtly. The creaking became a banging. The noises made the ceiling shiver.

"What the hell is going on?" Ella cried out.

I tried to contain the very instinctual reaction I had to the sounds, that of running. Something up there wasn't happy.

Moving towards the noise made the beast inside me rear up and demand to know what the hell I thought I was doing. If we couldn't fight it with fists and guns, then we needed to leave. The djinn remained unhelpfully silent on the subject. Despite the desire coursing through by blood, I knew running never gave me answers to questions.

The banging became so loud Ella put her hands over her ears and hunched her shoulders. "We need to leave," she cried out over the noise.

"We need to find out what's going on," I countered, then flinched as the noise stopped halfway through the sentence, making my shout obscene in the sudden silence.

Together, we approached the stairs. I peered around the wooden banister, the torch beam too frail to reach to the top. A stair carpet of deep blue had dusty footprints all over it from the police, and other daylight intruders.

Ella gripped my arm the moment I moved to take the first stair. "Wait. Let me pray first."

I should ask her to leave, but to be honest, the curling, rising fear made me hesitate. I didn't want to face this alone. Besides, it was kind of nice to know it wasn't all happening in my head.

You really are a selfish bastard.

Not much point in denying it.

Ella held my hand and offered a prayer of protection. I let her soft words of appeal wash through me, and visualised that blue bubble she liked to use. Just as in the cave when we'd been subjected to who-knew-what forces, while rescuing teenagers the first time we met, I felt her calm faith and bowed to its presence.

"Come on then, soldier, let's see what's happening."

With Ella half a step behind me, we breached the stairs in ominous silence. They creaked under my boots, and each sound made me flinch. Reaching the top, we stood on the small, narrow landing and just listened.

The creaking began again, but this time it came from the sprung wooden floor below us, the one in the hallway we'd just left. Ella turned with me and the torch's feeble beam. The creaking continued until the very end of the torch's light danced over the front door.

Then the banging started.

The entire cottage shuddered, as if a door crashed repeatedly against a wall too fast for any living human to accomplish.

Ella covered her ears and pushed us backwards.

She cried out, "Peggy, stop it! You're hurting me!"

A silence so encompassing it became overwhelming in its implications.

"Fucking hell," I breathed out in a whisper. "She's still here."

"We don't know that, Lorne."

"Seriously?" I asked, looking down into a very pale face. I had no doubt mine looked just as disturbed. Eyes too wide, skin clammy, nerves shredded, pulse pounding. "You're the one that likes to tell me if it quacks like a duck…"

"Maybe this one quacks like a dog barks," she mumbled.

"What's next?"

"I bless the cottage. Lay it to peace."

Dust and sand.

Oh shit. "Can we do that now?"

"I ought to prepare at the church, get the sacrament—"

"I think we need to do it now." My urgency came over loud and clear.

Ella slipped behind me and went to the bathroom. I followed, keeping an eye on the looming darkness beyond the torch, just in case. The room smelt of old lady's talc and soap, the very mundane accoutrements to life. A chilling counterpoint to the swirling feeling of panic growing outside the small room.

"We need to hurry," I whispered. "Whatever is causing this, it is growing stronger again." Panic, it was panic I felt out there in the cottage.

Removing a plastic cup from the bathroom cabinet, Ella filled it with tap water. She paused, and I felt her centre shift. Once she had the correct headspace, she offered the Lord's Prayer over the water and blessed it.

"I need you to find her Bible," Ella said. "It'll be beside the bed. If you can't find it, look for a Book of Common Prayer." She flicked out her necklace, the small gold cross bright on her dark shirt.

"I'm not leaving you on your own."

Her lips thinned. "Seriously, Lorne? It's the Bible you're after, in an old cottage in a Somerset village, not the Arc of the Covenant from some Nazi lair."

I huffed, trying to come up with some protest, but couldn't find one. Feeling oddly exposed, I left the bathroom and went in search of the Bible. I opened one door, and the torch revealed a nest of blankets and other knitted objects, sufficient to cover Dunkery Beacon in wool to keep it warm. I tried another door. Bedroom. Obviously the main one because Peggy's dressing gown and nightdress remained on the bed, waiting for their occupier who would never arrive.

Tears pricked my eyes at the very innocent scene.

Shaking off the sadness, knowing I had a mission to complete, I went to the bedside cabinet. No Bible on the top, rather a racy looking romance, a half-naked pirate on the front grasping a woman in his arms. It made me smile. I crouched and opened the little door. There sat a Bible. A warm red cover with gold lettering. I opened it and recognised the King James text. I stood up and almost screamed.

On the edge of the bed, her back to me, sat the image of a little girl. Indistinct, flickering, made of starlight and shadows, but definitely there. As real as a phantom could be in a world of mobile phones and electric light.

Dust and sand.

We needed to do this blessing, and fast.

Backing away, rather than turning, I tried to forget every damned horror movie Heather had made me watch over the last few months. The figure could turn at any moment and scream at me with maggots in her eyes, or a mouth full of fangs.

Making it to the door, I paused. The image didn't move, just flickered on the edge of my awareness and the only sense I had from the faint being, was one of sadness—terrible, terrible sadness.

I slipped out into the hallway and retreated to the bathroom.

"I've just seen her again," I confessed.

Ella looked at me in shock. "In the bedroom?"

I nodded. "On the bed."

"Was it Peggy?"

I shrugged. "Don't know. She was hardly there and wasn't aware of me."

Ella sucked in a deep breath. "Okay, well, let's get this job done." She took the Bible from me and started to pray aloud while dipping her fingers into the mug of water, and flicking it around the room. This went on for each room.

Only when we reached the kitchen did the banging start again. This time it came from the kitchen table, but it didn't shake the timbers of the roof. Ella patiently repeated the blessing ritual and the banging, half-heart as it was, relaxed. In the cottage, the dense atmosphere eased.

We stood by the back door.

"What do we tell the others?" I asked.

Ella looked at her watch. "It's almost four. It'll be light soon."

"So nothing then?"

We left, closing and locking the door behind us. "What's to say, Lorne? We have no proof."

"I can't hide this from Heather. I can't hide anything from Heather." Except for the desperate need I had to surrender to my growing fascination. She'd laugh in my face.

"You don't have to hide it from Heather, but don't mention it to the others. Paul isn't ready. Eddie and Lilian don't need to feel weirder about living in

Luccombe. This is, this was, something for us to deal with, Lorne. The cottage is at peace, even if Peggy isn't."

I helped Ella over the wall onto the road near my bike. "Okay."

"It might not have happened at all without you being there."

"That's a comforting thought."

She smiled. The night lifting its dark veil in the east. "You're a trigger, an enabler, for these things. It's time you learned to admit it."

I climbed on the bike, reluctant to admit anything of the kind. "I'll see you later."

A solemn nod was my only reply as I pulled away, keeping my revs low so I didn't disturb the start of the dawn chorus.

8

DESPITE MY LACK OF SLEEP, THE following day with the executives went well. It turned out their lowly new member of staff was a corporal with the Royal Signals. After she'd let the alpha male sales team fight it out, she took those who were fed up with listening to the arguments and brought them back to the farm without a problem. She opted on the scenic route mind, so they found themselves dragged through rivers and woodlands, but they had a good time.

"Most fun since I passed out of my regiment," she said to me.

"You're welcome. If I'd known, I'd have made it more of a challenge."

She grinned at me. "Any time, soldier." Then she winked.

I watched her saunter away. I wondered what Willow did when men flirted with her in the shop. It must happen all the time. To me? Not so much. I didn't quite know what to do, except feel a little peacocky.

Heather sidled up. "She's been flirting with you."

"Yeah, feels nice."

She scowled. "You know what your superpower is with women?"

"It's not my good looks, that's for sure."

Heather huffed. "No, it's because you talk to us like we're human beings. You expect the same from us as you do the men. Not saying you expect us to be like soldiers, just competent humans. It makes a nice change."

I blinked in surprise. "Oh, right. Thanks."

"Just don't use it on women you don't want flirting with you." She sounded peeved, but I didn't understand why.

I watched her go until one of the other people on the course wanted to talk. This bit of my business I found hard, the small talk, but it was good for me to meet new people and build relationships with the outside world. Stoke Pero was isolated enough to give me peace when I needed it, but the days I worked with groups provided the balance that kept me in the present.

The group left the farm, and we retreated out of the heat of the day. In idle moments during the long hours we'd watched the groups on the moor, I'd told Heather about the night before. She'd been amazed, annoyed at being left out, and pleased I seemed to be coming to terms with my 'other-self' as she described it.

I'd also been considering Paul's discoveries. Despite myself, it sparked something I wanted to chase down. I hadn't forgotten the dream the night before, either. That shadow around the woman, the one from the cine film, it meant something. The soldier in Eddie's field also tugged at my conscience. Maybe I could lay a few things to rest for Paul if I dropped down to Luccombe and helped him figure things out? His grandmother, being some big Soviet secret scientist, also interested me.

All the pushing and pulling of the Cold War left me—well, cold—who could untangle it when they were knee-deep in the muck and bullets of the next big war? It did interest me from a different perspective than most. The effects of the Cold War were still being played out in the Middle East and places like Korea, Afghanistan and now Ukraine. All of which had an effect on my life.

After I'd cleaned up the group's bags, and stowed them away, I found Heather with her head in a book. An actual paper book this time, one of the academic ones she needed for her college courses.

"I'm popping down to Ella's so I can check on Paul. Wanna come?"

"Not tonight. I've too much studying to do right now."

"Oh, okay." I failed to hide my disappointment.

She glanced up. "Unless you need me to come?"

"No, it's okay. I just enjoy your company."

Good way to manipulate her. I said you're selfish bastard.

She uncurled from the armchair and put the book down. "It was sending me to sleep anyway. I could do with some Ella time."

I took the longer route down to Luccombe again, enabling us to enjoy a more relaxed ride on the bike.

We rode down to Horner River and the small bridge. The summer light dappled the road as it poured through the ancient tree canopy, dancing in the light breeze. The narrow lane, at the combe's bottom, barely looked like a road. We could almost be in any century.

I slowed to take the corner, Heather's weight tight to my back.

Several things happened at once.

A figure stepped out in front of me.

My foot hit the brake. The back wheel flicked out. I took the weight of me, the bike, and Heather on my left leg. She cried out, but kept her balance in line with mine. I gunned the engine and pushed us upright. The bike screamed in protest, but did as ordered. In the process, we turned one-hundred and eighty degrees.

On the bridge stood a man. He wore a uniform of brown wool, and a tin hat. Black boots covered in mud from a foreign land. Not this one. He carried a .303 rifle.

"Fuck," Heather snapped out from behind me.

My hands tightened on the grips. My eyes met those of a man who fought in a war I didn't. He didn't appear transparent in the defused light at the bottom of the combe. He didn't flicker or fade. He raised his rifle to his shoulder. He dropped his head to take aim through the iron sights. A finger lay over the trigger. Those eyes, they shone with a sadness I recognised.

He had to take my life.

Just as I'd had to take so many lives.

He didn't want it, but he had to obey orders.

Just as I had done, so many times.

"Lorne…" Heather's fingers clutched my sides, digging into the scars.

"Hold on." I gunned the engine, leaned the bike on my left leg again, and flicked the back wheel out once more. We did the other half of the circle and roared off down the lane.

"What the hell was that?" Heather yelled.

I had no words to share. For the first time, she'd seen something I thought existed only in my head. This wasn't my PTSD. This wasn't the djinn. This was all me.

We pulled up outside the bungalow.

I trembled and Heather almost fell off the back of the bike.

For the first time, our eyes met. "You okay, kid?"

She swallowed hard. "Yeah. I'm okay."

"Sorry for almost dropping you."

"I'm okay, boss."

Paul wandered out into the sun, blinking and mole-like. "She's at church. Evening song or something."

Heather didn't even bother looking at him. We'd both removed our helmets, and she leaned in to kiss the side of my face without the scars. "I'll go up the church and catch you later. No harm done."

"Erm, yeah, sure." I watched her walk away, the black jeans snug.

Paul also watched her. "That is a challenge."

"*That*, is called Heather, you oaf. Leave her alone or I'll rip your balls off." I needed to keep in the present. I needed to put the weird to one side. Paul didn't believe in…

Say it.

Okay, ghosts. I saw ghosts. I made other people see ghosts. I was a fucking enabler for the damned things.

Well done.

Paul glanced at me. "Okay, okay, no touching the local wildlife. You're a lucky man, especially with your face." He waved a hand at my jaw and cheek. "What happened to it?"

I locked my helmet to my bike and tried to keep the irritation out of my voice. "Shot in the face in Iraq. The burn marks are from Syria, but it mostly left my face alone."

"And yet still you bag a woman half your age."

"Paul, stop being a prat. If you want my help, just know that anything to do with Heather is not up for discussion. She means a great deal to me and hearing you say things like that makes me want to knock you on your arse." I stared hard at him and watched the colour rise up his pale cheeks.

"Fine," he mumbled. "Come inside, I've done more digging."

I sighed in relief as he strode off. "Of course you have."

Before I went into the bungalow I stood still, closed my eyes, and breathed deep of the late summer evening. The very faintest hint of autumn now graced the air, that loamy chill mixing with the scent of grass cuttings. I still needed to figure out a birthday present for Heather and I wondered if I could bottle this smell. She'd like it so long as Paul's expensive aftershave didn't taint the air.

Inside the bungalow I realised Paul had spread more paper around and Ella's printer chuntered away in the background, pressed into use for something other than making posters for the latest village jumble sale.

"I found this and wanted to ring you to get you down here, but Ella made it clear you were working." He didn't ask me what I was doing, or how it was going, but that was Paul—all work and casual sex. Other people just existed to help further those two goals in his life. He needed to find more, just like I had by living in my small community.

"Have you any more news from the police?" I asked.

"They're bloody useless."

I doubted this, but I let it go. DI Kate Mackenzie didn't strike me as useless, and Eddie trusted her.

"Show me what you have?"

"Sure your PTSD can cope?" he asked, snarky bastard.

"Yes, Paul, I'm sure. And until you can hold a weapon and shoot it at a target without losing your lunch, I'd wind your bloody neck in."

"Bet your girlfriend—"

While scanning the paper I said, "She's a damned fine shot actually, so be careful."

I tuned him out while I read. The letter was another between Captain Dick Westbrook and his Russian bride.

My love,

I can't believe our news. A baby on the way already? This is just the perfect beginning to our fairy tale. I am a lucky man. The way we found each other, the terrible events in Berlin, the stress of your defection and work in Somerset, have all been so hard on us. Not to mention my posting back to West Germany, so soon after our marriage. It has been brutal. Now, though, my dearest, we have a baby coming. I shall be home soon and together we can make the most perfect nursery. I wonder if the baby (saying 'it' feels so wrong) will be a boy or a girl. Which would you prefer? I would love a girl, I think. Someone as clever and beautiful as you.

Captain Westbrook went on for some time like this.

Paul held out another letter. "My mother was born in 1948, here in Luccombe. Then I found this…"

My love,

I found her. I found Bettina. I can hardly believe it. This letter cannot be long or detailed, but I have her here, in West Germany, and she will be coming home to you. We'll be a proper family, you, me, Peggy and Betty.

"Who is Bettina?"

"I think it's the sister. My grandmother must have had a child already and been forced to leave her in Berlin for some reason. Then my grandfather must have found her and brought her out."

I remember the stoic child in the film and my dream. They could well have different fathers.

"This means she was married before?" I asked.

He snorted. "You know as well as I do what occupying forces are capable of during a war."

I'd like to say I didn't, but I'd had to sit in during the questioning of female soldiers about alleged rape by their colleagues. One of the hardest damned things I'd done was admit to my team some of their own were going to prison for such crimes. It made me sick.

We were good soldiers in The Regiment; it didn't mean we were necessarily good men.

"How old did the girl look in the film?" he asked, dragging me away from the misery of those sad days.

I blinked. "Um, about this old." I held up my hand to about a metre off the ground. Then lifted it a bit.

"How's that help?"

"I'm hardly an expert on children, Paul."

He smirked and I could see the next sentence out of his mouth.

I pointed at him. "If you say one word about Heather, I'll smack you."

He held his hands up for peace but didn't lose the shit-eating grin.

"Let me get this straight. Your mother moved here after her retirement with your dad, but she had no real memories of the place. Both of her parents were dead when she was quite young, right?"

"Ella tell you that?"

I nodded.

He said, "Yes. She was nineteen. It was a car accident, apparently. She met my dad a year later. They had me fairly late in life." He didn't meet my eyes at that point, and I guessed there was an unhappy family story behind his reticence. "She was always drawn to the South West. We used to holiday in the area all the time. When they retired and realised they could afford a nice cottage down here, she pushed Dad into coming. Just a shame they were so far away from a hospital when he had his heart attack."

"But she had no memories of her time here as a small child?"

"None she could recall clearly enough to tell me."

I thought about the film and the scene in it of Eddie's graveyard. I worked hard to be objective and not to dwell on the odd haunting images I kept catching. "Tomorrow we need to go and visit Eddie Rice again. I want to take a look at something, but it needs to be light, and we'll need a mower or strimmer." I'd appreciate there being no ghosts either, but I guess I didn't have control over that particular problem.

The front door opened and closed, the women coming in from the church.

Ella looked exhausted and Heather worried. I rose and put the kettle on.

"Good turn out?" I asked, trying to fill the tense silence. Had the women had words?

"The usual," Ella said, slumping into a kitchen chair. Last night must have exhausted her. That, on top of everything else...

"Can we borrow your strimmer tomorrow?" I asked, hoping the question would draw her out.

"Sure."

Clearly, I needed to do more poking. "Have you seen the letters Paul found? It looks like Peggy's sister was Russian or East German."

"Really?" Heather asked.

Paul explained in more detail. Ella kept quiet. I wondered how many people she'd buried who'd died of cancer over the years.

"I'm going to crash. You can let yourself out, Lorne," Ella said and rose from the table.

Heather and I shared a worried glance. "Okay," I said.

"I'll clean up if you like?" Heather said.

Ella left after saying, "No need, it'll all be dirty again tomorrow."

Paul looked confused but managed to hold his tongue until Ella was out of earshot. "What's going on? I'm better with data than people, but something's obviously wrong."

"I wish you'd come and stay at the farm," I muttered.

"No, it's too far away."

"Just tidy this mess up so Ella doesn't have to come down to it in the morning and keep the noise to a minimum," I said. "I'm going home now and you're going to be ready to do some work come morning. I'll be here at zero-eight-hundred hours."

"Or eight in the morning for us normal mortals," Heather mumbled, collecting her bike helmet from the kitchen counter.

We left the bungalow.

"Do we have to go home now?" she asked. "I need to decompress."

"No, we can go look at the sea for a bit."

She smiled. "You know me too well."

"You and Ella okay?"

The smile dissolved in a vat of sadness. "Yeah, I just... She's terrified, Lorne. I kept saying it could be nothing, it could be easy to treat even if it is something—she's already got one foot in the hospice. I tried to talk to her about what you saw last night, but she just said, *'All part of God's great works.'* Which seems very un-Ella like, in my book. I didn't even bother mentioning what had happened earlier."

"She's seen a lot of people die, I guess."

We climbed on the bike, and it burped into life.

Heather said, "So have you, but you don't think about it like that. Do you?" She twisted to look at me through the bike visors.

"Let's go to the beach," I said, avoiding the question.

I didn't want to tell her about the way my thoughts ambled over to the dead if I didn't fill every waking moment with work or her company. It was that or drinking, and I'd noticed how much it escalated on the weekends she was away and I didn't have Willow for company.

We rode down to Minehead, and I thought about popping to Willow's shop, Magick Minehead. She might like to join us for chips. Then I thought about how she'd poke into my latest nightmares, and I figured I could do with a rest from the psychoanalysis. I wanted to eat chips with my friend in silence, and watch the sea race up the beach as the tide switched.

9

THE FOLLOWING MORNING WE ARRIVED in Luccombe at eight sharp and Paul stood outside the bungalow with Ella's strimmer. The shimmering menace of the supernatural no longer dogged me under the beauty of another summer's day. I'd slept soundly for once.

The evening before had warmed my dreams. We'd watched the distant shore of Wales come to life as the sun abandoned the day. Thick chips, battered fish, and so much vinegar it'd made our eyes sting, filled our bellies.

Being with Heather made my life simple and easy. She didn't challenge me to 'get well' and I didn't challenge her either. We were two damaged souls that fitted around the cracks in each other. Being with Willow meant work. I'd have to work on me—my least favourite thing to do.

Haltingly, we'd talked about the ghost in the woodland. Neither of us had any answers, and the questions mounted the more we talked. Heather's main focus lay in the obvious—could a ghostly bullet have killed us? I had no idea. I didn't plan on testing any of the theories we posed either.

We took the shorter route to Luccombe, avoiding the darker parts of Horner Wood. When Heather climbed off the back of my motorbike, I saw Paul's eyes darken at the sight of her slim legs flexing. I wanted to rip his head off. He was good looking, younger than me, and wealthy in comparison. No way was I losing Heather to his philandering ways.

She walked past him without a glance and headed to Ella's front door.

"Morning," he said, still watching her.

"Paul," I growled.

He turned to look at me with a knowing smile. "I was just admiring the view."

"Stop it."

He shrugged. "I have the strimmer all set up. I've put some shears in the car. You rang your police friend and warned him we're coming?"

I nodded. Eddie hadn't been pleased, but I promised to explain. Once I'd told him about the letters and other evidence, I was certain he'd understand.

"You going to follow us down there?" I asked.

He nodded.

Ella and Heather came out of the bungalow. "We'll walk down," Heather said. "The exercise will do us good."

I chuckled. "Nothing to do with the fact we'll be done by the time you rock up?"

"It didn't occur to me at all," she said, expression one of astonishment at my words.

"Innocent doesn't suit you."

She stuck her tongue out and handed over the heavy bike gear so I could carry it down to Eddie's cottage in Horner.

I took the journey at a sensible pace and as I rode around the final corner, a very sleek Mercedes Benz AMG GT C Coupe in black with tinted windows pulled out. Not the kind of vehicle we saw in this area. If people had money to burn, they usually bought an over-the-top SUV.

Pulling into Eddie's drive, I saw him standing in front of his cottage with a worried expression on his face. I put the bike on the stand and dismounted.

"What's up?" I asked.

His eyes were still on the long-vanished car. "A woman's just offered me twice what I paid for the cottage."

I felt my eyes widen. "Really?"

He focused on me. "What the hell is going on, Turner?"

"What was her name?"

He handed me a business card. It just said Heartcore on it with a London phone number.

Eddie said, "She's their solicitor, apparently. But that's the company."

"You Google it?"

"Not yet."

Paul pulled up in his car and I told him what we'd seen, handing him the card.

He grinned. "Leave it with me." Wandering back to the car, I watched him retrieve his laptop. We'd soon know everything the internet knew about Heartcore.

While we waited for Paul to do his magic, Eddie leaned against his car and crossed his arms.

"Spit it out then, Turner. How are you about to complicate my nice simple retirement? Me and Lilian, we moved down here from Bristol to escape city life—and I don't mean the nice bits with museums and cafes serving twenty different kinds of porridge—I mean real city life. And now we have a murdered woman and some sinister solicitor wanting us to sell our dream home."

I felt for him. Since my retirement, I'd been forced into action a few times. In the drama of action, the old zest returns, then you remember why you left and a bizarre sadness creeps over the threshold. The kind of sadness that shows you all too clearly, you never really leave violence in the past. Once you've dabbled, as Eddie had, or sunk neck-deep in it like me, that violence never goes away. For me, it fitted like an old pair of boots.

"It'll pass, Eddie. Something about this stinks, but we know it's not your boss this time, so if we have enough evidence to give DI Mackenzie, we should be able to walk away."

He grunted, obviously not happy.

Paul came over with laptop in hand and a light in his eye I didn't want to see. The last time he'd looked at me like that, I'd been in Sangar, and nothing went right on that mission.

"Heartcore doesn't exist," he said.

Eddie just looked at him.

I said, "Clearly they do." A weight filled the space where my breakfast should be and turned a shiny morning into something more camouflage brown.

"No, it's a name registered at Companies House and there are even accounts presented each year, but it's a shell. It's a shell of a shell. Its background is so murky you'd be hard pressed to find a single piece of evidence as to what they actually do."

"What does that mean?" I asked, my brain already aching.

"It means someone wants this land, but it isn't Heartcore. So who does? And what does it have to do with my mother's death?"

Or the ghosts I kept seeing. I suppressed a shiver.

Eddie's eyes turned sympathetic, but he said, "I understand you want to find a reason for such cruelty, but crimes like these are all too common. Maybe not in places like Luccombe, but violent robbery—"

"It wasn't robbery."

The tension mounted. Ella and Heather walked into the drive, and I watched Ella laugh. It warmed my heart to see. Heather really was our sarcastic, and somewhat bitter, ray of sunshine.

"Let's put the strimmer to work and we'll see what the graves really look like," I said. "Then we might find some evidence to help our cause. Just because someone is rich enough to offer an obscene amount of money for a chunk of land, and hide who they are, it doesn't make them evil incarnate."

Eddie nodded. "Fine, but I've got things to do in the house. Don't cut down too much. Lilian wants to leave the field alone, so the seeds come back next year and we can encourage more bees to the flowers."

"Agreed." I returned to the car, and after Paul popped the boot, I retrieved the strimmer.

We marched up the field, Heather staying with Ella at the caravans to sample Lilian's breakfast scones. My stomach informed me that sounded like a better plan than the current one, because it turned out Paul didn't really understand the fine art of strimming a field.

After a sweaty hour, in which grass cuttings and dust infiltrated every crevice in my body, we had a strip cleared. There were five small, arched headstones, all of them crooked and illegible.

"Sandstone, weathered too much," I said. I lived next to a graveyard; I knew more than I wanted about headstones. "It was cheap to carve though, so it would suit a Methodist community like this one."

Paul sniffed. "No easy evidence of a disturbance like you saw in the film?"

I crouched down next to one of the gravestones and put a hand on the stubble of grass. "No, but none of the headstones have remained upright. That's unusual. Maybe one or two would shift over time, but this is rare. It's indicative of soil disturbance underground. Can you get satellite imagery up of the area?" A tingle began to spread up my arm, and I hastily drew my hand away from the grave.

We sat in the grass and Paul whizzed about the secure servers he used for work. I concentrated on making sure the area stayed clear of Second World War soldiers with bolt action rifles.

"This do?" he asked, handing it over.

I squinted at the screen, changed the angles so I could see, and examined the area in detail. The image looked recent, maybe this year, because the ground had the scorched look that covered most of England right now, and last summer had been wet enough to keep a field like this very green. Letting my eyes rove over the familiar landscape from above made chills race over my skin. I'd ordered up and pored over maps like this all the time while in theatre, using them to plan attacks, routes, meetings. Over the years, I'd grown adept at interpreting the signs of a human presence and the differences between historical and actual.

The lads joked I'd find Atlantis one day.

"Look at this," I said.

Paul shuffled around to stare over my shoulder. "What?"

"Here." I pointed to the area in which we sat. "Look at the lines in the dry field." A series of small, darker humps were obvious. "Then look at these, closer to the cottage." More humps, but less dark and obvious in the dry soil. I moved the image around a little to take in the trees. "And look at this." I pointed to the tree canopy. "These are dark, taller, older trees." They covered the rising hill like a deep green woolly hat. "But these aren't as dense, and they aren't as old." A large patch in line with the cottage and graveyard looked lighter in colour than their neighbours.

"There was something under the canopy," Paul murmured.

A disturbance in my periphery made me look up from the screen. Heather approached with napkins full of food and some water. I breathed out in relief.

"Found something?" she asked.

"Jackpot," Paul said. "We need to dig these graves up." He grinned at her as if it would frighten her to think of such a thing.

"It'll be hard going getting through the dirt this time of year. It'll be baked solid," she said, meeting his gaze, not fazed in the least.

I fought to hide a smirk. In a pissing contest, my money would be on Heather. "I think we'd best served by finding out what happened to the tree canopy back there." I pointed to the woodland beyond the field.

"I'm up for that," Heather said. "Ella's taking Lilian into Minehead for some shopping."

"You don't want to go shopping?" Paul asked.

She rose, looked at me, and said, "You coming?"

I watched her stride off as I scrambled up from the ground. "You really need to stop trying to put her in a box, Paul. Also, how the hell do women fall for your misogynistic patter?"

"She's pissing me off. Most women find me boyish and charming."

"Yeah? Well, she doesn't, and she's made it clear she's not interested, so for all our sakes, knock it off. Besides, how much longer is 'boyish' going to work for you? Or are you going to start dyeing those grey hairs?"

His hands flew to his head. "I am not going grey."

I laughed and followed Heather. On the way to catching her up, I rang Ella. "You need to come up to the woods and find us. Bring Eddie. I think we might be on to something."

"Hello to you as well," she said, an amused tartness in her voice.

"Yeah, alright, just get your arses up here. It'll be more interesting than shopping." I hung up.

It didn't take long to reach the trees, maybe twenty metres, but Heather stopped by a barbed wire fence.

She looked back at me. "You sure this is Eddie's land?"

"Worrying about trespass? My, how times have changed." I'd been party to her B&E antics in the past.

The glower on her face didn't quite hide her excitement at the coming adventure.

We waited for the others to catch us up. To be honest, I didn't want to go tramping about on Eddie's land without him being aware. A part of me couldn't afford to forget he was always going to be a copper, like I'd always be a soldier. You don't just walk away when you serve for twenty years or more and leave it all behind. Considering both Heather and I 'might' have ended the lives of people 'prematurely', it didn't seem wise to stumble into more trouble.

Both Eddie and Lilian came up the field with Ella, so we all climbed over the fence. I helped Lilian, but Heather and Ella made short work of it.

"Thank you," Lilian said. "I'm not quite the country girl the others are."

I smiled. "You might struggle with a fence, Lilian, but I wish I could cook like you. That's an alchemy I'll never capture."

She blushed. "Thank you. I can teach you. I used to run cooking classes for single men in Bristol so they'd be able to feed their kids. It was a way of helping them after they'd been widowed or divorced or came fresh out of university."

"Really?" I had no idea.

"I loved it and was reluctant to leave my boys. Some of them were so angry at the beginning of the classes but give them an hour of making bread and they soon settle down."

"That genuinely sounds like fun," I said.

"Then maybe I'll talk to Ella about finding somewhere to set up a group.

The nearest school would be best, because they have larger ovens than most village halls."

"Well, I'll sign up. Me and Heather are okay at cooking well enough to survive, and I can make most things edible on an open fire in a single pan, but to have real kitchen skills would be good."

Lilian smiled and the sun dapple through the leaves took years off her. I liked Lilian. Eddie Rice was a lucky man. We stepped over a fallen section of wire fence that must once have been substantial. I glanced left and right, assessing my surroundings without conscious thought. The fence rose off the ground, rearing out of the undergrowth and was topped with more barbed wire.

Lilian glanced at Heather. "She's a little firebrand. You're a lucky man."

A strange curl of *weird* snaked up from my stomach to my heart and tapped on the door. "Oh, no, we aren't... She just wants Paul to leave her alone and I'm the safe option. Her 'beard' I guess. Heather deserves more than I can offer."

Lilian's eyes widened. "I'm sorry if I stepped over a line, Lorne. But are you sure that's all it is? She clearly adores you."

"Holy shit," Heather said from some way ahead.

Alarm shot through me and before I knew what was happening, I'd left Lilian and raced ahead of the others to prevent whatever trouble Heather had found this time.

10

HEATHER STOOD NEXT TO A young alder tree. Nothing had leapt out of the dark woodland to swallow her whole.

"Wow." The ruins of a building rose before us, covered in ivy and brambles. Trees grew through the destroyed windows and collapsed roof like some post-apocalyptic vision of the future, when nature reclaims the land.

Heather grinned at me. "There has to be something interesting here. Come on."

"I doubt there'll be anything interesting. The local kids would have had it away years ago."

"That fence came down recently, Lorne. It's not really covered in enough undergrowth to be hidden properly."

I nudged her. "Okay, smarty pants."

Ella caught us up. "Do you think that's the building we saw in the film?"

Recalling the image of the place, I thought about what we saw now. "Yes. I think so." I pointed. "That's the place we saw the doors. That woman stood—Paul's grandmother, maybe—stood in front of them." Apex square walls, roof long gone, appeared to be the main entrance.

"The other woman in the film wasn't Peggy's mother," I stated. In my dream, this was the place I'd seen the austere woman standing, the black shadow rising behind her, reaching out. Did it reach for me or for her? The memory of hate and pain in the dream made me shudder.

Heather tugged on my t-shirt, distracting me. "Come on, let's go look inside."

"It's not going to be safe," Ella said as we followed Heather.

She waved a hand in dismissal at Ella's concerns.

Ella sighed. "I'm not sure her living with you is good for her life expectancy."

"Better than it was with her previous bloke," I muttered, the image of his ruined face floating into my mind. I had no remorse about that particular death. I should have killed him in the damned biker bar and saved Heather from the final beating he gave her. We talked about it, occasionally, but the wounds still bled in her heart and mind, despite it being almost nine months.

We all gathered near the front of the building.

"So this is the hospital type place you saw?" Eddie asked.

"Looks like it." I turned and stared back through the trees, assessing the viability. I couldn't see Eddie's cottage, but I thought I'd be able to do so if we removed all the greenery. "This plot came with the rest—the cottage and graveyard?"

Eddie shook his head. "I checked the land registry again, and this place is just beyond our boundary. We have the only legal access by vehicle, not that you can get one up here without destroying the fence. Which means we have no right to go poking about." He stared meaningfully at Heather.

She snorted. "Well, I'm going. You can clap me in irons if you like, but I want to know what's in there."

I had to agree with Heather and Paul was already moving off.

Clapping Eddie on the shoulder, I said, "Looks like you're about to enter the real world, mate." Part of me quailed at the thought of walking through the broken doorway, but this time I chose to ignore it. No one with a suicide vest or assault rifle waited in the soft, dark green interior.

Eddie sighed from the bottom of his boots and trooped after us. Lilian was more than happy to break a few laws for the sake of curiosity. Not fully aware of it, Heather and I took point and peeled left and right, setting up a perimeter of safety for the others. Going through the hole in the front of the building, we clambered over the fallen masonry and twisted metal doors. Broken glass blinked at us when the sun caught a shard or two. Ivy smothered everything, twisting around and embracing the secrets of the building. The dark green, heavily-veined leaves clothed all in their path. I had the sinister feeling that if we remained still for too long, it would overwhelm us in its pernicious embrace as well.

The walls, once white, now held host to a creeping disease of grey and brown. Rather than breeze blocks, it appeared the building had been made out of concrete slabs, like so many of the old and very cheap council houses in Somerset. This place was not meant to last.

A large reception room contained nothing but the remains of the pillars holding a crumbling ceiling in place. Weirdly, at least for me, there was no graffiti, or signs of people treating the place like a doss-house. Every building in the world I'd been through that looked something like this one had been used as a refuge for dislocated. Floors covered in filthy mattresses, needles, old food and worse. Sometimes a fresh corpse or two. The different life of West Somerset from the hellholes of the world. I'd never quite get used to it.

Several exits were obvious, some even with doors. The light wasn't great as the canopy of young trees filtered the bright sun. The temperature drop made goose bumps break out over my arms.

Paul came to my side. "I found this." He handed over a metal sign. It read: Warning, Live Fire Exercises in the Area. Keep Out.

That could mean anything. I'd seen similar notices on military land where no live fire was permitted, but arms' storage facilities and bunkers were hidden away.

"The plot thickens," I muttered and tossed the sign. It clanged and made us all flinch. Ella cursed and scowled at me.

"Shall we split up?" Heather asked.

I checked my mobile phone reception. So far it seemed to work okay. "Yeah, sure, why not. You, Ella, Eddie and Lilian go that way. I'll go this way with Paul." Keeping Heather and Paul separate seemed wise.

"I'll go with you," Ella said. "Heather and Eddie can handle anything between them."

Heather shrugged and looked relaxed about the arrangement, so I let it stand. Paul and I headed west with Ella; Heather and the others went east.

Ella walked beside me, Paul just in front, eager for answers.

"You should talk to him about Peggy," she whispered.

I glanced at her in surprise. "What? Why?"

She sighed. "He needs a friend, Lorne. He hasn't phoned anyone to talk about what happened to his mum. I don't think he has anyone close in his life, except you and Peggy."

I shook my head. "We don't have that kind of relationship. We're blokes who worked together."

Even in the dim light I could see her jaw grinding in frustration. "Lorne, he needs a friend. He needs to talk. You need to listen. You have listening skills I've seen you use them with Heather, so make him talk about his feelings. This behaviour isn't healthy."

"Feelings?"

"Yes, Lorne, feelings. I'm sure you know what they are if you think about them hard enough." She stopped walking and pushed at me, to make sure I joined Paul.

Feelings, I could talk about feelings. I had female friends, we talked about feelings. "You okay?" I asked Paul.

"Yeah."

We pushed hard against a double set of heavy doors. They creaked open and a dark hall presented itself. I switched on my phone's torch.

"If you need to talk about Peggy…" I let the sentence drift.

"Not yet. I want to find out what happened. Then I can mourn. I loved my mum very much, but grief isn't going to help her right now. This might help me though. I need to understand." The tension in his voice I understood, but it masked a world of pain waiting around the corner.

"Okay, just know we are all here for you, if you need a friendly shoulder." So much for talking about feelings.

~ 94 ~

"Thanks, Lorne."

Nothing hid the pressure in his body and face. I had the sudden idea his reactions to Heather, wildly over the top even for Paul, hid a sadness and shock we'd misunderstood. I'd known Paul to be this manic in the past and the more I thought about it, rather than just being defensive over Heather, the more I remembered the extreme circumstances that caused his behaviour. Sangar swam once more into my mind before I pushed it back. Memories wouldn't help.

We stumbled down the darkened corridor and arrived at a set of stairs. They went down, the bottom too dark to see even with my phone torch.

"That doesn't bode well," Paul muttered.

Ella backed up a few paces. "I'd rather not go down there if we don't have to and, guess what? We don't have to."

"Do you think they built underground so people didn't see the height of the building over the treetops?" I asked, not listening to Ella's warning. Since entering the building I'd focused purely on the mission. I didn't want to consider anything else. I didn't want to sense anything else but those living people around me.

Paul thought about my question. "Could be. We both know what the government is capable of doing when it's trying to hide the truth."

I grunted as Iraq flashed up in my head. At least it took my mind off Sangar.

We heard voices heading in our direction. I moved off, ready to go down the stairs. Into the darkness. Into the black hole below ground.

Dust and sand.

I almost gagged. The black heaved out of its hole. I back-pedalled and almost tripped over the fallen masonry. The black tried to lunge for me, a scream shuddered to a stop as it hit a blockage of dust tightening my throat.

The grit of sand between my teeth, coating my tongue and nose, shocked me. The crawl of sensations over my scalp and spine made a sharp breath hiss between my teeth. The attack came with such speed I had little to no control.

Shivers raced over my skin, my scalp crawled with the sensation of a thousand tiny electrodes being switched on and off in rapid succession. I grabbed Paul's shirt sleeve.

"We need to leave." I didn't, *couldn't*, hide the panic in my voice.

"What?"

"We have to get out now!" I pulled on him and pushed at Ella, who backed away.

"Lorne, that doesn't—"

"Have I ever led you wrong on this?"

He studied me for a moment. I tried not to flinch away. A hand gently eased my white knuckles off his sleeve. "Okay, mate, okay, we're going."

I spun on my heel and called out, "Heather, get everyone the fuck out of here! Stat. Ella, get after her."

She ran up the corridor, more than happy to listen to me. Just like all the recent additions to my life, she knew to trust my instincts.

Paul tried to stop me. "Don't be—"

I strode away from Paul. "Come on, we're leaving."

Blood and bone.

This time, I felt my breakfast heading for the exit. I bent over and puked. The rush of adrenaline made me dizzy for a long time, and as I tried to breathe through the rising panic, I felt hands on my back. Soft words became a buzz in my head, but I managed to make my feet shuffle through the debris, guided by unseen care. I had my eyes closed, and I tried to rein back the collage of images crashing around inside my mind.

A basement full of men and women in white coats.

I was strapped to a table.

The terror as someone approached. A woman. A sense of confusion at the betrayal. Waking. Blank mind. Blank... Empty... Adrift...

"Lorne? Lorne. Listen to my voice. Come back. Come back to us."

I gripped the hand holding my shoulder. "Ella?"

"Good man. Heather's on your other side."

"Hey, I'm right here."

Tears sprang into my eyes. "Heather..."

With great care, Ella turned me, and Heather wrapped her arms around my neck. Only fifteen centimetres separated our height, making it possible to bury my face in her shoulder.

I heard Ella from a distance. "I know, Paul, but we've learned how to handle these episodes. We did warn you. He's not the same man you knew. He's not the man he remembers being, and he forgets that, which means things like this happen. Go back and we'll catch you up. He's going to be fragile for a while."

"Sorry," I murmured into Heather's neck.

She pulled back, stroking a hand over my scalp. "What happened?"

I glanced into her face but couldn't hold her gaze yet. "Don't know. Need to sit." My legs felt like wet cotton wool.

With her shoulder under my arm, Heather guided me to a fallen chunk of wall. I didn't want to sit on the building, and I didn't want to sit on the ivy. "No, can't. We need to move away."

She didn't argue, merely helped move me back into the woodland. I managed to focus on a fallen tree and sat, leaves crunching under my boots.

Ella returned, puffing from the effort. "Water." She thrust a bottle under my nose.

I took it and rinsed my mouth out before swallowing. It helped ground me. She took my hands and muttered a prayer. I visualised blue and gold around all three of us, as Willow and Ella taught me in their separate ways, and the world started to straighten out.

"What spooked you?" Heather asked as she felt me relax.

"There's something dreadful about this place. Something really dark. Eddie needs to build a bloody great wall in front of it." I sucked in several lungfuls of warm air, rich in the scent of the woods.

"He's going to need something more specific than that," Ella murmured. "You've scared the crap out of them. Paul thinks you need to be sectioned."

He might be right. That was a bad one, mucker.

I stared at a bramble bush and its small black bobbles of fruit. "A sense of dread roared up the stairs at me. Almost strong enough to be a wind. A series of images along with a terrible panic from someone... small... a small person." I frowned and rubbed my head. "Christ, Ella, it was a child. That child, from the cottage, strapped to a table in a room full of people in white coats. Utter terror, then—then nothing. No emotion. A void. A vacuum. Somehow that was worse than the terror."

I looked at Heather and she swam, my eyes blurry from unshed tears. "I'm sorry."

"What for?" she asked.

"For being so weak. You just wanted to explore, and I spoiled everything. I'm so bloody broken." I buried my face in my hands, too ashamed to acknowledge their compassion, feeling it as pity.

"Lorne, look at me, please." Heather gripped my wrists, and pulled my palms away from my face. Her hands were small and unblemished against my thick, scarred forearms. "Listen to me. You are the strongest man I've known. Nothing holds you back. There is nothing to be sorry for, but you really need to get a grip on this psychic business."

"I'm not—"

"Really? This isn't enough of a clue for you? This, what happened on the bike and last night?" She waved a hand at the hospital.

I glanced at Ella. "Aren't you supposed to disapprove?"

She shrugged. "When something barks like a dog..."

"It's a duck?" I suggested.

She chuckled. "Heather's right, Lorne, we can't keep ignoring it. You've a rare talent and we need to use it without doing you any harm. Besides, I spend my life listening to the Lord speak to me and give me guidance. The only thing that worries me is that we don't understand this... well, this hitchhiker of yours. We don't know if it's batting for the right team."

"I have the feeling that it doesn't care. It's my decisions that make its visions good or bad. I've read that djinn can be ambiguous at the best of times. This time it just wanted me gone from that place. But last night it wanted me to do something useful." I peered through the trees at the vague shapes of a building I could see among the trunks and undergrowth. "I'm going to have to go down there. Something dark might be lurking, but there's also something suffering, and I can't walk away from that pain. Not again…"

My memories, sparked by Paul coming back into my life, dragged at my mind. We were at an old school, dating back to when Afghanistan was under the control of the Russians. The Taliban used it as a base, and it was supposed to be an FOB for us once we'd cleared them out. Only this forward operating base made me suffer the worst insomnia of my life. Every damned time I closed my eyes I'd hear them, the screams of girls.

One of the interpreters took pity on me one night and told me the story he'd heard in the marketplace.

The Taliban had gone in there and beaten every girl in every classroom. The female teachers weren't so lucky. The playground had run red with the blood in the sand. The walls echoed with screams for hours. The townsfolk were too terrified to help them after the first few died in the dusty street, shot in the head.

My throat closed as I thought about it happening all over again in that abandoned country. Only it wouldn't be AK47s shooting, it would be MP5s or AR15s. How many weapons had we left in-country?

"Lorne, come on, we need to get you into the light," Ella said, as if she could read my thoughts. Christ, I carried so much pain in my memories, it's a wonder I managed to lift my head off the pillow each morning.

The three of us left the woods. Back in the sunlight, I stood still, face to the sun, eyes closed, and just breathed. I felt Heather's hand in mine. Her reluctance to let me go warmed me just as much as the sun.

"We're going back in there," I said. "I just need to find a way to do it without losing my breakfast."

11

ONCE MORE AT EDDIE'S COTTAGE, everyone looked at me as if I'd blown the heads off a dozen teddy bears. Just as well they didn't know about the events at the cottage or those with the dead soldier. After five minutes of their shock, I'd had enough.

"Alright, I had an episode. They happen. I'm not going to hurt anyone or myself, so just relax. We need to figure out what that building was for, who owns it now, and if any of those old Methodist graves have been reused. We also need to find out why Paul's mother, Peggy, was killed. I realise it's hard to trust me right now, but the police can't act on anything we've found so far, which means we need evidence." I looked hard at Eddie.

"True enough." He was worried. "If you're up to it, we'll go dig up a grave."

"No!" Lilian said. "We can't do that. It's wrong. We need to find out more first. The last thing we want to do is cause more problems because we disturbed the dead. This is our home."

"Lil, love, they're just dead—"

"Don't you give me that, Eddie Rice," she snapped in return. "You know that's not true, and I'd have thought poor Lorne's attack of the collywobbles is evidence enough of a problem."

'Collywobbles', I hadn't heard that word used since my mum died. It made me smile. I quite liked the thought of my PTSD being an 'attack of the collywobbles', sounded a great deal less scary.

"What about the archives?" Heather said. She'd been quiet since we'd arrived back at the cottage. "Like at the museum in Taunton, or old newspapers at the library?"

Paul snorted. "Yeah, let's go look up books and microfiche." He shook his head. "It'll all be on-line."

"Alright, smart arse," Heather shot back, "what if you're wrong? What if it isn't? Somerset is hardly the most sophisticated place."

She had a point, but I didn't want to let them argue it out.

Ella twitched and a shrill rendition of Love Over Gold, by Dire Straits, leaked from her jeans pocket. "Bugger, it's the bishop. I have to take this."

"Interesting ring tone," Eddie mumbled. "I need to phone Kate anyway."

I wandered off from the others and stared out to the distant hills, keeping the ones at my back firmly out of my eye line for a bit. Other than a terrifying episode back in the winter when I'd been carrying a bag full of bad juju to Spud's special place, I'd not experienced an attack like the one in the woods. My insides still trembled, and I was knackered. Ten miles over rough terrain with a full Bergen would make me less exhausted. I just wanted to sleep.

What if Ella and the others were right? What if I'd spent my life in denial and I actually had some kind of ghost sniffing gene buried in the back of my head somewhere?

You're an idiot for this coming as a surprise. Especially after last night.

I agreed. After all the experiences I'd had both in the army and out, I had the proof. I just didn't want to do anything with it because it smacked of airy-fairy-peace-loving-hippy-dippy-nonsense. I was a highly trained warrior. Not some acid taking dope fiend who couldn't hold down a job.

Judging much?

Yeah, alright, a tad judgemental.

I glanced at Heather; we'd shared some mellow evenings over the summer. She looked up and smiled, obviously feeling me watching her. Christ, I should cut her loose. We were too close by half. She needed someone her age and with considerably less damage.

Pushing all the noise to one side, I tried to think about our current situation. Whatever had happened in Luccombe during the Cold War hadn't become public knowledge. They'd obviously built the place in the middle of nowhere for a reason. Even now, the Army still hid its secrets in odd locations. Mind you, keeping something like a hospital hidden in a small community seemed unlikely. Maybe we needed to talk to some of the original residents? If any of them still breathed.

That seemed the place to start. Nothing here made me think our investigations were time critical. The police would handle the investigation into Peggy's death, and I had some confidence in them figuring out her link to the mysterious building.

My musings were interrupted by Ella yelling, "Bastard!"

The bishop tended to drive her nuts at the best of times. This clearly wasn't a good time.

She stormed towards me, and I found myself wanting to retreat, but I managed to hold my ground.

"I have no idea how that man became bishop, but I swear to all I hold holy, I want to cut him open to see if he's actually able to bleed red—or if he was born with purple blood so thick the Church and everyone in it belong to his idea of what the clergy should be." Her tension vibrated through her small body.

I had the disturbing image of Ella ordering the bishop's head on a platter— Salome style. "What's happened?"

She glared at me. "Someone told him I've been asking questions about Peggy's family. I've been reported for disturbing the dead here." Her arm snapped out to encompass Eddie's graveyard. "How? How does he know this stuff? It's like I have an invisible GoPro attached to me." She huffed out a breath. "I shouldn't have called him a bastard."

I refrained from commenting. I'd have called him a great deal worse.

"We haven't disturbed the dead here, so how does he know?" I asked.

"Drones," Paul called over from where he sat in his car, ensconced once more with his laptop. "I'm checking the ones I have access to, and we've had a recent visitor."

I glanced up at the sky. "Seriously? Why? Who would bother redirecting a drone over our position? Then take the time to contact Ella's bishop?"

He didn't look up but muttered, "Who indeed? I've been sweeping the skies as a matter of course since I arrived, just in case."

"In case of what?" I asked.

Dextrous fingers continued to dance over his keyboard. "It's just something I do. You would too, if you knew some of the stuff I did," he muttered. "Damn it."

"What?"

"I've been blocked. A damned firewall it'll take days to crack just slammed down on me. They're tracking me as well." He looked troubled.

"That's bad, right?"

He scowled. "Very."

"But why bother my bishop?" Ella asked.

Paul shrugged. "To put you off? To force us in a different direction? They picked an easy target to manipulate. You're the only one with a boss they can bully."

"So is this our Security Services?" she asked.

Paul's mouth thinned as he thought about it. "It could be, or it could be someone saying they are from MI5 or MI6. You're an easy target."

"What do I do about it?" Ella asked.

"Depends on how much you like your job, I guess," Paul said, ever helpful.

I put a hand on her shoulder, "It won't come to that. Someone is trying to disrupt us."

Eddie came over, tapping his chin with his phone. "Heather, you know someone called Monkey?"

She glanced at me. Any reference to her old life disturbed her. "Why?"

I watched Eddie fight his smile, as if he knew her reasons for being evasive. "Kate wants him in for questioning."

"Monkey?" Heather rose from where she'd been sitting on the ground. Dusting her hands off, she said, "He's an addict and a thief, but he's not capable of hurting an old lady."

"How do you know him?" I asked.

She shrugged. "How do I know most of the bottom feeders in the area? My ex would bring me up here so we could spend time together in public without his wife knowing. Or that was his thinking. Little did I know it was so he could meet the Gnostic Dawn idiots with some eye candy floating about." The scowl on her face said being eye candy wasn't her life's mission.

The Gnostic Dawn was the society of wealthy would-be immortals we'd stopped in January. Heather's ex had been their hired muscle.

"Still doesn't explain how you know this Monkey," Paul said.

"Not that it's your business, but my ex shifted gear through him. He is, or was, one of Smoke's distributors this side of the moor."

Smoke was the president of The Devil's Mercenaries motorcycle gang. "He better not be supplying for Smoke now," I said, guts tightening. Smoke and I had an arrangement. I taught his people some handy skills to improve their self-worth. He'd leave Exmoor out of his less legal businesses. I wasn't naïve enough to think our agreement would keep the drugs out of the area, but it might help a little.

"Her ex is a drug dealer?" Paul asked me.

Acutely aware of Eddie's presence, as one of the police officers at the crime scene of the untimely and rather sudden demise of the biker in question, I didn't quite know what to say.

Eddie knew I'd shot him in the head, but he couldn't prove it and wasn't terribly interested in doing so. Still, the law is the law.

"My ex *was* an evil bastard who deserved what he got." Heather's stance on the subject never varied. She knew what I'd done. Her unspoken gratitude removed any sense of guilt I might have over killing outside the rules of engagement as a British soldier. I'd seen her bruises.

"Still, if we get to Monkey before the police…" I let the sentence hang.

Eddie said, "I can't hear this." He stuck his fingers in his ears, making Ella chuckle.

"Okay, I think we go find this Monkey and have a quiet one-to-one meeting before the police catch hold of the little bugger," I said.

"I know where his squat used to be in Minehead. No idea if it's still there mind, but if it is, he won't be too far away." She retrieved our bike gear from a pile near the caravan. "Let's get this done. The later we leave it, the harder it'll be to find out where he is."

I looked at Ella. "You okay here?"

"I've a service soon, so I'll have to work."

"What about the bishop?"

She shrugged. "To be honest, what about him? They going to keep flying drones over the site just to keep an eye on the local vicar? I don't think MI5, if it is them, is that bothered about me. Paul's right, they just want to freak us out."

Lilian shifted, rubbing her thighs with her palms, a nervous gesture. "Are we in trouble or danger? Are MI5 really involved? It's all very strange. I mean… isn't it all a bit farfetched? Shouldn't poor Lorne just have a lie down and try to forget what happened in that horrible building? We don't own it, so we shouldn't be affected by it."

"I'm not leaving this alone," stated Paul. "Whatever is going on killed my mother. I don't intend to let anyone bully me into backing down. And that drone might not be one of ours."

"Besides," said Eddie. "If we don't know what happened in there, we could all be in danger without knowing why. I'm sorry, love, but I agree with the others."

Lilian sighed. "I had the feeling that would be the case. I had to try. I guess we'll be the centre of operations for the moment?"

"Sounds wise," I said, pulling on my heavy Kevlar bike jacket.

"I better get to the shops then and buy some more biscuits."

IT DIDN'T TAKE LONG TO reach the seaside town. We picked up the A39 at Holnicote and doubled back to the *'metropolis'* of Minehead. I wondered how Heather would feel seeing her old life. I didn't know how I'd feel if I returned to Hereford.

"It's on Marlett Road," she said, her visor up, as we rode into town.

I sat straight on the bike, the congestion thick. Weaving in and out of heavy traffic would just draw attention to us, so I was happy to go with the flow on this occasion. "I thought that was a posh bit of town?"

"It's an old building that's been empty for years. To be honest, they keep the location quiet and try to remain out of sight. The locals kinda ignore them and so long as no one is stupid enough to break into the nearby houses or cars, they can stay."

The easiest way to Marlett Road was past Willow's shop, Magick Minehead. I slowed going past and wondered whether to stop. Then I had to, because the damned traffic backed up. The door to the shop opened, and a man walked out, tall, good-looking, young and dressed in expensive flowing clothing—probably organic hemp. Willow also came out of the shop.

Heather straightened on the back of the bike. Pulling away from me.

Willow, her tawny hair wild around her beautiful face, leaned into the man and they kissed, more or less chaste. They smiled, then embraced, full body hug. To my dawning horror, I watched him lean down, clasp her face in his hands and kiss her full on the lips. She responded in kind. My heart tripped over itself, and my guts plunged into a stinky soup of emotional sludge. Although we spent less time together these days, she'd never called a halt to our intimate connection.

I couldn't help myself. I twisted my hand and revved the bike's engine so hard the exhaust roared. Willow turned to the traffic. She knew my bike. Our gaze locked. I watched those cat green eyes widen in shock. The cars in front of me, mostly holidaymakers, started to move towards the beach.

Heather leaned back into me, her arms around my waist. "Just go, Lorne. You don't want this conversation in public. Trust me."

The engine barked as I pulled out of the queue and roared down the white line.

Well, at least I knew why she'd not been up to the farm very much the last few weeks. She'd met someone new.

"It might not be what you think," Heather said as we slowed for the junction.

"Of course it bloody is," I snapped. Then I reached back and rubbed her thigh. "Sorry. Not your fault."

Heather remained silent.

We trundled up Marlett Road, and I chose to focus only on the mission ahead, not on the vision—engraved on my brain—that we'd just seen. To be honest, I couldn't blame Willow. We kept trying because we genuinely enjoyed spending time together but... *Meat is Murder* in her view, and I used to kill people for a living. Two very different lifestyles and my PTSD... that was a lot for any woman to deal with long-term.

Didn't stop me being angry, hurt and very sad. I knew full well I wasn't much of a catch, but a bit of honesty wouldn't go amiss.

"Here," Heather said, tapping my shoulder. "Pull over here."

I slid the bike into a space between a flash BMW and a Merc. We'd pulled up among expensive detached houses tucked behind well-maintained hedges and large metal gates. The property we needed to infiltrate stood out because the hedge splodged over its low wall and covered half the pavement. The metal gates weren't rusty, but the blue paint had faded and peeled back. Weeds choked the gravel drive.

Heather stood still for a moment. "You gonna be okay in there?"

"What?"

"Lorne, not even you can compartmentalise that well."

She was talking about Willow. Heather's big blue eyes were sad and a little worried.

I stared at the house for a moment, not seeing the damage to it, but the damage to me. "I'm fine. Let's get this done." The hurt radiated out from the centre of my being, but I was trained to ignore pain, fight through it, and continue to the function. I had a mission to complete, and complete it, I would.

With a sigh and a shake of her head, Heather walked through the overgrown lawn. Strangely, the recycling bins were all in order and correctly stacked.

She noticed my expression of confusion. "Gotta blend in, right? The neighbours would soon complain if the rubbish built up too much."

"We used to do the same thing when on long obos in a clean community. I'm just surprised."

Heather didn't reply. I watched her as she led the way around the side of the house. Tension made her small body tight, and anger hovered around her. A defence mechanism. She didn't want to be here, and I suddenly wondered about the wisdom of putting her through it. By walking away from her life, that day she'd asked for my help, every decision she'd made pulled her further from the past. Returning as a visitor must create a lot of conflict.

I realised, with shocking clarity that I never wanted to go back to Credenhill. The longer I was out of my old life, the less I wanted to return. Or maybe that was the company I kept these days.

We stopped behind the house, and I did an external check. A large two storey nineteen-thirties style detached property with big windows and a large garage. It would be worth a small fortune. How had it become a squat?

Some of the windows had glass panes replaced by chipboard, now covered in graffiti. The backdoor had a certain rugged brutalism about it, the wood banged up and replaced by sheet metal screwed into place. The smell oozing out of the open door made me reach for Heather and pull her back.

"Let me go first."

"It's fine, Lorne."

"That smell—"

"I know what it is, and I can handle myself well enough. Let me do the talking. I know the people we need to mention so we can find Monkey."

The smell in question combined human bodily fluids, decay and drugs. Not the sweet smell of dope, but the bitter stink of Class As.

Heather stepped over the threshold and the atmosphere flipped. From an idyllic seaside town, kissed by warm summer sun and fresh breezes off the sea, to an inner-city den of addiction and disease.

I couldn't accuse the kitchen of being clean, and I certainly saw evidence of spoons used for something other than making the tea, but it had an organisation to it that denied total neglect. Heather ignored everything and strode through another door. I wished she'd let me go first so I could clear each room. I didn't like seeing her operate in a place this dark. She didn't deserve to know how to survive in this environment.

I knew, logically, places like these littered her past, as familiar to her as barracks are to me, but it didn't make it easier to see her navigate it so easily. She'd been part of this world for almost ten years. Many operators didn't last that long in The Regiment. She knew her environment better than I did right now.

We came to a closed door and Heather knocked. Not hard and not in a way that would make the occupants think we were police.

The door cracked open. A woman's face, too thin and hollow-eyed to be attractive, with cheap and tangled blonde hair. "Who are you?" she snarled through the crack in the door.

"I'm looking for Monkey. Smoke sent us," Heather snapped.

The woman looked Heather up and down, then eyed me. "Answer the question."

"It doesn't matter who I am, and it really doesn't matter who he is," she jerked her head in my direction, "you just need to tell me if Monkey is here because Smoke wants him for some business. I take it you still need Smoke's business?"

The woman cocked her head, like a malnourished puppy sensing steak nearby, or at least a rubbish bin full of cheap burger meat.

"Monkey's upstairs with his missus." She nodded towards the stairs behind us. "You got any fags on you?" the woman asked.

"No," Heather said. "I do have this though." She pulled out her wallet and removed a five-pound note. "Try to spend it on food, yeah?"

The woman took the fiver with a delicacy I didn't expect. She looked down at the floor and mumbled, "Thanks," before shutting the door in Heather's face.

"There but for the Grace of God," Heather breathed.

I watched her heart ache for the victim on the other side of the door. I put a hand on her shoulder. "You okay?"

She turned and glanced at me long enough for the tears in her eyes to shine in the dim light of the house. "Not really. Let's get this done, then get drunk."

We turned as one, and made our way to the stairs. Wood stripped of dignity. The paint a forgotten pride, the stair carpet a memory to someone other than the current occupiers. The walls, once covered in expensive wallpaper, were now a mesh of failed images, thoughts, and foul looking smudges. The graffiti here held none of the poignant politics of a Banksy, and all the self-loathing of an addict.

At the top we heard the dull thump of a bass beat, so we followed the sound to a room at the front of the house. The door was open, and I looked into a bleak summation of a man's life. I'd seen families all over the world exist in a single room this size and somehow, they made it look like a home. Not so in this once elegant address.

Needles littered the floor along with the empty detritus of other addictions; cider bottles, over filled ashtrays, empty wraps, and half-eaten meals. A man lay on a mattress on the floor, a woman next to him, tucked in tight to the wall. Both looked emaciated. The room stank of fetid human and drugs.

"Monkey?" Heather called out, not yet breaching the entrance.

The lank haired figure turned his head. "Who wants to know?" A surprisingly deep but heavy cockney accented voice.

Heather stepped into the light from the half-covered window. "Remember me? I'm one of Smoke's girls?"

How much did it cost her to say that? Why wasn't I just pounding heads into walls to get answers?

"Yeah, man, I remember you. You're the sweet ass that Smoke's VP was banging. Who's your friend?" His eyes slid to me. They were black, but whether that was the true colour or my perception…

"New muscle. He wants a word." She looked back at me. "I don't know how to get answers out of him."

"Step outside," I told her. For some reason, I reached up and touched her cheek. "Go back to the bike and wait for me. This isn't going to take long. Then you will wipe this place from your mind, and I will never ask you to do this again." I wanted to tell her how sorry I felt for putting her through it.

Wordlessly slipping past, she left. No protest or attempts to 'see it through'.

The man on the bed watched all this with growing awareness and gradual fear.

"I don't want no trouble. I don't owe Smoke nuffing."

"I'm not here about Smoke." I approached the bed. The woman didn't stir. "I need some information and you're going to give it to me. Then I'll leave you in peace and you'll never see me again."

"Give me money and I'll tell you anything, even suck your—"

"That won't be necessary." I shuddered at the thought. The sores around his mouth, even if I were that way inclined, would be enough to put me off. I took out my wallet this time and removed a twenty. "I want to know about a burglary in Luccombe."

He snatched for the note, but I pulled it away.

"I done it."

Yeah, I was going to fall for that.

"Which house?"

"I done them all."

"Monkey, I am not in the mood. I've had enough of being in this hellhole. Where were you two nights ago?"

At that, his mouth snapped shut and his eyes widened. Now he was with the programme.

"Tell me what happened." I maintained steady eye contact.

"Fuck off."

"Tell me what happened in Luccombe two nights ago, and I'll go away."

"You a copper?" The words a well programmed sneer.

"I'm far worse. I don't have to keep you in one piece to answer questions." I smiled.

He looked at me in alarm. "I don't know anything about a burglary in Luccombe." His fragile gaze slid away, body jittering, hands twitching.

I still wore my motorcycle gloves, so touching him didn't feel like a betrayal to my skin. I grabbed the front of his ratted shirt and hauled him off the bed. He screeched in alarm and tried to punch me. The woman still didn't move.

With his back to the bedroom wall and my hands in his chest, pushing him tight, I could see the rock and hard place having the right effect on his natural inclination to lie. I'd be having the truth this time.

"I didn't know he was going to kill the old woman. I goes into a house, does the job and gets out, sharpish. I don't hang about and if the owner wakes up, I'm off on my toes. I'm not doing time for some old video machine and a bit of bling."

"You took the projector?"

"Yeah, the bloke wanted me to take it, but he took the film in it."

Shit. "Describe this bloke."

Monkey tried to shrug. "Dunno, just a bloke. Drove me out there, told me to turn the place over."

"What kind of vehicle?" I demanded.

Again with the attempt at a shrug. "One with four wheels and a fucking engine. What does it matter?"

I leashed the beast long enough to snarl, "I want a description of the vehicle used."

Denied his shrug, Monkey huffed. The whiff of air made me want to gag. "A van. A black van like a Transit, only it was a Merc. New, shiny inside. Nice wheels."

A large black van and a make, if not a model. I didn't bother asking about a number plate. I didn't have that much time. "Go on."

Monkey said, "When the old woman set off a racket, the bloke came storming in and beat the poor old dear. I just left."

"You didn't try to stop him?"

Confusion passed over Monkey's face. "No, why would I? He was a vicious shit. Just like you." He squirmed in my grasp.

I wanted to sigh, but the thought of inhaling that much air around this pond scum made my nose think twice. "Tell me what happened. Exactly. And I want a description."

Monkey rolled his eyes. "Not like I can paint a fucking portrait. The man had an accent. He was dark, bigger than you."

"What kind of accent?"

"I dunno. Just an accent. Maybe European, maybe Russian."

I ground my teeth. "Could you be a little more specific?"

The woman in the corner mumbled and rolled over. I grabbed Monkey by the back of his neck and dragged him into the darker hallway. "I want answers, chimp man, or I'm going to start snapping fingers." I grabbed two of his fingers and bent them back.

He whimpered and dropped to his knees. "Who the hell are you?"

"I'm the good guy. The bad guy is the man who beat an old woman to death."

"Dead?" His eyes cleared for the first time. "She died?"

"Yes, and when the police find you, which they will, you'll be done for her murder. So, talk to me. I have more chance of finding the bad man than the police, which will prevent him from coming back to find you, to make certain you don't talk." My internal beast slid from the dark where he'd been napping for weeks and leaked through the barriers protecting the world from his desire to hunt. Maybe I could have treated this pond scum with a little more care, taken into account the fact that most people in this situation didn't choose it, but fell into it because of some tragic life story.

However, I was angry and in a rush. I wanted out of here before the police arrived and I wanted to vent some of the agony gathering in my chest. My phone vibrated in my jacket.

Monkey's eyes betrayed his panic at the shift inside me. "Okay, it was Russian, but he had a mate with him, and he sounded American. I didn't hear much, but they wanted that tape real bad. They wanted me to turn the place over, find it for them and anything else it was with. I can get into most places without breaking any locks and stuff. But the old lady, she was asleep in the front room and woke up. She came at me and started to scream. Then they came in and started asking her questions, like 'Where is it? We want the files. We know she took them from the lab. Where are they? Tell us what we want.'

All that stuff. She had no idea what they were on about. None. I swear I didn't know they was going to kill her."

"But you let them hurt an old woman?"

His mouth moved, but he couldn't speak.

"You have anything else you want to tell me?" I asked. The anger surging through me at the thought of this scum bag being one of the last people on this earth a woman like Peggy had to see made me dizzy with the need for violence.

My phone buzzed in my pocket—again. I'd have to check. With my free hand, I retrieved it. Heather. I swiped to answer. "Yes."

"Police. Get out."

"Walk up the hill. I'll come find you."

She hung up.

"I need more intel, Monkey, or you'll be picking bits of you up off the floor."

A shiver started at the base of my spine and prickled up my back. The shadows around the hallway danced and crept towards Monkey. I tried to ignore them, but it proved impossible. I glanced up the hallway, and the shadow became denser, thicker. It shifted form, turned into the shape of a man.

My heartbeat rose for the first time since we'd arrived. I stared into the dark eyes of a dead man. A man holding a .303 rifle.

Monkey wrenched me back to the present. "The man, the Russian bloke, he had a tattoo on his wrist. It was a weird red flared star thing."

I knew what he was talking about. I'd seen it on Russian soldiers in Siberia and Syria. The flag of the dreaded GU, or GRU, Main Directorate of the General Staff of the Armed Forces of the Russian Federation. Bloody great mouthful in English. They owned the Spetsnaz boys.

Car doors banged outside. I needed to move. The soldier stood, impassively at the end of the hallway, weapon held across his body, not pointing at me.

Releasing Monkey from the finger lock, I jogged down the stairs and back through the kitchen. Once outside, I heard the police on the gravel at the front. A wildly overgrown hedge covered a small gate.

I made a dash for it, hunkered down, and pulled it open. It protested, then fell to pieces from my abuse. It gave me the exit I needed. I squirmed through the hole and found myself in a narrow alley. Turning left, I jogged down the passageway, the gates and hedges all neat and nice in the other houses, then turned left again and returned to the road.

Two police cars and a van now filled the road. I guessed they came from Taunton because Minehead's police force wasn't large enough for a raid.

With calm purpose, I walked up the street, back to the bike and stopped by the police car. A young officer stood near the van. She looked gutted at missing out on the action.

"Afternoon," I said, with a sharp nod. "About time someone did something about that place. Thank you."

"Just move on, sir."

I gave a brief smile, climbed on the bike, and carefully pulled away. I found Heather at the top of the road, sat on the war memorial. She mounted the bike and pulled on her helmet. We rode off without a shared word.

12

THE INTEL I'D GLEANED FROM Monkey needed to be given to Paul so he could direct his computer wizardry, but I wanted a little time to gather my thoughts. The shock of seeing the soldier in the building added to the mystery gathering around us.

Back in the winter, I'd had to avoid the Gnostic Dawn's manhunt, so I'd done battle with the weather and the footpaths of North Hill to reach Culbone on the other side of Porlock Bay. Now, however, the sun shone and—despite the tourists—we could ride up North Hill without any problem on the road. I pulled over at the summit, driving into a well-maintained bridleway, before switching the bike off. Wales lay in the distance, a hazy line in the afternoon light. The sea before it, looked benign. Rosebay willow herb littered the bracken and heather. Sheep dozed in the heat.

My companion dismounted my trusted steed.

We both stared at the view rather than face each other. The soldier in me knew I needed to organise my thoughts and focus on the mission. The man inside me wanted to figure out what the hell Willow had done and what I wanted to do about it.

"You need to talk to Willow," Heather stated.

"I'd rather talk to you."

She glanced at me. "Why?"

I frowned. "Because I care about you and going to that house upset you."

"My emotional wellbeing is not your responsibility, Lorne, and the fact you think it is, confuses and hurts me." She walked away from me for a moment before turning back. "Fuck it. If I don't say something, you're never going to understand." This came out as the kind of growl you'd expect from a Doberman just before he snapped your arm off. She sighed and straightened her shoulders. "You've made it clear you aren't interested in me—romantically—but I can't help how I feel. I don't want to jeopardise our friendship or my living arrangements."

Oh fuck, we are having the *conversation. Time to step up, fool.*

I'd played this out in my head many times. If I didn't admit that, I'd be lying to myself. I wanted to get this right because it felt more important than the vision of seeing Willow with another bloke. Or the dead man with the rifle. I stared at my petrol tank for a bit.

Raise the objections first. "Eighteen years is a lot, Heather. I'm an old man."

She barked a bitter laugh. "You worked with men eighteen years your junior, right?"

"Well, yes, but—"

"And yet I'm still a kid in your eyes?"

She definitely wasn't, despite the nickname.

"I don't want to lose you," I blurted, feeling the heat creep up my face. The speedometer needed wiping clean of dust, so I focused on doing that for a bit.

"What?"

"You have so much life to live. I want to help you do that, provide for you, but..." I exhaled. "I don't know. I just..." I finally managed to meet her eyes. "I'm not..."

Her blue eyes shone with mirth. "God, you're insufferably cute sometimes."

I frowned. "Cute?"

"Yes. Cute. Though I'm sure none of your enemies ever think that. Can I ask you a question without it screwing up our living arrangements?"

"Of course."

"Do you find me attractive?" She stood before me, her short dark hair windblown and spikey from the bike helmet, in black jeans and Kevlar jacket which I'd bought her because it was safer than her old leather one, wearing a t-shirt that said: *Attempted Murder* with two crows on the front. It always made her chuckle.

I laughed. "Yes. Yes, I think you're one of the most beautiful women I've met, Heather. I always have."

She held her arms out wide. "Then why do you treat me, by turns, like I'm a child, a soldier, a piece of blown glass, but never as a woman?"

"Because I didn't want to take advantage. I don't want to be like all those other men!"

"Take advantage, Lorne, because I'm bored with waiting."

Oh, okay, gold invitation, right? Just try to think with the larger of your heads.

"I should end things with Willow properly first."

She rolled her eyes. "Yes, okay, do that if you must."

My phone vibrated. I pulled it out of my jacket. "Willow," I said, looking at Heather.

"Of course it is," she snarled. "Fucking witch probably tapped into your..." She walked off down the path, still muttering, and left me to it.

I suddenly wished for a car load of fascist Russians to drive up and start shooting at me. I'd know how to handle that. How did a man like me attract two such remarkable women into his life? One of which was kicking stones with some passion, muttering under her breath.

I took the call. "Turner."

"Lorne, I..."

"Just answer me a couple of questions. Are you happy?"

"Yes."

"Is he going to treat you well?"

"I think so."

"Are we still friends?"

"I hope so."

"Can I come and eat cake with you when I'm in town?"

"I'd really like that, Lorne." There were tears threatening. I didn't need to be dealing with tears.

"You should have told me." A certain hardness crept into my voice. I couldn't avoid it.

"I know. I'm sorry."

"Why didn't you? And if you say you were scared, then we have a problem."

"I wasn't scared. I was just being a coward. I thought things with Heather would take the decision out of my hands. I didn't want to hurt you. We were so close to making it work, but..."

"I'm a soldier." What did she mean about Heather?

"Sorry." Willow sounded genuine. "It's not just that, but it is a big part of it."

I sighed and watched Heather, who seemed to be pulling the heads off the dandelions. "Don't be. You were honest. That's not a bad thing."

"We're done?" she asked, and I heard the note of relief.

I paused. I'd felt the stirrings of something deeper than lust with Willow. I'd been so close to falling in love with her, but she'd always pulled back when she sensed it, so it had never become real. I really wanted something real. "Yeah, we're done."

"Thank you, Lorne."

"I'll always be there for you, Willow."

"I know. Me too." She hung up on a sob.

I put the bike on the stand and walked up to Heather. Well, I couldn't really get a more romantic setting for our first kiss than the top of North Hill in the glorious summer weather.

Cupping her face in my scarred old hands, I looked into her eyes. "I'm very fond of you, Heather. I don't want this to go wrong. If it does it's going to be hell, but I can't let you go without trying to make you happy."

The smile on her face outshone the light of the sun. She held my wrists and whispered, "I'm not going to break your heart." Our lips met, and the world bled away on summer breezes full of the warm earth, the sea and the sound of a buzzard's joyful screams overhead.

THE RETURN TO LUCCOMBE CAME as a shock. It felt like we'd been away for weeks, not just a couple of hours. Heather slid off the back of the bike and removed her helmet. I couldn't help but smile at the slightly glazed look in those blue eyes.

"No good smirking, Turner," she said. "You look exactly the same."

"Not exactly." I took a piece of bracken out of her hair.

"We keeping this quiet for a bit?" she asked.

I stared at the caravans in Eddie's garden. "I don't want to keep it a secret, but Paul already thinks we're sleeping together. The Rices aren't going to care and it's none of their business, but..."

"Ella."

"She'll have a moan the minute she works it out."

"Which will be the second we walk into her company."

"Yep."

"Confess when we need to," Heather said. "Other than that, we keep it quiet. I'm not interested in other people's opinions." She kissed me and a surge of heat so intense I didn't have words to describe it flared brightly from the core of my being. She whispered, "Don't break me, and Ella won't kill you."

I managed a tight smile. "There speaks the voice of experience."

"I've been lied to and betrayed so often it became a game in the end. The *'let's see how many more ways there are to break a heart'* game."

"I'm sorry, kid. You shouldn't think like that." I stroked her neck, because I could.

"Says the man who remained firmly single his whole life because the army couldn't be unfaithful, and relationships confuse him."

"Hey, I'm not like that."

She just raised a single dark eyebrow and strode off towards the caravans.

"Turner? That you?" Eddie asked, rounding the corner of the cottage.

"It is me, Eddie." I put the bike on the stand and walked over to join him. "Where's Ella and Paul?"

"In the garden. Heather's still with you then?" His police skills were astounding.

I nodded at her retreating back. "Apparently."

He scowled. We walked around the cottage. Ella smiled when she saw me. Paul frowned.

He said, "You took your sweet time."

"Had things to do," I said, forcing myself *not* to look at Heather right now.

"Did you find him?"

"Of course I did, and we have things we need to talk about." I went on to describe my interview with Monkey. Leaving out the bits where I saw the shade of a dead man and when I'd threatened to snap Monkey's fingers off. Eddie didn't need to know about my finer interrogation skills. I knew Monkey would probably grass me up to the police. There weren't too many men in the Minehead area who are fairly small, fit, and bald with heavy facial scarring on the right side. I had to hope Smoke's reputation might keep his mouth shut.

While I talked, Paul scanned the databases for images like the tattoo I described.

In short order, he turned his laptop around and showed us the result. "You're talking about these guys, right?" The image covered the computer screen in various versions.

I nodded. "Why would someone with that as a tattoo be hanging around with an American?" I asked him.

He shrugged. "Doesn't make sense on the surface, but we know Russia's GRU has been interfering in politics all over the world. What's to say they don't have boots on the ground here as well? Or he could be a merc?"

"In Somerset?" I thought about the poisonings in Salisbury, just a short drive up the road for a Russian Special Forces operative, even if it did mean doing battle with the A303. Did I want to be tangling with Russians? No. I did not.

"My bishop is being leaned on by the GRU?" Ella asked in confusion.

Paul shrugged. "It might not be them. It might be our security services. It depends on the secret everyone is trying to hide. And whether it really is the GRU or Putin's private army. Two different things these days. Or an independent contractor. Or hired security for a private company, which is most likely."

"What is this secret, then?" Heather asked, bringing me a beer and sitting beside me on a straw bale we were using as a sofa. Ella's expression remained carefully neutral, a warning sign if I ever saw one.

Paul ran his hands through his hair. "That's the question I still can't answer."

"We need to find out who your grandfather was. If we can't track your grandmother, maybe we can learn more about him," Heather pointed out.

That sounded like a lot of internet stuff I didn't want to think about. "I need to find the men who paid Monkey."

Paul hummed, thinking the problem through for a few seconds, then said, "Well, we keep tabs on those Russians we know about. Not the Americans so much, but I should be able to find a few faces to show your new ape-ish friend."

I glanced at Eddie. "If we find some faces, what are the chances of you getting me into the police station to show Monkey—assuming that's where he is by now?"

Eddie sucked air over his teeth. "How much of Monkey did you break?"

"Hardly anything."

"And if he gave Kate a description of you, rather than the real bad guys?" Eddie asked.

I sniffed. "Yeah, that did occur to me, but he thinks I work for Smoke, so…"

"You're using the fear of Smoke to keep him quiet?" Eddie asked.

I shrugged. He sighed and shook his head.

Watching him consider the issues surrounding me accompanying him to the station in Minehead made me acutely aware of our different working practices.

He eventually said, "Well, I reckon we could try to get in to talk to him. Kate might allow it. She does owe me a favour or six. She's a good copper. If we can get Monkey on record fingering the Russians, it could open a few doors." He didn't look pleased at the prospect. Who could blame him? Going back to work just weeks after retiring wouldn't please most people.

"Best we get in there now," I said, standing up.

"I'm not going anywhere on that death trap you ride," Eddie stated.

I grinned. "To be honest, Eddie, I don't think she'd cope too well with the weight. I'll follow you in."

He sighed, probably wondering how he'd been roped into helping us, but ambled off to find his keys without complaint.

1 3

I STOOD OUTSIDE MINEHEAD POLICE station leaning against a tarmack-strangled lime tree. The building rose above the road on a bank of grass, stained brown by the sun, its red brick exterior full of neat square white windows. As police stations went, it looked okay. Firm but accessible.

It felt good, being here, being practical. The overwhelming sense of rage from the black mass of shadows in my current dreams made me deeply uneasy. The soldier and his behaviour baffled me completely. I kept glancing over my shoulder, expecting him to show up. I didn't understand any of this supernatural stuff. I didn't know how to figure out what they wanted, where they came from, how to make them back off. I didn't know if they presented a danger to me, or my family. Doing this, something I'd done a thousand times, this came as a relief.

Eddie had asked me to keep back, so I'd given him the images of various Russians that Paul had gathered from the databases, who might fit the profile of a Russian mercenary.

Not wanting to be seen lurking outside the nearby school, I'd wandered up the road. With an old army cap, and my wrap-around sunglasses, I doubted anyone would identify me easily. Just to make sure, I stood out of view from the nearby CCTV cameras monitoring both the school entrance and the police carpark.

Keeping still for long periods came easily to me after years of practice, so I just settled in and waited. Twenty minutes into my observation, I watched two men leave the building. That whispering instinct, trained into all operatives, sharpened my senses without making my body twitch. The last thing you want to do is draw attention to your presence when you detect a potential target.

Both men wore suits and carried briefcases. One had dark hair, the other was fair haired. They both wore good suits. On the surface, they appeared to be solicitors. However, they walked in step, their bodies were heavy and square under the suit jackets. They moved with predatory grace, in exactly the same way I did. Watching their surroundings, eyes on swivel. These weren't solicitors. I was torn between following them and waiting for Eddie.

Glancing up and down the road, I realised it would be almost impossible to follow them for long without them seeing me clearly. With so little foot traffic, I'd be made in no time, and I had no one else to swap out. For a good tail to be placed on a target, you needed at least a four-person team.

Damn it, I'd give it a go anyway. I pushed off the tree to follow, when a wail of noise began to drift out from the inside of the police station. I turned back to the building. Smoke rose from the back and Eddie hurried towards me.

Jogging up the wide drive to meet him, the sound of sirens came from a distance on my left.

"What the hell's going on?" I asked.

"Monkey's dead."

"What?"

"On the surface it looks like he OD'd in his cell. Which should be impossible. There's also a fire broken out."

I glanced down the road. The two men were out of sight, but I saw a dark BMW 7 series prowl towards our position. I made certain not to stare into it, but the moment it went past I memorised the number plate.

"I saw them leaving," Eddie nodded at the retreating vehicle, which kept under the speed limit of twenty miles per hour.

Already moving, I called over my shoulder, "I'm going to follow them."

"Turner!" Eddie called out, to stop me, but he cursed when he realised I wouldn't listen.

I ran back to where I'd parked, tugged on my bike helmet and gunned the bike into action. The speed limit became an advisory note as I roared after the car so I didn't lose visuals. I saw the tail end of the vehicle vanish into a road on my left. They were heading for the main A39. With no plan in mind other than to keep 'eyes on', I used my bike's blue tooth to call Eddie.

"They're heading out of Minehead on the main road. Going north."

"Turner, we can't engage. We have no authority."

"No, but if we have a location, we can report in. Come catch me up." I ended the call. I didn't like talking on the phone and riding. The two were incompatible for safety.

Keeping several vehicles back, I watched the sleek BMW drift up the road. I glanced over my shoulder and several cars behind my position ambled Eddie's little Ford Fiesta. Despite being a main artery to this side of Somerset, the A39 wasn't the fastest of roads, especially during tourist season. With roundabouts, traffic lights and short dual-carriageways, it could be hectic.

I remained back from the target vehicle and followed. Eddie caught me up and sat behind the bike at a safe distance. The BMW made it to the junction for Dunster and drifted into the right-hand lane. I indicated to follow. Only one car separated us. The turning for the small castle town was usually busy with tourists, but by some alchemy of the traffic gods, on this occasion, it was clear. The traffic lights turned green, and we crossed the large junction. The BMW drove up the hill into the town and I flashed my indicators, hoping Eddie would understand as I slid into a side road for the tourist information centre.

He drove past and picked up the tail. I followed him. We moseyed, the only speed available in Dunster, straight into the main street and past the medieval Yarn Market. A collection of cute medieval buildings with tourist shops and cafes ran along the wide street on either side. Families wandered about eating ice cream and enjoying the late summer sun. I knew the main road led to the large and well-maintained castle, not that I saw it from this angle.

The BMW turned into a low archway belonging to The Castle Hotel. It was a tight fit. The arch was designed for horse and carriage, not wide BMWs. They were parking, which meant they were staying, and they hadn't spotted their tail. Shoddy.

I flashed my headlight and Eddie answered with a waggle of his indicators. We'd continue on until we found somewhere to pull off the road. Several sets of traffic lights, some narrow streets and more twee houses went past, before we pulled off into the carpark of the Foresters Arms. A beautiful stone-built pub.

Eddie wound down his window as I parked next to him. "What do you want to do?" he asked.

They probably murdered a harmless old lady, so go in there and beat them until they talk.

I said, "Call your DI mate. If they are Russians, or even Americans, and they're Special Forces, I don't want to tangle with them unless I have to."

Eddie looked amused. "Scared?"

"Old," I observed. "And I have something to actually live for these days."

Eddie chuckled. "I noticed." He picked up his phone and called DI Mackenzie. "Kate, yeah, I know, just listen for a second. Turner saw two men leave the station just as the alarm went up. We followed them to Dunster. I think you might want a quiet word. That's right, the two that looked like solicitors. We're outside the Foresters right now, but we'll make sure we can keep an eye on the Castle Hotel."

I waited.

When he hung up, he said, "She's coming over. There's not much she can do at the station. There are enough cooks in that kitchen."

"You'll never get parked close to the Castle."

"You will though. Get back there. Keep an eye on the front. I'll park around the back as if I'm going to stay at the hotel and see if I can get a lead on names from reception."

"Sneaky."

He wagged his eyebrows.

I PARKED THE BIKE IN the main street and walked back up to the Castle Hotel, but on the other side of the road. Not wanting to be noticed among all the families eating ice cream, I entered one of a litter of cafés overlooking the entrance to the carpark. The cool interior brought out a rash of goosebumps and it smelt of clotted cream and sun lotion.

Ordering a cup of tea and a sandwich, I took a seat at the small-paned medieval window. I had a clear view of the front of the hotel for as long as the café remained open. My phone rang.

"Eddie, you okay?" I asked.

"I'm talking to one of the cleaning crew here."

Always a good option. Cleaners go everywhere and no one pays them much attention.

"And?"

I heard muttered conversation on the other end. "She says there are two men staying in a twin room. They haven't checked out. Supposed to stay one night but have now booked for two weeks."

"So they can clean up their mess?"

"Looks that way, doesn't it?"

"What do you want to do?"

"Sit tight until Kate gets here."

Of course he did. Eddie used to be a detective sergeant, not a rank known for making risky decisions by the time they reach retirement.

"I can go have a quiet word," I said. The beast inside me lifted his ugly head at the thought but didn't seem interested. Returning to Heather, now that thought made him perk up.

"No, you stay put." Eddie's voice brooked no argument.

We hung up, and I tucked into my rather nice ham sandwich on thick, fresh bread with loads of salad. I'd known worse places for obos.

Eddie walked in after thirty minutes and sat down. DI Mackenzie followed him.

"What's happening?"

Mackenzie looked frayed. "Christ, this place is so cute it makes you want to puke. Eddie, can you get me a beer?"

Once a sergeant, always a sergeant. I wondered if one of my old COs turned up, I'd be the same, or whether I'd been out long enough to stop jumping at orders.

"Do we have intel?" I asked.

Eddie returned with a beer and a huge slice of chocolate cake. Mackenzie looked ready to weep. "God, I miss you, Eddie."

He chuckled.

"Do we have news, DI Mackenzie?" I asked again.

"Kate, call me Kate. And I'm not sure why you're involved." Her eyes narrowed.

"I happened to be there." My gaze held steady.

"So you're not the one poor Monkey was squeaking about, trying to break his fingers?" she asked.

"No."

"Some other bald thug with scars all over his face, then?"

"Must be."

She dropped her gaze first and sighed. "I can't be bothered to bollock you both for this, so we'll just move on. To be honest, I need all the help I can get. There are two businessmen staying in the Castle Hotel. However, their descriptions don't fit the CCTV of the 'solicitors' from the station. I didn't see the buggers myself. They must have used disguises at the station."

"Are either of them Russian?"

"Eastern European for certain. That's the passport details."

"Fake?"

"Who knows? I can't go in there without just cause or a warrant or something like proof of a problem. I can run the names given through the database and Border Force but that's it right now."

"How did Monkey die?" I asked.

"He drank a coffee they brought in with them."

I sat back a little, my paranoia kicking in. "If he was poisoned, and it's the Russians…"

Kate nodded. "I know. The place is being locked down for a radiation threat. I was out of the building already. It's why I'm here. They also started a fire in a bin on the way out. They knew how to keep us chasing our tails, that's for certain."

The thought of something like the disaster at Salisbury hitting Minehead made my stomach crawl. Polonium was not a substance to take lightly.

"What do we do?" I asked.

"Build a case. We can't arrest people and then look for evidence."

"Are you able to sanction a team to watch them?" I asked.

She shook her head. "Not without more of a budget and I'd need to present a compelling case to my DCI for that. How they link in with the murder of an old lady is pretty slim, and I need the tox report back from the post-mortem before we decide if Monkey's death was murder or not. He was the only witness we had, and the only man we could place at the scene of the murder. He made a brief statement saying he hadn't been there during the killing, but we don't have a formal statement. Those men turned up, claiming to be his solicitors. Their ID checked out, so they were allowed time with the suspect. It's an almighty balls up. Glad it's not my station."

I didn't relish the idea of spending the night somewhere in the area trying to keep eyes on the targets. I could tell Eddie didn't want to either. We both had places we'd rather be—like a bed.

Kate held her hand up. "Don't think about setting up your own operation, you two. I'll request drive-bys from the plods and I've asked reception to ring me directly if anything changes regarding their status. I need to talk to my DCI because I suspect the Security Service will be involved if this is anything like Salisbury." She devoured the last of the cake and beer. "Which means I should be leaving now."

"You want us to inform you if we stumble over anything?" Eddie asked.

"Of course, and thank you, Eddie, for your help. We'd never have found them without your quick thinking." She smiled at him.

I raised an eyebrow. He shrugged. The bugger wasn't going to tell her that my intervention meant we'd located them.

14

I STOOD IN A TUNNEL. It didn't smell right, feel right, not my tunnel, and a chime called out. A song I recognised. Where...?

"Lorne? Wake up."

That voice, I knew that, and the hand on my chest. Though it felt new.

"Fuck," I muttered, rolling over and grabbing my phone off the bedside table. "Turner."

A tight voice snapped out, "It's Eddie. Get down here. There's someone in the woods."

I blinked. "What?" To be honest, I'd had a busy night and dragging my mind out of my present proved hard work.

"There's someone in the fucking woods, Turner, and I need your bloody help. This is your fault," Eddie hissed.

"Call the police, surely."

"You think they have the resources to deal with this and whatever is going on at the Minehead station? By the time they get here from Taunton, Lilian and I could be dead in our beds. Just get down here."

He had a point. It would take the police nearly an hour to reach this spot from Taunton, never mind making it into the woods at the back.

"On my way."

Heather was already out of our bed—*our bed*—that felt...

"You're not coming," I stated.

"Fuck you," she muttered. "You think Eddie can back you up?" She headed for the door.

I grunted. I didn't know if I was proud of Heather or dismayed at the little monster I'd unleashed.

I headed for the gun cabinet under the stairs and put in the security code. I took out the SIG Sauer P226 I'd snaffled from the Quartermaster's stores in Iraq and the Heckler and Koch P30 I'd taken from an idiot in Scob. I wondered about removing the assault rifles, but they'd be harder to handle in the woods. I picked up the two shoulder holsters for both handguns and two clips each. That gave us enough 9mm rounds to do some serious damage.

I handed Heather the P30. She preferred it to the SIG.

Despite seeing me check the weapon, she did it as well, just as I'd taught her. Clearing the chamber, before inserting the magazine, and putting it into the small shoulder rig I'd bought her. It had extras so she could carry a knife and an extendable asp.

"Ready?" I asked.

"Ready, boss."

The last items I grabbed were a pack of radios. After our experience in Scob with the toy ones, I decided I needed better comms units to hand, so bought four black Retevis Walkie Talkies and ear pieces to go with them. I also stuffed a full-face balaclava in my pocket, a familiar tool for operators all over the world.

We grabbed the bike gear and headed into the night.

It took me eight minutes to reach Eddie's place. We rolled in on silent running with lights out. Still in silence, Heather slipped off the back and headed for the caravans while I walked the bike into the shadows of the cottage. I jogged to catch Heather up and found Eddie in dark clothes outside. A moon rose overhead, half full and bright, the stars a wild cacophony of light overhead.

"Lilian alright?" I asked first.

Eddie gave me a tight nod. "She's inside."

"Lilian will remain here. If there's a problem, she can leave in the car and head for Ella's place. I need a threat assessment."

As if summoned, Lilian left the caravan wearing dark clothing but looking extremely pale.

"There are lights up in the woods. I'd estimate at least three individuals. They didn't come through my land to get up there, but I don't know the footpaths to know where they might be parked."

Heather said, "There's a carpark and a footpath into the woods that runs from Crook Horn Hill up to Webber's Post. It would be easy enough in the dark. Then you can pick up the path that follows Horner River and from there it would be a quick jog over dark fields with no farmhouse to disturb."

Eddie frowned. "How do you know all this?"

"Dog walking. I did a lot of dog walking for people when I moved into the village. I'm not scouting for properties to rob," she snapped.

"Alright, settle down. I don't think he meant it like that," I said, placing a hand on her shoulder. She quivered with tension.

"So it's likely we're dealing with fit and confident people if they came that way. Without tramping over the properties fronting the lane, like yours, Eddie, they had to have come some distance. There's only the three of us against the possibility of three, maybe more. We don't know if they're armed or trained."

"I'm guessing you didn't come unarmed?" Eddie said.

Heather didn't look at me.

"No comment," I added. Handguns were not popular among the constabulary of Great Britain, and I didn't want mine confiscated. They'd be aggravating to replace.

"Good," Eddie replied. "I'm bugger all use, Turner. Running around woods in the dark is not how I managed to produce this," he patted his stomach, "so I'll follow you up, but you have command."

"Understood."

Eddie looked at Heather; she stared back in confident defiance. "I'm more use than you," she stated.

I didn't bother getting into the rights and wrongs of what I planned. I just told them, "I'll take point. Head for the doorway of the hospital. You'll be backup only." I gave Heather, Eddie and Lilian the walkies. I put one on my jacket and fitted the earpiece. "Radio check."

We went through a radio check.

"We have numbers. Lilian, you'll be Red Four. Eddie, Red Three, Heather—"

"I'm pretty sure we understand," she said.

I lifted an eyebrow but continued, "Heather, I want you to follow, but the moment we cross the fence you head east and take the perimeter, then work your way forwards. If they get spooked, they might leave the way they came. Do not engage. I want obs only. Understood?"

"Observation only, boss, understood."

"This is not a hunt and capture mission. This is recon only. We do not engage unless lives are endangered. We need evidence. We need to know why they're here. There's nothing up there we can protect, so let's not go silly. The most important thing we do is protect Lilian at the OP. We also need to make sure they aren't heading towards Ella's place. If they suspect she has intel, then it'll be a target."

"Should I go there?" Eddie asked.

I considered it for a moment. Paul was bugger all use in a fight and wouldn't be any use protecting Ella, but it would take time to get over there and the enemy didn't know this location like we did.

"No, I don't want her worried if it's not necessary. If Lilian's okay with keeping an eye down here, we'll track them to make sure they aren't causing problems in Luccombe. Eddie, you're backing me up. I need you on the edge of the woods, this side, so you can report movement if they flank my position."

"I can do that."

"Let's move out, people," I said.

Heather and I jogged up the path, and Eddie did his best to keep up. It sounded like we were being followed by a set of bagpipes without the pipes but a lot of bag. When we reached the graves, I had a moment of shivering murmurs race over my body. An almost-heard collection of voices rose together and swept over me. It drowned me in raw sound for several seconds, loud enough to make me stumble, before withdrawing to form a sinister whine of tinnitus. I shook off the feeling of wet cobwebs on my skin and kept pace with Heather. The image of a soldier loomed in my periphery but I wouldn't be distracted by the dead, not this time.

We crossed into the treeline and left the bagpipe bag behind. In near silence, we raced over the uneven ground, able to see, thanks in part to the bright night and years of practice with night runs and no NVG. Though I'd give a fair amount of money right now to have some night vision goggles.

Stepping over the fallen fence, we moved with greater care, just in case we set off a metallic sound. Once done, Heather glanced at me and nodded. She peeled off to the left, taking it slow but steady through the undergrowth and trees. So far, we hadn't seen anything to indicate a problem in the area. No lights, no voices, and no people. The woods, though, the woods felt heavy and there was an absence of wildlife that had my senses pinging. No owls, badgers or foxes. I'd seen evidence of all three during our daytime trip up here.

The shadows below the night canopy of trees kept me watching for more than just some human interlopers. As I slipped between the trunks, I wanted to brush them off my shoulders, a sense of the shadow's sticky residue clinging to me, edging me ever closer to madness. I paused, to take a steadying breath, pushing away the bizarre fantasy.

After the earlier episode in the ruin, my guts informed me that returning tonight might just lead them into betraying me. Knowing I had to go anyway, I pushed the warning back and hoped another PTSD flashback, or whatever they were, wouldn't take me out of the game. It didn't prevent me from approaching the building's gaping doorway with even greater care than usual.

Keeping my profile low, I scrambled over the debris. The moonlight fought to lend a hand, but the dark dominated and slowed me down. I reached the main reception room and paused, crouching low, listening with my entire body. A faint scent of washing powder drifted on the cool air. People were here, and recently.

I neared the doorway leading to the steps I'd been unable to conquer that morning. The tangos we hunted could be anywhere in the remains of the building. However, my luck just wasn't that good, so I headed to the stairs leading under the ruins. My heart considered abandoning my chest it beat so hard. I really didn't want to go down there, but...

The corridor seemed a lot shorter this time than the last, an unpleasant trick of the mind. I didn't want to reach the stairs, so of course, I made it in double quick time. If I had an episode now, I'd be fucked. I had no close backup, and I was armed, which made me dangerous. Keeping calm and focused would be a priority. Reaching the steps to the subterranean level, I paused, half expecting the same rush of panic and fear to swipe at my sanity. The same black rage sweeping upwards with nightmarish greed, aiming to swallow the minds and souls of the living who trespassed on their hallowed cavern.

Instead, I saw shadows shifting about at the bottom.

Not shadows intent on spilling up the stairway to suck me down into Hell. Rather, shadows caused by unshielded torches. The muffled sound of angry whispers joined them. I grinned. My imagination had been on overdrive since Eddie rang and woke us up. Now I had known combatants to face, this was easier—a lot easier.

I took the balaclava out and tugged it over my face. Next, I drew my weapon, the SIG a familiar shape and weight in my hand, and I stepped down. Moving with care, I kept my back to the wall, the weapon close to my chest, barrel pointing towards the ground but flush to my body with a firm two handed grip. Smooth movement, well-trained confidence, it made me silent and calm. The lights gave me enough vision to see the steps had no debris on them, and I made it to the bottom without being detected. They had no one on watch.

Standing still, I listened to the sounds.

"I don't like this. We shouldn't be here," hissed a young man's voice.

"So you've said, just get on with it. We're being paid good money and you, being a twat about it, isn't going to make any difference." Another voice, an older man. Both had Somerset accents but not Worzel strong. More like mine.

"If you keep talking, I'm going to batter you," hissed another. This one sounded European. Polish maybe?

At least three of them are in there. In theory, no problem. I had twelve rounds in the SIG, and it wasn't like I could miss, with them carrying torches and me having the element of surprise. However, I'd been very lucky—and a damned fine shot—when I'd taken out the men in Scob without killing anyone. No promises I'd manage it again. Killing them would be hard to justify.

I needed to check to make sure it was just three men I faced and what the layout of the room looked like. Any more than three men in there, and I'd be sneaking back up the stairs and thinking of Plan B. Replacing the SIG in the holster, I lowered myself to the ground, keeping my weight on my toes. The torchlight shifted away from the stairwell, making me risk a head poking look-see around the corner. In no more than two heartbeats, I confirmed three bodies in an office type room. A corridor ran down the length of the building, matching the one above us, with a series of doorways. Nothing but darkness lay beyond the first room.

The three men in the nearest room sounded like they were attacking metal filing cabinets. The doorway was close to my location, just one step from the exit I crouched in. It gave me a clear sight of the interior. The next look-see peek, I took my time. I mentally confirmed it being an office room. I saw old fashioned wooden desks, grey filing cabinets, like the ones you'd see in films from the fifties and sixties. Dirty laminate flooring and walls with posters on them, unreadable in the dark.

I reached into the narrow pouch on the belt of my combats and silently removed my asp. Rather than flick it out and cause the click you couldn't avoid, I pulled it and gave a firm tug at the end to lock the mechanism. Waiting to make sure they remained focused on their mission, I waddled in my crouched position, to the other side of the office's doorway.

Slowly, making my thighs groan in protest, I rose, keeping my back to the wall. These guys were searching for something and if I let them leave with it, then I'd never know what that 'something' might be, and I really wanted to know. With the local accents, I figured someone hired these bozos, so they weren't going to be heavily invested in stopping me with terminal intentions.

Sounds from behind me quivered up my back. A whispering skitter of noise. Rats? Badgers? Please let it be badgers.

"What's that?" hissed the youngest voice.

"Just fucking concentrate," said the Polish voice. He was the biggest of the three.

"I don't like it down here. Place is fucking creepy."

He wasn't wrong.

Dust and sand...

Oh no, I wasn't having an episode now. The feel of grit began to gather in my mouth. The skittering behind me grew more pronounced. Over the last few minutes my heart rate and breathing had been fine. Now it increased with such speed that dizziness swept over me for a second or two. I breathed through my nose and knew I had to act. If I remained in the dark the monsters in my head would take over far more quickly than whatever lurked in the blackness behind me.

I leaked around the corner of the doorway, and on silent feet approached the biggest man in the room. No point giving them a warning of my presence if I didn't have to. I had no obligation to play nice like the police.

His senses picked up something, because just as I was three short strides from his back, he twisted.

The light from his headlamp almost blinded me and his yell, bordering on a scream, made the younger man screech. I lashed out with the asp, keeping it low, not making a sound. Contact. The asp hit firm and hard, but not bone crunching because the man moved fast for his size. He threw something at my head, the light ruining my vision. I put my arms up to protect myself, and whatever it was hit the hand grasping the asp. Pain shot through the bones and my grip loosened. The asp fell.

So much for my advantage. A shape stepped towards me with a fist coming first. I dropped my weight, balanced on my left foot, and lashed out with my right. The contact was good, and I felt the man stumble back, hitting the filing cabinet.

The beast surged out of the sleepy corner he'd been in for months, and my shoulders rolled in anticipation of a real scrap. The youngest and smallest of the three rushed towards me, carrying a chair, yelling like a medieval peasant being forced to face an enemy army.

I knocked the chair to one side, pivoted on my left foot by ninety degrees and punched him hard in the side of his head with my left fist. He did the oddest wobble, like a mister bobble-head, for a second or two before his legs gave and he hit the floor.

That made my job easier.

The big man gave shouted orders, but I wasn't listening. It didn't really matter. They weren't leaving unless I allowed it. I picked up the fallen chair by the leg nearest me and threw it at the big man. He backed away, trying to untangle himself from the metal legs.

The other Somerset accent muttered, "Fuck this." He rushed for the door. I could have stopped him but didn't see the point. I wanted them gone—or some of them anyway.

Now I pulled the SIG, aimed for the wall behind the Polish guy's head, and squeezed a single round from the barrel. The sound even made me start in surprise, contained in such a tight space, the world around us so silent. The man froze.

"Leave," I snarled.

He didn't waste time thinking or arguing. Those sturdy legs took him out of the door so fast I suspect it was the first time a human might have broken the sound barrier without the aid of mechanical intervention.

15

I CROUCHED BY THE FALLEN body and removed his headlamp before shining it back in the face of its previous owner. A young man, as I'd suspected. I frisked him. A standard hunting knife was all I found, apart from a wallet and some car keys. I flicked open the wallet just as he groaned. The driver's licence said Peter Tucker. There were a lot of Tuckers in this area, but I had the feeling I knew this lad.

Picking up the asp, I poked him. "Your mum calls you Pete, right? You're from Ashcroft farm. The youngest, if I'm not mistaken?"

The lad scrambled to escape, so I rose and stepped on his ankle to pin him to the floor. It worked. Scared and doubtless not used to having his brains scrambled, he froze with a yell.

"Le'go."

"No."

"Fuck you." He tried to tug his foot free. I ground it into the concrete flooring under my boot.

He screamed. I put the asp in the same hand as the torch and pulled the SIG. Those mud brown eyes widened in horror.

"Get up. Don't piss me off. No one will hear you die in this place if you piss me off." I kept my voice even, growly and unemotional. It scared him, as I knew it would.

"You broke my ankle. I can't get up."

"No, I hurt your ankle and it'll hurt as you walk, but it will prevent you from trying to run and that'll keep you alive. Now move. Repeating myself makes me angry." I shifted position, as if preparing to fire the weapon.

Bless the poor little bugger, he didn't notice my index finger lay against the side of the weapon, not on the trigger. Even if he found the courage to attack, I wasn't going to shoot the silly bastard. I might pay his mum a visit to tell her what a knob-bucket she'd raised. That would be worse than anything I could do to him. The Tuckers at Quarme Hill had a farm about ten miles from Stoke Pero, down near Wheddon Cross. Their father and I had gone to the same school, so I knew just how much trouble this young man would face at home if word of his exploits leaked over the hills.

Lifting himself off the ground, hands raised like a good little boy, he shuffled out of the room. Taking each step, with groans worthy of an Oscar, he made his way up the stairs. I now had the lamp on my head, making his back very clear to me. The sight of old style DPM combats made me smile. He'd been raiding the army surplus store in Taunton. I didn't blame him. Well-made and cheap, it kept many of the farmers in Somerset clothed.

The darkness in the underground rooms rushed up the stairs behind me, a tangible weight wanting to wrap around my chest and pull me back for a visit with its secrets. I forced my shoulders back.

Dust and sand...

"Boss?" hissed a quiet voice to my three o'clock at the top of the stairs.

The taste dissolved on my tongue once more, the shadows rushed back and away. They were just as surprised as me to find Heather at the top of the stairs.

"Here, kid. Coming up with a tango to escort. Don't shoot."

"Roger that."

The lad whimpered.

We made it to the top, and Heather, scarf wrapped around her face to disguise her features, stood with the P30 held firm in her hands and pointing at Pete's head.

"Hands," I ordered.

"What?"

"Lace your fingers together behind your head and move forwards." I almost laughed at his efforts. His hands shook so much he found it hard to keep them locked.

Heather came to stand beside me, behind the lad. I pushed the barrel of the P30 down and shook my head. She rolled her eyes but holstered the weapon. Trusting her with the weapon during practice was not a problem. Trusting her in the field was another kettle of potential piranha. I searched about in the pocket of my bike jacket and removed a length of bailing twine. Almost everyone on the moor carried at least one length they'd found somewhere.

"Tie him," I ordered.

The lad stood a little taller than me, so Heather reached up and yanked his right arm down hard, then the left. She made short work of tying his wrists together.

"Move, Pete," I ordered.

He shuffled forwards, and I might have caught the very faint sound of a sob. His night-time adventure had turned to rat shit.

It took a while, and some piteous mewling from Pete, but we made it to the fence separating Eddie's place from the ruined building. The retired detective stood watching us with an amused expression on his face.

"Looks like you've been busy."

"Caught a poacher, Officer Rice," I said. "Citizen's arrest I reckon."

Pete gasped. "You're police? Thank God, this lunatic almost shot me!"

Eddie raised his eyebrows. "Is that so, sonny? Is that so? I don't see a firearm present. I don't even see the bruise on the side of your ugly mug. So let's get you over this fence and let's get some answers to some questions, shall we?"

Heather removed her asp, flicked it open with a click so loud Pete flinched, and poked him in the back. "Get moving."

"I can't climb over the fence without my hands free," Pete whined, then sniffed.

"You'll manage," she snapped. A swift jab to the ribs made him raise his leg over the fence. I may, at that point, have hoofed my boot under the barbed wire and lifted it a little. The sharp barbs hit the lad's groin.

"Ow! My fucking bollocks, you bastards."

"Now, now, ladies present," Eddie said, trying not to laugh. He took mercy on the lad, I knew he would, and helped him with the final manoeuvre.

I put the SIG away and, with me on one side and Eddie on the other, we gripped Pete's arms, marching him down the path to the cottage. We passed the caravans, which were in darkness so appeared empty.

Heather peeled off and went to report to Lilian. Eddie and I pulled young Pete into the shell of his cottage.

"Shouldn't you be taking me to the police station?" squeaked Pete.

Eddie sighed. World weary and patient. "Well, yes, son, under normal circumstances I should, but that man," he pointed to me, "works for the Security Services and he wants a word in your shell-like."

Pete's eyes were like dinner plates and a growing panic oozed out of him. "My what?"

"Ear," I snarled, doing my best to sound like a vicious bastard. It wasn't hard. I'd scared the truth out of nastier lads than this poor excuse for a bad guy.

"I don't know anything." His West Country accent thickened the higher his voice rose. He spoke to Eddie, trying to ignore my dark shape in the shadows of the cottage's interior.

"I'm sure that's not true, son. But you be a good lad and tell my friend here everything you do know. I'll be nearby once the SIS have finished with you."

"The what?" Pete asked.

"Secret Intelligence Service, son. MI5 and MI6, plus a few others we can't discuss. I think it's probably one of them my friend works for... You heard of Black Sites, Pete?"

Pete shifted on his feet, as if struggling to stay upright. "Like Guantanamo?"

"That's not a Black Site, son. We all know about that one. There are far worse places to be. That's the kinda place people end up after they've spoken to men like my friend here." Eddie nodded towards me. "Though, as a member of the British Constabulary, I'm hoping that won't be necessary because I prefer to uphold the law, and I'm not convinced what they do to their prisoners is legal." He shook his head.

I fought the desire to giggle. He was enjoying himself.

I didn't blame him, all the little scroats he'd have lost over the years because of annoying things like the rights of suspects to rest-breaks, legal counsel, health care and more. All those who worked in the emergency services must suffer from bouts of rage when they had to abide to the rules of engagement rather than just let loose. Of course, there were some of us who did lose it, and when caught, the price usually turned out to be even heavier. Still, this bordered on fun.

Pete was practically in tears by now. "They... they... came to the pub. The Stag's Head, and they were looking for a couple of locals who knew the woods."

I pushed off the wall. "Who are 'they'?"

"Just some blokes."

"Weak, Pete. Really weak." I began to pace around. He tried to turn to watch me. "Eyes front. You don't want to see my face, boy." I barked the command, and he locked in place. Even Eddie flinched. "I want names, I want descriptions, I want times, locations, I want their fucking dick sizes. Do you understand?" More barking. His shoulders rolled forwards as if I were smacking him around the head with each word.

"Yeah, okay, yeah. I was in the pub, two nights ago. Two blokes and a woman comes in, she's real pretty, posh clothes, nice hair, them expensive heels with the red soles."

Odd thing for a lad to notice.

"She had really nice legs, feet, you know?" he stuttered.

"Someone has a foot fetish," muttered Eddie.

"Names," I snapped.

"No names. We were just in the pub, you know? The woman, she comes over. We're playing pool with Vlad. That's what we call Tadeusz. He's Polish. He works on our farm, but he's been around, was in the army in Poland. He, um, he was in Afghanistan. He was discharged for killing Tallis when he shouldn't—though he says they all deserved it. He... he... Oh fuck..."

Eddie put a hand on Pete's shoulder. "It's better you give us the whole truth, son. You're in a lot of trouble, but I can smooth it out if you're honest."

"He's a nasty bastard, sir. He'll take me apart. He might hurt my mum."

I struggled to imagine Pete's dad allowing such a man on the farm.

Pete sobbed. "Dad, he's... he's got Parkinson's. We needed the help with the farm."

Oh fuck. I repressed my sigh. It wouldn't help.

"They offered me a lot of money to show them how to get through the woods. I knows Horner Woods really well. Do a bit of hunting."

"Poaching?" asked Eddie.

Pete shrugged. "There's a lot of pheasant and deer to spare," he muttered, sullen now. "Free meat."

He had a point.

"I don't care about your dietary habits. I want facts," I ordered. I'd have to think of a way to help the Tucker family.

"This lady, shiny dark hair, real slim and tall, she said there was a building they needed to find in the woods. I knew the ruins was there, been through the fence a few times but..." Pete shrugged. "It's a nasty place. I never went in. None of the animals I tracked went in either, far as I could tell, and I'm good at tracking. Anyway, Vlad, he says we can find it. She says she needs details about the place. Then she takes Vlad off on his own for a bit."

"What happened?" I asked, coming in a bit softer this time as a reward.

Pete, relieved I wasn't shouting at him, continued, "Vlad comes back, looking well pleased with himself, and says we have a job to do. Mikey, that's his mate, he says he's up for it and I... well, we needs the money, see. I didn't think there'd be any harm. These blokes, they look like bodyguards for the woman. Big guys, army type haircuts, dark suits. They follow the lady out.

Vlad says we gotta come here, covert like, and get some information about the ruins. When we gets into that room, we find all these cabinets and he says we need to start going through them, looking for information."

"What information?" Eddie asked, all business now.

Pete shrugged. "Dunno, really. There was lots of empty drawers, but some had paperwork in them. Science stuff I didn't understand. All the paper was real old. No computers in the place, just these old books with notes in them and people's names on empty files. Then this bloke comes in and starts beating us to death."

I snorted. "I tapped you. Nothing more than a love bite, trust me."

"Cut him loose," Eddie said.

"What?" I asked, pushing off the wall.

Eddie turned to look at me. "Cut him loose. He doesn't know anything more. Besides, you know where to find him, right?"

"Yes, I know exactly where to find him." The snarl made the boy flinch.

I stuffed Pete's wallet back in his pocket before smacking it a few times. He stared into my eyes. Despite being taller than me, I saw the fear. Balaclavas have that effect when all you see are cold and empty eyes looking back at you. I removed my knife and held it up to Pete. "You'll behave yourself when you get home. Tell Vlad you escaped, and you ran free, away from their location, because five other men were chasing you. Understood?"

Pete nodded.

"You keep that lie going because it'll save your life. They find out you've spoken to me, they will kill you. I have no doubt about it." I really didn't have any misgivings on that front. Pete had a target on his back if he didn't keep his mouth shut. I cut the bailing twine and Pete backed away from me, rubbing his wrists.

"Run," I suggested.

He glanced at Eddie, who nodded, and Pete took one last look at me before turning and racing off into the night. We heard his boots on the lane heading west. He'd probably make for Minehead and call someone to come get him back to the moor.

"Christ, Turner, you're a scary bastard."

I pulled the balaclava off my head, swiping at the sweat the warm night had caused. "Training. Years in the field." I didn't want to elaborate, so changed the subject. "We made a good team."

Eddie chuckled as we walked back to the caravans. "It was fun. Poor little bugger was shitting himself. Thanks for coming down. I shouldn't have woken you."

I put a hand on Eddie's shoulder. "You, of all people, know how wrong things can go. This is a remote location, and someone's been murdered in your village. You need to be alert and cautious. I'd rather be woken in the night than find you and Lilian in trouble. Besides, we now know we have to go down under the ruin to get some answers. They won't be back before we can raid the place." I gave him a lopsided grin. "But I'm not doing it in the dark."

16

WE RETURNED TO THE CARAVANS. I told Heather I'd take her home to sleep before coming back to Eddie's keeping 'eyes on' until daybreak. She moaned like a squaddie on night patrol in the rain, so I lost the argument, she was staying. I wanted to remain because, despite my assurances to Eddie, the wannabe thieves might return looking for their accomplice. Lilian tried to insist we bed down in the caravan, but the night was warm and being stuffed in a tin box didn't appeal. Lilian gave us a couple of blankets and Heather arranged the straw bales until we had something resembling a double bed.

"Guess things have changed then, Turner," Eddie murmured as he watched Heather's antics.

"Make any comment about the age difference and I'm leaving you alone," I growled.

He looked at me in surprise. "Why would I do that? You're perfect together. I'm feeling sorry for any poor bastard who upsets either of you. I have the feeling that she's the more dangerous."

"Oh, well, yes," I said, surprised by his acceptance.

"I'm happy for you, mate. She's a better fit than Willow. She's never going to want you to change. As a long-married man, that's an important advantage for happiness." He clapped me on the shoulder and ambled off to bed.

Heather looked up and smiled. Everything inside me did an odd flip and jiggle at the sight.

"Come on," she said, "time to catch an hour or two." She held her hand out, and I joined her on the bales.

In no time she'd snuggled up, using my jumper for a pillow, and fallen asleep. I listened to the soft breaths coming and going in peace while I watched the boundless dark above. I'd seen amazing night skies in some far-flung places. African nights, full of the sounds of strange and dangerous animals, the stars a blaze of white in the eternal void of space. Arabian nights, so cold after the heat of the day you thought you were in that empty void far above, the stars more plentiful than the grains of sand. Afghanistan's mountains, where you reached up, wondering if you could pluck the light from the night. But this one, this I loved the most. I knew exactly where Orion lived, and his dog. I could find the Plough with no effort and Cassiopeia. And on a good night, like tonight, the Pleiades. These gave me safety, they murmured of home. The moon always stayed the same in her cycle. Just like the trees and the smell of the moor, they located me, and it gave a sense of reassurance I craved after all the chaos of my life.

I thought back over the day, replaying it from the beginning, and found myself lingering over the events with Willow and Heather. That felt pretty major. An odd sense of relief filled my being. I'd fallen into a relationship with Willow by accident because of the circumstances surrounding Shaw and the Gnostic Dawn. Seeing her with someone else, sliced into me, because— well, she'd lied to me, basically. She'd lied about my place in her life, and that betrayal stung. The flip side was I didn't have to think about her reactions to my decisions any more. I also didn't have to handle her judgement about my service.

That led me on to Heather's reaction to Monkey. It pained me to see how it shook her. The new version was still too fragile, and her fear of the past surged over those strong shoulders, threatening to drown the strong spirit. I'd burn the world to the ground before I let anything happen to that woman. It would take time for her to heal, and I'd give her that time. With no blood family of my own, Heather's place in my life filled an empty space. I needed her, and I needed her to be successful. Wanted her to be safe. I'd give her that and so much more. Her heat warmed my flank, and I knew I just had to let go of the reins and I'd be in love. That made me smile. I had the feeling I could plan a real future with Heather, and I looked forwards to exploring it with her beside me.

Ella's news, something I'd been trying hard to ignore all day, rushed to fill the quiet spaces of my dozing mind. The prickle of unshed emotion made me blink and my hands formed into fists. Ella was the centre of my world. I needed her calm confidence. I needed her faith and certainty in the goodness of people, her belief in something greater than all the evil I had faced over the years. Her compassion, her understanding, about my monsters, the deaths I'd caused, all of it. I needed it like I needed food. I'd remain at her side every step and we'd cope. Whatever news came our way, we'd face it together.

I sniffed and forced away thoughts of full graveyards. Too much... too much.

Yanking my heart back from the brink, I used the night to trail my wandering mind through current events. We had a mysterious woman who once worked for a company that didn't exist and it wanted to buy Eddie's cottage. A murdered pensioner who'd discovered a box that belonged to her father. A missing film tape with two small children on it, one of which was rescued from East Berlin. A scientist who'd escaped the Soviet Union before the city was walled off. We had some Russians and Americans looking for intel. The mysterious woman paying locals to find said intel in the ruins of an old building, which could have been a hospital, lab, or something else. It was definitely secret. We also had a dead addict at the police station, possibly poisoned by something horrible. We had no evidence and no idea where all this was going.

That's what we needed to do come morning. We needed to gather more intelligence and formulate some theories. Paul would help.

I ignored thoughts about the ghosts now haunting my waking hours, as well as my dreams.

I dozed on the bales for the rest of the night, relaxing into the scent of the straw, Heather's breathing, and sounds of the night. Nothing disturbed us, and as dawn breached the skyline, I rose, leaving Heather asleep, and went to the caravan the Rices used for a kitchen and sitting room.

ELLA, WITH PAUL IN TOW, turned up soon after seven. I filled them in on the night's adventures, Paul cursing me for being left out. I just stared at him until he shut up.

"My plan this morning is to talk to the old woman who was resident here during this period. Do we know who she is and where?" I asked Ella.

She sat on a bale, nursing a black coffee whose colour matched the bags under her eyes. "We can talk to Sherry. She'll remember Peggy's father if anyone does. There has to be a reason the box ended up with the amateur dramatics society."

"Okay, that's where we'll start. Just the three of us. We don't want to overwhelm her. Then we go check out those ruins."

Heather frowned at me but stayed quiet.

"What if someone goes back to the ruins while we're talking to the old woman?" Paul asked. "I should speak to her. You should go to the ruin."

"I can't go in there alone, Paul. I coped last night because I could focus on the violence but..." I looked at my hands, embarrassed by my mental weakness. I'd been around people who understood the fragile state of my daily life for a while now, and it made admitting it to an outsider, one who'd known me at my strongest, difficult. I didn't like the way Paul looked at me, as if I'd suddenly become this foreign thing unworthy of his respect. "Basically, if I go in there alone, or with you, and have an episode, I might hurt either myself or you. Neither of which will help, so you take it, or leave it. We do it my way, or you can go to the ruins on your own."

He scowled but muttered, "Fine."

I stared at him for a moment, wondering why he was being such a prick. I never used to find him this irritating. He must have changed since we served together.

It's not him who has changed, idiot.

I shook my head and focused on Ella. "When do you think we can go and find Sherry?"

"She's too old to sleep much, so any time. We'll know if she's up and about. She's one of the regulars at church, which means she won't mind talking to me. She's in Rosebay Cottage, just up the lane from here." Ella nodded towards Luccombe.

"Right, let's get to it then," I said.

"I'll keep an eye on things here and call if something suspicious turns up. I want to look at some of those graves," Heather said.

I nodded. "Good idea, thanks."

We walked back towards Luccombe, and I enjoyed the rising warmth of another day. The verges danced, full of rosebay willow herb, their pink flowers vivid against the drying grasses and hardier bracken. Blackberries filled the hedgerows and sloes would soon be ready for picking. Heather and I could make Sloe Gin this year. In fact, we could do a lot of things together at the farm. The future beckoned with tempting fingers.

The small cottage belonging to Sherry took its name from the riot of tall pink flowers marching about in the morning breeze.

"Sherry," Ella called.

A small pink head moved around somewhere below the height of the towering flowers. "Is that you, Vicar?"

Ella opened the wooden gate, and I followed. We found the elderly woman on her knees among the flowers pulling up dandelions.

"Sherry, you're supposed to let your gardener do that," Ella said with some exasperation. "Besides, they're good for the soil."

"He keeps telling me they are good for the wildlife. That might be so, but I don't like them," she said, her conviction reminiscent of my dislike for liver and kidney pie.

"Who are you?" she asked, eyeing me with the shrewd gaze of a military interrogator.

"Lorne Turner, ma'am. I'm a friend of Ella's."

"And the other lanky one?" she asked, turning her laser focused gaze onto Paul. Her eyes held the colour of winter dawn blue.

"Paul Cole, you knew my mother, Peggy Cole."

She frowned. The age of her face increasing as the wrinkles merged into a skinned walnut-like structure. "Ah, I wondered if I'd be seeing you. Very sorry for your loss, son." She looked like she meant it as well.

"Thank you." Paul clamped his mouth shut, holding back the obvious pain.

Sherry sucked on her false teeth. "Dear Peggy said you worked for the government. I don't much trust them." Her Somerset accent marked her local from birth to death.

I tried to hide my smile and failed.

Sherry noticed. "No good smirking, young man." She held her arm out and I took it to help her up off the ground. When she stood, she didn't increase in height much beyond the flowers. "If he's government, what are you?" She waved a hand at me, more swollen knuckles than fingers. "No innocent, that's for sure."

"No, ma'am. I was a soldier."

She gave a single nod. "Army I can live with."

"I'm so pleased," Paul muttered behind me.

"Can we have a little chat about Peggy?" Ella asked.

Sherry studied the vicar for a long moment. "I think it would be wise. Let's go inside and I'll tell you everything I can remember."

Her cottage was not what I was expecting. I thought it would be like most of the older residents of Exmoor, full of a lifetime of clutter and images of family. Sherry's place reminded me of some monastic cell where the monks weren't permitted personal items, crossed with spartan Feng-shui minimalism.

"Wow," Paul said, clearly as surprised as me.

"Shoes off," barked Sherry, removing her outdoor shoes and replacing them with white slippers. "I don't like clutter and I don't like cleaning, so don't make a mess."

I liked this woman.

We walked through the small cottage to a kitchen that would make an operating theatre in Harley Street look cheap and grubby. Gadgets covered the surfaces, but each carefully separated and new-shiny. The tea towels lay in regimental order on the cooker's door handle, pressed into sharp folds and the dishcloth shone bright white, draped over the gleaming tap. I'd seen adverts for cleaning products with less sparkle. Sherry might have a bit of a problem.

Ella's lips pursed when she looked around. "It's very nice."

Sherry gave her a look that said, 'I know I have a problem, and don't you dare say anything more or I'll use it as an operating theatre and show you how to remove a liver without anaesthetic.'

My friend decided to add, "Now I know why your cakes are always so beautiful. It pays to be organised. Don't suppose you can come do my kitchen?"

Sherry raised an eyebrow. "No, I've seen your kitchen and your attempts at a sponge, Vicar."

She had a point. I'd tried Ella's sponge, just the once, and if we were ever invaded by hordes of zombies, I was fairly certain I could use them as deadly Frisbees.

"Take a seat and I'll make you all coffee."

I opened my mouth to ask for tea, but the pale eyes pinned me to the spot and the words froze in my mouth. "Coffee would be lovely, thank you."

She gave a nod and set a machine going. We all sat and kept our hands off the dark wood of the table top. Personally, I didn't want to smear the polish.

"You knew my mum?" Paul prompted. He sounded delicate for the first time, as if desperate for some connection to her. I had to keep reminding myself she'd only just left him. Poor bastard.

Sherry turned and regarded him for long moments. He dropped his gaze, and I watched his shoulders slump.

"I did know her, Paul. She loved you very much and was very proud. I am deeply sorry for your loss and for the manner of her death. I feel horribly responsible. If I hadn't found that box..." Sherry sighed. "People can be so cruel."

I watched Ella's reaction. If she hadn't started poking about in the various archives to find information for Peggy about this mysterious sister, no one would know the box had been found. The tension in Ella's body spoke volumes.

"The only people at fault for this terrible crime are the ones who did it and those who ordered it," I said in my best NCO voice. "No one could predict what happened to Peggy. We must honour her suffering by uncovering the truth and seeking justice."

Sherry nodded. "I know, I just wish…" She rubbed her hands together, as if her knuckles were painful. "Well, perhaps the truth will set her soul free." Sherry studied Paul for a moment and a smile softened her face from walnut to aged cider apple. "You look a lot like your grandfather, Paul. A handsome man, he was. I was barely more than a girl, but he turned all the heads of the women hereabouts. I'll never forget the sight of him in uniform at church. Those RAF boys were always the best looking in uniform."

She was right. The Royal Air Force still had the best uniform for pulling women, we all knew it.

"I suppose the story starts when they built the hospital and your grandmother arrived from Germany just as the Soviets started to blockade Berlin. He brought her over, so my mother said."

"Can I ask how you remember all this?" Paul asked.

"I have little left but memories," Sherry said with a terrible sadness I didn't want to contemplate. "Besides, it was the first time I saw your father and trust me, a girl never forgets her first crush. We rarely left Luccombe in those days, so none of us knew much about the outside world and suddenly we had this dashing hero among us. We also had countless strangers all over the place, from scientists to workmen, though they didn't mix with us villagers often."

"Scientists?" I asked.

"Yes, dear. They built a hospital with a laboratory attached. Many of the village women found employment as cleaners. Mother among them. Paul's grandmother was one of the scientists. She headed up the place in the end."

Ella stirred at last. "What was happening there?"

Sherry's face clouded, the pale walnut features collapsing into more folds. "Nothing good, from what we gleaned. There was a great deal of gossip at the time, dangerous gossip, but we were used to keeping secrets, so it didn't spread far. The entire country didn't speak out of turn in those days. *Loose lips sinks ships* and all that. We didn't have *the* social media."

"What did people think was happening?" asked Paul.

"Experiments on people's minds, dear. They were changing people. Ambulances with no markings on them would drive up past the cottage next to the Methodist church. My old mum, she was one of those allowed to clean up in the labs. She didn't talk about it until I was caring for her and the old marbles wandered off." Sherry tapped her head. "But she said they was soldiers, some in a real bad way. Screaming and hollering. Then, they'd be quiet little mice. I dug a bit deeper once. She used to get to fretting if we talked about it for too long, and she said..." Sherry's eyes grew very sad. "She said they was trying to make new soldiers out of broken ones, because we all feared there would be another one. Another war. Maybe the Russians, or the Chinese. Much like now, I suppose. Almost a century later and we still haven't learned a damned thing."

We were wandering off topic; I didn't have time for it.

"What kind of experiments?"

Sherry's tiny shoulders lifted. "I can't tell you that. I don't know. Lots of rumours, but most of it was plain impossible. Frankenstein tales so tall you could use them to pick the stars from the sky. One always persisted: they were using Soviet and German research to control people's reactions to fear and memories. But in those days, after the war, people said a lot of daft stuff about the Germans and Russians."

"What about my mother's sister?" Paul asked.

"Hmm, that's still a mystery. I didn't know Peggy was the little girl I have vague recollections of. She was a great deal younger than me in those days. The sister I remember better. One day, a girl we didn't know turned up at church. She didn't understand our language, so couldn't come to play often. Gradually, she became part of the village, but she was troubled, often violent, when pushed by teachers or us children. Then she vanished. We all assumed she went back to wherever she came from. With the evacuations during the war, we were used to odd youngsters coming and going. Everyone struggled with having German-speaking people in the village. Maybe they left because of that. You have to understand, dear," she said, noticing the distaste in Paul's face over the prejudice, "we couldn't help it, not then, we'd been programmed to be scared of Germans and Russians so anyone with an accent was suspect."

Paul grunted. "Not much changes on the Russian front, trust me."

I tended to agree but kept my thoughts private. "Do you know what role Peggy's father had in the hospital? Or her mother?"

Sherry looked at Paul again. "Your grandparents, they were odd people. Peggy's mother, she was some foreign bigwig in the labs. Your granddad, God rest his soul, suffered terribly with the shell-shock when he finally came back for good, and he tended to stay home with the children."

"When did they leave the village?" Paul asked.

Sherry pursed her tiny mouth. "Well, the hospital was closed down in the nineteen fifties. Something about it going to America. They could continue their work better in the States. Peggy didn't go, though. I think her father kept her in England, but they moved away from here. Before you ask, I don't remember there being a second girl with them when they left, and I don't know if her mother made it to America. I don't know much, to be honest. From what Peggy told me, both parents died in the car crash, so maybe they stayed as a family."

"Do you remember any deaths being reported?" I asked.

She nodded. "Yes, several times my dad was called out to dig graves. Might be why the place was closed down. I was away working by then mind, at the hotels in Minehead. Mum used to weep about a lost child from the hospital. I never thought about it until Peggy mentioned a sister. Maybe they was the same thing?"

We all sat in the oddly sterile kitchen and contemplated what we'd learned. Paul shifted in his seat, bringing our attention front and centre.

"I think we need to go up to the ruins," he said.

Personally, I'd rather be anywhere else in the world—anywhere—but I didn't have the luxury of a choice.

Ella looked worried. "I don't think you should, Lorne. Not after yesterday."

"I know what to expect this time. I'll be fine."

"Then I should go with you." Her gaze held mine, and I nodded. We'd been in some tight spots, literally in some cases, so she knew how my 'episodes' worked. "And you'll never keep Heather out of the place."

That made me grin. "No. I won't."

Sherry rose off her chair and began gathering the coffee things together, obviously wanting us gone from her tidy kitchen. As we filed out of the sterile cottage, she took hold of Paul's hand. Ella tugged me away, out of earshot, but I could see the effect of Sherry's words. Paul bent down and engulfed the tiny woman in a fragile hug. He didn't speak as he walked past us with his head down. We chose to keep quiet, his grief a living creature wrapped firmly around his back.

17

BY THE TIME WE RETURNED to Eddie's place, emotions firmly under control, Paul decided to hide the grief under the shiny armour of 'bossy git'. It even had the dead nerves in my face beginning to twitch in irritation. I saw Heather down at the caravans, which made us both smile, and we caught everyone up on the news while Lilian dished out a breakfast of scones and mugs of tea. She apologised for not having more, but I'd never had jam and scones for breakfast. It was awesome.

Turns out the way to a man's heart isn't through his ribcage, it is through his stomach. I loved Lilian and wondered if I could keep her at the farm.

"No, you can't. She's my miracle," Eddie grumbled beside me.

I looked at him in surprise. "I said that last bit aloud, didn't I?"

"Only just, your gob is full of scone again, so I managed to decipher the code after years of dealing with stoned idiots."

"I sound stoned?"

Heather laughed. "You look stoned. Any minute now, you're going to pass out in bliss."

"But they're really good. You lot have no idea what army scran is like," I grumbled.

Paul didn't seem to have much patience with us. "So, who is going up to the hospital? We need to get a move on."

"Fewer people the better," I said. "We need to keep the perimeter secure while the rest of us are under the building."

"Do you need to go down there at all?" Lilian asked. "After what happened during yesterday's visit, it might be awhile before you're safe in that environment."

I sniffed. "I'll be fine."

Heather said, "Lorne, being psychic isn't like being a sniper. There's little body armour once you've been attacked, and you've been attacked more than once." She looked apologetic while she spoke. "Sorry, I gave Willow a call, told her what happened yesterday. I was worried…" Her voice trailed off at whatever she saw in my face.

I didn't know whether to be grateful she cared enough to check, or angry she'd gone to Willow, of all people, for advice without talking to me first.

Paul grunted. "I'm not listening to this old bollocks. He's about as psychic as an armchair." He waved at an old armchair that basked in the morning sun. "If you knew some of the things he'd done, like in—"

"That's enough, Paul." He knew too much about the beast and what *he* was capable of doing. I didn't need Heather or Ella hearing about the hell we'd brought down on the Taliban when necessary.

He shook his head and said, "They don't know you at all, do they?"

"I am not that man, and I am not under orders. I left The Regiment, and I left that version of me in the desert along with my men."

Heather watched us with concern. "And that's why he can't go charging into that hospital." She pointed at Paul. "You might not believe in what's happening to Lorne, but we've seen enough to want to protect him."

"Maybe we should just let Lorne decide for himself," Ella said, her voice unusually small and tired.

Heather looked at her as if betrayed.

"Sorry, love, but he's a big boy and can make his own decisions. You wanted to be a part of his life; you need to know you can't control it."

I frowned, not liking this conversation. Heather flushed red, and looked ready to snap at Ella in return.

Placing a hand on her thigh to still her tongue, I said, "I think you're both right. I shouldn't go, but I can't let Paul in there alone. He needs help and I owe him. I will need help though, and you're both able to offer me that, so let's do what we do best: work as a unit."

Spending time with Regiment men meant I had a handle on how to blend strong personalities into a fighting unit that would cooperate under fire, even if they couldn't be friends outside work. I was a good NCO.

The others snapped to, Ella looking like she wanted to apologise, but one glance at Heather's face made her swallow her words. A horrible feeling crept over me. What if they'd butted heads over the change in my relationship with Heather? I needed to check-in with the pair of them, but not now. I certainly wouldn't allow Ella to derail my future with Heather.

Barking orders made me feel better, normal, so they kept coming and four of us trotted back up the slope of the graveyard to enter the woodland at the top. Lilian and Ella kept watch at the caravans. Due to our phone signals being unreliable, I gave them a radio. I didn't want to be out of comms range, it made us all vulnerable.

Eddie kept to his side of the barbed wire fence and the three of us went into woodland together.

The moment we crossed the spiky barrier, the world fell silent. Somewhere outside the glass bowl of our reality the birds sang and cows mooed, but in this wood, in this moment, silence held sway. I fought against the sensation of the sticky shadows. I would not be distracted by the creeping intensity folding itself around my shoulders and tightening my guts. I would not be driven out by the strange murmur of sound, not quite tinnitus, whispering in my ear. I would not back down from the sense of dread rising and blocking my throat.

Heather kept silent beside me, but Paul grumbled about our slow pace to the point I wanted to knock his head against a tree.

If I was psychic, then perhaps applying the same tactics I used in The Regiment might work. In other words, keep going, keep fighting and dominate your landscape. In this instance, my internal landscape. My hitchhiker needed to keep his opinions quiet as well.

If I wasn't psychic, then I'd have a breakdown in private and the rest of them could bugger off.

We entered the ruin through the absent front door, and I found the chill of the old building seeping into my skin. The smell of crushed poison ivy and rotting concrete filled my nose, making it tingle. I was primed for a battle. Tension hummed in my blood making me feel sick, because the chances of having anything to fight were slim. I didn't like holding tension when it wasn't necessary, it led to stress symptoms—like nightmares.

Taking the right-hand corridor, we walked towards the stairs. I stopped at the top and took a breath to centre my scattering thoughts. Each step down those stairs made the dark push back against me. The previous night there had been enemy targets lurking, keeping me focused on the real-world potential for violence. This time I had no such luxury.

One step down at a time, my skin tight, the murmur in my ears rising and falling like a tide, a sing-song quality I couldn't quite catch. I signalled for Heather to stop.

"We need light," I whispered. "We can't go in blind."

Paul huffed behind us. "I think you're being paranoid."

"You weren't the one fighting three men," I muttered.

Paul flicked on his light and walked past me down the final few steps and into the corridor. I almost grabbed him and pulled him back, but I remembered this wasn't Afghanistan. We weren't hunting insurgents; we weren't going to be blown into red mist and body parts. I almost felt the weight of my body armour, webbing full of mags for my SA80 assault rifle and battle helmet, making my brain ache from the burden and heat.

Dust and sand...

"Not today, mate," I murmured, breathing the thought to make it more real. The creeping sensation of grit gathering in my mouth eased back, and I swallowed.

The grating sound of metal on metal screeched through the dark. Heather yelped in shock.

"Bloody hell, Paul," I snapped out. "Stop fucking about."

"Sorry, drawer stuck."

"Drawer stuck. Bugger me sideways," Heather cursed. "I thought it was Freddie Kruger and those talons on his fingers."

I chuckled. "Or an axe."

"You're not helping. With or without your creepy vibes, this place is doing my head in." Heather's eyes were wide and on permanent swivel.

Touching her arm, I said, "Go and wait with Eddie. You don't have to be down here."

She focused on me, not our surroundings. "And what if you have another meltdown?"

"Then Paul will get me out."

"He's as much use as a teaspoon bailing out the Titanic," she said, walking into the underground hallway at last.

She had a point.

We left Paul in the office, where I'd clashed with the thieves the night before, and walked further into the underground complex. The hallway only had rooms on one side, our right, and all of them had half and half walls. Half solid to waist height, then glass. Every pane remained intact despite the passage of time and crumbling ceiling. The paint peeled in various places but otherwise seemed in good nick.

"Jesus," Heather mumbled. "This isn't good." Her torch swept over the third room along the corridor. A bed was pushed back against the far wall, thick leather straps hanging from the side nearest us. In the centre of the room stood an old-fashioned dentist's chair, only this one belonged in a shlock horror film, maybe on the poster to advertise the depravity of the antagonist. It even had bindings on the stirrups.

"No way I'd want a cervical smear sitting in that," she added.

I had no comment. A sense of panic, not coming from me, swirled around our feet. A low pain that matched the rising wave of internal noise drifting through my head. The panic closed my throat, making it ache and my free hand, the one without the torch, flexed constantly.

The next room held the remains of a lab. The hallway began to curve to the left, and we found another laboratory, or the remains of one. They'd left the heavy equipment but removed anything of value, so old fridges, tables, chairs, shelves and large distillery type items stood as silent sentinels to distant crimes.

"I imagine North Korea like this," Heather whispered.

"It might have been like this once, but not now. It's tec savvy these days. Though the rural areas are probably more like this, I guess."

"You been there?"

I glanced at her. "Inside North Korea? No, thank God."

We came across a series of rooms with heavy metal doors containing small hatches at eye level. Heather pulled one door fully open. It screeched at us, and she dropped her hand, flinching. Inside was a bed formed from the same brick as the walls and painted to match, a deeply tarnished metal sink and toilet, with a desk screwed into the brick.

"These were cells." Heather's tension made her voice wobble.

I continued down the hallway to a pair of double doors. She caught me up, and we stared at the wooden barrier for a while. What lay on the other side?

"Gotta be done," she said.

"On three?" I asked as we reached out for a door handle each.

"On three."

"One, two…" we pulled without saying three. A long, low room full of beds and shifting shadows. The sense of panic around my legs, thick and grease-like, rose around us with every step. Heather swallowed hard as we crossed the threshold.

I swept the torch from side to side, the light nudging at the dark rather than pushing it back.

"Lorne…"

"Yeah, I know." We both sensed it.

We stopped moving forwards. This place rose on my creep meter way above anything we'd experienced at Scob in the Rectory. Whatever lived in the layers of reality I'd touched, but didn't understand, they weren't happy. Heather retreated a step and my feet decided this might not be a bad idea. They followed suit. We backed up until something stopped me.

~ 164 ~

"Wait," I whispered, holding my hand up.

"What is it?" Heather hissed, and I heard her fear.

I reached out and lowered her light, so the room fell into a gloom, rather than pure black. The shadows rushed forwards but didn't quite reach us. They seethed on the edge of the torch's pale glow. I caught the shifting images of military men in uniforms, some sailors, some airmen, one wearing the familiar beret of the Paratroopers. Then, the slowly forming image of a man holding a rifle. He lifted the muzzle.

A soft and pure sound reached me. A song. A song as sweet as a blackbird's spring celebration. It made my head cock to catch the words.

"That's Russian," I murmured with a frown, the rising dread forgotten in the beauty of the melody.

"What is?" Heather didn't hear it.

"Bayu-bay, all people should sleep at night

Bayu-bay, tomorrow is a new day

We got very tired today,

let's say to everyone 'Good night',

go to sleep

Bayu-bay..."

"I didn't think you spoke Russian?" Heather's panic made her sound about as old as the child I now saw on one of the beds.

"I don't. Not much anyway."

"Then how...?"

My gaze didn't waver. "She told me." I pointed to the bed.

Behind the child stood a shadow wrapped in smoke and dust. It formed a thob and an almost there face covered in a veil. He held out arms of pale darkness. The small form on the bed, with pigtails down her back, clothed in a white sundress covered in tiny flowers, reached for his protection.

The djinn lifted the child, and I sensed no fear from them.

"I don't see anything," Heather whispered. "But I feel plenty, and I don't like it."

The moment the djinn held the child in his arms, the shadows rose from the ground and pushed at the torchlight. The soldier dropped his head to his shoulder and set the rifle, just as he'd done before. Only this time, it came with a sense of rage so deep and vast I feared its touch would burn my skin like acid. All that fury focused on me and Heather.

My legs threatened to collapse, and Heather whimpered.

"We need to leave, right now!" I cried out, turning away.

The shadows, a swarm rushing towards us, as if the torches no longer held the power of light against the dark, became almost tangible. I didn't want to wait to see the shades coalesce into whatever was left of the dead. I didn't want to discover what damage a .303 might do to my spine if the soldier fired on us.

Together, we ran back up the hallway.

"Paul, get what you want, and leave!" I bellowed. The pounding of our feet matched the pounding of my heart.

He appeared in the doorway of the first room as we rounded the corner. "What?"

"Leaving, now!" Heather yelled, almost screeching.

His eyes widened in alarm, but they weren't looking at me or Heather. They fixed on something over our heads. We barrelled into him, each of us turning and pushing him before us as one. We scrambled up the stairs, hit the leaking sunlight and stopped, forcing Paul back against the far wall.

Breath heaved in my chest, fighting past the lump in my throat. We shone our torches into the black of the stairwell despite the daylight.

The shadows remained where we left them.

Neither torch remained steady.

18

WE REACHED THE SUNSHINE IN double time. When we found Eddie, I opted to lie down on the baked soil with my eyes shut, trying very hard not to think. Heather sat beside me. We didn't touch, not quite, but if she reached out for my hand, I wouldn't say no to the comfort.

"What the ever-loving fuck was going on?" Paul asked.

I kept my eyes closed, the light making them almost translucent. "Did you get any actionable intel?" The croak in my voice came from the fear still lurking in my throat. Nothing on the wide Earth would make me go back to that hospital. *Nothing.*

"Yeah. I think I found what they were looking for last night."

I opened my eyes and squinted against the light.

"Amateurs aren't trained in searching professional environments and they didn't know what they were after." Paul reached into his crumbled linen jacket and pulled out a notebook with a hard blue cover. "It's in Russian though."

"You can read it?"

"Me and some software."

"Get on it. I want to know what the hell happened down there and why it's after us."

A pause among the group.

Eddie cleared his throat. "Lorne, it doesn't seem likely it's *after* you... It's just a black hole in the ground that can't move."

"Tell that to my fucking psyche, mate. I feel like I've run a bloody marathon with a succubus and the Kraken along for shits-and-giggles. I need to go home."

"Erm…" Eddie shifted his feet on the edge of my vision.

"What now?"

"Kate called."

I groaned. "DI Mackenzie can sort out the bad guys. I'm not interested."

"You will be. Monkey's body has gone missing from the morgue. She wanted to know if we'd seen anything macabre turn up here."

It took a while for that to be processed. "They killed him and stole his body?"

"Could be."

"If they thought he was poisoned with Novichok, wouldn't it be in a special location?"

"The police soon realised it was a bluff. Whoever killed Monkey made him OD on heroin. Someone had a jammer for the CCTV and an injection site was found on his toe. So, they made sure it looked like a chemical attack, but it wasn't anything that sinister. They just created chaos in a provincial police station to cause a distraction. It wouldn't have happened in a city, but…"

"It's Minehead not Scotland Yard."

"Or even Bristol. Security is not the same down here." Eddie sighed. "She's a worried woman. And, to be honest, Lorne, I'm a married man. This is masquerading as a foreign government attack, but…"

I heaved myself off the ground. "I know. It's missing something intangible to make it government. We need to find out what they want, give any information we gather to Kate. Maybe she can go public, and it'll make whoever wants the intel back off. Sound like a plan?"

"I just want Lilian safe, and this place doesn't feel too safe right now."

My phone burbled in my back pocket, and I pulled it out. Ella. I swiped up. "You okay?"

"Get down here." She spoke softly but with enough urgency to get me off the ground, as if pulled on strings.

"On my way."

Heather picked up enough of the conversation to already be racing down the field. I powered up behind her, my longer legs just about keeping pace with her flat-out sprint. Breathing hard, we made it back to the caravans and saw Ella and Lilian talking to a woman in a dark suit, with heels. A couple of men flanked her; they made the average SEAL team member look like a Ken doll.

The conversation had a polite intensity that civil women manage to do so well. The kind designed to make your teeth ache with the barbed politeness.

I decided to barge straight into the middle of it. "Hello. How can I help?" As if the women weren't already dealing with it perfectly well. In my defence, I wanted to take the heat off them and transfer it to me.

The woman in the heels, face of an angel who'd been sucking on lemons for a few millennia, looked me up and down very slowly. "Who are you?"

"Lorne Turner." I stuck my hand out. Her fingers tightened on her briefcase. No way was she touching me. I continued to talk while watching the heavies. "I'm a neighbour. Going to be helping out with the renovations. Thought I could give you a tour of the graveyard. Do you have relatives you're worried about in there?"

The woman's eyes were dark brown and heavily made up with a subtle understatement only the very classiest of office drones manage. "I'm sorry?"

"Well, it's the only reason to be on private property, isn't it?" I asked, giving her a smile that I knew made the most out of the scars littering my face. "The dead. In the graves up there. They've all been moved. I'm sure there must be records. What was it? Grandparent?" A form flickered on the edge of my vision. I gritted my teeth, trying to shut it out.

"I'm a solicitor, Mr Turner."

"Sergeant Major," I clarified.

"Excuse me?"

"Sergeant Major Turner. British Army. So what is it you do want if it's not the dead?" I asked, switching subjects again.

She blinked. The most expression I'd seen on her face so far. "I'm here to make Mr Rice a very good offer."

"Really? I think he's perfectly happy with his home. You like it, don't you, Lilian?" I looked at Lilian and managed to step between her and the woman. The heavies shifted; their dark suits matched as if their mother had dressed them to be the perfect twin boys. Their white shirts reflected the sunlight so brightly I thought they'd learned to weaponise cotton.

"I love it, Lorne," Lilian agreed.

"So, there you have it. No sale. Perhaps you can fuck off now and take your goons with you before this gets personal. What do you say?" I asked, with the same smile, but this time the smile did not reach my eyes.

The woman stepped back and licked her thin lips. I made her nervous. Good.

"The people I work for are offering a great deal of money for the cottage and associated land." Women like this didn't give up easily. It's how they smashed through glass ceilings.

"Does that include the woodland?" I asked.

She drew in a breath. "I believe that's part of the property. It's on the deeds."

"Then we aren't interested." I made shooing gestures with my hands. "Go on, off you fuck."

Eddie and Paul were now down from the woods.

The former police officer took up a position beside me. "I thought I'd explained myself well enough yesterday."

The woman looked at Eddie, her expression just as disappointed in him. "We have come to offer considerably more for the property."

"Nope. And whatever you want with the old ruins, you can't have it, Ms Fletcher. The only way to legally access it is through my land, and I don't want you here. So, do as you're told. And if you send anyone else to trespass during the night, I'll be forced to have my people pick them up rather than having my friend here break some bones."

I didn't smile this time. I just stared hard at the heavies. It didn't make much of an impact on them, but to be fair, I'm a small bloke and they were the size of dumper trucks. It wouldn't stop me, of course, if it kicked off.

The woman's jaw bounced with tension. "Well, we'll have to see what else can be done to encourage you to our way of thinking."

"If that's a threat…" Eddie snarled.

I glanced at him in surprise. This was a side of Eddie I'd never seen before, not even when he'd been convinced his old boss was one of the bad guys. It sounded like Eddie was ready to start banging heads together, old-style police.

The woman managed a sort of smile, a tenuous upward lift of her mouth as if it didn't quite understand the instruction. "I'm a legal representative of some very wealthy people, Mr Rice. I don't need to make threats, just promises." She turned on heels so sharp I'd be done for carrying a lethal weapon if I had them in my hands, and walked back to a very expensive black Merc SUV. The men flanked her but remained silent. I watched them. They moved stiffly, a sign of too much weightlifting, not enough aerobic exercise and a lot of steroid abuse. Some savage attacks to the knees. They'd go down and stay there.

"Heather," I said, keeping my voice low.

She stepped up beside me. "Yes?"

"How would you disable them?" I nodded to the heavies.

"Knees, lower back, but you'd have to stop them fast. They hit me with one of their shovel-hands and I'd go down for the count."

"Good."

Ella tutted but remained quiet.

"God, those shoes would be more money than I earn in a year," Lilian said.

My eyes flicked down to the heels. Red underneath. Did that mean something? I'd never seen anything like it before. Bloody funny place to have something so flash. But then, all the women in my life wore boots.

"I think it's time we found out what they're really after," Eddie said. "This is getting disturbing."

"Then we need to look at the notes and make sense of them," Paul said. "I'll head back to Ella's and start decrypting the Cyrillic so we can read some of the entries. Get a feel for what's happening."

I sighed, weighed down by what had happened in the hospital and the black void we'd run from earlier. "We need to find out what's happened to Monkey's body if possible and..."

"And?" Ella asked.

"And I think I need to talk to Willow about some seriously nasty spooks."

Paul glanced at me in confusion, and I clarified, "Not the Intelligence Service kind, mate."

Heather tensed beside me.

Ella's eyes narrowed. "Maybe you could talk to a priest and not a witch. How does that sound?"

This snappy breakdown in vicarly behaviour caught me unaware. "Sure, I'll talk to a priest, but you have said you aren't an exorcist, so I thought discussing it with someone who understands the occult might be wise. We don't have time to dig out some dusty Church of England specialist."

"Then I suggest you get moving." Ella turned away from me, her jeans too loose and her t-shirt hanging off narrow shoulders.

Heather watched us, concern etching her face. "I'll keep an eye on her. Go if you need to."

"I won't be long, but I do need to talk to Willow."

"I'm not sure you do, but..." She shrugged. "If that's what you want."

Her withdrawal from me stung like a rubber band retreating at speed against my heart. I reached out and caught her arm. "Whoa, slow down." Forcing her to face me, I gave up on the whole idea of keeping us quiet in front of the others. "Listen to me. If it bothers you, I won't go. I don't want to confuse or hurt you."

I watched tears pooling in her eyes, making the blue turn into the deep colour of the Mediterranean summer sky. "It's fine." She tugged out of my hand and walked away, shoulders bowed. Ella stood watching us, her face a closed mask of anger.

I'd done bad. I didn't understand what exactly, but I didn't have time to process these new and complicated shifting boundaries between the people I cared about most in the world. I rarely felt the gulf between my gender and those closest to me.

Sadly, I needed time to think about the external threats facing us, not interpersonal relationships.

Why would these crazy people murder an old woman and a drug addict? Then steal his body? Why would they offer so much for Eddie's place? Why would they send in some thugs to raid an abandoned building? None of this made sense.

I climbed into my bike gear, left Horner, and rode towards Minehead. It helped clear my head of the detritus, and I chose to concentrate on what I felt from the underground adventure. Willow said that trying to understand the emotions I picked up on in these places would help me control their effects. I wove through the summer traffic and thought about the rage that darkness held. The shades of the men in uniforms from wars fought long ago. The Devonshire soldier raising his rifle towards us… How did these men die to be so angry? Why were they in the hospital, and why were they stuck? In other graveyards I caught flickers of memories, not full manifestations. Something dreadful held these poor buggers trapped in the dark of this abandoned building. And a child found herself trapped with them. A horrible fate, evil even.

I thought about the image I'd seen of my desert djinn picking up the girl. That's twice I'd seen him care for her. She must be Peggy's sister and she must have died at the hospital, but why would she be there as a patient?

If her mother worked for the hospital, then perhaps the child was ill? The dark rage in the place swirled around her; it didn't attack the djinn, just me and Heather. Rage often came from fear, so…

I pulled up outside Willow's shop, Magick Minehead, and continued to sit on the bike in the shade. I shouldn't involve her in this adventure. If the dead in the hospital were full of fear, which made them angry, then I needed to find out what made them fearful. I didn't need Willow's advice to figure that one out.

How would I help them, though? How could I move them on, and with them, the little girl?

"Since when are you a ghostbuster, Lorne?" I muttered aloud.

My priority should be the human element. Live people were the dangerous ones and yet... I couldn't shake the feeling the suffering of the dead under that hospital, buried in the old graves of the Methodist church, was far more important.

The police could deal with the humans.

I dismounted from the bike. I was here now. It would be weird, but I could talk to Willow, see where the new rules of engagement left us. Pulling off my bike helmet, I began to concentrate on crossing the street, my mind bouncing from one subject to another, completely distracted from everything but the summer traffic clogging the main road.

Which had to be the only excuse for what happened next.

A heavy hand landed on my shoulder. I turned the bike helmet, swinging up in defence before my eyes even registered a potential problem. A sharp pain in my neck, a wasp sting, had me stepping back towards the traffic.

"Whoa, steady there, my friend." An American accent.

"What the fuck...?" The world spun. I stumbled forwards as the big man pulled me from the traffic. Horns blared and my bike swam off down the road as my vision doubled, tripled...

I tried to keep my senses online. A black van with shiny wheels pulled up behind me and opened a large black mouth into which, I fell...

19

HOW MUCH HAD I DRUNK to feel this deep in the well?

I breathed hard through my nose, trying to control the rising nausea. Wherever I was, I remained seated, so not in bed or on my sofa. I rarely drank enough to feel like this, maybe by accident, but if I drank, the hangovers had a habit of dragging with them depression and I didn't need that temptress wiping me out.

Another problem faced my confused brain. Why weren't my eyes opening? I'd had episodes of waking in panic after contact with an enemy, covered in blood, and my eyelids might be crusted closed. Oh, now that made sense. This felt like an anaesthetic. My brain slowly coming back online over a period of time and my body taking far longer to wake. I'd been hurt then? How?

If this was anaesthetic, what had happened to me?

What was the last thing you remember?

The sun-drenched cottage, the bike ride into Minehead, reaching Willow's shop... The sting to my neck.

Christ, this wasn't some weird flashback, and I hadn't entered some kind of time vortex, waking up in one of dozens of conflict zones. I'd been snatched off the street.

My stomach flipped, bile rose, and I twisted to avoid puking in my lap. Once the heaving stopped, I realised my left arm hadn't moved from the chair.

I tugged to wipe my mouth clean. It didn't come free, and I registered the restraints for the first time.

I couldn't see or move. The smell of my vomit rose, and I dry heaved several times before managing to gain control.

Assess the situation, soldier.

I returned to breathing, trying to stem the panic. Sitting back in the chair, I knew that much at least, I realised tight restraints held both arms and my legs. I also wore a blindfold, which meant I wasn't injured. I wiggled my toes in my boots just to make sure.

Well, if someone watched, they already knew I was awake, so no point faking unconsciousness for the moment. I sat still and listened for a while. No birds, no wind, only the scent of my vomit and stale air. Under my hands, I felt either leather or vinyl covering hard foam and metal. My back pressed into a cushioned surface, as if I sat in a dentist's chair, and the straps covered not just my ankles, but thighs as well.

I clicked my tongue in an attempt to gauge how large the room might be, but I lacked the skills for a good assessment. If we were outside on the moor, I'd know blindfolded if I sat in woodland or on the heath, but caged in a building I had no chance. It seemed large, no sense of echo, but the sound flattened out, so tiles? Concrete, probably.

"Oh, fucking hell," I whispered.

The laboratories under the old hospital... No, no, no, this was not a good place for me to be. My panic began to rise again, and I tugged harder at the cuffs holding me down. They were leather, like the ones I'd seen on the chairs and bed in the underground, very haunted, rooms. I yanked, pushed, pulled, whined and gnashed my teeth. Nothing moved. I tried to bend down to savage the leather, but the angles of the chair meant I couldn't curl my spine enough. I should have taken Willow up on the offer of yoga classes.

"Fuck!" I bellowed. I tried rubbing my head against the headrest so I could remove the blindfold, but the damned thing remained firmly in place.

One of the absolutes you learn when you go through your first torture session at the hands of the British Army's training for Special Forces is to conserve your strength. You'd need it for the long hours ahead. We all broke, eventually, we had to face that failure, that vulnerability, so we knew, and our people knew, what we were made of. Somehow, despite facing our own people, never made it any easier.

A sound reached me at last. Footsteps, more than one person, and they headed in this direction. I drew in a few deep breaths to bring myself back to the centre and close down my rage. It wouldn't help me think and gain the advantage I needed for escape.

Next came the sound of a key scraping and opening a lock. So, I sat in a room with a locked door. That must mean I hadn't been taken back to the hospital. The sense of relief this gave me was mildly humiliating. The fear that place manifested in my head overwhelmed the worry surrounding my current circumstances. The door opened, and I leaned forwards, straining to pick up on some clues.

A light step, a heavy one, movement of fabric, a sense of at least two individuals and their smells. The first, light and fragrant, the second heavier and musky. Female, male, almost certain. An unusual combination for torture.

Just keep breathing, Lorne, and try not to panic. If you lose control, who knows what will march out of the darkness?

I thought about the djinn, the beast inside me and their current passivity. What would happen to me the moment they surfaced? The drugs still coursing through my foggy mind, must be holding them at bay. I didn't imagine them waking to find my body locked in place, being a positive situation for me or those who held me captive.

The woman walked around the chair.

That meant I didn't have my back to the wall, which made things worse—if they could be worse right now.

"Dear, dear, seems we might have overdone the sedative," she murmured. "I cannot work in this smell. Not to start with at least. It might come later, but not at the beginning."

The voice wasn't directed at me, and I kept my lips locked. She moved away. I heard a tap. I heard water and thought of Abu Ghraib. It made my heartrate kick up. I forced my breathing to slow, combating the rise of panic. I did not want to endure water torture, not after what happened in Scob. The water sloshed on the floor and the smells shifted around me, dissolving.

While the floor cleaning occurred, I thought about her words, her accent. It wasn't British-English, more American-English, but that could mean she'd learned it in America or from American TV. A lot of people picked up the accent when they worked for the American Armed Forces overseas. Underneath, barely detectable, I heard the harder rolling letters of Eastern Europe, maybe Russia. At least I knew this had something to do with the current investigation and not my past. That helped a little.

"Good, now I can think more clearly," she said with brevity that made the hairs on my arms stand up.

People shouldn't sound that happy with a prisoner tied to a chair. Something tapped my left arm, and I realised for the first time they'd removed my bike gear, so I sat in a t-shirt and jeans. Stupid, should have logged that sooner.

"Sergeant Major Lorne Turner, latterly of the Special Air Service 22nd Regiment, was on active duty until four years ago—more or less. Twenty years' service in total, most of it spent in theatre because of the War on Terror. Discharged for severe post-traumatic stress disorder due to something finally snapping in your head while trying to escape the Islamic State in Syria, most of your unit died. The Americans hauled your backside out of a fire." While she spoke, she traced a line down my right arm, and I shuddered from the contact, the scars making the light brush come and go with various amounts of sensation. I remained silent during this rendition of facts she shouldn't have any access to in any open network database.

Almost all my files were redacted, except for those people at the top of the totem pole.

"Nothing to say?" she asked.

I fell back on training. "Sergeant Major Lorne Turner, *retired*," I said, putting a heavy emphasis on the final word.

"I had a feeling that might be all the information we'd share," she cooed.

"We'll move you on from this phase in a minute. I really don't want to spend hours asking you questions to get that answer in return. It becomes very boring. Boring makes me tetchy."

'Tetchy'? That's an unusual word for non-natives to use. I logged it.

She continued. "I want to speak to you, to give you a chance before we move on, about what we've discovered during the last few days. Information about you and your little friends."

I couldn't repress the flinch that surged through me at the thought of them knowing about Ella and Heather. Did they also know about Willow? This made the world infinitely darker.

A small chuckle made me realise she'd said it to provoke a reaction, and it worked. Damn it.

"Still nothing to say, Sergeant Major? I understand. You have no idea who I am, what I want, why you were taken, but you do know you are in deep shit. I should think your training is kicking in and you think you'll resist despite knowing that at some point you'll break. You also hope a rescue will occur before that happens. However, you will not be found. We will release what is left of you when we are ready. Or we will kill you—which to be fair, is far more likely."

That didn't sound even vaguely like a good thing, and it made me curl my fingers and toes up.

"Oh, no, we don't resort to physical abuse, much to the dismay of my colleague here. It's your mind I will be attacking."

Good luck with that mess.

It did make my breathing heavier though, because I'd come to a gentle coexistence with my haunted mind these last few months and I didn't want the monsters, the ghosts and demons, dug out and revived. In fact, the more I thought about what she'd said, the more it scared me. What if I lost myself in my nightmares? I'd been lost in the hospital in Cyprus for days until the medication brought back some control. They'd taken me off the anti-psychotics soon enough, but I'd never been the same man.

I loved my small life on Exmoor with Ella Morgan, Heather Wicklow and the others. I did not want to change. I started repeating their names in my head, a mantra to keep me in the present—my present.

The heat of a body came close. A whisper in my ear made me jerk away but I couldn't avoid her voice, "I will take you to places you never thought possible, and you will tell me everything you know about the old woman, the hospital, the formulas and what your friend from GCHQ might know about us."

Paul... If he'd been taken, they already knew everything. We'd been separated once in Lashkar Gah's backstreets. I'd found him eventually, sheltering behind some overflowing bins in an alley. He was babbling about being taken by the Taliban for questioning—they hadn't been anywhere near. I grabbed him by the scruff of his neck and shoved him in a RWMIK Land Rover, telling him what a bloody idiot he was and how he needed to grow a pair of balls.

I didn't think like that any longer. We all had our limits. His were far saner than mine.

Fingers started to beat a tattoo on my chest. "Maybe I can get more information out of you than just the stuff Winter Sun wants to buy? That could be handy. I do so love playing with soldiers. They really are the most fun to break. You never know what will come tumbling out. I've spent my entire professional career trying to find that hospital. The old woman, and your vicar, led me right to dear old Peggy's back door, which then led us to you. That's the bit I love the most, one link in the chain leading to another, until you find the barking dog at the end. That's you. You'll be my barking dog. I've read your psych-eval and you, Sergeant Major, are fucked in the head."

I kept my mouth shut and logged that name, Winter Sun. All I'd do by answering was give her ammunition and I didn't want to encourage the bitch.

"We will be moving on shortly," she said. "It is not going to be pretty, Lorne. You are going to know fear and pain. If you give me what I want now, I can make it a trip of fluffy clouds, blue skies and tweeting birds. If you remain silent, I will turn your worst nightmares into reality, and you'll never escape. You'll be trapped in whatever hellscape broke your mind. You will never hold the hand of your young love again."

She meant Heather.

"Then I will find Paul and the vicar and start asking them questions. I thought to spare them, but if you remain silent, they will suffer. If you retain enough of your right mind, you might even be aware of it happening. Sounds bad to me. What do you think?"

"Sergeant Major—"

She slapped my face. "Alright, boring. Enough. I might be a total bloody narcissist, but even I need a break from listening to the sound of my own voice."

Personally, the longer she talked, the less likely I'd become her victim of choice, but it seemed my time had run out.

2 0

I FELT, RATHER THAN HEARD, her move away. Some metal against metal sounds started on my right, and the creaking of plastic made the skin on my scalp creep and crawl. My breathing hitched upwards again, and I tried to count breaths in and out to balance them. The faster my heartbeat, the faster things would change for my situation. I needed to remain in control for as long as possible.

What happens when you lose it, soldier?

Christ, I didn't know. It had taken years to work some kind of peaceful balance into my life. To find people who understood and acted as a net for me—whether they knew it or not. What would I do to them if something in me was triggered?

I thought about Heather, how much she trusted me, how much she'd grown in such a short space of time. How much I loved watching her laugh without the bitter cynicism I knew always hovered on the surface, like oil-stained water. If surrendering to this mind-rape would help protect her and Ella, then it would be easy to give up. Unless the sacrifice of three people meant the safety of many more. It all depended on what *they* wanted in exchange?

Whoever these people represented it must be something far larger than the simple murder of an old lady on Exmoor. They wanted Soviet secrets that had been smuggled into the UK during the beginning of the Cold War.

Those secrets lay hidden in laboratories in a quiet wood in rural Somerset, far away from the machinations of Washington, London and Moscow. Concealed, kept secret by the handful of locals who lived here, and guarded by entropy. What mysteries did that notebook Paul took from the lab hold? Surely this woman had the resources to hack anywhere on the planet to steal the information?

"You heard of MKUltra, Lorne?" asked the woman.

The information from the notebook must be invaluable to be worth risking so much attention from local law enforcement. Why fake a radioactive attack and steal Monkey's body? Red flags were being waved like Liverpool supporters abusing a dozen energy drinks mixed with vodka. The government had to know what was happening down here in Somerset.

What if you're not in Somerset? You don't know where you are. You could be in a Black Site somewhere in Africa.

Helpful, really helpful thought, thanks.

Arguing with myself wasn't going to help. Answering questions might.

"I've heard of MKUltra."

A small cheer went up. "It speaks! Wonderful. We'll get on so much better. I'm about to give you a simple dose of scopolamine. It comes from the nightshade family. Did you know that?"

"Not on the reading list for the average grunt," I said. "Not sure it's a good idea. I've some nasty boxes you don't want opening."

"I'm sure I'll manage, between the chair and my security blob, you're well contained. This particular dose will ensure your metabolism retains more of the other drugs I'll be using. Anyway, back to basics. MKUltra was an American programme, but the Soviets had something similar going and the British, even the Canadians. MKUltra is still the largest known experiment of its kind and as they destroyed much of the work involved, the naughty CIA has never been held to account by its victims. When they were caught with their paws in the cookie mix, the work they started segued into the private sector and that's where I come in."

"So you're a torturer for hire?"

The woman laughed and patted my belly. It churned. "Oh, you're funny, no, I'm actually a highly qualified scientist but I don't have much of a conscience, which is why I'm handy on a team of people trying to find a way to create the perfect soldier by controlling a human mind. Hitler loved people like me." The emphasis on the word *loved* made me shiver.

At least I was managing to see the bigger picture for the first time. All I had to do now was survive long enough to tell Paul.

"What's that mean?" I asked.

"Do you know how much it cost to train you?"

"Somewhere north of six million pounds, I've been told." My hands flexed against the chair arm and the leather binding my wrist.

"Exactly, and before you hit forty, your mind turned you into cabbage. What a bloody waste. Imagine how much money we'd save if we could keep pushing you out there despite the horrors of war. If we removed the emotions around the memories, reset you like a computer game, and sent you back out, you'd last a lot longer. You'd also be more use after your body starts to fade or you suffer catastrophic physical failure as well."

One of my muckers with his legs blown off drifted through my mind… 'Catastrophic physical failure…'

"Imagine if we could have kept you in the field for another five years? We'd have saved so much money. And what of the younger men, men who left with the same weaknesses you have, but broke so much sooner? How much money was wasted on them? Multiply that across all the Armed Services and you have a lot of waste."

"My memories made me a better soldier. My emotions make me a better man."

"Until they didn't. They made you weak." Her anger at my failure hurt my heart.

I'd given my life to becoming the best soldier possible, and in the end that dedication took my mind, not my life, not my limbs, my mind.

I felt the scratch of a needle against the back of my hand. It jerked hard against the leather restraint.

The words of pure panic tumbled out of me. "Please, don't do this. Please. You have no idea how much damage you'll do to everyone around me. I don't know anything. You've told me more in the last five minutes than I knew this morning—assuming it still is the same day. I'm totally fucking harmless to you."

"Don't worry, anything you say will be erased from your mind, and we'll have control over you for as long as necessary. You won't remember any of this."

"Then why do it?" I asked, the anxiety now clear in my voice.

Beat the shit out of my body and I'd handle it, attack my mind with prolonged programming I'd do alright, but this? A hatchet job deep in my psyche? Too dangerous, too scary, I wanted out. I'd done LSD once, and it was enough; mushrooms of the psychedelic kind, never. My work meant too much to me, being wedded to my career and the dedication it took to be the best soldier I could be, kept me on the straight and narrow—I couldn't do this... I had no safe place to hide inside my head.

A hand trapped my useless thrashing. "To be honest, Lorne, I'm doing this because your discharge papers interest me and I want to know more about your type of psychopathy. You see, the woman who worked for the labs you stumbled over, she had some mad skills. She left England to work on MKUltra for a short time but returned. She never reached her full potential and when she realised they used civilians and soldiers without their knowledge, she wanted to blow the whistle. Not only that, she destroyed much of her work. When she returned to her family in the UK, she died from an unfortunate 'accident'. The Winter Sun has spent billions trying to replicate her work, but they've never managed it. I'm close, so bloody close, but I need just a little more from her—so we came here. To merry old England and found you lot playing Scooby Doo."

A set of heavy knuckles rapped the back of my hand, holding it down with bone crushing intensity.

"Do behave. I'm only putting in a cannula."

"Fuck you." I heaved my entire body up and used the muscles in my legs to really fight the restraints. Every fibre worked to snap my way free of this lunatic. I pushed my head back into the chair. The structure groaned.

"He can't actually break free, can he?" asked the woman, sounding a little scared as I drew in another breath and thrashed.

"No." Not enough for me to determine the country of origin. It didn't matter, I just needed to escape this chair, and he'd find himself a new line of work.

Within moments, I broke out into a heavy sweat. A few more moments and my beast howled in rage as he surfaced for the first time. You don't collar a hyena. We fought and snarled and savaged, but nothing worked. We couldn't break free. We were losing, and we knew it.

I stopped struggling and sealed my fate. The woman touched the back of my hand as my breathing strained just the right side of panic. "You really are very strong," she murmured in my ear. "An ugly brute perhaps, but something beautiful lurks under all that savagery. Let's see if I can find it. I might even decide to take it and nurture it, rather than destroy it, but you would make a fine addition to my collection of broken toys."

"I hope whatever comes out of me kills you," I growled in return.

The cannula slid into my hand, and I felt the tape go on. It jiggled about a bit, and something cold filled my veins, heading first up my hand, then back up my arm as my blood whipped it towards my brain. I had no way to protect the delicate chemistry between my neurones, and whatever happened in the spaces between them.

I focused on memories from the summer. Heather and I lying in the garden smoking weed and drinking beer after a long weekend of work with wealthy London city bankers. Heather learning to safely use the P30 out on the moor somewhere quiet so we wouldn't be caught with the illegal firearm. Her joy at controlling the weapon far outweighing any conscience I might have over teaching a civilian to use firearms correctly. Heather turning up after her first weekend away with the Army Reservists, exhausted, dressed in muddy fatigues, and never looking so amazing. She needed me in her life, and I would not let her down.

The drugs hit my brain and her face dissolved.

To be replaced by upswept black eyes, kohl rimmed, a veil over a mouth and nose. I thought male, but to be honest, the djinn might be female. Genderless then, but angry—there was no escaping the powerful anger.

"Name and rank, soldier?" came a softly spoken question from a thousand miles away.

I sat on a dune of fine golden sand, the ripples from a warm wind making it shimmer like water. A dark-skinned hand gripped my shoulder, held it tight, and pushed me down into the sand. The grains of the dune rose, just like water, and lapped at my crossed legs, engulfing my knees, my hips, my passive hands. Up, up, the sand rose, and I sank, sank, sank into the dune as the robed figure became stronger, darker. The soft colours of the woodland in his robes changed into something else, becoming more ragged, the surrounding wind lifting the tatty robe like wings. I gazed upwards and realised he looked like a human crow. Or maybe she...

Old legends came back to me, the Morrigan, goddess of war, picking her way through the dead of the battlefield, a crow for company.

A desert djinn born from dust and sand, war and hate, the black flags snapping in a wind full of screaming and pain. Fear in every breath, drowning a small, but ancient, desert town in Syria.

The sand of the dune now covered my shoulders. I asked with my eyes, 'Will you save me?' I felt no fear, only peace.

The djinn did not answer, merely pushed harder, and the sand closed over my head.

"I don't understand a word he's saying," said a woman from the other side of the desert.

"It sounds a little like Kurdish," said a man, Russian accent strong. "I worked there once."

"Everyone worked there once," she snapped.

"He won't stop talking."

"It's gibberish." She sounded really pissed off.

"It sounds old," said the Russian.

"Oh, what would you know?"

"More than you, apparently," the Russian said, no longer hiding his contempt for her. "He is elite soldier, broken, not a toy. Something in him. I see it. I see too much in men like him. He is haunted by something other than his memories."

"There are no such things as ghosts, you provincial fool," she snapped.

"Then you are fool. I am from Siberia. We know of the creatures who live in the wilds. They live in the mountains too, in places like Afghanistan, they will live in the deserts. They live here if you fool enough to find them. We need to stop this."

"No."

"Little scientist, we need to stop and kill him. If we do not, he will kill you."

"You said he was safe in the chair."

"Perhaps a man is, but he is no longer a man."

A vague and distant feeling of something cold entering my hand again. I felt my mouth moving and air rushing into and out of my body. I felt my heart beating and my body kept still in its bonds, but from so far away I knew I had no control.

I'd been absorbed by the dust and sand of a distant desert.

21

FLASHES OF IMAGES I DIDN'T understand. Blood staining a wall, warmth covering my arm, down my neck, on my face. A broken head under my boot. Another screamed in terror. Words echoing around me, many I didn't know, couldn't know. Something dark and *other* sucked at my mind.

A door. A boot.

Keys.

Fingers not wholly mine fumbled and fought but won in the end. A corridor with grey walls, pastel green floor, metal door and recessed windows. A whimpering sound behind me proved easy to ignore. The images tumbled away.

Screams of rage, weapons I didn't know how to use, lifted and glinted in the desert sun, blood and shit mixed with dust and sand. Horses pounding the sun-baked earth so far from the misty woodlands I knew and understood. Camels in a long train, spread over miles, carrying all manner of goods for sale in distant lands. Women dancing under the full moon in worship of ancient gods. Men wrestling together in celebration of a hunt or battle. Again, war, blood red swords, AK47s, bullets screaming through the night to hit the moon-drenched blades of ancient warriors.

Pyramids of white and gold. Gardens of pleasant green hanging throughout a city. Clean water, plentiful one moment, gone the next, as crops fail, rivers move, flooding stops. The desert flexes its might and buries villages, towns, cities...

We slept.

You woke.

You came and woke us.

The devil came and woke you.

Yes. The devil is you. Men with hate in their hearts. Blood and bone woke me. I fled in fear. I found you.

Can you leave me?

No. Yes. Perhaps. You are not my kind. Your soul tastes of mud and rain, of trees and moors.

You taste of dust and sand.

As I should.

It scares me.

As it should.

The dunes rose everywhere, and I stood alone, lost, trapped in a place I didn't understand. My body was… where? Doing what?

I stood alone in a vast wilderness I didn't understand.

"I'm a survival expert," I whispered at my hands.

Young and unscarred. Hands that knew how to kill. Hands that knew how to find the way in a desert. I took my watch off, 09:53. Close enough. I pointed the little hand at the punishing sun overhead… Wait, I didn't know where I was which meant I couldn't work out GMT. Bugger it, south would be close enough, an hour or two wouldn't matter, it was the effort I made that mattered.

I built a small pile of sand to help check the position of the shadows as I marked off the direction my watch told me was south. I began to walk, my boots sinking into the sand of the dune, sinking but not vanishing.

"I will not be lost here," I yelled out. "You don't get control."

The colour of the sky shifted from a blue so hard it could be made from the heart of a diamond, to black, a void so vast my existence proved irrelevant. I looked at the swimming stars. They swirled and tumbled in the dark ocean, the constellations unknown. One bright, unblinking star hovered on the horizon. Venus. The planet of a goddess known for love, grace, beauty, young in the days the djinn was old—I knew that now. I walked towards love.

I walked towards love.

I walked...

"Lorne!" screamed a voice that reached through the inky sky above me. It tore the veil asunder, ripped a tear in the fabric of my reality and sucked me into a vortex. I raced into it with a wild heart full of burning hope.

Burning.

My skin burned, my mind screamed, the technical shuddered as the weapon barked *ratt-tatt-rattattat*. Robed faces shuddered under the pressure of controlling the barking machine gun. My fingers closed over the grenade. I pulled, the pin came out as it detached from my webbing, and I hurled the explosive through a gaping maw...

"Lorne, come on, come back, please, you're bleeding. Please, don't leave me. Please, I can't do this alone. Please come back."

Venus, a bright star in the *dust and sand, blood and bone.*

We stood on the dune, together, a strong arm around my shoulders.

Go home, brother, it is now safe.

Stay with me.

It seems I have no choice. You must stop this evil. Many souls are trapped. You will free them. They need the light. This is now your task. I will guide you, warrior, as I have many before you.

As you wish.

I am your djinn, warrior. I will guide you in war.

I am yours to command.

"Lorne?" asked a weeping voice I knew so well.

"Heather?" I croaked. My eyes peeled open and snapped shut under the glare of a vicious sun coming up through the waves of the sea.

"Oh, thank God."

"Don't think he helped," I mumbled.

"What?"

I shook my head as small hands took hold of my inert body.

"Most of this isn't your blood," Heather whispered.

I tried to focus on her face. "What?"

~ 191 ~

Blue eyes peered into mine with concern. "Lorne, where have you been?"

I thought about this question for a while. "In the desert." Honesty did seem the best policy right now.

Or not, as Heather sucked in a sharp breath. "You've been gone almost three days…"

I blinked. "Where am I now?"

She clutched my forearms as if some vanishing act might snatch me away again. "You're, *we're*, on the beach at Porlock Weir. Look around, we're below Culbone Church."

"The sea," I turned and looked up at the woodland cliffs, "the forest. It's all here. I'm not in the desert?"

"Lorne, where did the blood come from?" Heather asked, her voice deepening in concern.

I licked dry and cracked lips. "I don't know. I don't know what happened. I don't remember, Heather. I just… I was—the desert… the djinn. I don't know what happened."

She stroked my head and my cheeks warmed from the tears I shed. I shivered despite the heat suffocating me. A thought ripped me out of her arms and upright. "You shouldn't be here alone!" My legs didn't want to keep me standing for long, so I hit the stones again.

"It's alright, Lorne. I'm not alone. Eddie is just down the beach. He couldn't keep up with me. We need to get this blood off you. Can you come with me into the sea?" Her concern rippled through me as though my skin were made of cobwebs.

I looked down at myself and realised I was indeed covered in blood, none of it fresh. I had torn the skin on my wrists at some point, but scabs now crusted in the wounds. I had bruises everywhere, my muscles hurt, many to the point of being ripped. Bits of my face hurt as well.

"Come on, we need to wash you off." Heather rose, stripped down to her sports bra and pants, but left on her tactical boots. She took my hand and pulled me towards the lapping waves, the tide high and close.

I went, meek and calm, a lamb following his shepherd. The water hit my legs, and it was cold, then it stung, and I yelped. A figure waved at us from down the beach, Heather waved back. She continued to walk into the sea without for a moment flinching until it rose over her waist and each wave bounced her up and into me. Being heavier and taller, I remained still.

"Come on, I need your help here, boss," she murmured.

With soft hands, she started to scrub at my skin. I got the message and washed my face and scalp. It helped. I began to breathe more deeply, see less colour but more detail, the feel of Heather against my body began to be familiar and comforting, even needful.

"How did you find me?" I asked as she used her hard nails to dig blood out of my skin.

"Paul. Most of the CCTV in the area is set up to download onto remote servers rather than sit on a hard drive in the business or home. It overwrites every few days, but he set up some kind of alert through GCHQ. I don't pretend to understand, but basically, every piece of spyware they used to track terrorists was used to track you as well. He added you to the list. The system picked you up because you happened to walk under the cameras of The Ship Inn. Then I knew you'd head here rather than anywhere else in the area. He's scrubbing you from the lists now."

"He's good at his job."

"Yes, he is, thank God. We would never have found you otherwise. Right, you're clean as you can be. Let's get you fed and watered. You look like shit." She started to pull me out of the water.

I resisted. "Wait."

Heather turned back. "It's cold, Lorne."

Taking her face in my hands, I whispered to her, "Thank you for keeping me safe for as long as possible." I leaned in and I kissed her gently on the lips.

Small hands clutched my waist but didn't push me away. When I released her, a sad smile made her blue eyes dark. "I thought you'd left me, then... I've been so scared, Lorne. I thought I'd lost you forever. I can't be betrayed by you, of all people. Please..."

"They broke me, Heather. I don't feel right."

She nodded. "I can see it. Don't worry. We'll get you squared away, then we'll talk."

"I know what they want."

Eddie arrived at the edge of the water, huffing and puffing. "Get out of there before you freeze to death." He rummaged in a bag he carried and pulled out a blanket.

Heather started walking me out of the water. "We'll talk about it back at the farmhouse. Everyone is staying there. With you missing, we needed a defensible position. I know the land there better than at Horner, and no one can sneak up on us. We need a dog."

"I'd like a dog," I said. "I get lonely when you go away."

She glanced at me, still concerned. "You have no filter, Lorne. You might want to think before you speak."

"No. I think I need to tell you everything."

Now her concern flickered into panic. "Yeah, because that's a good idea for someone on acid."

"What?"

"You're still tripping, Lorne."

"How do you know?" I asked as Eddie wrapped a blanket around me.

"What the hell were you daft buggers doing in the sea?" he asked.

"He stank, and it's a good way to ground someone who is on a bad trip," Heather lied without blinking. I opened my mouth, but she pinched my arm as she helped rub me dry, so I snapped my mouth shut. She continued, "He can't remember where he was or what he was doing."

I did remember something. "They took me from Willow's place—shit is she—"

"Fine, Lorne. She's fine. She has someone staying with her in the flat and he's helping in the shop. That's how we knew you were missing. She saw your bike and found a vial on the ground. You were dosed before you even left the area. I can see it's something like a hallucinogenic, you get to recognise the symptoms. Come on, I'll keep you safe until you feel better."

Eddie had emptied a large bag on the ground; it contained food, water, and clean clothes. He talked to someone on the phone in his reassuring police voice.

"No, it doesn't look like he's physically hurt, but Heather thinks he's been dosed with acid or something similar. He's a bit of a mess. No, I don't know if he hurt someone…"

"Look at me, Lorne. Don't listen to Eddie, it won't help."

I leaned close to Heather and whispered, "I think I killed someone."

She clutched my face and stared hard into my eyes. They gleamed like dark sapphires. "It doesn't matter right now. We'll talk about it later. Please, just do as you're told, okay?"

I nodded and her hands released me. "Eat, drink, then we walk back to the car." She thrust a water bottle and high energy nutrition bar into my hands. I stared at them for a while before she tutted and opened them both for me.

I smiled at her, and those blue eyes rolled. She muttered, "I can't believe I dumped my life just to find it all over again. You on acid and me playing grown-up."

"God, this food is amazing," I murmured.

Heather laughed and wrapped her arms around my waist to give me a cuddle. "I'm so glad you're alive."

"Me too, you're awesome."

Eddie came off the phone and watched me for a minute before chuckling. "Oh, this is going to be fun."

We started to walk back towards the village of Porlock Weir, and I drifted in and out of the weird hyper-reality that resulted from the drug abuse. I didn't like it, but with Heather there, I felt safe.

22

THE CAR JOURNEY TO STOKE Pero turned into a nightmare. The trees blended together, no matter how slowly Eddie managed to drive. The corners made my stomach lurch and the sky threatened to swallow us in one gulp. We sat in the back of Eddie's small run-around and Heather maintained a running commentary in a low voice, holding my hands to help me breathe.

When we pulled up outside the farmhouse, it felt like I'd done a full tour of duty, lasting years, not months.

"Come on, shower, more water, food, then bed," Heather ordered.

"Ella," I managed to blurt out without vomiting.

Heather gave me a crooked smile, a sad mask covering her obvious worry. "Okay, Ella." Her approval of the request felt all warm and spicy.

As if summoned, Ella came out of the front door and into the yard. I fell out of the car, my legs not completely under my control.

She rushed over, halting my foal-like attempts to get off the ground. Not a word, just a small body pressed into my arms. This felt good as well. I just wished I was the smaller body and could be held safe. I just wanted to be safe.

"Go steady, Ella, he's not well."

Ella pulled back and studied my face. "What happened?" she looked at me but aimed the question at Heather.

"We found him on the beach," Eddie said. "He's completely out of it. Heather's been guiding him the whole way. It's like he's not in there."

"He's in there," Heather said. "It'll just take time."

I had my doubts. I didn't feel right. Not at all. The world shimmered and shifted around me, making movement difficult. The memories flickered and flashed through the present and I found it a struggle to tell the difference. My hearing behaved like it was being governed by a radio dial, the static humming one moment but the next, tuning into gunfire, or some old briefing, half-remembered conversations in the mess hall, funerals of muckers... Then it would shift back to the present and I'd locate Heather's gentle voice in the swamp.

The kitchen, I stood in the warmth of my kitchen, but it resembled a war room in a FOB. A bank of monitors sat on the table and hard drives hummed.

"What?" I asked, pulling back on Heather's tug in the doorway.

"Paul had to find you. He raided the local PC World and networked everything. We needed the computing power. We also had to upgrade the satellite internet."

A face that looked a great deal less put together than it did the last time I'd seen it, popped up over the bank of screens. "Good, you're back. I need more intel."

"Paul..." Heather said, drawing the name out in warning. He looked at her with a hunted tinge to his haggard face. "We talked about how we would handle this if he came home in a state. He's in a state, so let's park the questions for now."

Ella stood next to me, and Lilian stood by the sink. Food littered the kitchen counters, and it made my mouth water.

"Food," I announced, ignoring everything else.

"Hey, Lorne, we have all sorts here, or I can make you a fry up if it'll help," Lilian said, her voice just as gentle as Heather's or Ella's. They were not like the *other* woman...

I picked up a pasty and said around a huge mouthful, "Woman, Eastern European maybe but very American as well, scientist. Working for a private company to make perfect soldiers. Name, name, name... She wants to make soldiers forget their minds—no—emotions, so they can keep fighting cos we cost a lot to produce. She fucks with the brain. She hurt me. I vanished into the desert. There was a man, Russian, but spoke English, until he didn't anymore."

"Whoa, Lorne, please don't say anything you'll regret," Eddie said, stepping in front of me so I could see him.

"Wasn't me. Was my… companion…"

I watched everyone share significant looks while I continued to stuff the pasty in my mouth. It tasted of heaven with a side order of Shangri-la. Swallowing it almost in one piece, I picked up a Danish pastry next and pulled it to pieces while eating. Heather and Paul were arguing, and I didn't like it, so tuned them out and stared at the garden. Mum's flowers looked amazing this year. Heather seemed to like making things grow.

"Lorne, I need more information!" Paul shouted over Heather.

I focused on him. "Don't shout, I don't like it."

"What did you see?" he asked, ignoring me.

"Nothing."

"What?"

"Nothing, blindfold. They held me down, until they didn't anymore. Don't remember much after that because I went away, into the desert."

A soft sob came from Ella.

I smiled. "It's okay. *He* kept me safe. *He* dealt with the problem. I came home." I finished the Danish and picked up another pasty.

Heather took it from my hands. "Let's go steady on the carbs, Lorne. You'll be sick. We're going to have some more water, then a shower, then bed."

I grinned. "You're coming?"

She chuckled. "I'll be there. I'm not going to bed with you, because you need some space, but I won't leave until you're okay."

Paul arrived, far too close for comfort. "I really need his intel. He's trained for this, Heather, and the more I know, the better at this point."

I looked at the ceiling for a bit and said, "She wants the notebook. She doesn't know it's a notebook, but she wants the formula. Your grandmother was something of a chemist savant. They haven't been able to replicate her work. They've been looking for it ever since she died. MKUltra is important. The company is in the private sector so took over the CIA's work when they got sussed back in the seventies."

"Anything visual you can remember? Please, Lorne. I need something to search for. You must have seen something as you escaped."

I sucked in a sharp breath as my mouth filled with dust and sand. "I saw a logo, a bird like a hawk inside a circle on her lab coat." Which meant she'd been there as I escaped. Had I killed a woman? "There is writing but I didn't understand it. I didn't have control. I left somewhere barren, somewhere I didn't recognise. A... a barn? A shed? I think. Abandoned, isolated, I needed to get us somewhere safe, but I..." My rising sense of panic made my voice pitch and wobble. I couldn't access any more.

The day vanished as my brain shut down.

The last thing I heard was Paul saying, "He'd have told them about the notebook..."

I WOKE WITH A MOUTH full of cotton wool and a brain full of barbed wire. I groaned, and the sound shifted a weight on the bed. Yes, a bed that felt, and smelt, familiar.

Peeling my eyes open hurt, but the light in the room lifted only a little from the darkest part of the night. I stared into the greyest of shadows near the window, and saw *him*. Not my djinn. The soldier. He stood in my home, my bedroom, with his rifle held across his body. Those eyes, they shone in the shadows, fox bright. They shone full of loss, fear, rage and, I realised, terrible grief. Terrible. As if sensing my awareness of his heart's misery, and the anger that intrusion caused, he lifted his rifle to his shoulder.

I heaved in a breath to scream a warning, to scramble from my bed—

"Hey, you're waking up?"

A body next to me and I turned. "Heather?" The ghost near the window vanished on the warm breeze huffing at the curtains.

She turned onto her side. "Don't panic, you're safe. We have a houseful, and Ella's worried because I didn't sleep much when you went AWOL. Eddie and Lilian have my room, Ella's in the office on the camp bed, Paul's on the sofa downstairs."

Most of what she said confused me, so I blanked it out. I blinked several times, my brain still trying to come online. "What's the time?" It sounded like I'd been smoking forty fags a day for my entire life.

"Early." Heather rose up enough to look over my shoulder at the alarm clock on my bedside cabinet. "05:30, so the rest of the house is asleep. How are you feeling now?"

"Better, I think." A rush of sorrow hit me from nowhere and tears stung my eyes, then escaped to slide over my nose and hit the pillow.

Heather reached out for my hand. "Hey, it's okay. You're going to feel really drained and emotional for a while. LSD can bring up a lot of trauma, so whatever drug you've been hit with is going to be worse. You were out of it yesterday when we found you."

"I need to talk," I whispered.

"Okay, do you want to talk here?"

I nodded. It felt safe. Heather wore leggings and a t-shirt, and I'd been stripped down to t-shirt and boxer pants. While she watched and listened, I talked. Everything I could remember spilled out: the desert, the djinn, the flashes of cooperation and my total surrender to the creature inside my mind. Heather made no comments, and there was no judgement.

"I think I killed them, Heather, but I don't remember anything. How can I kill someone with my bare hands and not remember? What does that make me?"

"A highly trained operative with a streak of self-preservation and something to live for?" she suggested. "I understand you're disturbed, Lorne, and I don't want you to think that giving into this djinn is a good idea, but it sounds like he saved your life and your mind. Can you imagine if you'd become lost in your trauma? He hid you, like…" She thought about it for a bit, then squeezed my hand. "It's like the way someone with DID behaves." The blank look on my face made her say, "Sorry, dissociative identity disorder. They have a dominant personality—that's you—then, there is the person who can cope with the bad stuff."

"What if that's what is actually going on with me? What if I'm going properly mad?" Fear curled in my belly. I didn't want to spend my life on drugs or living in a modern equivalent to a padded cell. Did they still have those? I couldn't be separated from the moor, from Heather and Ella.

She released my hand long enough to stroke the left side of my face. Her fingers were gentle, and the kindness released more tears.

"I'm scared, Heather."

"I can see that, but I don't think it's DID. I think you are genuinely haunted. That being said, you should see a professional psychologist just to make sure."

"They aren't going to believe I'm haunted. They're going to medicate me like they did in the hospital when I couldn't stop screaming."

"Then you take up Willow's advice and see someone who understands mediumship and spirit guides."

I felt my guts curl up at the thought of making myself that vulnerable to a stranger.

"Or we could get the thing exorcised? Ella could talk to the bishop. She'd need you to talk to a psychiatrist to make sure it's not a process that'll harm you, and then I guess we go Exorcist on you."

I chuckled. "You have such a way of giving me confidence in the process."

"I think we just need to wait it out, Lorne. I think LSD has a way of buggering up people's minds until you don't know if you're part of the Matrix or not. I've seen a lot of long-term users on many substances, from legal highs to crack."

"You ever done that stuff?" We rarely talked about her time with the bike gang, and I knew little to nothing about her life beforehand with her family.

"Some," she admitted. "I'm not proud of it, but I spent a lot of time trying to survive and being off my face helped. I like alcohol best though, so stuck with it in the end. You ever done it before this?"

"Once. My job—"

"Meant everything to you," she said with a smile, paraphrasing me. "That's good."

"It's also very limiting when trying to deal with the real world. All these emotions, all these people, decisions… I liked following orders, knowing my objectives and sticking to them. I feel really lost out here and I'm scared of the djinn. I shouldn't have been able to shoot those men in Scob. It was too easy. I couldn't do it in Credenhill during my last review."

"You were acting on muscle memory. You had no time to think, no time to brood or know fear. You had to stop them, or I was going to die. I don't think it's any more complicated than that. I don't think the djinn had anything to do with it. As for feeling lost… We all feel lost, Lorne. Out here in the real world. I know I do most of the time. You've given me a foundation I build from, but I know it could vanish any time. I just have to work hard to keep it and form a foundation of my own."

"I would never take our life away from you," I whispered.

It was Heather's turn for her blue eyes to swim with tears. "You're too good to me. Sometimes I wish I could hate you a little bit, then moments like this wouldn't hurt quite so much."

I frowned. "Hurt? I never want to cause you pain, kid." I hadn't called her that for days and it felt… odd suddenly. I lay in bed with a beautiful woman, not a 'kid'.

"Lorne, we need to talk—"

A phone rang beside the bed.

2 3

"THAT'S NOT MY PHONE," I said.

"It's your new phone."

"What?"

Heather reached over me. We were almost nose to nose as she reached for the bleeping annoyance. We both breathed in too deeply at the movement. She dragged her eyes from me to check the screen. "It's Paul." She swiped.

"I thought he was downstairs?" I struggled upright. Christ, my body ached, and dehydration made my head spin.

"Paul?" Heather asked over the phone. She frowned hard, removed the phone from her ear to check the screen, and put it back. "Paul? Answer me."

She hit speaker on the screen. A soft wheezing sound came out of it and birds tweeting with crows in the background. The dawn chorus a riot of sound.

"Paul, buddy, where are you?" I asked. He clearly wasn't on the sofa downstairs.

The phone murmured a soft sound. I almost caught it. "Repeat, Paul."

"Ella's." It sounded like the simple word cost him more than he could spare.

"Hang on, we're coming down now. Heather will stay on the line, she'll talk, I'll drive."

She looked at me. "Is that wise?"

"Probably not, but do you want Ella to see whatever's been done to Paul?"

"Good point. Get dressed and we'll text the others when we know more."

We dressed, scribbled a quick note to the others saying we'd gone to the village but not giving details, then ran to the truck. The drive down proved difficult for both of us. Heather trying to keep Paul conscious on the phone, me trying not to fall off the road with every corner. The world refused to remain predictable. Whatever they'd pushed into my body, it just kept rolling back, less intense with each wave, but still too strong to be safe.

We made it to the bungalow without bouncing off more than two hedges, and Heather clambered out of the truck. She ran across the lawn while I tried to make my legs move in the same direction. A body lay on the grass.

I dropped down beside Paul's head and what remained of his pretty face.

"I'm here, mate, I'm here," I murmured, while my mind started an injury assessment.

Broken nose for certain, split lips, possible break to the left orbital socket and cheekbone. One hand badly damaged and breathing shallow, too fast, and noisy—possible broken ribs. Legs lay at an odd angle, but he might not have moved since hitting the ground. No major blood loss covered the parched lawn. Just a beating.

Just? He's a friend, show some heart.

Okay, one helluva beating.

I heard Heather on the phone calling for an ambulance and explaining, not too patiently, that we needed help asap.

Paul's hand, the one not smashed, fluttered and his only visible eye rolled. "Lock—" the word barely recognisable.

I frowned and glanced down at his body. Bodily fluids stained his red jeans. His left hand fluttered over his front pocket.

"Okay, mate. Okay. Just keep still and save your strength." I stroked his head, the blood hot under my palm. I didn't want to see this, not in my current state.

Heather dropped down on his other side. "Hey, it's okay, Paul. You'll be okay. We're here now." She glanced at me. "Why don't you go and check the bungalow, Lorne? And find Paul a blanket, get us some water. We can't move him, but we can make him more comfortable."

"I should be here," I whispered.

"Not now. You're not handling this very well."

"How can you tell?"

"You look like you're about to puke all over him."

I grunted. "He has something in his pocket."

Heather nodded just the once. Her small fingers fished into the tight jeans and pulled something out, a chain with a pendant on it. She handed it over. I turned it over and pulled it apart. A USB of some kind.

"It unlocks your laptop?" I asked Paul.

He managed to close one eye.

I nodded. "I'm going to find you a blanket now. Have they left?"

Again with the blink. "Sorry…"

Heather made a small noise. "Never the fault of the victim, Paul. Never."

I had the feeling I'd regret my next question, but it popped out, anyway. "Someone did this to you?" I asked Heather.

The haunted look I received in turn said all I needed to hear. "Get some water, Lorne."

I nodded and rushed into Ella's bungalow. My insides churned and rolled, my heart ached, and my mind spun in crazy circles. I barely knew which way to turn or what to think. A sense of panic once more started to gather in my chest, closing my throat and lungs.

Dust and sand. Blood and bone.

I pressed my hands into the wall beside a picture containing the three of us, Ella, Heather and me, at a cliff face in the Cheddar Gorge.

Calm washed through the rising panic. The vision of a soothing wave rushing up a stony shore, tumbling pebbles, with the accompanying acoustic swish of gentle water, rose to calm my jittering mind.

Relax into your training. You know what to do next.

Did I? Clearly my mind had more faith in me than I did right now. The calming vision and sound helped, though. Next, a vision of the moor with a buzzard crying overhead and the wind against my face. I moved away from the wall and further into Ella's home. The place resembled a china shop after the invasion of the bull. Blood smeared the carpet where Paul must have dragged his body outside to be found, or he'd been dragged by someone else.

The beast woke for the first time. Snarled, snapped his mighty jaws, and the anger surged over the lingering effects of the narcotic cocktail still surging through my blood. I stepped between the smashed glass frames of a dozen pictures and tossed furniture. In the kitchen, I recognised the location of Paul's beating. The table stood, slung sideways, across the floor to hit the backdoor, which was obviously the place of entry, and the chairs lay scattered. I didn't touch anything, forensic evidence being in the forefront of my mind, and opened the cupboard I knew contained a few bottles of water in case of being cut off from the mains supply.

Ella didn't believe in bottled water generally. Between the plastic, cost of transport by truck and stealing it out of the ground, along with living in a country able to supply safe drinking water, she tended to rant about it if given the opportunity. I left the kitchen, walked into the small living room, fairly untouched, and took a blanket from the sofa.

Back outside, Heather sat on the grass and held Paul's undamaged hand. She spoke in a soft voice while stroking his hair back. Dawn coloured the sky a pastel orange and pink, and the birds continued to welcome another summer's day. I knelt beside her and covered Paul in the blanket while she moistened his bloodied lips. He looked better than when we'd arrived and managed to move a little.

"Steady, mate, you don't know what's been done to your back."

He managed a sort of lift towards a smile. "You've known worse." A hissed croak.

I nodded. "Maybe so, but they paid me to learn to take the hits. What the hell were you doing down here? You knew the farm was safe. You knew what they did to me." A flashback to the chair and I rubbed my scabby wrist, swallowing the fear and trying to box it away. The results could best be described as mixed.

"I got an internet call on the laptop. Said they wanted to meet. Voice was machine altered. I tracked the call, busted through the VPN, and found it routed through Ella's Wi-Fi." He coughed and bright red blood misted his lips.

Heather glanced at me.

I mumbled to her, "Don't worry, normal." I offered him more water. "You didn't think it might be a trap? They know you're a GCHQ boffin, mate. They lured you with the perfect bait—your ego."

"You wouldn't have let me go, would you?" he asked, his fingers flexing against mine.

"No, fella. I'd have come down here, weapons hot, and destroyed them. That's why they did it now. They know you have me back, and the state I'm in. Did they get the intel they wanted?"

Paul managed a slight smile, showing the damage to his mouth. He'd be paying a lot of money in the near future to revive that cheeky boyish grin. "I didn't bring it with me. All at the farm."

Alarm shot through me. Heather cursed.

"Don't panic, mate. They think I'm dead. In the house. They aren't going to the farm until dark. You have time."

I gripped his hand a little tighter. "Thank you."

"Lorne, what if they've planted something in your head?" he whispered.

The sound of an ambulance screaming through the lanes reached us. "I'll go to the end of the road and show them where we are," Heather said, rising and sprinting into the dawn.

"She's a good one, Lorne. She never gave up on you. I've never been loved like that." Tears leaked from his eyes.

"Maybe you never let yourself be loved like that, Paul. What did you mean by saying they might have planted something in my head?" Worry murmured bitter words of unknown vulnerability in my mind.

"It's what they did to some of the victims of MKUltra. Weaponised them. So the urban legends go. Be fucking careful, mate. Keep Heather posted and give her the guns."

Wouldn't the djinn know? Could I ask him?

Yeah, ask your imaginary friend if someone's turned you into the Manchurian Candidate, that sounds like a plan. Idiot.

The ambulance pulled up. "Listen, Paul. You're going to be taken to Musgrove in Taunton, I expect. They'll want you overnight at least and they'll call the police. Tell them to contact DI Mackenzie. She needs to talk to you. One of us will come to collect you when they release you, but…"

"You don't want anyone hanging around the hospital because it splits your resources in case they are using me as bait?"

We'd done this game before in Helmand. "Yeah."

"Find them, Lorne. Stop them. Whatever they are planning with these drugs they are making… men like you don't deserve it. *You* don't deserve it. Tell Heather, I'm sorry for being a shit. Get me evidence and I'll post it online—everywhere—and we'll close them down."

The emergency crew jogged up the drive towards us.

"Just rest, Paul. You just need to rest, leave it to me. I'll find out who's behind this and we'll stop them."

"Move away please, sir," said the burly paramedic.

I released Paul's hand and watched, Heather tucked under my arm, as he had a neck brace, back brace and arm sling put on before they lifted him off the lawn.

HEATHER DROVE US BACK TO the farm. She might not have a licence, but it turned out, she drove a lot better than I did on the way down.

When we reached the farm neither of us moved from the cab. The pair of us felt the weight of the last few days and the coming fight.

"How are you?" Heather asked.

I heard the question behind the question. "Truth? I don't know. I don't think I have it in me to do what we managed at Scob. I can't fight, I'm wrung out and I'm scared. Paul's worried I have some autosuggestion bullshit in my head."

Heather's eyes widened in alarm. "What do you think?"

I shrugged. "Who knows? I can't remember anything they did to me." I looked at my scarred hands, passive in my lap. "I have no idea how dangerous I might be to anyone around me." Our eyes met, and she reached out to lace her fingers with mine.

"You'll never hurt us, Lorne. It doesn't matter what they've done to you. Nothing could make you hurt us."

I wished I believed her.

We watched a couple of pied wagtails potter about the farmyard.

She said, "The reason I don't think you'd hurt us is just logic. I know a bit about hypnotism, Kicker was into it for a while to help with his esoteric study. I let him use me as a subject."

"Really?" I asked in surprise. "That doesn't sound like the kind of thing you'd do."

A self-deprecating smile. "I did say me and Kicker were good friends for a long time. I know I have trust issues, but he always looked after me. Anyway, he explained it all in detail and even the most susceptible people can't be made to do things they really don't believe in. So even if they programmed you to hurt us, you can't. Your training and emotions would prevent you."

"What about the people they did programme with MKUltra?"

She shrugged. "If that's what they did, then those people were already troubled and set against targets those people might be inclined to destroy. I mean, they'd think about it, never planning on acting on it, but the hypnotism made it possible for them to act."

"You don't think, even with the added drugs, I'd hurt anyone unless I wanted it?"

"That's my belief."

I raised an eyebrow. "Belief?"

She smiled. "I've always believed in you. That's not going to change. You will never hurt me."

I nodded. Not exactly satisfied, but what could we do about it? I didn't really know at what point the djinn took over. They might have held me for three days and released me, or I escaped at some point during the process by killing people. We just didn't know, and that scared me more than anything else I'd faced. Being betrayed by your mind, having it fracture and break under your feet, it took away a level of trust and confidence you never recovered. You became a reforged sword, a possible flaw in the blade that might cause it to snap again, no matter how skilled the blacksmith was at repairing the damage.

"Well, whether I'm safe or not, we have a job to do and that means explaining to all these people what's happened to Paul and that they need to leave the farm."

"We need more of a plan than that, Lorne. They're going to come after us. If nothing else, we know too much to be left wandering around the world. And what happens when they know Paul is alive?"

More staring out of the window took place while I thought about the problems facing us. "We can't be passive and let them come to us."

"No, they'll destroy us," Heather replied. "We need to take the fight to them."

I shook my head. "I don't think we can fight. I think we just need to find them, find evidence of the corporate influence and make it public. That's what Paul would do."

"We don't have Paul."

"He'll get fixed up and come back. He might be crap in a fight, but he's no coward, not really. He wants his mother's murderers brought in or dead."

Heather's fingers started to strangle the steering wheel. "When you vanished, and Willow found the bike. I..." She sucked in a breath and shuddered. "I kept seeing Peggy. I know I didn't really see her, but..." Tears made her big blue eyes shine. "I thought you—"

I leaned across the console and kissed her. "I didn't die and I'm home. We aren't going to lose each other, Heather. I promise you." She shouldn't have to deal with thoughts like this.

She nodded and fought back the tears. "Plan."

"Well... I have something of a plan."

"Tell me."

"Let's get the others up and I'll explain. Eddie should be able to help, and we need a very good map." I took the small USB stick out of my pocket. "And Paul can still help."

Heather grinned. "Let's take the fight to them."

24

WHEN WE REACHED THE KITCHEN, we found everyone up and Lilian using Ella as a sous chef for a mountainous breakfast. My stomach didn't rumble so much as cause an earthquake in its desperation.

"Hey," Ella said in welcome. "Where's Paul? We found your note."

"What's happened?" Eddie picked up on the body language straight away.

I told them. Ella sank into a chair. "My house?"

"It's secure, Ella. We'll help clean it up. The police will want in at some point. Eddie, can you liaise with DI Mackenzie?"

"Of course. How is Paul?"

"Bad, but he'll be okay. It's mostly surface damage. He needs some x-rays and there's a few broken bones in various places, but he'll live."

"Only because we found him," Heather muttered.

"Christ, this is bad," Ella said. "What do we do?"

"That's the thing. They know we have the intel they want. Paul couldn't keep it secret and he's not to blame for that. He thinks we're going to be targeted tonight."

"So we need to leave the farm?" Eddie asked.

"Yes." I tucked into the fry up Lilian had put down in front of me. The whole house smelt of food in a way it hadn't since mum died. It brought a lump to my throat until my stomach informed my throat to button it down and eat.

"Where do we go?" Lilian asked.

Eddie took her hand. "Don't worry, love, we'll B&B it until this is over."

I made eye contact with Ella. "You too. I want you well clear of this. Get yourselves down to Lynton. Somewhere busy with grockles crawling all over the moor."

Ella waved a hand. "I have services."

"You have a routine that could get you killed. Call your verger and get someone else in for Sunday services. I'm serious, Ella."

She nodded consent, but I made a mental note to check she'd obeyed. I didn't want her pacifying me now, only to discover she'd gone off somewhere I didn't know about and stumbled into trouble. Civilians rarely followed orders.

"The people that held me threatened all of you." I made meaningful eye contact with each of them in my kitchen. "They know we've been working together and you're all on their list. Until we stop them, we have to remain careful and vigilant. I don't know if I gave them a bloodied nose when I left wherever they held me, but even if I did, it won't stop them long."

Glancing at Heather, I said, "We have a plan."

"Don't tell me," Ella muttered, "it involves shooting someone." She glared at Heather.

"I'm not sitting on the sidelines, Ella. That's not who I am."

"Guns aren't always the answer."

"They are if they turn out to be part of the question." Heather's snapped reply surprised me.

I tried to pacify them. "We're not shooting anyone. Apart from anything else, I don't think I can be trusted with a weapon right now. I need to be on a range before I try anything in the field." I closed my fist on the table to stop the tremor. Visions of the Kill House at Credenhill flitted through my head and my failures. Dealing with Paul in the moment had been easy, but this— knowingly building a plan that could involve conflict—made my skin feel paper thin and my mind a wibbly-jitter of alarm bells.

I'd felt like this on the drive back to base after my dad's funeral.

A warm hand on my shoulder started to calm me, Heather once more sensing my distress. That drive had happened over four years ago. A lot in my life and mind had changed since then and I could do this. I could stop these people and expose their plans to the world. They needed stopping. Men like me needed protecting, not being constantly used until we were so broken we weren't safe to be allowed out in the world. If Winter Sun turned us into emotionless warriors, they'd never let us have normal lives for obvious reasons.

I took a breath and squared my shoulders. "I've been thinking about how I ended up on the beach at Porlock Weir. To end up there, considering the state I was in, I had to be somewhere close by. It's a safe place for me, but so is this, which means why didn't I come home?"

"Because you were held closer to the coast?" Eddie asked.

"Maybe. Or I had to stop because I hit the sea."

"So you think you moved in a straight line from that location to the beach?" asked Lilian.

Ella rose and vanished into the house. I heard her go upstairs to the office and knew she was fishing for the maps.

"It's a possibility. We also have that young scroat we caught at your place, Eddie."

"Young Pete Tucker," Eddie murmured, nodding. "He could be handy."

"So could the Polish bloke he was talking about," I said with heavier meaning.

Eddie nodded. "Tadeusz was his name, right?"

"Roger that," I said.

The former policeman rose and said, "Give me a minute while I make a few calls to the station down in Minehead."

"Why is he important?" Heather asked.

"Because the whole thing with Pete seemed off. He believed what he said, I don't doubt that, but this Polish farmworker who helped them? It's wrong. How did they know to find them in that pub? And why hire them? They have muscle. This Vlad, he knew how to fight, and he knew when to run."

"You think he's worked for them before?"

I shrugged. "I just think it's all been a bit too easy for the bad guys."

Eddie came back, still on the phone. "Yeah, okay, just hang on a minute while I put you on speaker. Kate, you're on with Lorne and the others."

A map appeared under my nose and Ella sat down, laying a hand on my arm in apology. I smiled at her and the worry in her face eased.

Kate said, "Hi all, not sure why I'm sharing, except I'm aware our resources are stretched, and I trust Eddie to help keep you all out of trouble."

All eyes landed on me. "Thanks," I said, trying to be diplomatic.

Mackenzie said, "So, we know now for certain the chaos at Minehead police station was nothing more than a diversion to keep us busy while the men in the hotel packed up and left. No one was supposed to know where they were in Dunster. It was you, Lorne and Eddie, that tracked them. We'd never have found them otherwise. They vanished during the night, leaving their bill paid for by a company called Heartcore."

"We know of them, Kate," Eddie said. "They're the ones trying to buy the cottage off us."

Kate took in a sharp breath. "Right. Well, they don't exist."

"We know that as well," I added.

"Then why are you wasting my time?" she asked with a distinct lack of amusement in her voice.

"Because we need to make sure we all have the same intel. I have a logo we'll email over, and we have Paul's notes to help us. I think Heartcore are on the moor somewhere and I think we might be able to find someone who can tell us where."

"Do you know what they want?" Kate asked.

I explained what I knew about the Winter Sun, who took over the MKUltra studies. "But to be honest, Kate, I don't remember much. It's all Hazy-Jane and not in a fun way."

"Let me get this straight. Your working theory is that the experiments from the Soviets and Germans during the Second World War led directly to the knowledge that the Americans, Canadians and British used for mind control experiments? The ones using LSD and anything else they could think of at the time? And Peggy's mother was the lead scientist on this, some kind of savant who kept a notebook?"

"Yes," Heather said.

"You have the notebook?"

"Yes, but it's in Russian," Ella said.

"They want the notebook because they are close to cracking the secret of making soldiers forget their trauma, enabling them to continue fighting long after most people would turn into cabbages."

"Yes," I said.

For her part, Kate seemed to be taking all this remarkably well. "You have no proof, do you?"

"Other than someone beating the shit out of Paul? No. And I don't know how much he's going to remember. We have the notebook and a sort of plan." Here came the tricky bit.

"What do you want from me, Turner?" Kate sounded very tired.

"Can you check a name on the system for us?"

"I'm not Directory Enquires."

I kept silent.

"Fine, let me login." Muttering ensued and some slanderous accusations about my parentage and military career. "Shoot."

"A Polish guy, name of Tadeusz. Works on the Quarme Hill farm called Ashcroft for the Tucker family down by Wheddon Cross."

"Any other name?"

"Sorry, that's all I have, but he's not afraid of a fight, is probably legal because he's worked for the family for a while. He's big, blond and in his early thirties. I can't give you more because it was dark."

"You left him in one piece?"

"He decided leaving my general area would be the best for his health."

She tutted. "Eddie, you need new friends."

"I think you might be right, Kate. Give us a call when you have something. We'll be on the move."

"Fine." She hung up.

Ella had the map on the table and found the breadboard to make a sharp edge. "It's a straight line from Quarme to Porlock Weir, but you'd have gone past here and Luccombe to get there. Why would you bypass both?"

I shrugged. "Maybe I just ran north? Maybe I worried about turning up out of my head? Maybe I just happened to end up at Porlock Weir? Maybe a part of me was heading for my old barracks. I don't know, Ella."

"You really can't remember anything?"

"Nothing. But I don't remember much after waking up in the hospital after Syria, so it could be all in the same black hole." I needed to move this conversation on. "What's the plan? I think we go to Quarme and find Pete, then Vlad, and ask them politely to give us all the information they have on the woman who hired them."

Ella's eyes narrowed. "Politely?"

"To start with," I said and grinned.

"Lorne..."

I held my hands up. "I promise I don't intend to hurt anyone."

"I'm going with you." Her hazel eyes turned hard, and she crossed her arms.

I laughed. "Absolutely not."

Ella scowled at me. "Bollocks to you, Lorne Turner. You're not dragging Heather down another rabbit hole as dangerous as the one she faced in Scob."

"Erm—" Heather raised a hand in protest.

Ella shot her a look. "No, you don't get to talk right now. I'm sick of the two of you behaving like a couple of Wild West cowboys, pretending the rules don't apply to you. They do, and the pair of you are going to get caught or killed. I found Peggy Cole dead in her home barely a week ago. Dead, Heather. Beaten to death by terrifying force. Can you imagine what these men would do to you if Lorne makes a mistake?"

I hadn't told anyone about Heather's culpability when it came to the dead man who worked for Prescott in Scob. No one needed to know he'd died because she smacked him with an asp. They all thought it was me and it needed to remain that way. The fault lay at my door because she shouldn't have been there in the first place.

I took Heather's hand. "She's right."

"What?" Heather looked at me as if I'd betrayed her by sleeping with the enemy.

"She needs to come with us, not to stop us, but to help. Vicars have a way of making people talk that Eddie and I can't manage alone. Not without hurting someone and," I looked at her with some of the confusion in my heart poking through, "I don't want to hurt anyone right now."

She breathed out and rubbed my knuckles. "Okay. Okay, I get it, we'll go together but you can't confront this Vlad on your own. You understand that, right?"

"I don't want to. I don't think I can."

Eddie rose from the table. "Right, well, I need to make sure my wife is safe, so if you don't mind, you can count me out."

We all gaped at him.

"What?" he asked. "I'm a retired copper, not a fucking martyr or superhero. I don't want these people finding us. I'll help now, but when you leave, we go in the opposite direction."

Lilian rose and crossed the room to her husband. "My love, I can look after myself. I'll go book us a room in Lynton and wait for you, as I have every damned shift for almost thirty years. Just make sure you come home." She kissed his poor old hang-dog face. "I love you, but you'll never live with yourself if something happens to them, and someone needs to help Ella keep SEAL Team Six out of the shit." She nodded at me and Heather.

He rolled his eyes. "Fine. But I'm not running after any bad guys. I don't want to give myself a heart attack."

"Alright, we have a team. Now all we need to think about is how to deploy our resources," I said.

Ella muttered, "I hate it when he uses army speak."

"I don't," murmured Heather with a flush.

Ella rolled her eyes. "I guess I need to go to the bungalow and find out how much damage has been done. Could you come with me, Eddie? Then we'll leave for Quarme."

25

WITH THE OTHERS GONE, I opened Paul's laptop, plugged in the USB, and waited for it to do something magical. Heather tutted and shoved me off the chair. She logged in without any effort. I stared hard at her.

She grinned. "I watched him whenever he looked for you so I could learn how to get in to his computer while he was asleep and keep looking."

"Ella's right, I'm a bad influence on you."

She leaned over and kissed me. It felt oddly intimate and beautifully casual all at once, like we'd been doing it forever and yet it was the first time for this kind of moment. We both looked a bit shocked and confused, like we'd missed several steps in the gradual increase of our romantic connection.

"Erm, I'll work on finding his translation. You find the paper copies he's made and see where he'd got to with it all," she said, now studiously not looking in my direction.

I hid a smirk, simply glad I wasn't the only one struggling to come to terms with our sudden, and increasingly dramatic, change in circumstances.

Rifling through the paperwork spread among the breakfast things on the table, I found the notebook, its hardback cloth blue cover marking it as mid-twentieth century. When I opened it, I found neat blue ink in Russian with English notations in a different handwriting, both in text and numerals. Formulas, they could be Egyptian hieroglyphs for all they meant to me, covered several pages towards the back.

It needed putting somewhere safe, so for the moment, I stuck it in my daysack hanging on the kitchen chair. I'd hide it with my assault rifles in the barn when I had a minute. Next, I gathered up the papers and started to examine them in detail.

The translations definitely looked like English, but I didn't understand them. The words blurred together to form a mess of chemistry, just like they did when I'd been in school. The only chemical reaction I understood, consisted of what made things go boom.

I was about to give up, when a name caught my attention. I remembered reading it in the letters Paul gave me that his grandfather wrote just after the war. *Bettina* headed up several sheets.

"I've found some information about Peggy's sister. The one who died," I said.

Heather glanced up from the screen. "Anything that'll tell you how to free her from the underground hell she's been locked in for the last seventy years?"

"What do you mean?"

She turned fully in the chair. "You don't think this is just about stopping the Heartcore company, right?"

I opened my mouth to say exactly that when she inhaled and exhaled in a way that made me realise I might be making a mistake. "It's a good place to start," I tried. Though I remembered my conversation with the djinn. He wanted the souls trapped under the hospital saved.

In return, Heather rolled her eyes and tutted. "Look, I'm not psychic, but I am sensitive to places and people. Kicker taught me. He knew a lot of my problems came from picking up errant emotions and sensing wells of unhappiness in the places where I found myself stuck. It's why I like the farm so much. Despite the graveyard, there's nothing sad here, or violent or soul sucking. It's why I understood what happened in Scob with Efa, Donne and Adams. Somehow, being around you makes it stronger and I'm starting to catch glimpses of things. Like the soldier we saw in the lane. It's the first time I've seen something so clearly, and that's down to you. Bloody scary but amazing at the same time."

I'd never really thought about it being amazing. Mostly, it scared me, because I thought I was going mad.

"Why have you never said?" I asked, slightly horrified by her ability to hide things from me.

"Because it's not a big deal, and it's nothing compared to what you go through. The thing is, Lorne, you're easily distracted by the mundane because it makes the world a simpler place for you. We need evidence to take to the police about this group who kidnapped you, I get that, but not once have you said anything about what we found under the hospital and how we help them." Heather studied me, watching for a reaction. I just didn't know what she expected.

"We have to prioritise the living and the safety of those involved," I said. "Besides, I've no idea what was under that place or what to do with it." I paused for a moment. "Did you... did you see the djinn?" I felt like such a numpty saying it aloud.

Heather considered the question for a few seconds. "I saw something. I felt a whole lot more. I caught a glimpse, nothing more, of a small shadow, a girl maybe, and something larger. I..." She frowned, checking her memory. "I think I saw the soldier again. I certainly felt rage and hate boiling out towards us. The safer I feel here, the more like home it becomes, the more open to this stuff I seem to be, it's like—"

"The barriers are dropping and it's letting more stuff in," I finished for her.

She nodded. "We can't just leave them down there."

"Why not?"

Heather's eyes widened in horror and she said, "Because they deserve some peace, and that little girl deserves to be with her family."

Her shock at my callousness made me defensive. "Heather, I'm not even sure how much I believe this stuff. Never mind how I'm supposed to deal with it. Surely, it's a job for a priest or something? Maybe Willow. I'm just an old soldier."

She threw her hands up in the air. "God, I wish you'd stop saying that.

You are not old, you're not just a soldier. Something magical woke up inside you, and it's giving you an opportunity to right old wrongs, save souls, and make a difference in the world."

I raised an eyebrow. "I thought being a soldier did that."

Her mouth tightened and thinned. "You know what I mean."

I did. I also realised I was being a stubborn grunt. "Okay, something needs doing about the dark under the hospital, but it has to wait until we've dealt with the more prosaic problem of actual human enemies."

"Good and don't for a minute think I'm going to forget." She crossed her arms and glared. Feisty and cute, I was doomed for sure.

"God forbid," I muttered, turning my attention to the paperwork in the hope it would close the conversation down.

I stared at the papers for a while without reading them, mulling over Heather's side of the conversation. Her knowledge and acceptance of the esoteric didn't come as a surprise. She'd been living on the edges of society for almost a decade and these things tended to go hand-in-glove. I just wished she'd told me about being sensitive to places and people. Much of her micro behaviours made more sense to me now. The way she hesitated around some people, locations, her rise in anxiety and anger, which often made no sense to other people, but it reflected my behaviour. We sensed layers in the world others didn't, and it made us vulnerable.

The obvious differences lay in training, background, experience, and age. Maybe gender played a part as well. I usually had greater control over my emotions. I also had a level of denial and ignorance which Heather wouldn't tolerate in herself. If her suppositions were correct, then being around me might harm her rather than help her in the long run. I hated this murky otherworld the djinn forced me to occupy by throwing visions into my head. I hated feeling places and dangers lurking. Even in the army, when it saved lives, I'd come to begrudge the talent because it meant I stood out from the men around me and somehow added to the increased isolation from my peers. I often sensed their emotional distress and grief, but couldn't do anything with the knowledge, and it became a burden.

"Stop mithering, Lorne, we don't have time," Heather said from behind the computer screen.

I sighed. "It means being around me hurts you."

She looked up. "You're an idiot. No, it doesn't and don't even think about using it as a way to push me out of your life because you think you are 'doing the right thing', and, 'it's for my own good'. I won't stand for it and it's why I haven't mentioned it until now. We are going to learn how to make more out of it, I just haven't figured out how yet. Now, what do those papers tell you about poor little Bettina?"

I scanned the documents. "Quite a lot, actually." Now I was paying attention, I realised Paul worked on these more than the other notations in the notebook. "She arrived in Britain in late 1948, just after Peggy was born. So it took them time to get her out. She only spoke German. They found her in an orphanage in Berlin. She was just three years old. They don't record who her father was, but I'm guessing that's not good news, considering what happened in Berlin after the war."

Heather blanched. "No, so let's not go there for the moment."

I scanned more information, mostly describing her physical details and state of health, which read like a list from someone suffering malnutrition and possibly starvation. The bit that interested me, lay at the bottom of page two. "It looks like they had concerns over her mental health, especially as she grew older. Behaviour problems like extreme tantrums, screaming so bad she'd make herself vomit, nightmares, then long periods of unresponsive behaviour, almost catatonic. The only person to impact on her was Peggy, by the looks of things." I frowned and muttered.

Heather asked, "That's a bad face. What's wrong?"

I tried to moderate the frown. "They started to treat her with the same drugs they used on the soldiers and other adult trauma victims."

"Oh. That explains a lot."

"Yeah." I put the papers down. I didn't need to read the details. It wouldn't mean much, and it felt like a form of invasive betrayal to be reading the sad and prolonged demise of a child I'd seen locked in that dark place.

"What have you found?" I asked.

"Much the same as you, more names and health records of men who they 'treated' with their cocktails. A list of regiments."

I scanned them and found the one I wanted, the 2nd Devonshire Regiment. The soldier had died in that hospital.

Heather said, "Many of them seem to have died. They had tuberculosis in the hospital. Maybe that's what killed Bettina. Thank God for vaccines," she muttered. "I'm now looking into what Paul uncovered about Winter Sun once he had that logo you described."

I rose and stood behind her, putting my hand on her shoulder and giving it a tender squeeze. "So what have we got?"

"Heartcore doesn't exist as such, this we know, but it seems it's a shell company attached to a large pharmaceutical conglomerate called Winter Sun and he's made a note here to say it matches the name of the project his grandmother worked on. They are American, but on their current board of directors, they have British and, get this, Russian investors. They've been active since the nineteen-fifties and Paul's made notes of what he thinks were projects pushed over to them when the CIA were caught doing bad things to people during the Cold War."

"Like MKUltra?"

"Among others."

"Do I want to know?"

She looked up at me. "Probably not, considering most of it is experimental stuff on soldiers with PTSD, from Vietnam onwards. It all reads like some dystopian capitalist hell. They even have stuff relating to the reprogramming of the Uyghur Muslims in China."

My knees turned into custard at the thought, so I sat beside her. "Does he know what was done to me?"

She flicked through more files. "I can't see anything but to be honest, Lorne, if he wasn't so anal about his labelling system, I wouldn't have gotten this far. I'm not a computer whizz like Paul. I just watched him for hours and I'm good at remembering stuff."

"You're doing great. I'd have beaten it to death trying to find the password."

"It's odd, because he's keeping all the intel on the USB drive, rather than a cloud."

"Air wall," I stated.

Heather chuckled. "Like you understand what that is."

"I can talk groovy geek."

She raised both eyebrows in surprise, and a burst of laughter filled the kitchen. "You really can't, Lorne."

We heard voices outside, and the pair of us moved away from the direct line of sight from the kitchen window. I headed for the backdoor, Heather moved to the knife rack. Then we both recognised Ella's voice.

She came into the kitchen, with Eddie and Kate Mackenzie in tow. Seeing both Heather and me on full alert made them all stop.

"Everything okay?" Ella asked.

"Fine," Heather said, peeling her hand away from Mum's carving knife.

"Where's Lilian?" I asked Eddie to distract everyone.

"Gone up to Bristol in the car to stay at Kate's place. Feed the cat, water the plants, until all this is over. It's easier for everyone if she's well clear of the area for the moment."

My stomach plunged in misery. "Don't suppose you can cook?" I asked Kate.

"Excuse me?" she asked. Eddie smirked.

I sighed, and so did my stomach. "Never mind."

She frowned at me but took off her jacket and ran the cold tap before finding a glass and making herself at home.

"Erm, why are you here, Kate?"

"I was in Taunton taking a statement from Paul."

"A bit of a lowly task for a DI," I said.

"Know much about police procedure, do you, Sergeant Major?"

Ha! She's got you there, fool.

"No. Not much. Is he okay?"

"Not at the moment, but he will be, physically at least. I think events are beginning to catch up with him, so if he has anyone close, they should be informed of his condition."

I glanced at Ella, who shrugged. "He's your friend."

"That was years ago," I said. "I don't think he has anyone close. He never mentions anyone."

"There isn't anyone close," Heather said.

I looked at her in surprise. "How do you know?" A curl of jealous fear snaked through me. Paul's handsome face and charming smile rose up from the depths, ready to strike.

"We bonded while you were gone and he apologised for being a dick, so I cut him some slack. He's okay once you stop him from behaving like a sixteen-year-old boy trapped in a man's body."

"Guess he'll be coming back here for his recovery then, unless he wants to go to Cheltenham. I'll talk to him once we've found you the evidence you need, Kate."

"That's why I'm here, a kind of unofficial sign off from my DCI to go for a bit of a poke about, to see what wriggles out of the stinky stuff. He can't sanction anything this tenuous, but we need a break. Right now, we have very little evidence that isn't circumstantial. Ella's place, despite the chaos created and Paul's blood everywhere, is going to be as clean of forensics as Peggy's cottage. We only found Monkey's prints and DNA in the cottage."

I glanced at Ella. "You seem remarkably calm."

She shrugged. "In the grand scheme of things, I'm just glad Paul's alive. Stuff can be repaired or replaced. I wasn't burgled, which is an oddly comforting thing after some of the crap I dealt with in London. Being gay and a female vicar tends to put a bullseye on your back regardless of people's, so-called, faith."

We'd had conversations about some of the prejudice she'd faced over the years, from her parishes and her peers.

"So, I guess we're ready to go to Quarme, then?" I asked everyone present.

26

THIRTY MINUTES LATER, A FEW arguments with my satnav, and some dismay from a wandering herd of sheep in the lane, we covered the ten miles from Stoke Pero to the outskirts of Wheddon Cross. The heat of the afternoon brutalised me. Heavy, thick, humid and brewing for a storm, it sat on the mind with all the subtly of a baby elephant. The heatwave would be ending with a spectacular thunderstorm at this rate. In the meantime, we all suffered.

I still didn't feel ready for driving. My ability to concentrate was shot to ratshit. I definitely posed a danger to the public, so Ella opted to drive me while Eddie drove Kate. With waves of the poison still rolling through my mind, I sat in the back of Little Gem, and tried not to be sick whenever the corners elongated and dips in the road turned into rollercoaster tracks.

Driving up an endless lane, the hedges dark green, the grasses brown from the sun's attentions, I watched the world drop away. Quarme Hill rose high over the area, and it opened up into a fine patchwork of small fields and hedges. The narrow lane ran straight over the ridgeline of the hill and a row of beech trees broke the view and the wind. Bracken filled the verges, its dark green fronds common on the moor. In the winter, I had no doubt the weather tore over this hill, ripping at the fields, just like it did over Dunkery and my farmhouse.

Both Ella and Heather stayed quiet on the drive, and I wondered why, but kept my counsel. We faced uncertainty, and I didn't have my usual resources to hand. In fact, I didn't have very much of anything to hand. I sat in the back of the old SUV and tried to remember something, anything, of the time I'd mislaid. When I returned to the last thing I did remember, the drugs being pushed into the back of my hand, a wall rose, and everything went dark.

Was the wall created by my mind to protect me from the potential deaths I caused? Or by Winter Sun, and their chemical cocktail?

I rubbed the back of my hand. A large bruise and small hole the only physical evidence of the cannula.

"You okay?" Heather asked.

"Yeah," I replied. What else could I say? I sure as hell didn't want to be alone at Stoke Pero, but I didn't think chasing dangerous people over the English countryside constituted the wisest of ideas, either.

The entrance to a farm lane opened up on our left, and Ella took the turning. Hard-baked earth led to a working farmyard in front of a large house. When I climbed out of the vehicle and looked around, I saw the evidence of a once wealthy property now struggling to keep a pack of starving wolves from its door. A fine nineteenth-century farmhouse, with lots of windows and a wild coat of wisteria smothering the south-facing wall, stood among a smattering of barns and farm vehicles. Everything looked tidy, but the stress of modern farming lay everywhere.

Age bit hard into the farm. The barns must have suffered under many storms, and the layers of repairs now looked desperate rather than just routine maintenance. The tractors, arranged as if parked in a supermarket, all wore the patina of rust and brutal weather. Trailers and farm equipment suffered the same, many with balding tyres and some with grass climbing the wheels.

The house itself looked to be in better condition, until you noticed the peeling paint and loose guttering, the wooden windows corroded by damp and the render on the walls cracked and missing under the beautiful ambling plant. The barns looked to be empty of cattle and sheep. I guessed they'd be out on pasture, or perhaps this farm concentrated on arable rather than livestock.

The views, though, they stole the breath. Rolling hills, coloured a hundred shades of green and brown, tumbled off towards a horizon dressed white-blue, bleached by the sun. Woodlands and hedges smothered the undulating hillsides, as if a giant lay asleep under the fabric of the earth and a blanket of chaotic wools kept him warm and docile. Not wild and rugged this land, until the harsh weather tore at it, but a long-tamed wilderness.

However, for all its bucolic charms, secrets and horrors lurked in the folds and creases of that giant's tumbling blanket, which is why we now stood watching three big men walk towards us.

Normally, I'd want to empty Stoke Pero of civilians, come here under the cover of darkness and see who or what crept out of the woodwork. Then I'd find some person, or thing, to exploit and get the answers I wanted. On this occasion, I didn't have operational control, DI Kate Mackenzie did and to be honest, her way was probably sensible—for the moment, at least.

One of the men walking in our direction I recognised. Vlad, the Polish man from the night I'd last felt like a soldier. The smallest of the three was Pete, and due to the family resemblance, I guessed the older version of Pete was his brother.

"Can I help?" asked the brother.

Pete glanced at Eddie and frowned. He'd been stressed and surrounded by enemies in the dark. He didn't immediately recognise Eddie or Heather, that would change fast. Unless I spoke, he'd not recognise me either. Vlad, though, he knew something unpleasant lurked in his near future. I moved away from the others, cutting off his best chance of escape. He'd have to run back the way he'd come now, and it would be down to who was faster, me or him.

Kate stepped up. "DI Mackenzie, we have a few questions. Nothing to worry about." She flicked open her ID.

Pete put a hand on his brother's arm. "It's okay, Rick, I'll deal with this. You go inside. Dad wants to talk to you about the top field and hedging."

To be fair to Rick, he looked knackered. "Fine, but if you're about to get arrested for doing something stupid, then at least come inside and tell Mum so she doesn't have to cook for you." He shook his head and strode off to the house. I felt for him, I really did. Farming could leave you wrung-out and empty.

Kate smiled the smile of a hungry croc, sensing a herd of buffalo nearby. "So, Pete, why would Rick think I'm here to arrest you?"

Pete opened his mouth, but all bets found themselves called-in when Vlad bolted.

The idiot chose to come in my direction. Going through me looked like the easy option in comparison to the others on offer. Fortunately, I'd been focused only on him, so when he sprang into action, I held my ground. He dodged to move around me, instinct taking him to my left, because the others stood to my right. I predicted his actions and stepped into his direction of flight. He made it very easy for me.

I grabbed his arm, used his momentum to turn him and pushed down on the back of his head to control his motion. We spun in a small circle, and he toppled over, face planting onto the hard surface of the baked farmyard. I followed him down, pulled his wrist up against my chest, locking his shoulder and knelt in the centre of his torso to keep him pinned and still.

"Nothing like giving the game away," Kate muttered. "Thank you, Turner."

"You're welcome, ma'am," I said in my best fake police voice. It sounded a lot like my normal voice, but the tangos didn't know.

Or rather, Vlad didn't. Pete looked at me with alarm and I smiled. This didn't reassure him at all.

Vlad started to squirm and curse, but Kate handed a set of plastic cuffs to Eddie, and he came over to restrain the fool.

She stood over us. "Tadeusz Szymborska, I am arresting you on an international warrant issued by the Polish authorities for murder."

Eddie and I turned to look at her in open astonishment.

Pete back-pedalled into Heather. She said, "Please remain calm, sir. I have a Taser touching your spine at the moment." He locked solid, and she winked at me.

"Why the hell didn't you warn me?" Eddie barked at DI Mackenzie. He hauled the big Polish lad off the ground with practiced ease. I didn't blame him for being angry. I'd be bloody furious if Kate's actions didn't suit my agenda so well.

Kate shrugged. "I was worried you'd insist on backup. When I found him on the database and I looked up the location of the farm, I knew it would be impossible to catch him if we came up here with the carnival. Like this, we have low impact, for a great result."

"Who did he murder?" Ella asked, looking shocked at the cursing oaf.

"Parents apparently. He's a proper little charmer. Involved in Neo-Nazi groups in Poland, likes to think of himself as a mercenary. Give me a minute. I need to read him what rights he thinks he has."

"Can I have him first?" I asked.

"No, Turner, you can't. Eddie, with me."

"We're having words about this," Eddie snapped at her.

"Think of it as a retirement present, Eddie."

My eyes settled on Pete. "You'll do for a start." Though now I had the chance to look at the lad properly, I realised someone other than me had set about him with fists and possibly more. Both eyes looked like they'd been coloured in by a demented five-year-old. A large bruise also covered his mouth, and he moved stiffly.

"I don't know nothing about no murders," he squeaked, Somerset accent thick again.

I took hold of his shoulder and propelled him towards the house. "Let's go find your dad and see what he has to say."

He balked, like an obstinate sheep. "No, I'm not going in there and causing my dad any trouble. He's not well. Do I know you?"

I remembered what Pete had said about his father being treated for Parkinson's. He was my age for goodness sake. "How bad is it?"

"They're trying to find medication to slow it down, but it's not working, just making it harder for him to function. He's really poorly. If you need to talk to me, you can do it out 'ere." Pete squared his shoulders.

Unable to help myself, I glanced at Ella, but it looked like she hadn't heard. She seemed very interested in watching DI Mackenzie doing her job.

"With me," I said, pulling Pete in the direction of the nearest barn.

Heather came in our wake, and I realised she'd brought the asp I'd given her. The shortened version is the perfect size to hold at someone's back in a threatening manner. Poor Pete wouldn't know it wasn't a Taser size or shape.

Inside the barn, I glanced around to make sure we remained alone. Nothing but small bales of hay and several large round bales of silage. The smell transported me back to my childhood like nothing else on this wide Earth. To be honest, it poleaxed me for several seconds, my brain tripping out with a series of images dredged from my work on the farm before the army took me away.

When I returned to the present I saw Heather, asp now extended, and Pete sat meek as a maid on a bale of hay beside her. How did that happen? I had no idea.

"You okay?" she asked.

I checked our surroundings again, uncertain whether I'd forced Pete down, or not, on entering. "Yeah, fine."

"You're the bloke from the other night, aren't you? The SIS man. You working with the police in daylight now?" Pete asked. He sounded depressed, exhausted, and hurt. The lad was in shit-state.

No one forgets the first time they meet a member of Britain's Secret Intelligence Service.

"Why don't I ask the questions?" I said, pulling another bale over so we could talk face-to-face. "Tell me about your dad. How is he?"

Pete shrugged, then rubbed his nose on his bare arm covered with thick black hair. I noticed more bruises covering the wiry frame. "They're hoping the change in medication will help in the long run, but I think Mum's given up. Why do you care?"

"I went to school with your father, Pete. I've known Martin Tucker for a long time. I don't work for SIS, well, not anymore, but I am worried about the trouble you're in and I'd like to help if I can."

His eyes welled up with tears. "You're not here to lock me up?" Pete might be into a bit of poaching, but hardened criminal activities went far beyond his understanding of the world.

"No, son. I'm here to help if you help me. I have the feeling you're in some trouble. Does your father know?"

Pete looked up at me with big wet brown eyes and almost sobbed. "I don't know what to do. I just wanted to help and the money…"

"Yeah, I know, the farm's struggling, your brother looks exhausted as well and your parents are sick of the worry. Let's see what we can do to help. How well do you know Vlad?" I used his nickname because frankly the shitbag didn't deserve anything else and now I knew he was up on murder charges, it seemed oddly apt.

"Vlad's been with us a few months. He knows how to farm, but he's bad with the animals. The dogs hate him, it's just he was cheap, and Rick gets on okay with him."

"But you don't?"

Pete shrugged. "Not now I don't." He touched his sore mouth and Heather winced.

"He do that because of the other night?" I asked.

Pete nodded and touched his belly. He didn't even realise the lad told me more with his body language than he ever could with words. I glanced at Heather and her face mirrored mine, concerned sympathy. We both knew what it felt like to get a good kicking.

"You want to know what he's been doing on the farm?" Pete asked.

I nodded. "I need to know everything. Lives are at stake, and I'm not bullshitting you. People have been murdered over what you were looking for in the hospital that night."

"Did you find it?" he asked.

I nodded. "We also found out what it said."

Pete stared at his hands, knuckles undamaged. The poor sod hadn't fought back. "We hired him from an agency. He had references from a company called Heartcore."

Heather hissed and swore, rubbing her hand over her short hair.

"Okay, then what?" I asked, swiping at the flies gathering around us now they had victims to plague.

"Then he just started work, like anyone else, but he's proper nasty. No patience with the cows. We stopped him milking in the end. Then he starts asking about the holiday homes we have down the other side of the farm. They're the only thing that makes enough money to see us through most months. The milk prices—"

"Bad, yes, stay on topic, Pete. We don't have time to debate the price of milk or lambs right now."

His shoulders hunched a little more, and I felt like a bastard. Not enough of one to apologise, but still.

"He said he wanted the holiday lets. He'd pay a good price for them. There's three cottages down there, some nice barns for parking and stuff. Much nicer than home, we put a lot of money in them in the hope they'd save the farm. Trouble is, the people that's moved in, they don't look like grockles."

"Big men with suits?"

"Big men with suits and guns," Pete admitted. "There's a couple of women staying with them. The one from the pub I told you about. I've gone into the woods behind the gardens and watched 'em." Then he realised what he'd said and glanced at Heather. "Not in a pervy way, mind. Just cos I was worried about them."

"What about the story you told me and DS Rice about the woman in the pub?" I asked.

"That's all true. It's only now I knows it's all connected. Rick says I'm too thick to be a doorstop sandwich."

Heather snorted a laugh. "I like Rick."

I glared her into silence and received a one-shouldered shrug in response. "You're not stupid, Pete, just naïve. There's no reason to think any of this is your fault. Though, I am going to need your help."

"Me?"

"I need you to get me into a position where I can watch those cottages as well. Can you do that?"

He glanced at me and at Heather. "Erm, yeah, sure, but why?"

27

WE NESTLED AMONG THE LATE summer undergrowth, trying to ignore the dive-bombing bugs and those that crawled, watching the rear of three small holiday lets in a scrape designed for one. Their natural stone walls and red-tiled roofs marked them out as labourers' cottages. I guessed they'd been built when the big farmhouse made serious money. Now I wondered how the Tuckers would keep at the farm beyond the next twelve months. These had serious earning potential if they marketed them correctly.

Seems I'd learned quite a bit from Willow and Heather about marketing a business. It felt good.

Pete drove us through the lanes to our observation point, the final hundred metres done on foot through the back of the woods that arced around from the lane to the cottages. On the way, he told me how deep in the slurry pit his family found themselves. Heather kept quiet, but she watched our surroundings with a care she'd learned from me. To be honest, I struggled to maintain concentration on Pete's ramblings. He seemed anxious to redeem himself and tried to justify his decisions. I could have done without either, but knowing the noose the Tuckers faced made me sympathetic.

The small defile we currently occupied meant I lay between Heather and Pete. Despite the scrape, we were higher than the cottages, so the view proved to be a fine one.

"Can't the National Farmers Union help?" I asked.

Pete shrugged. "What makes us different from the other thousand farms in trouble this week? The NFU are doing what they can, but we're a leaking sieve."

"You need a business consultant," Heather said, squirming and cursing at another bite.

Pete peered around me. "What, like an accountant?"

"No, not like an accountant. They will go through your accounts and everything you own."

"My dad won't allow that."

"Then he's an idiot," Heather said. "You have any number of assets on the farm and its land. If Lorne had brought in a business consultant before selling everything off and still ending up with a massive mortgage, he'd have made far better decisions. Farmers are stubborn and think they know best, you don't. You have an emotional history with the land and that makes you vulnerable. You need a clear eye and a sensible plan." She lifted the binoculars Pete had found for us to stare at the cottages.

"How the hell do you know about business consultants?" I asked.

"My father is one."

That was the first time she'd ever mentioned him willingly in my presence.

"Okay, and farming?" I asked, a little afraid she'd say something about him working for the Duchy of Cornwall or something.

"Exeter, rural city, he specialised in rural businesses. Focus, Lorne, we have movement in the centre cottage, upstairs window on the left." She handed over the bins.

I wanted to know more about her family, but with Pete breathing down my neck, now wasn't the time. Watching the cottage, I saw the same thing Heather did, several people moving around in a small space. That odd tingle began in my spine and my teeth ground down on sand.

"Lorne? You okay?" Heather whispered, putting a hand on my arm.

"Yeah, but these people are something to do with all this. I know it."

"You don't think you were held here?" she asked.

I shook my head. "No chance. There was water on tap and a drain for cleaning up set into a concrete floor."

"You sound like you're talking about a cow shed," Pete said.

I turned to look at him. "You're right. I am."

"We have one that's been condemned so we can't use it for the cattle, but Vlad's been talking about growing weed in there." Pete didn't sound happy about the prospect, and I didn't blame him. Any mass production on a farm meant you lost your home and your business if caught. The fines alone crippled any who tried it out of desperation.

"They tortured you here," Heather said, taking the bins back off me.

Pete started yammering at the mention of torture, but I tuned him out.

"I need to get down to the cottages, see if we can hear or see anything that gives us an edge," I said.

"Kate said not to get involved and you're in no fit state for a fight," Heather pointed out. "I'll go."

I laughed, which earned me a hard glare. "No, Heather."

"They'll never suspect me, and I can say I wandered down there because I've found myself lost and I can't find the car."

"They know who you are. There's no way I'll sanction you going down there alone."

"I can go with her," Pete said. "She can be my girlfriend and I'm just the owner's son asking if they need anything."

"No," I almost shouted. "No girlfriend bollocks."

Heather's mouth twisted in amusement, but she had the good sense to say nothing. Pete looked disappointed. I regained control of my desire to strangle Pete and took the bins off Heather. I scanned the lane in front of the cottage, looking up and down the thin strip of tarmac, and smiled.

"Oh no, I know that smile," Heather murmured.

"It's the Merc SUV we saw at Eddie's place," I said, handing the bins back to Heather.

I watched the vehicle race, at a speed indicative of panic rather than controlled urgency, and pull up outside the cottage.

"Give Pete the glasses. Pete, I need you to ID the woman that'll come out."

Pete focused and gasped. "How did you know?"

"Experience. Lots and lots of experience. We've rattled the snake's cage and now she's going to strike." I squinted against the sun. A woman with three minder types stepped out of the big black SUV.

"It's her," Pete whispered.

I snatched the binoculars off him and looked. "You don't want the sun glinting off the glass, son. Makes you easy to spot. I'd have thought a poacher would know that."

"I don't have much call to go out during the day, Mr Turner."

"Don't suppose you do," I said. "Heather, can you hear anything?"

We watched the woman and her entourage enter the middle cottage and no amount of double glazing could hide the almost immediate verbal explosion.

"She's not a happy woman," Heather said. "I can't make out much, but seems they've discovered Paul's in hospital and the police know about it. You really are as deaf as a post, boss."

"Try being blown up a few more times and having an SA80 rattling through your head on a daily basis. See how well your hearing works," I muttered, watching through the bins again.

"You've been blown up?" Pete asked Heather.

I felt her swell with pride at my side and tried not to grin, leaving her to handle his awe.

"Only the once so far, but I'm an Army Reservist now so..." She shrugged with casual decadence.

"They're leaving," I said. "Time we went to find out what's going on in the lion's den. Pete, do you have a key?"

"Not on me, but I know where the spare is kept. We only tell guests when they've been foolish enough to lock themselves out."

We waited for a few minutes as two women and six men left the cottage. The smaller woman caught my attention. My breathing sharpened, and the world lurched to the side, just enough to make my stomach roll.

"Lorne?"

"What?" I flinched, making her wince.

Heather touched my arm. "They've left, boss." Her concern made a flash of anger warm my skin.

I blinked. No vehicles. I'd lost several minutes. "Let's move out." I didn't look at Heather, couldn't bear the thought of her pity as she figured out my broken mind had absented me from the game. I didn't need understanding or sympathy.

I led them through a narrow field and into the garden from an angle. Pete knew enough to stick to the hedge line and stay in the shadows. We didn't know if someone remained in the cottage and if I had to deal with multiple x-rays, I'd rather they stayed unaware of us for as long as possible.

With no alarm called, Pete found the spare key in the log pile, and we entered the kitchen of the middle cottage.

"I'll do a sweep of the premises. You check the table," I said to Heather.

Small and compact this kitchen. A table just large enough for four chairs stood against one wall, the rest of the room filled with a modern set of units from any DIY store. Heather handed me her asp, and I flicked it open. Pete made to move with me, but Heather put a hand on his arm and shook her head.

"He's better off without you cluttering up his space," she explained.

The kitchen opened straight into a lounge with a nice log burner in a traditional fireplace and a good quality three-piece suite. The interior of this house stuck with plain fabrics and paintwork, but everything looked bright and very clean. They'd spent good money on the things that mattered to grockles, a nice TV with a satellite box, a good-looking log burner, and nice carpets. The artwork represented the moorland at its romantic best and didn't overwhelm.

I saw evidence of the people staying in the cottage, but not much. Professionals didn't tend to leave anything lying about: we trained to be tidy and private.

Taking the stairs with caution, I made it to the landing without incident. To be honest, my gut told me we were alone, and I'd take that instinct to the bank every time. Three doors faced me, and I guessed one was the bathroom, and numbers two and three were the bedrooms.

"Lorne," Heather called.

"In a minute."

"No, now."

She knew better than to interrupt a sweep of an unknown location. What the hell had she found? I ignored her request and opened the first door, bathroom, clear. Second door, twin bedroom, clear. Third room, I pushed the door open, stepped up and the damned thing smacked back into me so fast I didn't have a chance to protect my face. The wood bounced off my forehead, saving my nose because I'd been looking down at my feet for some reason. I stumbled backwards, dazed and shocked. Why no warning? Why hadn't my famed instinct kicked in?

"Fuck," I growled.

A big shape filled the doorway and came at me, smooth and sleek as a young tiger. I back-pedalled, balance shot, vision blurred. A heavy fist landed on my head, and I failed to block it. Another landed deep in my guts, knocking the air out of my chest. I dropped to the ground, the asp clutched in my hand but my brain unable to tell my arm what to do, the scramble of visual stimulus too fast.

"No!" screamed Heather.

The shape moved away from me.

"Run, little girl, because I will not be beating you, unless you deserve it," said a deep voice, a naturalised American accent.

I heard footsteps. Heather coming to the rescue. He'd kill her, or worse.

Time slipped sideways. Something inside me moved. Dust and sand filled my mouth, but no dread. I went away…

"LORNE?" A GENTLE HAND ON my arm. "Lorne, give me the asp. You can stop now. It's okay. I'm okay."

I blinked. I stood at the bottom of the stairs. A man lay at my feet. Face bloody but he groaned. His lower left leg didn't look right.

"What happened?" I asked, dropping the weapon in Heather's hand.

"You did. He came for me before he finished you off and... well... you smacked him in the leg, then gave him an uppercut with the handle of the asp in your fist. He bent over. You hit him with a strike to his spine before pushing him down the stairs. I jumped out of the way so he didn't crush me."

"You okay?"

"Yes, you don't remember?"

"I didn't know he was there. I didn't feel him. Why didn't I feel him?"

"Lorne, do you remember what you did?" she asked me, peering into my face.

"No." I shook my head, catching sight of Pete in the doorway to the kitchen, mouth open, eyes wide. "Why don't I remember?" Fear curled in my guts, real fear.

Heather's small hands fished about in my combat shorts until she found my knife and the ubiquitous piece of bailing twine I always seemed to have in a pocket. "Go into the kitchen with Pete. I'll sort this idiot out, so he doesn't choke on his tongue." With shooing motions, she forced me into the kitchen.

Pete backed up to the furthest corner away from me. No way you'd have room to swing a hamster, never mind a cat.

"You demolished him," Pete burbled.

"Training."

"You weren't going to stop."

Wasn't I? I swallowed and tried to focus on the intel laying all over the table. It blurred together as unaccustomed emotions lay siege to my barriers of manly honour. Shuffling pages around didn't make much difference, and I soon gave up.

"Check the computer," Heather yelled from the front room.

I glanced at the laptop on the table and drifted a finger over the touchpad. It woke with startling clarity. Email web browser, but the kind Paul used, not the domestic variety.

The words, 'They are at the farm, undefended, they have Szymborska' glared at me from the screen.

"Oh shit."

Heather strode in. "Oh shit is right. We have to get back. They must have a drone over the farmhouse to keep eyes-on."

A switch flipped back in my head. The confusion vanished under a wave of training. "Fastest way back to the farm," I snapped at Pete.

"Across the fields."

"Can we make it in the truck?" I asked, already moving to the door.

"Yeah, I guess."

Heather and I tumbled out of the cottage and ran towards Pete's old Land Rover Defender. We'd parked it behind a large logging pile. Pete struggled to keep up with the sprint Heather set.

"I'm driving," I said, holding my hand out, breathing hard but even.

They both looked concerned about this decision.

"Who's had the most training in combat situations on Salisbury Plain where we spend all day in these things being chased by tanks?" I asked.

Pete handed over the keys, panting. Heather pulled out her mobile phone and speed dialled Ella. I gunned the engine.

"You have stock in that field?" I asked, nodding to the one on the other side of the line.

"No, it's arable, big, no hedges. Why?"

"I'll owe you a gate."

"What?" Pete asked from the back.

I knocked the old Landy into second gear and slew her around in a tight arc. We smashed into a fairly new five-bar gate. The headlights exploded. Pete yelled in protest. I ignored him and threw the Landy into third. With the hot weather baking the big field and the wheat stubble giving me clear tractor tracks to follow, we flew towards the farm.

"I can't get her on the phone," Heather said, panic in her voice.

I didn't say anything, just cursed my stupidity. I knew we'd arrive too late. Why had my instincts broken down? What the hell had they done to me? Being too broken to be an effective soldier was one thing, but being so broken, I couldn't save my family...

My foot grew heavier on the throttle, and we raced over the brow of the hill. The farm lay before us, and I aimed for the other gateway. This one, fortunately, stood open.

"Brace," I yelled.

Heather followed the order. Pete wasn't so lucky. I slammed on the brakes, and we shuddered to a halt, the ancient ABS kicking in on the dirty farmyard surface. I saw Kate's car, Ella's SUV and a police van.

"Ella!" Heather screamed, tumbling from the still shuddering vehicle.

Banging started on the side of the police van. Heather ran to the back. I clocked something more disturbing. Vlad lay in a pool of fly infested liquid beside the old seed drill, the turning blades splattered with blood and brain matter.

The back of the Transit van opened, and Kate stumbled out. "I need a phone," she barked.

My mobile rang with Ella's ring tone. Heather looked at me. I nodded, and she handed over her mobile to Kate. We needed the cavalry.

I took the call. "Where is she?"

"Lorne Turner, you are something of a pickle for us. It seems you have more lurking inside that mind of yours than I bargained for, such a shame we didn't have more time to play. We only want the notebook, then we'll leave you and your people alone." A woman's voice. *The* woman's voice.

I swallowed a lump in my throat. "Fine, you can have it, but I need proof of life." My heart froze hard, and the beast rose, shaking off the cobwebs and dust to snarl and snap.

A pause. "Lorne?" came Ella's voice.

"I'm coming."

A soft cry came from the phone before the female voice I recognised said, "You know the drill, soldier. I promise not to inject her with anything too nasty, and you bring me the notebook."

"Where?"

"Well, that's the thing. I need you somewhere secure, and we aren't in an environment I have control over, so I'm opting for the old hospital. It'll have a room I can lock you up in. You've made quite enough of a mess of my people and plans. Come in, unarmed, and without your girlfriend, let us leave with the notebook and I'll make sure you can find your vicar friend."

I snarled down the phone.

"Use your words, Turner."

"Agreed." What choice did I have?

The line went dead. I stormed towards the Land Rover. Ella had the keys to Little Gem in her pocket so I couldn't steal that, but my daysack sat in the front foot well. I retrieved it and the notebook. Heather came towards me.

"Get in the Landy. I'm driving. Your job is to keep me focused."

"The police…" Heather said, glancing at Kate. I'd never heard her voice have that waver of doubt. It made a shudder go through me like an ice bath.

I stared at her. "You don't trust me?" She'd never side with the police over her confidence in me under normal circumstances.

Her hesitation said it all.

"Fine, stay." I climbed in the big Landy.

"Fuck it," she growled. "Even on a bad day you're better than the wooden tops."

The wave of gratitude for her trust in me felt a little humiliating. So many damned emotions demanded my attention, and they confused me. I needed to focus on one thing—retrieving Ella.

Kate moved to stand in front of the Landy as we climbed in. "Oh, no you don't, Turner." She put a hand on the bonnet. "I'm calling in the armed response unit." Eddie stood behind her, they both had bruises on their faces and Kate held her side. The two young, uniformed police officers called in to help with Vlad's arrest looked unhurt but shaken.

My guess? The tangos had pulled up, waved guns around, a small scrap ensued, hurting Ella, Kate and Eddie, all of whom were unarmed because I hadn't been there. They'd been cowed and Vlad was shot to prevent him talking, making everyone compliant when the van arrived. In order to escape, the tangos then forced everyone into the van and locked it, taking Ella with them. The most obviously compliant hostage and the one person they knew would motivate me into obeying their instructions.

"If you don't get out of the fucking way, woman, I'll drive over you," I said out of the open window.

Eddie grabbed her and pulled her out of the way. "Let him do his job, Kate. It's her only chance. Turner, you'll find a little something special in the caravan under my side of the bed. Key taped under the table we've been using. Don't break anything, Lilian will kill you."

"Thanks," I said. "Get the ARU to Eddie's place but keep them quiet if you can, I'll need back-up when they run," I said turning to Kate.

"And what if they kill you?"

I shrugged. "Then I'll be dead, and you'll have operational control over a manhunt." I shot out of the farmyard and into Quarme Lane. In the rear-view mirror I saw them helping Pete's father and mother out of the police van and his brother who hugged Pete. It gave me a brief moment of something like pleasure.

The beast though, he knew only one thing would make me happy. The voice on the phone, the voice from my imprisonment, silenced, forever.

28

HEATHER STAYED QUIET BESIDE ME, doubtless thinking about our escapade in Scob and how close she came to losing her life. We raced through Wheddon Cross, going at a speed designed for rally driving, rather than speed limits. By some miracle, everyone kept well out of the way, even the grockles.

"We'll need weapons," she said, holding her seatbelt tight to keep still.

Huh, okay, I was wrong.

She continued, "We don't have time to get back to the farm to collect the guns."

"Eddie implied he had something in the caravan," I said, overtaking a tractor on a blind bend making it swerve to avoid knocking us into a ditch. My blood hummed, and my focus was almost superhumanly sharp. This switch from my previous emotional muddle came as a relief. I didn't enjoy being vulnerable. I couldn't afford to worry about anything other than Ella's survival. These people beat Peggy to death and thought they'd done the same to Paul. They'd also killed Monkey and Vlad.

Heather snorted in derision. "Eddie's idea of a weapon may well consist of nothing more than a baseball bat."

"Which can be a very effective weapon."

"Not against an assault rifle, Lorne."

She had a point.

"I have the notepad, that's all they want. I'll do a simple exchange and we'll get Ella back."

Heather grunted. "You don't really believe they'll let us leave, knowing as much as we do?"

We slumped once more into silence. I powered the old Landy, rattling and bouncing, around the bottom of Dunkery Beacon, heading for Luccombe. Only ten miles, give or take, but each mile wove through narrow single track country lanes with horses, bicycles, tractors and day-trippers all conspiring to turn me into a sweary angry man.

We screamed up the lane, through Luccombe and into the small hamlet of Horner, Eddie's place arriving on our left. I hand braked into the gate, and we shuddered to a halt, the old Landy taking a deep breath and relaxing. I shouldered the door open only to have Heather pull on my arm.

"Wait, we need a plan. For all you know, there's a sniper out there in the field, or taking cover in the cottage."

"They want the notebook," I repeated, still half out the door.

"For God's sake, just think for a minute, Lorne. They can take the notebook from your dead body, just as easily as from your living one." Heather's exasperation covered her fear. "You aren't firing on all cylinders. Please, just give yourself a little time. Ella needs you on your game. We know they have multiple hostiles in play, highly trained, armed men. These aren't hired security like Prescott had. These are professional soldiers, real mercenaries."

I looked at her, assessing her panic. "You don't trust me?"

"I don't trust what they did to you." The words blurted out of her, then her teeth clamped tight on her bottom lip, hard enough to turn the soft skin white. "Sorry," she whispered.

"There's nothing I can do to make you trust me—"

"Lorne," she pleaded, "I trust you. I'm just worried about what you'll be walking into, and I have no way to protect you, or Ella, if something goes wrong. What happened in the cottage just now wasn't you, and I don't know how to deal with that. Please…"

Throwing myself back into the driver's seat, I stared out of the window. We both sat and sweated while I pondered options.

"You're right. I'm not thinking straight. We have no intel on what we'll be facing and no weapons." I pulled the daysack out of the footwell at Heather's feet and hugged it to my chest. "I don't give a shit about the formulas, and I don't care much if they escape with the notebook. I have to get Ella back and keep you alive. That's all I want."

Heather relaxed a little. "Okay, so, my thinking is, if they want the exchange at the hospital, maybe they know something about what's under it. Maybe they know it'll unsettle you, make you vulnerable."

"I'm already vulnerable. I think they're using it as the exchange point because they can keep hidden under the canopy of trees from drones they don't control. They can set observation posts in the ruins, and they'll be hard to spot in the gloom of the woodland. They are also desperate enough to go looking for more intel in the rooms underground. Maybe the woman who injected me wants to look at the place before they bug out. She's obviously one of those in control."

"All valid points. So what do we do about them?" she asked, relieved by my detailed assessment.

"We need to see what Eddie has before we make any decisions. Come on." I debussed and Heather followed suit. We jogged up to the caravan. I ducked down under the table and found the spare key taped to the underside. Letting myself into the small, neat interior of their sleeping caravan, the heat inside suffocating and humid, I fished about under the bed. My hand closed over a metal box.

"What have we got here then?" I murmured, pulling it out and putting it on the small table. I opened it and found a Taser. "Damn, Eddie, you naughty boy."

"Not much use," Heather muttered. "I hoped it would be something with a bit more gunpowder."

"Give me the asp, you take this. I don't want you anywhere near here without a decent personal protection weapon."

"I'm comfortable with the asp, Lorne."

"It's great for close work, but I'd rather you stop someone from a distance." I hesitated before adding in a quieter voice, "Also, if I trip out, you might need to hit me with it before someone gets hurt. Better this than the asp. I'd never let you hit me with that."

Her face crumbled up. "I couldn't—"

"You can, I know you can and I'm trusting you can. Paul was right. There might be something lurking in my head I don't know about. Please, Heather. It'll make me feel safer." I offered her the dull, black, gun-looking weapon with a bright yellow business end.

She sucked in a breath of hot air and nodded, picking up the weapon with obvious reluctance. Then she handed over the asp and I tucked it into the belt on my old combat shorts. I found our radios on the small surface designed for a quick cuppa in the mornings and handed one over. Heather fitted the earpiece in, and we did a quick comms check.

"You want me to take the left flank?" she asked.

I nodded. "Report what you see, scout where you can, but most importantly, don't get between me and any weapons they have. I'll find a way of ensuring they don't have all the advantages once I'm close enough to Ella and can make a real assessment."

Heather nodded, but rather than look like the bedraggled elf of mischief I'd fought alongside in Scob, her expression remained worried and scared. All this began with the death of an elderly friend, and it made everything too real. Violence had a habit of doing that. The more you interacted with it, the more it scared you unless you had some control over the situation. Right now, we had no control and everything to lose.

Clasping her face gently, I looked into those blue eyes. "You mean a great deal to me, woman. Don't get hurt. Trust your instincts and keep me safe."

Heather, eyes awash and shining a blue I'd only ever seen in the deepest glaciers, leaned in and kissed me. So many words found themselves shared in that brief moment.

Breaking contact, she turned away, and we left the caravan.

JUST PAST THE BARBED WIRE fence, Heather and I parted company. I watched her for a moment as she blended with the trees and undergrowth, her slim form becoming one with the woodland. With her as safely out of the way as possible, I glanced over my shoulder at the graveyard. Storm clouds gathered over the distant hills above Tivington. Mean, rolling monsters pushing the hot air around in sullen protest. The sun continued to blare down on the valley, silencing even the most enthusiastic of birds in the hot afternoon. The promised storm approached, but would it break its back on the Beacon or roll onward?

Coming up here, I felt nothing, no warnings, no whispers, no dust and sand, no dead soldiers. Had I been cut off from my internal self? All soldiers in The Regiment develop a sense for danger in situations most people would find mundane. Our senses tuned in, working with such clarity the world became hyper-real, and never really became normal again. Mine reached beyond that point. In combat, we'd know clearing a house might mean facing a bomber behind a door, but I seemed to know which door and what lay beyond. That's the instinct my unit trusted, that I trusted. What if the cocktail of horror injected into me had burnt it from my mind?

"It doesn't matter, Lorne, you have to go in there and face the monsters. Ella needs you," I muttered, stepping into the woodland and handing my immediate future over to fate.

I checked my surroundings once more, and with a firm step, walked through the trees.

The green dark closed around me. The atmosphere cooler, but more stifling than ever. Insects droned in the dull light and the undergrowth stirred with resentful rustling as I passed. I kept the asp in my belt, under my blood-stained t-shirt and walked slowly, but fully, into the open. The daysack on my back caused a small tsunami of sweat to fall down my spine. I walked over the metal fence without making it bark in protest, and the hospital came into view. I hadn't seen any sentries thus far, but knew they'd be here somewhere.

I spotted them standing outside the broken entrance. They looked like clones from a GQ magazine Spetsnaz Special edition. Clearly aware of their surroundings, they stood with AR15s, the ArmaLite weapon as familiar to me as the SA80 I'd first been trained to use.

The moment I came into view, they turned to look at me and raised their rifles in well trained unison. I lifted my hands away from my body.

"I'm unarmed," more or less, "and have the notebook."

The man on the right stepped forwards. He called out, "Come into light, lift shirt and show us you carry no weapon. Then open bag and empty it on ground."

"No."

He looked confused. "You do it," he said, Russian accent strong.

"No, not until I've seen the vicar," I said.

"That not deal."

"It is now. Take me in or bring her out."

"What if I shoot you now?" he asked, dropping his eye to the scope on the rifle and taking aim. His finger remained on the side of the weapon, rather than the trigger, so I gambled on his intention to shoot me.

"Then you'll never know where the missing pages in the notebook are," I called out, wishing I'd thought to stash a few pages somewhere in Eddie's ruined cottage before coming up here. Heather was right, my game fell well short of safe. "You think I trust you to let us go? I'll tell you where the final pieces of the formula are, once I have Ella and I'm out of the way of your weapons." I nodded towards the AR15 in his very competent grip.

"Lift t-shirt."

I did as instructed, and turned in a circle, holding the daysack out from my body so they could see everything clearly.

"Walk," GQ number one ordered.

I stepped forwards.

The radio earpiece crackled to life in my ear. "I haven't seen anything or anyone, boss. I have eyes on from the remains of the roof above your head."

I didn't glance up, just gave a single downward nod, while I also fumed at her damned audacity for constantly disobeying orders. She'd never last in the Army Reservists at this rate. With Heather, it always amounted to 'Why?'

Why's it like that? Why do I have to do it like that? Why is it important? I was going to strangle her one day—if we lived that long.

The two GQ clones closed in behind me, GQ1 removing the asp, while GQ2 covered his approach. The earpiece and radio also found their way into his pockets. I entered the hospital. The world darkened further, and I had to stand still to wait for my eyes to adjust.

"Walk." GQ1 poked me in the back with the rifle. Never a sensation I enjoyed.

"Wait, unless you want to trip over the rubble," I snapped back. Blinking several times to help the process, the ivy-roped graveyard to cheap concrete and brick came into focus. I walked towards the large entrance hall of the hospital. The smell of the place, already programmed into my subconscious, made my heart start to beat too fast.

"Go right," came the order, with another poke.

I was going to take that bloody gun off him in a minute and smack him around the head if he didn't stop being an irritating twat. No way would a trained member of the military let someone like me get this close to their weapon. The bozo was lazy and arrogant. I'd seen men like him die all over the world. The anger helped ward off the fear.

Right led down to the underground level of the hospital. The place where the *dark* waited. The place where the whispers of the dead became screams of hate for the living. Fear churned in my stomach. I didn't fear the men with the guns. That would be pointless. They'd either shoot me or not. I did fear what lay under this hospital. The dark could, and would, rip my reality to pieces before spitting me back out a broken mess, unable to function in the world. That result I very much did fear.

Taking it slow down the corridor, I tried to summon the circle of blue and white light Willow and Ella talked about, both in their own ways, but nothing appeared in my head. A kind of vague swampy coloured sludge filled my inner vision, rather than the crystal bright bubble I'd been working on over the summer in quiet moments. It dried my mouth, but not with dust and sand, just plain, ordinary fear.

We came to the top of the stairs. Light tried to gush upwards, but it slunk to the top in an exhausted heap of attempted brightness, defied by the darkness that had nothing to do with the lack of light.

"Down." Another poke.

I couldn't help myself. He needed a lesson in the basics. Turning with a speed neither GQ1 nor GQ2 anticipated, I caught up the barrel of the AR15 in my elbow joint and used its solid length as a pivot point before cracking my left elbow into the side of GQ1's head. He dropped the rifle with a shout and GQ2 raised his weapon. I heard more shouting from below and rather than provoke a fight, I clicked the switch to drop the mag out of the weapon and let the rest of the rifle fall earthwards as well. It thudded into the dusty ground. I held my hands up and endured the pickle egg breath of GQ2 as he yelled at me.

2 9

I WATCHED THE SHADOW OF a small Heather shaped person flit towards us in the noise of the kerfuffle. GQ1 yelled at me for a bit, while nursing his hand, but I remained calm, mute, and passive. It earned me a smack to the guts with the butt of the weapon, but it was worth it, just to annoy the overconfident Russian. It also allowed Heather to follow without being noticed. If she wasn't going to follow orders, I might as well make the most of her skills.

"Down the stairs," GQ1 ordered.

"You really don't want to take me down there," I said. "Nothing good will happen to me, or to you, down there."

GQ1 stepped up so close to me that I needed to crane my neck back to maintain eye contact. He towered over me and tried to make use of every one of his extra inches. I'm a small guy for a Special Forces operative, so being towered over by other SF guys came as part of my training. I didn't flinch.

"You, little man, you tore the throat out of my friend. You lucky you still alive. When this over, we have a problem."

As far as the Russian knew, the only effect his words had on me was the slow blink I allowed myself. Inside, I wailed. Why couldn't I remember what happened? Why had the djinn made me do it? Or was I using my psychosis as an excuse for being a casual murderer? Christ, Willow was right to leave me, and I should cut Heather loose before I hurt her.

I made a decision. It didn't matter if I lived or died down in the black hell under this hospital. I just had to stop these people hurting Ella and Heather. That's all. I turned and walked down the stairs, a cold lump in my guts.

When I reached the bottom, I found the welcome party in the first office. Two men raided all the filing cabinets, taking everything and filling black sacks with any scrap of paper they found. Two women and Ella also stood in the room, making it a tight fit when I joined them with my minders.

I zeroed in on Ella. "You okay?"

She didn't look okay. A bruise coloured her right temple and her cheek. White gloss paint had more variation of colour in it than her skin, and she trembled. They'd plasticuffed her hands and dust covered her light blue summer shirt. Her pristine dog collar had a speck of red on its virginal surface, and it made my beast snarl in a way I'd never felt before. Fuck the damned djinn and whatever games it was playing with my head. Me and my beast had killed long before he showed up to make life difficult for me and we'd kill again.

"You going to get me out?" Ella asked.

"Yes."

"Then I'm okay." She managed a smile, but I saw the fear in her eyes. One of these bastards had shot a man in the head at close range and my dearest friend, my beacon of hope and light in this shit hole of a world I inhabited, bore witness.

"It's often the smallest of flowers that offer the most hope," I said.

Confusion flashed across her face before understanding dawned.

The shorter of the two women stepped forwards. She wore flat boots, black fatigues and a green t-shirt. Aged somewhere between fifty and sixty with iron grey hair in a tidy bob around her face, she stood just an inch taller and a lot rounder than Ella.

"Lorne, lovely to see you again." I knew that voice, the faux American accent would haunt my dreams for a long time—presuming I lived through the next few minutes.

"I didn't kill you then?" I said.

"No, but you certainly made an impression. Turned out the chair wasn't as sturdy as we'd been led to be believe. You are quite impressive despite your..." She waved a hand in my general direction. I guessed she meant I looked unimpressive. Considering these women surrounded themselves with pretty Russians, then yes, I certainly did look unimpressive.

Bantering with these idiots seemed pointless. It would annoy me and stress Ella. I wanted this done, so we had a chance of saving our lives.

Something drew my attention to the picture window in the wall adjacent to my position; a shifting in the shadow that I thought might be Heather. No. No, it wasn't Heather.

"We need to get this swap over with and we need to leave," I said. "I'm not interested in anything else right now."

Ella frowned and followed my gaze, her concern deepening further. I watched the wheels turning in her head.

The taller of the women stepped forwards a little, and I saw the weapon she had pointed in Ella's back. A small Walther PPK/E, usually loaded with a .22 calibre bullet, more than enough to kill someone Ella's size at close range, with or without training. The woman had swapped out her expensive heels for tactical boots that brought her height down to match mine and made her look a great deal more dangerous in my book.

"Give us the notebook and you can leave," she said.

"No, I'll give you the notebook. You can give me Ella and we all leave." I glanced through the window wall again. The blackness in the next room, the one with the chair and restraints, rose and swirled. A dark, thick mist. Faces flickered through it, too indistinct to make out anything but their rage. I flicked my eyes back to the people in the room. "We all need to leave this place. Now."

Both women looked amused by the urgency I'd injected into my voice. The evil pixie one said, "I think you mistake us for fools."

I glanced at the window again. The mist rose to the level of the glass, and I watched it slither along the surface, seeking weaknesses. "No, I know you're fools, or you wouldn't have agreed to the exchange here. Just hand over Ella and let's get out."

Pixie said, "You have an extraordinary psychosis, Turner—"

I focused on her. "Listen, lady, I really don't give a flying fuck, really I don't. You can babble at me all day about the monster living in my head if you want to. I'll answer all your fucking stupid questions, but what I don't want to do is stay here. Please, we need to get out into the light." Fear burrowed deep into my guts, a primal fear I'd never learn to control. Not the fear we bury to become soldiers. This was something that tapped into the most basic part of my lizard brain. A fear of the dark, a fear of the monsters dwelling in that dark.

It started to leak through gaps it found in the old wood surrounding the glass and I stepped sideways as I saw it squirming its way across the floor and into the open doorway. The guards all raised their weapons as I moved, but they didn't worry me.

Staring at the floor, I said, "Ella, when things go south in this room, run for the stairs and keep running. Don't stop. No matter what you hear, don't stop. And pray, pray for me."

"I'm scared, Lorne."

"Me too, mate."

The guards looked at me in confusion. The first tendrils rose to lick at the boots of GQ2.

I looked up at his face. "You might want to leave," I said in a very calm voice.

"Fuck you." Nothing like a Russian accent to give that gloriously simple phrase added gravitas.

My attention returned to Ella. "Now is the time to pray."

"You can see it?" she whispered.

I nodded.

The others gawped in confusion. GQ2 shifted, his subconscious clearly trying to explain the problem, but listening to the unseen dark didn't come as part of Special Ops training. Another patch of black slid over the old linoleum towards GQ1. Bollocks to him. I stepped away from the tendril trying to reach me.

"Ella, start praying aloud," I murmured.

The black gathering around GQ2 licked at his balls. I remembered Willow explaining chakras to me during a meditation exercise she wanted me to practice. The base chakra, the one through which the world enters, to rise up to the crown and back out in a continual circuit, which you could learn to control with some patience, if you believed in that kind of thing. I didn't have that kind of patience. I'd rather go for a run or spend some time beating the shit out of the bags.

Now, though, I saw the point, because the black tendril leaked upwards, stroking the man's groin, until… I watched in dawning horror as the darkness penetrated GQ2, right between his thighs. Once it gained entry, it surged. I glanced at his face. The torches they all carried started to flicker.

The evil pixie and the fake lawyer talked at me, but I tuned them out, because GQ2 shivered. He glanced over his shoulder and frowned, but he couldn't see the broiling blackness, now full of screaming faces, pressing against the open door, gathering itself for the tidal wave attack.

I heard Ella praying, and I started to visualise a bubble of blue and white around me, but I knew it wouldn't be enough. I didn't believe in anything enough. I denied myself. The djinn, Ella's faith, Willow's beliefs, even Heather's gentle suggestions it might be wise to learn more. Nothing I'd experienced with the Gnostic Dawn or in Scob prepared me for what surged through that doorway.

GQ2 screamed, clutched his head, dropping his weapon. I dived for it, training dominating my instinct to run. Mistake. The black, already familiar with me, lunged. My hand closed over the AR15 as my entire body shuddered. I screamed, the pain of the black unimaginable. Fire and ice filling my senses, the top of my head a ball of flame, the centre of my forehead deep-space cold. Next my throat, heart, belly, cock and the burning of lightning through the base of my spine so bad I arched up off the floor. GQ1 bellowed and backtracked out of the room, firing off rounds into the black. The noise shattering, the smell of gunpowder and hot brass all too familiar.

I saw the living people in the room, but through the film of thick smoke, it smelt of misery and rage. I saw Ella down on her knees yelling the Lord's Prayer, but it sounded like a whisper in a hurricane.

A pale blue light surrounded her though and as I lost the battle to keep the dark out, I knew she'd be safe from it, even if it took me.

The sucking black filled my mind, and I drowned inside it, formless, witless, an innocent inside a void of pain and grief so vast I couldn't comprehend its enormity. Visions began to bombard me. Steaming jungles full of fear, where every step led to the trap of a landmine or a bamboo blade strong enough to pierce the green of a uniform no one believed in any more. A prison of more bamboo, the cage too tight to move. Another war, a different prison, this one cold, the death camps stinking and foul. More and more images of death and misery filled my head with conflicts I didn't know, conflicts that weren't mine, until the sucking black found my pain, found the boxes I kept locked up tight and threw the lids open.

It shattered me. No dust and sand to protect me this time. I faced my life square on and witnessed my suffering and the suffering of all those I touched. Horror after horror. Bodies torn to shreds under a hail of bullets from my hands. Entire villages flattened on my orders, given through comms units to remote planes circling so high we couldn't see them until the last few seconds. Muckers downed by enemy fire, only for me to deny a family their father, brother, son… It went on and on and on…

Grief overwhelmed me. A grief so deep I had nowhere to hide and no excuses to use for protection.

This is hell!

I mourned. The depths of my soul screaming and thrashing in a pain so deep I knew it would haunt me for eternity.

Until…

Until a small spark of light wavered in the eternal dark. A small spark rushing forwards and becoming larger, changing form, growing and shifting even as I grovelled in the misery of my personal hell.

The sparking light turned into a shimmering figure with pigtails and a simple dress covered in daisies.

'Come,' she whispered, the simple command cutting through the tormented howls surrounding us. 'They are nothing more than memories. The wars of the past come to trap the wars of the present. They feed each other and need new memories to grow stronger. The men here are full of war and death.'

"So am I," I wailed.

She held out her small hand. 'Your worthy companion does not believe so, and he will show me the way home when the enemy has been van...' The little face frowned in concentration. 'Vancist.'

I placed my paw in her tiny hand and suggested, "Vanquished?"

Her face brightened, as if I'd just given her a pony with a ribbon in its mane. 'See, he said you are a magical warrior. One loved by God.'

If the djinn told her this, which god was he talking about?

Really, do you think that matters, fool? She's showing you a way out!

The girl, I guessed her to be Peggy's sister, Bettina, lifted me from the dark and brought me into her light. I heard Ella's voice, the soft murmuring of prayers, and the distant figure of my shadowy companion who bowed low as Bettina led me past him. From one reality to another I slipped, one orb of white light to blue, the colour a shade I'd only ever seen in Heather's eyes, wrapped around my dearest friend as she battled the dark to pull me back from the edge.

Ella fought her war as bravely as any warrior, her sword and shield more worthy than any weapon I'd carried. The dark washed back, racing away from the light as it always does, to cower and wait, biding its time until it returned.

MY SENSES CAME BACK ONLINE. I lay on my side, Ella's lap my pillow, Heather's body my blanket. She'd wrapped herself around me to hold me still. Both women prayed on a loop. I sucked in a deep breath and Heather's arms snapped open. Ella stuttered and fell silent on an Amen.

"Lorne?" she croaked.

"Yes," I whispered, my throat ragged.

Heather sobbed against my back, and I rolled, every muscle groaning in protest, to take her in my arms. A single torch lay on the ground, light dim but alive enough to give us this moment. I held Heather, and Ella whispered her thanks over our heads.

30

WE STOOD IN THE HEAVY heat of the late afternoon sun, the black and heaving clouds still not quite ready to right wrongs, and smite the unworthy, but certainly working themselves up to it. I felt like spun glass and had all the coordination of a stringless puppet. Heather looked wired and by turns tearful and furious. Ella had a peace about her I'd never known before, an awareness she'd touched Hell and survived because of her faith. It suited her.

"I need a sitrep," I croaked. I sounded as though I'd been screaming for an eternity.

It had taken us time to leave the underground lair, and we'd been so focused on escape we didn't discuss what happened.

"I saw them leaving," Heather said. "The yelling started. I heard you, but I daren't come down until I knew it was safe. I'd have been no use. The two women ran out, one armed man going with them, carrying some black plastic bin liners and your daysack between them."

"They have the notebook," I muttered. Damnit.

"The other soldiers?" Ella asked.

Heather shook her head. "I didn't see them leave, it's like…" She glanced at me.

"It's like the black absorbed them?" I asked.

Her eyes, wild and unsteady for several seconds, grew steady as I squeezed her hand. "Yeah."

"Maybe they ran with the others and we didn't see them?" I didn't want to consider the less rational version of that truth any time soon. "Whatever the scientists did to the souls and minds of the men in that place, the drugs they used made it a thousand times worse once those souls left the tether of the body. We need to stop them from getting that formula."

Now you believe in ghosts and that you're psychic. At last, you've read the memo.

My phone rang. It made us all start in surprise. Somehow, the twenty-first century shouldn't be a part of this epic battle happening in worlds only imagined by the likes of Dante and Blake. I fished it out of my pocket, hand still trembling.

"Turner," I said.

"Lorne? Thank God. It's Eddie."

"Yeah, your name came up."

He cursed. "Listen, we don't have time to bugger about. They're on their way to the coast. Can you get there? We're miles away."

"How do you know?"

"Kate got onto the coastguard helicopter. It's on training exercises off the coast at Ilfracombe. They're following two black SUVs seen leaving Horner."

"Where are they headed?" I asked, the three of us already on the move.

"We think Porlock Weir of all places. There's a fancy-pants boat in the harbour down there and the tide is on the turn."

"Can't they get the lifeboat out to block the harbour?" We were halfway down the field, and I pulled up short. One of the graves we'd uncovered with the strimmer shone bright white for a moment. Bettina's final resting place. I marked it in my head and ran after Heather and Ella.

"They're armed, Lorne."

"What do you expect me to do?"

"Kill the boat they want to use?"

I huffed. "I'll do what I can." I hung up. "Bastards." Meaning the whole of the rest of the world.

The old Landy stood in the sunshine, looking a little forlorn with its smashed headlamps. A roll of thunder growled overhead, and a fat raindrop hit my naked scalp, making it tingle.

"I'll drive," Ella said.

I wasn't going to argue. I'd left the keys in the ignition, so she sparked up the rumble and the three of us left the old cottage as the heavens opened. It took our combined concentration to wind our way through the lanes alongside the thin trickle Horner River had become over the hot summer. The rain smeared the world with the largest, fattest drops I'd ever seen. The sky overhead turned dark in a matter of seconds. Ella had no headlights, so we flicked on the fog lights and the hazards as we negotiated the slow-moving traffic on the A39 into Porlock village. When we came out the other side of the cowering streets, flashes of lightning scored the sky, and I saw the Coastguard's heli doing a one-eighty and heading back up the shoreline.

We sped through the tight two-way lane towards the small harbour of Porlock Weir and I couldn't help remembering the strange snow filled night I'd shared with Willow as we battled together to reach Culbone. Ella slowed for a camper van, picking its way through the rain, and we struggled to see more than five metres ahead.

"There!" Heather pointed to the carpark on the other side of the road to the thatched haven of The Ship Inn pub. How many pints had we shared over the summer in its tranquil and hallowed bar?

In the carpark we saw two large black Mercedes SUVs. They looked like cancerous lumps among the camper vans and family saloons caught in the sudden summer storm.

"They've debussed and headed for the boat," I said. "Get around the corner." I pointed past the hotel, now called Miller's at the Anchor Hotel. I had yet to figure out what that meant. Then past the Pieces of Eight. The old boatyard had a range of little businesses in them, the harbour diversifying as the fishing industry died.

Ella parked right on the summer scorched grass. I spilled out of the passenger side and Heather came more elegantly out of the back. Lightning snapped the world into monochrome and seconds later, a sound like ten thousand devils dancing on a tank's roof roared out over the sky.

"Fuck me," I yelled in the noise. The rain tore at the skin, monsoon heavy.

"There," Heather called out, hunched against the downpour, already soaked. Her dark hair lay flat against her head. She swept it back. At which point, I noticed a familiar shape in her hand.

"Heather?" I pointed.

She grinned and handed it over.

"It's a SIG P229." I checked the magazine, cleared the weapon, and racked the slide.

"I know. One of them dropped it."

"Lorne," Ella yelled. "Over there." She pointed towards the row of small cottages on the earthen part of the harbour wall.

Motoring out of the swollen harbour I saw a small boat that I had no doubt could get the three people aboard into Wales or further. In this weather, we'd have no way to track them either.

I started to run. The SIG's effective range was fifty metres. I didn't have much time. Racing the raindrops, I pounded up the well-worn path, puddles filling even as I splashed through them. I ran to the end of the concrete, hit the dirt and kept going, quickly drawing up on the slow-moving boat. Once it escaped into the Bristol Channel and opened up its engine, I didn't stand a chance, but the summer weather kept the harbour busy with touring and small fishing boats, so they had a job dancing through the maze of bobbing vessels and buoys.

Another bolt of wild lightning streaked through the world to smack into the shore. Or did it rise from the earth to strike the heavens? Thunder rumbled through me and made my body want to hit the deck to escape the roar.

Heather and I drew up alongside the boat. The only man aboard it had the wheel in his grip and handled it well. The evil pixie held the small PPK, and the fake lawyer held the AR15. They were so focused on escape, the rain so thick between us, that none of them saw me and Heather close the distance.

I took up a solid firing stance for the handgun, both hands on the grip, thumbs side by side, clasped firmly but still relaxed, hips tilting my upper body forward. Aiming down the iron sights at the man holding the wheel, I moved my finger from the side of the weapon to the trigger.

The world froze.

Every raindrop stopped its downward trajectory as my breath left my body.

I willed my finger to squeeze. All I had to do was squeeze and the air would be filled with a red mist. His body would slump, and we'd hit the deck as the AR15 let off a volley of rounds, but I'd fire back and take out the fake lawyer from a prone position. Then the evil pixie would have to surrender. Or I'd swim out and take command of the boat with Heather covering my position because the P229 had a better range than the small .22 calibre of the PPK.

But it didn't happen.

"Lorne?" Heather whispered beside me, her hand on my arm. "Shoot the engine. I can hear the police coming. They just need stopping in the water. Eddie said the firearms unit are on their way as well. They can't escape now. I can see the lifeboat from around the headland." She understood. Bless her battered heart. She knew I couldn't kill that bloody Russian idiot if I tried. Correction, I was trying.

I shifted focus. "She'll shoot at us. Be ready to drop."

I squeezed the trigger and round one, followed by the second tap left the barrel. Both found their mark. Black smoke filled the air. Lightning filled the sky. The AR15 barked, but we lay in the mud already, and the rounds sailed off over the harbour wall and into the dark and heaving sea.

Shouting filled the night-dark day, and the rain pounded around us. I lifted my head enough to watch the three fugitives start to fight among themselves, but the lightning dancing a jig around the bay from North Hill to our location, and the accompanying music of drumming summer rain and thunderous clapping from the clouds, made it impossible to hear. More shots found their way in our general direction and Heather cursed up a storm of her own, unused to the volley of sound.

I remained calm, almost detached from the chaos going on around me.

Events from the last few hours ran through my mind and I didn't know what to make of them. As I heard the police screech into the sleepy tourist village and shouts from the Armed Response Unit filling the air, I rolled onto my back, dropped the SIG in the nearest puddle, and stared at the clouds. If I held my eyes still, just blinking away the rain falling onto my face, I could see the individual droplets race towards their destruction, only to become part of the whole when they merged on the ground, in the sea, on a summer cooked leaf or wing. Is that all I was? A drop in the vast ocean of humanity, just one broken soldier in a long, long line of ruined lives that stretched back to the dawn of the first tribal war?

Yes. The djinn certainly showed me that I stood in a line of warriors he'd guided. Except I couldn't pick up that SIG if my life depended on it right now.

"If you want to keep that gun, you need to hide it," Heather said. She lay beside me but watched the ARU approach, keeping her hands laced behind her head as per their yelled orders.

"I never want to see it again," I murmured to the clouds.

I felt her gaze on me, steady and not the least surprised. "Okay," she said. "Maybe that's for the best."

The ARU guys, all in tactical gear and matt black, ordered me to roll over. They carried their MP5 and G36 variants with practiced ease. I rolled, laced my fingers behind my head, and waited to be handcuffed. I watched them take up positions to fire on those in the boat. The remains of Winter Sun's expedition to a quiet corner of West Somerset suddenly realised they'd never escape, and they surrendered their weapons.

The next few hours, even with Kate's arrival, consisted of a lot of explaining in some detail how we ended up chasing Russian and American citizens across the moor and into the sea. I couldn't explain about the black mass of madness under the hospital, but we did begin explaining about the links to MKUltra until a helicopter landed in the carpark and everything ground to a halt. The slick heli didn't look like something the Coastguard used, and I had a sinking feeling we'd be bundled into the back, hooded and silenced, only to arrive in a desert somewhere to face an uncertain future.

I found myself in the back of a police van that acted as a makeshift operations post. The woman sitting opposite me wore a very expensive pants suit and mackintosh.

"Hello, Sergeant Major Turner." She spoke with a soft English accent but from where, I couldn't tell, except it sounded expensive.

"You are?"

"Currently? Your best friend."

I doubted that, but I hadn't seen Ella or Heather for a while, and it made me nervous.

"MI6 or 5?"

She smiled. "No flies on you."

"I don't know, I can certainly smell bullshit," I muttered.

She chuckled. "Don't panic, you aren't being renditioned… yet."

I felt my eyes narrow. "It's that last part I'm worried about."

"Lorne, to be honest, so am I. From what we can gather from your viperous little friend—"

"Is that the vicar or my lover?"

She arched an eyebrow. "Both as it happens."

I grinned. "Sounds like my women."

She eyed me. "Well, from the younger of the viperous women, we gathered you were used as a subject by Professor Kammler."

"The evil pixie?"

Mrs MI6 opened her mouth and snapped it shut. "Okay, yes, the evil pixie. She used you. Now, we've had a quick read of your file and it leads us to a question."

"Am I safe to be a free man?"

"Hmm, 'fraid so."

I gazed at the metal wall of the police van for a while, considering the seriousness of her question. "Do you mean safe for national secrets safe, or do you mean safe as in going postal down at the post office queue safe?"

"Either, I'm afraid."

"I'll never tell anyone what's happened if that's your worry. I've more secrets in my head than you, considering our age difference. Am I safe with regard to the public?" I shrugged. "You can ask that of any of us from Special Forces. It's a risk every government takes when it lets us back out in the world. It's why so many of us vanish because we can't handle the stress and don't want to hurt anyone. I'm truly blessed, though. I have some people who keep me harmless and sane, give me a reason to keep going. I'm not a danger. I can't vouch for my vipers if you don't let me go…"

She smiled. "Good enough for me. You've proved your loyalty time and again. Your service record is immaculate. You cannot go public with the experiments the Winter Sun company has been doing. We are in discussions with the CIA and FBI about how to handle them. Perhaps we'll be able to bring their work under government oversight—"

My jaw clenched. "Yeah, that's reassuring, considering they're the ones who started it in the first place." Her neat eyebrow rose at my dark muttering.

"We'll also be talking to the European Union. It tends to act as a brake on the US's more esoteric shenanigans. We're more worried about what Winter Sun might be selling to the Russians and Chinese, so I think they'll pull together."

"No soldier deserves the fate they envisage," I said.

Mrs MI6 studied the metal floor between our feet. "No, they don't. None of this was sanctioned by the US Government. It might be an American company, but their recent exploits have not been sanctioned by any of their Federal organisations. I think, especially after Afghanistan, if the American public knew about this, the outcry could well cause chaos for the current adminstration. We need them strong and stable to face any Russian threat. That also means keeping this out of Russian hands."

I nodded. "I'm relieved. The Winter Sun have left a lot of dead in their wake," I said, thinking of poor Peggy.

Mrs MI6 nodded. "I know. It's sad, but it's over now."

I thought about the little girl trapped in the dark of the hospital. It really wasn't over, not for me.

"We'll have some paperwork for you, and someone will come to the farm to take a statement. I suggest you write everything out as you would for your CO after a mission. It'll make things faster. Try to get your girlfriend to do the same and if she could minimise the bad language, it might help."

"No promises on that score."

"We'll have the police release you now. Thank you for your service, Lorne. You did well. You've saved the lives of many men like yourself."

"I hope so. Just keep the boffins honest when they get their hands on the intel, please."

She rose and squeezed my shoulder, unable to give me such a promise. I sighed and surrendered to the inevitable. Someone, somewhere, would continue the work of Winter Sun, trying to create a soldier who didn't become a useless hunk of six million quid's worth of training because his mind snapped.

31

THE THREE OF US RETURNED the Land Rover to Quarme and Pete Tucker. Ella drove. I sat in the back, eyes closed, trying to make sense of the steaming bowl of lumpy custard in my head. It proved too much of a challenge and I ended up watching the scenery, the summer storm now over, and the daylight fading to a bruised purple twilight. The roads ran with water, the land too dry to soak it up, and the drains full of detritus. Localised flooding would be a problem for several hours, if not days. The air though, when we stepped out of the Landy, the air smelt of every childhood rainstorm and summer's day I'd ever had on the farm. I also heard my mum yelling for Tommy and me to come in and have supper before we crashed out in our latest den.

Moments like these made me miss my childhood friend, the first loss of my life and always the hardest. During the long summer, I'd considered visiting Shaw, but Heather and Willow convinced me it would do nothing for my peace of mind. Whatever had happened to Tommy that night so long ago, he was dead, and giving Shaw power over me because the bastard thought he had some secret, wouldn't help in the long run. I just needed to focus on the good times, so I stood in the darkening farmyard, ignored the police tape sectioning off the place Vlad had died, and breathed the cool evening air.

Pete came out of the house. "You brought it back."

Heather said, "What did you think we'd do with it?"

I didn't open my eyes but said, "I owe you two headlights. We'll look at some scrap dealers and find them."

"Don't worry. I'll replace them. I owe you that much, at least. I don't think my family would have been left alive if you hadn't been here."

Giving up on chasing happy memories, I turned to Pete. "No. They would have killed everyone in the family to keep you quiet. These are very serious people."

"Are we safe now?" he asked.

I nodded. "I wouldn't worry now. The police have the man left in the cottage. He won't talk much, so we won't be implicated. They're professionals and I expect they'll be extradited to the US to face questions about Winter Sun."

Pete shifted. "I'd ask you in, but Dad's in a bit of a state tonight."

I put a hand on Pete's shoulder. "Heather's right about the business consultant. Let me help you find someone you can trust. I don't know enough about farming to be much of a help, but I'm here if you need someone to lift and shift stuff."

"I talked to Rick. He says it's time we make some changes. Maybe sell some of the land, look to the future. Farming's changing. We have to change with it or die."

"Rick's right."

Pete shifted his feet and glanced at Heather. "Thanks for not reporting me to the police."

She sniffed, then offered him a smile. "Us reformed criminals have to stick together, right?"

Ella still leaned against the Landy but took Pete to one side and offered him one of her business cards. If the Tuckers needed some last-minute help from the Man Upstairs, she'd want to help. It was kind of her, considering the fear she had about her test results. I rubbed my head. That conversation felt like several lifetimes ago, not just a week.

The three of us bundled into the Little Gem and ambled back to Horner to check on Eddie at the caravans. By now, night threw a calming blanket over the day, and when we debussed, the only sound to fill the air came from the barn owl in the ash tree to my right. Heather snuck under my arm and pressed her head into my chest. I kissed her crown.

When we reached the caravans, Lilian greeted us.

"I couldn't stay in Bristol. It's too hectic," she said with a smile. "Besides, I figured you lot would want feeding, after your adventures."

I laughed. "You make it sound like we've spent the day in the woods with sticks and are coming home with skinned knees."

"Well, you look like that's exactly what happened." She had tea lights scattered about and some paraffin lamps.

With no moon and Exmoor's dark sky project keeping electric lighting to a minimum, the cacophony of stars overhead filled the void above us, making it somehow more, and less, intense. It still felt safe and like home, despite the horrors of the last few days. I tried to remain in the present, the immediate past too difficult to comprehend just yet, a tactic I'd learned over the years to survive the unsurvivable.

Ella and Heather helped bring food out, thick veg soup, dense bread and cheese with a cold ham. Eating calmed my frayed nerves and my skin started to feel like flesh, rather than glass. I had a beer, and we chatted about anything other than the day's events. I guessed Lilian had a lot of practice at normalising whatever horrors a Bristol police detective sergeant faced on a daily basis, and it worked for an old soldier as well. Ella stayed quiet, but she did eat, so I tried not to worry.

After a couple of hours, we all sat in silence, until Ella said, "We need to think about the hospital and what we do about it."

"What happened down there?" Lilian asked. Eddie placed a hand on her arm and shook his head, asking her not to probe. She hushed him, "We live here, love. We have to know what's happened. It's on our doorstep."

Ella and I stared at each other for a while. I didn't know what she saw or heard. I do know she helped save my sanity and probably my life.

She said to Lilian, "We had an experience down there that tested us all to the limit. Whatever is held in those concrete walls, whatever intangible threat, it needs putting to rest, but I'm not sure I know how."

"Yes, you do," Heather said. "It retreated because of you."

"Bettina showed me how to get back to you both," I muttered, surprising myself. I stared into the candle flame rather than look at anyone. "I was lost in the void. Lost in the memories of the men who died there in a state of fear and anger. The conflicts that shattered their minds, they are part of this black mass of anguish, soul deep anguish. Peggy's sister has been trapped with them all this time. We need to save her and put them to sleep. They deserve peace."

Ella stared into the same flame. "I'll need help. I don't want to go to the bishop, not after he told me to leave all this alone. Maybe we can ask Willow? She's good at barriers and sensing problems I can't."

Heather shifted beside me, but managed to stay mute.

I nodded. "Good idea. Get Thomas over from Ilfracombe as well. He's a good man in a fight like this one."

"I'd feel better with him here as well," Ella said, nodding. She was building a plan in her head, and it made me smile to see some confidence return to straighten her back. "The stronger someone's faith, the better."

"Paul will be back from the hospital in a day or so. We'll need him there as Bettina's family," I said.

Ella nodded. "Maybe make a morning of it, if Lilian and Eddie don't mind. I'll think about what prayers will help and we'll get some incense down there, bring the full regalia from the church. Then we'll say some prayers for Bettina in a separate ceremony."

"Oh, which reminds me, I know which is her grave," I said.

Ella smiled. "Then we'll do that as well."

"Shouldn't we inform the authorities about the extra dead bodies up there?" asked Lilian.

Eddie took her hand. "I don't think so, love. I think we can care for them. Maybe we can do some research and if we find living relatives, we'll consider the best way of approaching them, but for all we know, poor Bettina is the only one up there."

"I think we'll use the Exaltation of the Holy Cross on the fourteenth of September. That's in ten days. It'll give us all a chance to get our strength back, because we'll need it."

"My birthday," murmured Heather beside me.

I squeezed her hand. We had another large corporate gig to do before then that promised to pay rather well, so I wanted to spoil her.

We had a plan and a date. Now all we needed to do was see it through.

THE FOURTEENTH CAME FAR FASTER than I expected. The survival courses were fully booked now the school holiday exhaustion had ended, and I'd even done some work with the local primary schools as part of an experiment for the new term. Heather was about to start college and she'd cut back on the Army Reservist activities. Something had changed for us, and it wasn't just that she'd moved into my bedroom at last.

I'd never lived with a woman, other than my mother, unless you counted women on bases all over the world, which didn't come close to this experience. At forty-two it came as something of a shock having Heather wander about the house naked at random moments, but I'd be lying to myself to say I didn't enjoy the view. The intimacy, though, that was harder to handle.

I'd been alone a very long time, often in extreme circumstances, so having this vibrant and passionate woman in my life turned me upside down and inside out. Since she'd moved in during May, life had became more tolerable. Now, life became worth living. I'd never really understood it when people said they fit together like jigsaw pieces, the voids and joints matching up to make a perfect whole. I did now.

When we went out together, and made it clear we were a romantic couple, people found it difficult. It wasn't just the age difference. Heather's dark elfin features made her beautiful to me and attractive by anyone's standards. When held against me... Well, I didn't exactly measure up. It made me humble and proud all at once.

On the morning of the fourteenth, I rose very early, sliding out from under

Heather's arm and grabbed my battered black combats. The sun had crested the hills, and the sky glowed with a reddish tinge that promised rain later in the day. Not a bad thing after the endless hot days, but I'd be sad to see an end to this summer. Not least because Shaw's trial started in November.

I pushed the thought away. Today was about Heather and a ceremony to lay some angry spirits to rest. Also to say goodbye to a child. I'd asked Heather if she was okay with using her birthday for the event and she said it would always help us to remember Peggy and Bettina, not a bad thing apparently. In the barn, I uncovered a tarp, then dug around for a box of extras I'd stashed. I returned to the kitchen and made us tea and toast to start with. If she wanted a full English, I'd cook that later. I picked a few of Mum's roses—or Heather's now as she looked after them—and put together a tray.

I'd always wanted to try being romantic, to have someone special who accepted it from me, and now I'd found that person. In the bedroom, Heather stirred as I set the tray down and grinned at her.

"Happy birthday, sweetheart," I said.

She blinked and smiled. "Love you," she murmured.

The colour rose in my cheeks. We'd done that bit a few days before and the novelty had yet to wear off. I didn't care if people thought it was too soon. It didn't feel like that to us, and we were the ones who mattered. "Love you too. Now, your gift is outside, so tea—"

"Oh! You bought me something?" she squealed in a way I'd never heard before.

"Erm…"

She dived out of bed with the speed of a scud missile and grabbed one of my old jumpers she wore instead of a dressing gown. "Show me!"

I laughed. "I was trying to be romantic." I gestured at the roses.

She planted a very brief kiss on my lips. "Very nice, thank you, you're wonderful. Can I see the pressy now?" Her bouncing feet put me in mind of a puppy.

Shaking my head, I took her hand and led her to the barn. "Shut your eyes," I ordered.

Happy to be playing the game, she did as instructed and I helped her into the barn. "Open your eyes."

She did. "Oh my God, Lorne." And she burst into tears.

My guts dropped several levels into a Hell dimension.

"You bought me a motorbike?" she asked, tears making the words almost unintelligible.

"I thought it would be something you needed, and you work so hard on the business and farm, you won't let me pay you and—"

A small body hit me hard, knocking me back into some bales, and strong arms encircled my neck. "Thank you, it's beautiful and I love it and I love you and no one, ever, has been this amazing." She kissed me.

Relief made my stomach lurch back up the elevator of love, something I was never going to get used to, and we proceeded to open the additional gifts to make her safe on her new vehicle. I'd asked Smoke to help find me the right, and legal, bike for her. A Suzuki Marauder 125cc. Not the most practical bike, but I knew she'd love it and more importantly, its size made it easier for idiots in cars to see her, also, she couldn't go nuts riding it at speed. I needed her to be fully independent from me, caging a phoenix didn't seem wise. I'd bought insurance, which almost gave me a heart attack, and added some extra safety gear.

I chuckled at her antics as she climbed on the bike. "And I'm already legal with the provisional," she said. This was thanks to the ex-boyfriend. I didn't like thinking about him.

"Yep. I checked your licence. So, you're good to go. We'll take the bikes down to Luccombe and afterwards ride wherever you want. I'll be behind you the whole way until you know how to handle her."

"Dixie, she's called Dixie," Heather said.

"Okay, Dixie. Is that to match Duke?" The name of my bike, apparently. I still hadn't managed to find out if she'd named the guns, but we hadn't touched them since the Winter Sun, and I didn't like thinking about it. Heather didn't press, but I had the feeling my episodes made her want to stop being in the AR.

My thoughts derailed as Heather took it upon herself to say thank you for the gifts. We didn't leave the barn for a while.

By 10:00 hours we'd ridden down to Luccombe. I hadn't told Ella what I'd bought for Heather, and she didn't know whether to be horrified or really proud of me. She opted for proud in the end, because Heather was overwhelmed with joy. Ella bought her a necklace, a beautiful golden Celtic Crucifix. I'd taken Heather to several services over the last few weeks, and she'd found herself drawn to Ella's Bible reading evenings in the bungalow. It surprised me, but after what we'd experienced under the hospital, maybe it offered answers in a way nothing else could. I certainly didn't have any answers, just new variations on my nightmare.

"I have the test results back at last," Ella said.

Heather froze, and I grabbed the kitchen door to hold myself steady.

"After the muddle with the letters going to the wrong address, they ended up phoning my GP. It's benign, guys. I have to have it removed in case it turns bad, but it's just a mass of breast tissue, probably caused by that rock fall hitting me a couple of years ago and the resultant bruising." She barely managed to get the last of the sentence out before I squeezed the air from her lungs.

She rubbed my back and might have released a small sob.

"Best birthday ever," Heather crowed, joining the hug.

The sense of relief over Ella's lump came with the bittersweet knowledge she and I fell into the category of—check, get checked, then get checked again. We both knew people who weren't lucky in the cancer lottery.

A car pulled up outside. Ella said, "That'll be Willow." She rose from the table and went to the door, a real bounce back in her step.

"Maybe not the best birthday ever," Heather muttered with a scowl worthy of a ten-year-old.

"Play nice, you don't have anything to worry about."

She just lifted her eyebrow. I reached across the space between us and took her hand, kissing the knuckles and she released a breath.

Willow came in and smiled, then her eyes landed on my hand grasping

Heather's and I watched something odd flit through those expressive eyes. I didn't pursue it, just rose and gave her a hug.

"It's good to see you," I said.

"And you."

"Did you bring the organic boyfriend?" I asked, unable to let her off the hook completely.

She laughed. "No, and that's the reason why." She poked me in the chest. "Besides, he's organic *and* vegan, you prehistoric lump." Her smile took in Heather. "I take it that mean looking motorbike out there is yours?"

Heather grinned, unable to contain her joy. "Lorne bought it for my birthday."

Willow hugged her. "You deserve it. I have something for you as well." She handed over a small box.

Heather, expecting a knife in her back, flushed in surprise. "You didn't have to."

"It's what friends do for each other, Heather," Willow said very firmly, making sure they understood each other.

"We'll be singing kumbaya in a minute," I muttered.

Heather opened the box and gasped. Another necklace, this one with a quartz crystal wrapped in a silver dragon. I glanced at Ella, and she nodded with a small smile and a shrug.

"We should go," she said. "It's time to put things right."

32

A KNOT FORMED IN MY gut. I'd spent a lot of time over the last few days *not* thinking about this event and focusing on Heather's birthday. I hadn't seen the soldier, but the fear remained. I didn't want to do this. Whatever they'd done to me with their drugs, the healing fracture in my head had widened. Shadows around the farm and moor made my palms sweat, and I didn't trust that odd awareness which murmured warnings in my head. I hadn't seen the djinn, even in my nightmares, just the swamping black. Heather suffered them as well and some nights she woke me thrashing to escape some unseen tormentor.

"We walking?" I asked.

"Seems wise. It's grounding and will give us a chance to balance ourselves. Eddie and Lilian are coming with us." The doorbell chimed. "Ah, our final adventurer."

Paul came in, sporting the most spectacular bruises. I'd picked him up from the hospital ten days ago and taken him straight to the train station in Taunton. He didn't want to come back to Luccombe just yet, he needed some time. Time to mourn. When his mum's body had been released, he'd returned for the service at the church, led by Ella, and Peggy was buried. The whole village had turned out for the service, and Paul never left. That was three days ago. He moved into the cottage, opted to work from home and commute when necessary. He'd become subdued, and I worried he'd be lonely.

Willow, however, smiled when she saw him. "Hello, Paul."

His eyes widened a little. "Willow. I didn't know you knew these reprobates."

I frowned. "How do you two know each other?"

"Paul's a new member of our Moot," Willow said.

My mouth dropped open, and I did a fair impression of cartoon astonishment. "You're a witch?" I asked him.

Paul shrugged. "I wouldn't go that far but after what happened here…" His words and vision drifted, doubtless thinking of his beating. Shaking his head he said, "After what I've seen and heard, I went into Minehead, looking for something, but not sure what, and found Willow's shop. It could be something that fills a hole inside me, now Mum's gone. Not that she'd approve." He smiled, the bruising on his face bunching up making him wince. "I need to be more connected to the world, to nature, and this thing with Winter Sun," he didn't meet my gaze, and it made me sad, "it's changed things for me. Made me realise what's important."

I clapped him on the shoulder. "Good for you, Paul. I'm pleased."

"I shouldn't have dismissed your PTSD, or your gifts, Lorne. I'm sorry. You've given me the peace I need to heal. Thank you."

Opening my mouth to say something like 'don't worry about it' I found I couldn't. I just grasped his shoulder to acknowledge his words and accept them.

Together, walking down to Eddie's place, we kept our counsel, thoughts quiet and calm. I also had a bad dose of nerves working themselves into a Gordian knot in my guts. Heather slipped her hand into mine. Whether to give, or take comfort I didn't know. Ella had a Bible, a book of Common Prayer and her favourite wooden crucifix with her, as well as the holy water and some Sacrament wafers. When we arrived at the cottage, Eddie and Lilian waited with Thomas Hearn.

"Lovely to see you both," he said after introductions were made. He smiled at Heather. "You are looking very well."

She beamed at him. "Thanks. It's good to see you."

Ella called us to order. "Right, everyone, I need to make something very clear. I am not an exorcist, and this is not an exorcism. They are performed on people, not places. What we are doing here is laying a place to rest, asking the spirits of the departed, in God's name, to leave the hospital and go to His side in peace. We will all be asking Jesus Christ and the Holy Spirit to help us. If anyone has a problem with that, then you need to leave." She held Willow's gaze for a moment, but Willow merely nodded.

"After what Lorne, Heather and I experienced down there, things might get a bit…"

"Tasty?" I tried.

"Not as good as my scones, I bet," Lilian muttered, making us all chuckle, more out of nerves than anything else.

"We'll go with tasty," Ella said. "It's important we stay together, stay calm and know that whatever happened down there is in the past. We will be protected, and we offer no harm. This is a blessing and a cleansing. Then we'll leave and go to Bettina's grave, to offer her a path to join her family at last. These are not evil spirits, merely lost and scared memories of people who suffered too much in this life."

Ella and Thomas led the way, the Book of Common Prayer open and prayers being said between them. As the one most vulnerable to whatever lay under the hospital, Ella asked me to carry the cross as 'tailend charlie'. The others spread out between us. I kept watch over Heather, who walked with Paul and Willow.

Once we climbed over the fence and walked into the woods, the fear in me began to rise to the point it suffocated me. As a soldier, I'd been scared lots of times, but training always gave me a way to handle whatever I faced, and I usually had a four-man team to back me up. Here, I faced a darkness I didn't understand, and despite being armed with a cross and a Bible, I'd rather be armed with a G36 on fully automatic and about five hundred rounds. My palms sweated. The woodland held still and quiet, the day cooling now the clouds had started to gather in earnest, and it grew darker. Every instinct in my formidable arsenal of instincts woke up and ordered me to run, because this was an enemy I could not fight.

We reached the entrance to the hospital, where I'd first met GQ1 and GQ2 and stopped. Ella started intoning the Lord's Prayer, and Thomas started to bless the doorway. A hand slipped into mine and from the other side, an arm encircled my waist. Willow stood on one side, Heather on the other, and Ella placed her formidable gaze on me from the front.

I glanced to the right, deeper into the woodland, and the shadows shifted just a little. The flash of a pale dress covered in daisies vanished behind the trees, closely followed by a tall shade in flowing robes. Was my djinn playing chase with Bettina? Is that why I hadn't felt him for days? Was he here with her?

Or maybe the trauma of the drugs I'd been forced to take fractured and separated my long-term psychosis? Maybe these visions came from a mind jacked up on fear and anticipation of nightmares made real?

You know that's not true, mucker.

Still concentrating on the vision of the girl, I didn't realise Willow and Heather had managed to get me through the doorway. We walked over the broken parts of the building, the scent of ivy and brick dust combining with the damp. All of us joined in the prayers and plenty of holy water lay sprinkled about. Willow lit, and carried sage, giving one to Paul as well.

In the entrance hall we gathered, said more prayers and I watched the right-hand corridor, knowing what waited at the far end, at the bottom of the stairs.

So far, we'd only disturbed a flock of tree sparrows and some wood pigeons. We walked down the hallway, Willow ahead of me, Heather beside me. I tried to stop the wooden cross from shaking as I held it like a fiery torch overhead.

The inevitable happened; we reached the top of the stairs. More prayers, more amens, more holy water, and this time Ella broke the Sacrament, and left half on each side of the doorway. Symbols of faith helped the focus, the intent, of those who were part of the ceremony. Ella, small, short salt and pepper hair windblown, wearing her vicarly robes, led the way. How could someone so tiny be so brave? I didn't feel brave, not for a moment.

Eddie and Lilian followed, then Paul. On the stairs Willow turned back and looked at me with a small smile and nod.

Heather whispered, "We won't let anything happen to you."

"I've never felt like this," I admitted.

She gazed up at me. "I know. What they did down there, to men like you, it was wrong. What Winter Sun did to you, it was wrong. What we're doing now is right and I think they'll be okay."

I tried to nod agreement but barely managed a wobble of my head. We walked onto the stairs, the torches of the others lighting our way.

"We'll do each room down here," Ella said. "Remember, nothing can hurt us, and I think, I believe, they just want to be released."

In the office, where the darkness filled the room, I saw the chaos of violence that we'd left behind that day, but no blood. I closed my eyes and visualised the blue and silver bubble surrounding me, then pushed it out to surround the others. If I was psychic, if I was a warrior for the spirit as the djinn wanted, if I wasn't a complete nutjob, then I needed to embrace the trappings of the occult to give me the body armour and weapons necessary to fight and protect those I loved. I needed to train and become disciplined in my new skills. I needed to become a soldier, an operator in the esoteric.

The blue bubble grew stronger the moment I stopped being afraid of the future. I needed to stop denying my role in these strange events and stop denying this odd gift I'd been born with, and ignored, until the desert broke me. I needed to harness the djinn.

I opened my eyes and saw them. Shades of grey inside the dark beyond the torchlight that strained to push them back. They shifted form, but I saw many in uniforms I recognised from history books and regiment memorabilia at events we attended. Restless, jealous of our life and warmth, our sense of family, they crowded and listened. Front and centre stood a man in a brown uniform and a tin hat, carrying a Lee-Enfield rifle across his body. His dark eyes never left Ella.

My hand tightened on Heather's, and she murmured, "It's okay, they won't come in."

"Can you see them?" I whispered back.

"No, but I sense them."

I think we all did because Eddie and Lilian held hands, standing close together, raising their voices to join in the prayers. Thomas and Ella spoke with strength, designed to dominate a large nave, and Paul stood with Willow, their sage held out and smoking, filling the air with life. I found no voice to share, but I willed the spirits to listen to the others, begged them to find their peace, their battles done. Ella walked out of the office, Thomas behind her with the holy water and I watched in awe as they strode among the drifting memories of tormented men, offering them peace and safety.

The shades of memories started to dissolve. Becoming free.

The ghost of the soldier turned. He looked at me. The rifle in his hands relaxed, the wooden stock dropping to the ground. His muddy boots returned to parade-ground bright. He took up Order Arms, the butt of the rifle on the ground, legs shoulder width apart. Relaxed, at ease for the first time in over seventy years. He did not salute, but I think I saw him acknowledge me with a nod as he faded.

My cheeks warmed, the tears flowing as I watched in awe at the power of faith and belief. These were lost souls, driven mad by war, and our combined faith in their ability to find peace at last gave them the freedom to leave their torment behind. I wished I could leave my pain behind, my fear, the earthly shackles of my brutalised body, a daily reminder of the horror I'd caused and witnessed. I wanted to be free of it, free of the sadness, free of the guilt and shame. Free of the taint gifted to me by Lady Death and all the souls I'd fed her over the years. All the souls I'd lost to her.

I wept and my family closed ranks around me.

"It's over," I managed to croak.

Ella and Thomas continued their blessing, dosing each room, and we helped, but I knew peace flowed through these broken rooms and soon enough animals would start making it their home.

We left the hospital and walked back into a day of bright light and tumbling clouds. The leaves had started to turn in the woodland, and when we left it, fields of red earth littered the landscape. I led them to the grave I knew held Bettina. Standing behind the crooked headstone, I saw him, my companion, the djinn. Not quite solid in the earthy sunlight, he held the hands of a small child with pigtails and an elderly woman made of cardigans and lavender.

I smiled at them, as Ella and Thomas said prayers of peace and begged forgiveness for the sins of those who failed such a young spirit. It worked. The three of them walked away, heading towards a sudden shower of rain that coloured the skies with a vivid rainbow.

THAT EVENING, WE HAD A barbeque at the farm for Heather's birthday. I ate a lot of meat, much to Willow's dismay, but I didn't have to care. Heather kept vanishing to check on Dixie. I'd take her out for a long ride in the morning. I needed to know she was safe before I let her out on her own, not that I was over-protective or anything. Eddie and Lilian danced to the power-ballad album I played, because we were all of a certain vintage, and even Ella managed to rock it up with Heather, which was a sight to behold.

We all drank too much and as the evening wound to a naturally quiet phase, the scent of something sweet drifted on the air. Paul sat with Willow. I joined them on the bales.

"I need the loo before I pass out in a heap," Willow announced, reaching for my hand to ask for help to stand. I hauled her to her feet, then took her place.

Paul and I sat, drinking beer, and watched Heather dancing alone with the stars to a long and drifting prog rock album she loved.

"She's a good one, Lorne. You need to marry her and sharpish, so she doesn't escape," Paul said.

I chuckled. "I thought if you loved someone, you had to let them go?"

He shook his head and took another puff before passing it to me. "No, mate, you need to nail it to the floor so it can't escape."

"Like you'd know," I said, on an exhale. It occurred to me Eddie was about somewhere.

"I know."

I turned to take him in properly. "You've been in love?"

Paul nodded. "Just the once, so far, though I really like Willow."

"Hmm, she's rather special."

"Is that right?"

"Gentleman never shares secrets, Paul."

"You are that, mate, you are that."

I didn't know how true his statement was, but I had other things to talk about. "Tell me about this love of yours."

"It was after you left The Stan. I really wished you hadn't. She'd still be alive."

Oh, this wasn't a good story then.

I put my hand on his leg and gave it a squeeze. "I'm sorry."

He shrugged. "Her family was Taliban. Nazo hated it, hated the hate. She ran from them to Kabul, which is where we met. Suicide bomber took out a bus of school children, all girls. She was stood nearby. It's why I'm such a bloody idiot around women, why I was a dick to Heather. I'm jealous of what you have with her. It's love, mate, she's crazy about you."

"I'm sorry about Nazo."

"Just don't fuck it up with Heather."

I watched her continue her dance, beer bottle in hand. "I don't intend to. I want her here for as long as she'll have me."

"Good. This family you've built, it's good."

I bumped his shoulder. "You're part of it as well, fella."

Paul grinned at me. "Witches, vicars, psychics and police? What can possibly go wrong?"

I laughed. "That's family, mate, a weird patchwork of souls muddling through this weird world."

"I could do with some weird in my life, Lorne."

"Stick around. I'm sure I can find you some."

We sat in the dark, watching Heather dance with the stars and just let the cool night air bring autumn towards us.

Author Thanks

MANY THANKS FOR READING THE third of Lorne Turner's books. If you have a little time, I would appreciate a review. I really value my readers' thoughts about a book. It often helps me craft future stories. They are vital for indie authors like me. You are always welcome to get in touch directly at

joe@joetalon.com
www.joetalon.com
Or find me on Goodreads and BookBub.

I have free stories for you as well. All I'd like in exchange is your email address and you can unsubscribe from the newsletter at any time.

The first is called *Forgotten Homeland*. Just follow the link. It takes place just as Lorne leaves his regiment and returns home.

The second is *A Meeting of Terrors*. It's the fateful meeting between Lorne and Ella for the first time.

I'd like to keep in touch. Either via the newsletter I'll send out every few weeks, or you can join my Facebook group: Joe Talon Books. If you join either, there will be notifications of new stories, releases of covers and the occasional giveaway and special deals just for you. There will also be an opportunity to join my *Advanced Reader Team*.

ACKNOWLEDGEMENTS

FOREMOST, MY THANKS GO TO David Luddington for doing battle with my deadlines and winning. Jeff Jones, for his proofing skills, any such errors are mine. A special thanks to Alex Whisman who, despite his mad schedule, found the time to beta read the first version of this story.

When I started this story, the terrible events of Afghanistan had hit the headlines a few weeks before and we had no idea what was to happen in Ukraine. I've spent many years writing about the effects of war on those we ask to make the ultimate sacrifice. I have never served in the Armed Forces, but I've seen the effects on frontline workers, soldiers, airmen and sailors first hand and the lack of support for them and their families makes me very sad. Many end up living on the streets or in shelters. Men and women in Ukraine, who have no training, are taking up arms to save their country. I'm sure many of us find that both inspiring and terrifying. Many of us ask, 'Are we brave enough? Could we survive?' who really knows until we face the decision? I'm sure many of them feel like Heather. Picking up a gun is never the right answer, until it's the only question you're presented with. Conflicts don't end when politicians sign a piece of paper. My great uncle never spoke of his time in the RAF, flying over Germany. The Second World War never ended for him. This story is very close to my heart. I hope we never have to make decisions like those faced by so many.

On a much lighter note, do explore Exmoor on a certain search engine we know. There are loads of good Facebook groups (including mine) that often have beautiful pictures of the moor. I'll add some to my website with the next update. You haven't lived until you've gushed over the fluffy face of an Exmoor pony or seen the noble stags.

My final thanks go to the most amazing people I've met while writing this book, my ARC team (you guys are wonderful), my Facebook group, and those of you who email me to say hello. I answer everyone and it means the world to me. Thanks for reading and I hope to see you for the next book *Salt for the Devil's Eye.*

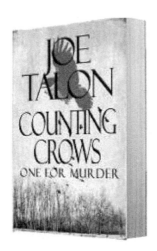

THE MOOR IS DARKENING. Lorne feels it in his bones.

His instincts, honed by years on the battlefields of the desert, scream in warning. Or is it the monster in his head?

When Detective Inspector Tony Shaw tells him the obvious occult symbols on the dead man are nothing more than faked staging, Lorne knows his instincts are right, and the police are wrong. There is darkness and it's spreading.

An ancient spirit line is awoken with violence and pain, seeping down from Dunkery Beacon, highest point on Exmoor, to the woodland church of Culbone on the coast.

Lorne Turner, SAS soldier and survivalist trainer turns to his best friend, Ella Morgan, vicar of the parish for help. Together they approach Willow Hunter, a pagan whose past impacts all their futures.

Time is against them as they battle the unseen forces of Somerset's aristocracy and the mysteries of an ancient moorland, never quite tamed. Its whispering dead are seeking justice.

Counting Crows on Amazon

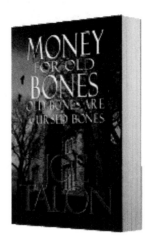

LORNE TURNER NEEDS A BREAK, so when he's offered the job of security guard and handyman at an old rectory in the Lyn Valley he takes it.

He thought he'd gain a little space and perspective. A little quiet from the noise in his head, from his demons, from his beast. Sadly, The Rectory doesn't provide the haven he needs.

As the rain falls, waters rise, and old graves move.

The grave of a witch, who cursed the village. The grave of a soldier, who tried to escape the Hanging Judge after the Monmouth Rebellion. The grave of a priest, broken by love and grief.

When the whispering of Exmoor's dead turns into a scream, Lorne has to act.

The original families of Scob must face their debt.

Lorne, Ella, Willow, and Heather need to find a way to balance the scales before more lives are lost.

Can they survive the haunting misery of the old bones? Can they save each other from the beckoning darkness?

And the rain. Always the rain.

Money for Old Bones on Amazon

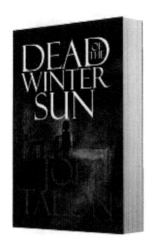

LORNE IS BEGINNING TO UNDERSTAND that the dead might not stay in the graveyards where they belong. He also knows it's time to start facing this disconcerting reality in the same way he faced his enemies in battle.

So, when Eddie Rice buys a rundown cottage on Exmoor, and an old graveyard, which should be empty, things become increasingly weird. It isn't empty for a start. Not of bodies, or the whispering dead.

After an elderly woman is murdered nearby, Lorne, Ella and the others begin to uncover a plot that links this quiet corner of the world with Cold War espionage. Soviet secrets unravel and the more Lorne discovers the closer to breaking point he gets.

The Winter Sun burns in his blood, eating his mind. Can his desert hitchhiker save him? Or will his sanity fold under the weight of Cold War madness?

Dead of the Winter Sun on Amazon

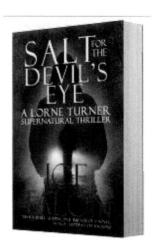

LORNE'S HOME IS TURNING INTO A dream. He's happy and at peace for the first time in his life. The nightmares are releasing their grip on his mind and he's learning to cope with the whispering dead.

Sadly, that's not the case for everyone.

An old friend calls about a missing boy from a traveller's camp on the Quantocks. They've been living on the site of an ancient hillfort, near the burial grounds of long forgotten souls.

These people don't trust the police, but they do put their faith in an old soldier to bring their boy home.

When Lorne discovers this disappearance has a link to his childhood friend vanishing, more than thirty years before, his oldest fears start to rise and take form.

The ancient sites of the Quantocks, the modern world of Hickley Point's new nuclear reactor, and ex-police officer Tony Shaw, start to weave a tapestry of darkness that threatens all the peace Lorne's worked so hard to find.

<u>Salt for the Devil's Eye on Amazon</u>

A freebie!

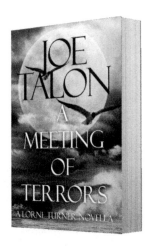

AFTER TEN MONTHS OF BEING alone on his moor, Lorne Turner receives a panicked call.

He needs to rescue some teenagers from an act of stupidity. Nice and simple. Fast rope down to a cave entrance, see if they are still alive, and get them out. Piece of carrot cake for an ex-operator.

When Ella Morgan is also 'roped' into helping, Lorne begins to understand the importance of friendship outside the military. The pair descend into the cave complex and that's when Lorne realises the dead don't always whisper.

Sometimes the dead scream!

This short novella takes place before Counting Crows and gives us an insight into how Lorne and Ella first begin their friendship. It's also how I first started to get to know the pair. I hope you enjoy it as well.

<u>A Meeting of Terrors Free on Story Origin</u>

And finally, the original story!

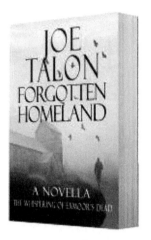

COMING HOME AFTER EIGHTEEN YEARS of service in the elite 22nd Regiment of the British Army should give Lorne Turner a sense of pride. Instead it fills him with dread. The shock of his last mission haunts him, rising from the dust and sand he never quite left behind.

The farm, in which he grew up, is isolated on the edge of a Somerset moorland. One covered in the barrows of the ancient dead, but he's more concerned with the recent dead.

Night after night a storm sweeps in from the north and Lorne can hear the crack, the bang, the scream of the wind... It is just the wind, right?

When his tolerance runs out he ventures into the darkness, to the church, as lonely as he is on the edge of the moor and he discovers that not all ghosts live in dust and sand.

Not all ghosts live in the nightmares of a tormented and haunted man.

Make sure you are part of the newsletter team and thank you for reading my books, it means the world to me.

Forgotten Homeland Free on Story Origin